American
Appetites

NOVELS BY JOYCE CAROL OATES

With Shuddering Fall (1964)
A Garden of Earthly Delights (1967)
Expensive People (1968)
them (1969)
Wonderland (1971)
Do with Me What You Will (1973)
The Assassins (1975)
Childwold (1976)
Son of the Morning (1978)
Unholy Loves (1979)
Bellefleur (1980)
Angel of Light (1981)
A Bloodsmoor Romance (1982)
Mysteries of Winterthurn (1984)
Solstice (1985)
Marya: A Life (1986)
You Must Remember This (1987)
American Appetites (1989)
Because It Is Bitter, and Because It Is My Heart (1990)
Black Water (1992)
Foxfire: Confessions of a Girl Gang (1993)
What I Lived For (1994)

American Appetites

JOYCE CAROL OATES

An Imprint of HarperCollins*Publishers*

HarperCollins books may be purchased for educational, business, or sales promotional use. For information please e-mail the Special Markets Department at SPsales@harpercollins.com.

A hardcover edition of this book was first published in 1986 by Dutton Books, a division of Penguin Group (USA).

FIRST ECCO PAPERBACK EDITION PUBLISHED 2014.

Library of Congress Cataloging-in-Publication Data has been applied for.

ISBN 978-0-06-226923-2

14   15   16   17   18   DIX/RRD   10   9   8   7   6   5   4   3   2   1

For my Princeton friends—

nowhere in these pages

My heartfelt thanks to friends for their expert advice in subjects crucial to this novel—Robert Morgenthau, Leigh Buchanan Bienen, Lynne Fagles, and Henry Bienen.

Everything is entirely in Nature, and Nature
is entire in everything. She has her center in
every brute.

—SCHOPENHAUER

The center of gravity should be in two people:
he and she.

—CHEKHOV

THE CREATION OF THE WORLD

They were young lovers, and married; and hand in hand, that first summer in Europe, they saw, among other inevitable sights, Michelangelo's "Creation of the World" in the Sistine Chapel; and after an hour stumbled back out into the traffic-clogged streets of Rome, into the blinding midday sun, each with a mild headache and not much to say, but smiling, dazed: no longer hand in hand. Then one proposed lunch, for they were famished after a morning of sightseeing, and the other said, as if waking from a dream, Yes, I suppose that comes next.

ONE

HELP

1.

What is destiny—a mechanical fact, a theoretical possibility, a concept, a superstition, a mere word? Ian McCullough was inclined to think one or another of these depending upon his mood. Destiny, the seemingly benign verso of fate.

He was a professional. He dealt in destinies, in the plural. Individuals' lives transposed into data units, threaded into systems, made to yield equations that were, it might be said, complex statements of reduction, a paring not back or down but surgically inward, to the individual's very essence—the statistic "self." That such a self existed nowhere but in demographic charts did not render it any less real. Existence, Ian McCullough playfully argued, often before audiences, is a matter after all of how you define your terms.

He was editor in chief of *The Journal of International Politics* and currently head of a five-year demographic study funded by the National Health Service, an investigation into the minute and mysterious correlations among age, employment, economic status, geographic mobility, illness, legal and/or criminal infractions, and death in a population mass of considerable size. He had long been a senior fellow of the prestigious Institute for Independent Research in the Social Sciences, Hazelton-on-Hudson, New York, and it was at the Institute he and his several associates and research assistants did their work of compiling, charting, graphing, predicting. Calibrating the diverse ways in which, so seemingly individual, the individual becomes a mathematical unit of a certain coherence—in a certain system, at least. In the system for which Ian J. McCullough had attained professional distinction, at least.

Though he never admitted it in public, but spoke of it readily enough in private, to his friends, Ian had always thought it rather terrifying that unrelated individuals, wholly unaware of one another, nonetheless cooperated in a collective destiny. Was there any other human phenomenon more mysterious, in fact—and terrifying? So many residents of a delimited geographic space will, in a delimited period of time, die of heart disease, cancer, AIDS; be victims of robbery, theft, assault, arson, murder; commit crimes themselves; commit suicide. (Ian's own father, with whom Ian had never been close, had drifted away from the family when Ian was a boy and was gone for years when news came of his death; and it was years later that Ian learned, accidentally, that his father had not died a "natural" death, not even an alcoholic's "natural" death; he had committed suicide: had shot himself in the mouth with a borrowed .45-caliber revolver. The knowledge had made little impression on Ian, since by that time he had more or less forgotten his father, to the degree to which, he suspected, his father had forgotten him and the family.)

Demography was not Ian McCullough's first love; pure historical research (into nineteenth-century post–Civil War America) was his first love, and, as he had been telling his associates for years, he intended to return to it someday soon: as soon as he completed the study at hand, acquitted himself of his numerous professional responsibilities, broke free of certain commitments. (The *Journal,* for instance, would be particularly difficult to give up. Ian had raised it from its prior status as an exponential and footnote-laden academic publication with a modest circulation, mainly to university libraries, to its current status as a publication of far more general interest and some controversy, not only eagerly read by, but contributed to by, the most renowned specialists in the field.) My success is my problem, he said, and his friends laughed with him and agreed, for many of them were burdened with the same problem: they were, like Ian McCullough, successes "in their fields," well into middle age yet "still youthful," comfortably well off beyond all dreams and expectations of graduate-student days yet still "ambitious"—though ambitious for what, none could have said.

Glynnis McCullough, Ian's wife, a food expert and a compiler of regional and ethnic cookbooks of uncommon originality and pictorial beauty—for Glynnis so loved what she did, at least while she did it, she could not entrust the design of her books to others—believed that they were, all of them, hungry; that ambition was in fact hunger: very nearly visceral, physiological, "real." And since hunger is nature, it is surely natural; isn't it?

The McCulloughs had one child, one surviving child, a daughter, Bianca, now nineteen years old. Another child, a boy, had died only a few days after birth, so many years ago now that Ian consoled himself with the possibility that the hurt and bitterness and inchoate rage that still rose in him at the memory, a rush of unwanted and even dreaded adrenaline in his veins, was factitious, and not genuine: what he believed, as a sonless father, he *should* feel, and not, fifteen years later, after all, what he *did* feel.

For surely he was recovered from the shock and grief by now. As Glynnis gave every sign, and had done so for years, of being recovered. "Just don't think about it, Ian," she'd said. "Think of other things. There is a world, after all," she'd said, smiling, "of other things."

But he was no longer young; he would be fifty years old in April, and this had something to do with it. Not compulsive thoughts but luxuriant thoughts. Of loss, grief, hurt, resentment.

IN HIS OFFICE on the top floor of the Institute, Ian McCullough's desk faced a large plate-glass window; he was not among the spartan-minded of his colleagues who insisted upon facing blank walls, out of a fear of being distracted from their work. And, yes, the view from Ian's window, a fourth-floor window, was endlessly fascinating to him, beautiful, in all seasons and all weathers: birch trees, juniper, oaks; a small man-made lake that looked, in its contours and bank vegetation, utterly natural; a hilly landscape very rarely interrupted by human figures—the Institute parking lot was on the other side of the building, the province of junior faculty and the less prestigious. (When Ian invited a visitor into his office for the first time he never failed to remark, with an air of embarrassment or tacit apology, that he'd been assigned this office—which was in fact two large offices, with a connecting door—because he had joined the Institute seventeen years ago, when such offices were more readily available; not because, in the notorious taxonomic structure of the Institute, he deserved it. His listeners bore him out, usually, in tolerant silence or regarded him with some perplexity. Did he not know who he was, or, knowing, did he not wish to acknowledge it? "The man's very modesty is an example to us all," Ian's friend Denis Grinnell had several times said, "but it is not a good example.")

On the office walls, as a counterpoint to the mathematical abstraction and fineness of his work, and as a rebuke to the view outside his window, Ian had long ago hung a number of reproductions of woodcuts, engravings, watercolors—most of them by Dürer, for it was Dürer who had enthralled Ian in late adolescence, when one is so particularly

susceptible to enthrallment. He had even imagined, and had been supported in his fantasy, at least to a degree, by Glynnis, the first young
woman he had ever loved, that he bore some resemblance to Dürer's
great self-portrait: the watchful doubting eyes, the bony nose, the rather
prim pursed lips: that look of self-critical intelligence, a shyly aggressive
sort of skepticism. He had never outgrown Dürer though he'd outgrown
his adolescent self; the woodcuts held a powerful fascination for him
still: a fascination of dread, as much for the artist's unsparing eye as for
his allegorical imagination. "Not what the eye sees but what the mind
imagines the eye must see," Ian said of it. So, in his office, in a rare con-
templative moment, he stared at the familiar images on the walls, the
meticulously rendered folds in clothing, creases in brows, impacted data
of grasses, melancholia, hair, fur, skulls, bones, living creatures in helpless thrall to the indecipherable drama of their times, and believed that
Dürer had captured not madness but the mind's triumph over madness.
With no structure to contain it—no human design, system, strategy—
such a flood of brute phenomena would have long ago drowned mankind. The very species would have gone under, become extinct.

Ian had always been drawn in particular to an engraving of Death
leading a handsome youth and a young girl on a horse: the two of them
stare ahead, beyond the frame of the drawing, in hope, dread, wonder.
In another, naked figures, evidently madmen, appear to be gamboling on
rather knifelike spikes of grass. Their activity suggests both futility and
dignity: since we are what we are, why not dance; why not dance . . . *also?*

2.

Out of nowhere the girl telephoned Ian, late one morning in February;
and though he rarely took calls from parties who declined to identify
themselves, and who insisted to his secretary, Mrs. Fairchild, that their
calls were "of the greatest urgency," Ian, already annoyed by a series of

things that had gone wrong that day in the office, picked up the telephone and said, "Yes? What? Who is it?"

He thought at first it must be a wrong number, the woman spoke so rapidly and so incoherently; he had to ask her name twice and then barely caught it. Sigrid? Sigrid Hunt? His wife's friend Sigrid? He had never heard her voice over the telephone before and would not have recognized it; they had had only one conversation of any duration and substance together, and that some months ago. And if it were true— and perhaps it was true—that, from time to time, at odd unbidden moments, Ian found himself thinking of her, and sometimes mistaking other women for her—on the street, in friends' homes, even in the corridors of the Institute, where, until recent years, there were few women at all apart from the secretarial staff—it was also true that he did not expect her, and did not much want her, in his life. For Glynnis after all seemed to have dropped her.

In a breathless wavering voice Sigrid Hunt was telling Ian that she had to see him: she was desperate, hadn't slept in several days, was convinced that something was going to happen to her, or had already happened. Ian interrupted several times to ask where she was—was she in danger, was she ill?—but Sigrid seemed scarcely to hear, saying that she had to talk to someone, had to talk to *him*, before it was too late. Ian said, "Are you alone? Is someone threatening you?" and she said, suddenly angered, "You don't even know who I am, do you! You don't remember me, do you! If I live or die, gutted like a fish, if somebody breaks in here and kills me, what does it matter to people like you!"

"Sigrid, please—"

"You and your wife, people like you!"

"—are you in danger? Is somebody there?" Ian asked, suddenly rather frightened. "Where are you?"

She began sobbing, panting harshly into the receiver, a warm moist desperate breath Ian could virtually feel. The last time he'd spoken with this young woman she had confided in him, half in worry, yet half, he'd thought, in pride, that she was involved in a love affair she couldn't seem to "control": formally engaged to a man, Egyptian-born, now living and working in the States, who was both "devoted" to her and "vindictive"; a man she loved very much, yet sometimes feared. Ian had had, only once, a brief encounter with this man, this rather exotic fiancé of Sigrid Hunt's, in the McCulloughs' house, in fact, at one of Glynnis's large crowded parties. Ian retained only the vaguest image of a handsome, quite dark, unsmiling face that looked as if it had been carved out of stone. He could not recall having shaken the man's hand.

Now Sigrid was saying, sobbing, "You want me to beg, don't you—you, all of you—" and Ian said, "Please don't say such a thing; tell me where you are, what I can do for—" and Sigrid said, "Come or don't come, what does it matter?"—her voice lifting in childlike despair even as it seemed to fall away from the receiver—"What does it matter?"

Ian said, "Wait, Sigrid, let me check the address I have for you—"

But the line was dead, a rebuke to his caution.

EVEN AS HE made his decision, Ian McCullough thought, But why me? Why is this young woman calling me? And he had no answer, could think of absolutely no answer. But he was flattered, in his maleness. That was, he'd recall afterward, the primary, the shameful, the exhilarating thing.

So he called Denis, to cancel out of their squash game and the editorial luncheon to follow, and he called his other colleagues, associate editors of the *Journal*, postponing the luncheon until later in the week: an emergency had come up, he said; he was terribly sorry to inconvenience them.

One of the men asked if it was a family emergency, if there was anything he might do to help, and Ian replied, hurried, vague, wanting to get off the line, "Thanks so much, Art, but I don't think so—not this time."

THERE ARE FINALLY only two categories of humanity in our social lives, as in Roman times there were Roman citizens and non-Roman: those whose names, addresses, and telephone numbers are carefully written into our address books, and those whose names, addresses, and telephone numbers are scribbled on tiny pieces of paper and inserted, with the expediency of the merely temporary, into our address books.

Sigrid Hunt's address was merely scribbled on a slip of paper and inserted into the tidy little book of permanent names and addresses Ian McCullough carried with him in his inside coat pocket. But how fortunate it was there at all! Ian studied it with singular intensity: *Hunt, Sigrid. 119 Tice. Poughkeepsie, N.Y.* No more than a half hour's drive.

Gutted like a fish. What, Ian wondered, had she meant by that?

He left the Institute by a rear door, half ran to his car, set off. Glynnis was in New York that day and would not be home until early evening, but that had no bearing of course upon Ian's errand.

South along the Thruway, the familiar route made unnervingly strange by a sudden snowstorm that seemed to erupt out of the sun, the sky beyond a hard ceramic blue: painterly, pictorial. Ian recalled an improbable turquoise sky in an oil by—had it been Parmigianino, or one of the others, of that odd stylized era?—contemplated, indeed, stared at, that summer in Italy, he and Glynnis hand in hand, at times gripping each other in sheer ecstatic joy at what they saw, as, at night, in love, they gripped in the ecstasy of passion. Ian thought, I must get there, I must get there before it's too late. Traffic on the Thruway was unexpectedly heavy.

Ian had taken down Sigrid Hunt's address back in November, a mild November day as he recalled, when the two of them had met, by chance, in Hazelton; Ian had dropped by the local crafts gallery, housed in a restored eighteenth-century mill, one of the several "historic" sites in the village, on an errand for Glynnis, and, returning to his car, dreamy, distracted, he'd happened to see Sigrid Hunt, or a young woman who closely resembled her, standing on a bank of the mill pond a short distance away. Ah, there, Ian thought, stopping dead in his tracks. There.

A family of tourists were rather too exuberantly tossing bread and seed out onto the pond for the ornamental waterfowl, but this young woman stood alone, unmoving, staring at the flat mirrored surface of the water: like Milton's Eve, contemplating her own mysterious reflection. She had not seen Ian but he had the uncanny feeling that she was waiting for him: knew he was there, knew he would see her, would come to her.

Which of course he did. An unavoidable social gesture, he'd thought it.

Ian's wife, Glynnis, was notable for taking up and cultivating, and eventually dropping, miscellaneous people of one kind or another: often people rather vaguely "in the arts" or "promising"; frequently young women of varying degrees of attractiveness, unattached or mysterious in their attachments, appealingly vulnerable or merely vulnerable. Her "specimens," certain of their friends called them, not without a degree of jealousy; and, indeed, it sometimes seemed to Ian that his wife collected individuals with the avidity of an old-time biologist, hauling in and examining and classifying species. Ian, whose energy was drained by his work, whose imagination floundered when confronted by the mere prospect of cultivating a new friend, envied Glynnis both her will and her ability; was not, on the face of it, jealous; yet one day he would ask, "Where is Iris?" or "Whatever became of—was her name Frances?—I haven't seen her for months," and Glynnis would look at him blankly for a moment, before remembering. At such times Ian felt a slight chill, wondering if, at the start, he had not been one of Glynnis's specimens himself, which she had decided to keep.

Where Glynnis had met Sigrid Hunt, Ian did not know, though perhaps he'd been told. The young woman lived twenty miles downriver, in a déclassé area, as she smilingly called it, of Poughkeepsie; she taught, or sometimes taught, or had once taught, modern dance at Vassar. (She'd murmured vaguely, with a child's reticent hurt, of university politics, academic jealousies and feuds, "budgetary restrictions," so Ian guessed her contract had simply been terminated.) She had begun dance lessons at the age of four, had studied for years with the Martha Graham Company, had worked with various companies in New York City, Los Angeles, London, until an injury to a tendon in her right foot forced her into more or less permanent retirement, aged twenty-one. ("A dancer's life is nasty, brutish, and short," she had said, with an enigmatic smile.)

Sigrid Hunt had told Ian these things at a large cocktail party at the McCulloughs' house, to which Glynnis had invited her. She'd shaken Ian's hand in a surprisingly hard grip and smiled happily, showing small, white, perfect teeth. "I've heard so much about you, Dr. McCullough," she'd said, and Ian winced and said, Please, call me Ian; Ian is quite enough. But she never did quite bring herself to call him by that name, at least not in Ian's hearing.

Sigrid Hunt spoke in a careful, quaint voice, a voice seemingly without an accent; she fixed her listeners with round, wide, childlike eyes, smooth as coins and the shade, seemingly soft and powdery, of tarnish: her gaze given a subtle but arresting magnification by the perfectly round pink-tinted lenses of her glasses in their wire-rimmed frames. Her face was narrow, the features finely cut and teasingly asymmetrical, the eyes and mouth down-drooping at the corners, the eyelids naturally shadowed as if stained, or bruised, a faint blue. She was tall, perhaps five feet eleven, with a slender, rather epicene body: her neck long, shoulders narrow, breasts small as a young girl's. Her hair, her spectacular hair, fell nearly to her waist, red-gold, ridged and rippled like a washboard, and wonderfully glossy. She wore, that evening, a lemon-yellow Thai silk dress, a beautiful garment, though soiled at the cuffs; well-weathered Roman sandals on her long narrow white feet; necklaces, bracelets, distractingly large and ornamental earrings that pulled cruelly at her earlobes. Talking to Ian and one or two others she smiled a good deal and showed her teeth, licked her lips nervously. Ian quickly perceived her intelligence, which was as much physical as mental: the young woman was conscious not only of her beauty but of its inevitable effect upon others—the resistance it aroused in them.

Look at me, she was saying. For here I am.

She had come to the McCulloughs' house alone but had not been there an hour before a man appeared beside her, to take her away; Ian, caught up with other guests, had hardly more than a glimpse of a dark-skinned, unsmiling, but strikingly handsome young man of perhaps thirty, with thick black glossy hair brushed back from his forehead, a manner both civil and restrained, and very sporty, surely very expensive clothes. He was slender and no taller than Sigrid, his upper arms and shoulders muscled in that hard, compact way Ian knew to recognize from the gym. Ian, as always rather awkwardly at sea in so large a gathering, would not have spoken to the man at all had he not happened to be saying goodbye to another couple, at the front door, when Sigrid and her companion slipped by—Sigrid clearly agitated, her boyfriend decidedly unfriendly—but there was a brief obligatory exchange of names and a hurried and perfunctory handshake, as Sigrid introduced

"Dr. McCullough" to "Fermi Sabri." And Ian closed the door after them and promptly forgot them.

That night, undressing in their bedroom, Glynnis asked Ian casually what did he think of Sigrid Hunt; and Ian said, frowning, "Who? Which one was she?" "The one with the long red hair, in the yellow silk," Glynnis said, adding, with a hurt twist of her mouth; "the one who didn't so much as trouble to introduce her boyfriend to me, or even to say goodbye to me." Ian said, yawning, "I don't remember, actually," and they went on to talk of other guests, of other more important guests: who had said what to whom, who had new and startling news, who had invited them to a dinner party the following Sunday if they were free. . . . There were so many people in the McCulloughs' lives, after all, and so few that really mattered.

But when Ian and Sigrid Hunt met some weeks later, at the mill pond, and again shook hands, Ian was oddly struck by a sense of—was it certitude? rightness? an excitement so keen as to feel, or even taste, like danger? He would not subsequently remember much of what he said, or how, slightly stammering, he'd managed to say anything of substance at all.

He would remember that they talked together with the nervous elation of old friends who have not seen each other in some time; that the corners of his eyes pinched, as if looking into Sigrid Hunt's face, at such close range, gave pain. It was not because Sigrid was a beautiful woman—in the sharp November sunshine she seemed in fact distinctly less beautiful than she had appeared the night of the party—but that, for all her guardedness, her self-consciousness, she was so vulnerable. And, being vulnerable, she aroused emotions in Ian he could not readily have named.

Though surely knowing that she had been dropped, or casually misplaced, in Glynnis's life, she asked after Glynnis nonetheless, with so gentle an air of regret one might have missed it altogether. Ian made a reply of some vague general smiling kind, alluded to the fact that Glynnis and he had been uncommonly busy these past few months and had not seen nearly as many people as they'd wished to see. And Sigrid, dropping her gaze, smiling enigmatically, said, "We never have time, do we, for all that we don't exactly want to do." And in the heightened pace of their conversation, the very setting a distraction—a gaggle of mallards had set up a terrific squawking, greedy for more feed than was forthcoming, and not far away, on the bank, a young mother was scolding her weeping child—it was an easy matter to change the subject, as if he hadn't heard. Yet it touched Ian deeply: that she had been hurt. That anything in his life could have enough significance to bear upon her at all.

Sigrid was bareheaded, and her red-blond hair blew in the wind, strands of it across her face, her eyes, catching in her mouth, so that, in quick nervous gestures, she had to brush it repeatedly away. Her eyes behind the pink-tinted lenses of her schoolgirl glasses were lightly threaded with blood and damp, and Ian felt a corresponding dampness in his own, an immediate sympathy, as he'd felt his daughter Bianca's pain when she hurt herself as a small child; and she was always hurting herself as a small child, falling and banging her knees, cutting the soft pink palms of her hands, bruising her forehead. My baby, my girl, he'd thought, how can I protect you, what on earth can I do for you, to keep you from being hurt? And it tore at his heart, to know that there was nothing.

They talked together for perhaps twenty minutes, and Sigrid confided in him that she was having difficulties with her "fiancé"; she could not determine whether she loved him very much or whether she wanted to escape him, to make an absolute break and never see him again. Ian laughed, saying, "That seems rather extreme." Sigrid said stiffly, "If you knew Fermi Sabri you'd understand."

Ian made no reply, thinking that Fermi Sabri was the last person he cared to know.

She told him that Fermi had been born in Cairo and had emigrated to the United States at the age of twenty; he was "brilliant" but "erratic," an engineer with an advanced degree in hydraulics from MIT. He loved her and wanted to marry her, wanted her to have his child ("a son, of course") as proof of her love for *him*. "The night I went to your party, he'd said it was fine with him, he didn't at all mind, but then, evidently, he followed me; I think he was actually watching the house from outside for a while, before he came in." Seeing Ian's look of distaste she added quickly, "It's just that he feels so possessive of me. I mean protective. He *means* well."

"Oh, as to that," Ian said, laughing again, though without much mirth, "we all mean well."

They were walking in the direction of Sigrid's car, at least Ian assumed it was her car, a foreign model, low-slung, sporty, lipstick-red but badly flecked with rust, its front bumper battered. It had the look of a car, Ian thought, not registered in its driver's name.

"I hope we will see each other again, before long, in Hazelton or elsewhere," Ian said; and Sigrid said lightly, "Yes, I hope so too." He opened her car door for her, then belatedly asked her for her address and telephone number, which he scribbled on a slip of paper, though this was information surely in Glynnis's possession already. After she'd driven away he stood for a while in the parking lot staring at the mallards, snowy white geese, black swans, as they paddled on the pond in ceaseless circles, now slow and languorous, as if on display, now wild and frenzied, fighting one another for feed. If any thought came to him, he would not afterward remember what it was.

HE HAD SOME difficulty finding 119 Tice, which was in an area of Poughkeepsie unknown to him, of run-down apartment buildings, row houses, taverns, railroad yards, rubble-strewn vacant lots—a neighborhood that, though largely black and Hispanic, reminded him of his boyhood neighborhood in Bridgeport, Connecticut. And when he found 119 Tice he discovered that Sigrid Hunt lived not in the house on the street but in an apartment above a garage at the rear.

A small yellowed card with SIGRID HUNT in childlike block letters had been tacked beside the door; beneath it, a wicker basket stuffed with advertising flyers. The door itself had been painted a bright robin's-egg blue, now covered in patches of grime and cobwebs. Ian peered inside its window but could see nothing except a narrow flight of stairs leading up into shadow.

He knocked loudly, but no one answered; knocked again, and called, "Sigrid? It's me, it's Ian." He peered up at the second-floor windows, whose blinds were drawn; no one responded. His heart knocked hard in his chest; he dreaded some sort of terrible revelation: a sudden scream, a smashed window, a man's footsteps rushing toward him down the stairs.

But no one appeared. Nor was any car parked in the drive.

"Hello? Sigrid? It's—"

He had the uneasy sensation that he was being watched, very likely from the house at the front, which, like other private residences on the street, wood-frame, shingled, shabby, had the look of a place in which welfare recipients and old-age pensioners lived. He felt exposed, a fool. An incongruous figure in his camel's-hair coat, black Astrakhan hat, green scarf: items of clothing bought for him by Glynnis. "Sigrid? Are you home? Come open the door," he called, cupping his hands to his mouth. He was quite alarmed by this time, envisioning Sigrid Hunt lying dead upstairs: partly clothed or frankly naked, strangled, stabbed, raped, murdered, her golden-red hair fanned out about her, as in one of those lurid photographs in detective magazines he'd examined surreptitiously as a junior high school boy. . . .

How sad, Ian thought, that a woman of Sigrid Hunt's beauty and pretensions should live in a place like this: above a garage of rotted shingles, peeling paint, broken and carelessly boarded-up windows, opaque with the grime of years. Trash had been strewn about the yard; broken concrete and glass were everywhere underfoot. Untrimmed trees and overgrown bushes, lightly touched with snow, were given a startling and rather inappropriate beauty, as in a Japanese watercolor of skeletal trees and snowy-white blossoms.

Ian tried the door again, could not think what to do—summon the caretaker, if there was one? Call Sigrid Hunt's number from a pay telephone? Call the police?—when, finally, a figure appeared on the stairs, descending slowly and cautiously, like a sleepwalker: leaning against the wall and gripping the railing with both hands. It was Sigrid Hunt, drunk or drugged or seriously ill, her face pale and drawn, her hair in a tangled braid behind her back. She wore an ill-fitting white robe that opened carelessly about her bare legs; her feet too were bare, despite the cold; though by now she must have recognized Ian, she did not open the door at once but rubbed the gritty window with the palm of her hand and peered out at him. Without her glasses her eyes looked raw and reddened.

Ian rattled the doorknob impatiently. "Don't you know who I am? It's Ian McCullough; you called me," he said. "Unlock the door."

Sigrid Hunt stared at him, seemed at last to know who he was, began to work the police lock, which took some time. When at last she managed to get the door open and Ian stepped inside, she flinched back from him and muttered, "Damned lock, works so damned hard," and turned away with no further greeting or word of explanation. She began to climb back up the stairs, again gripping the railing with both hands. "Watch the stairs," she said, "they're rotted; it's that kind of place. You can see, can't you, it's that kind of *place?*" Her voice rose on the last word as if on the edge of laughter.

Ian followed her upstairs, staring at the young woman's bare legs and chafed, reddened heels, the badly creased and soiled skirt of the robe hanging loose about her hips. She offered no explanation, no apology: simply led him upstairs to her flat. The stairway was poorly lit and unheated and smelled of dirt; it reminded him, and the memory came swift and unbidden, though not entirely unpleasantly, of the shabby boardinghouse in which he'd lived as a graduate student in Ann Arbor, a long time ago. "Here we are," Sigrid Hunt said, out of breath from the climb. "Here it *is.*"

The apartment, or flat, was quite large, stretching the full length of the building, a single room with a low blistered ceiling, windows whose shades—cracked, crooked—were drawn, bare floorboards upon which brightly colored woven carpets were scattered. Ian had an impression of mismatched furniture, including, most conspicuously, several sling chairs in a synthetic coyote hide and a six-foot swinging mirror with a heavy carved frame: a mirror that had the look, Ian thought, of a mirror that is much consulted.

"Come in. In*side.* I must lock the door," Sigrid said impatiently.

Small buzzing radio voices emerged from beside the sofa bed, over which, with evident haste, a soiled crimson silk comforter had been drawn. There were smells of cooking, and of unwashed clothes, talcum powder, perspiration. An eerie undersea atmosphere pervaded: the blinds drawn against the daylight, and only a single lamp burning, with a soiled flesh-colored shade.

Ian asked what was wrong, what could he do for her, and Sigrid, who looked both ill and nervously elated, as if on the verge of mania, began to speak in a rapid near-incoherent mutter, smiling and grimacing as if to herself. "I need to talk to someone," she said, "who doesn't know me and doesn't judge me." She pointed at a chair and said, "Sit down, *please;* you make me nervous standing." Ian wondered if he would have recognized her: her face was thinner than he recalled, her eyes bruised, her skin unnervingly pale. There was a pouty blood-heavy slackness to her lower lip, and the lovely ridged-rippled hair, in a coarse braid that hung down limply between her shoulder blades, had not been washed in some time. The terry-cloth robe, a man's robe, fell open to reveal, as if defiantly, her small shadowy breasts and prominent collarbone. "At least take off your coat," Sigrid said breathlessly, when Ian remained standing. "Your . . ." And her voice trailed off as if she'd forgotten the word for hat.

Ian took off his coat, his hat, and his scarf, and laid them neatly over the back of a chair. His mind was working swiftly but to no evident purpose. He said quietly, "What's wrong, Sigrid? Have you taken some sort of drug?"

And Sigrid said at once, in a low angry begging voice, "Don't judge me, don't *look* at me, I can't bear it." She was pacing about the room, too nerved up to remain in one place.

Ian said, following after her, "What is it, Sigrid? You can tell me, Sigrid; you know who I am, don't you?"

"I don't know who anybody is," Sigrid whispered. "You're all lying fucking hypocrite sons of bitches."

SHE WAS LYING, limp, across the sofa bed and looked as if she were about to fall asleep. Her face glistened with sweat, and her breathing was hoarse and arrhythmic. Ian, standing over her, uncertain what to do—call an ambulance? try to revive her himself?—saw in the corner of his eye a ghostly spectator: his own reflection, fair-skinned, fair-haired, attentive, rapt, alarmed, in the slanted swinging mirror. Why are you here, why you, and why here? The buzzing radio voices continued, like a demented chorus.

Sigrid lay unmoving, breathing shallowly; Ian could feel the heat lifting from her. "I want to die," she said softly. "I don't want this."

"What do you mean?" Ian asked. "What is 'this'?"

"I'm paralyzed; he's got me," she said. "I can't go forward or back."

"Who is 'he,' your lover?"

"Won't let me have an abortion, says he'll kill me if—"

"You're pregnant?"

"—if I kill *it*. Six weeks, only, and already it's beginning to—"

"Is that it? You're pregnant? Is that why you're so upset?"

"—exert its own *will*. Sucking the life from *me*."

She began, with no warning, to beat her fists against her belly. Ian caught her wrists, forced her to lie still. With surprising strength she twisted free, clawing and kicking, and, on her feet now, ducked away behind him. Ian saw to his astonishment that the back of his hand was badly scratched; tiny blood beads appeared between his knuckles.

He said, "You'd better calm down, you're making yourself hysterical."

"Go away and leave me. What difference does it make."

"If you are pregnant, it's a relatively simple—"

"I can't go forward or back." She pressed her hands over her ears, bent nearly double, and would not hear. Ian went to touch her, and she shrank away. "No. No. No. No. No." She stumbled into one of the coyote-hide chairs and, in a sudden rage, kicked it and sent it flying against a wall. Ian watched in helpless fascination, as he'd once watched his two- or three-year-old daughter in the paroxysm of a temper tantrum, as Sigrid Hunt, dazed and lethargic only a moment before, began to curse, slam, pummel, kick, throwing things about, overturning fur-

niture, tearing at her own hair. Ian thought, I will have to get help. I can't do this alone.

He was sweating inside his clothes. An old terror of sudden and unanticipated intimacy rose in him, a memory of other such situations when, thrown together with another person, whether a man or a woman, in one or two cases children, he had been taken off guard: had simply not known what to do. Glynnis would have known: would take the girl's hands in hers and embrace her, speak soothingly to her, brush the damp strands of hair off of her forehead. It's all right dear don't be frightened dear I'll help you dear there are people who will help you please don't be upset. But Ian dared not touch her.

He said, looking for a telephone, "I'm going to call an ambulance; you're hysterical, you're going to hurt yourself."

Sigrid cut her eyes at him and said, panting, "Leave me alone, just please leave me *alone*."

"Don't be silly, I can't leave you alone," Ian said. He advanced upon her and said, "I don't want to leave you alone."

Like Glynnis, though not so easily as Glynnis, Ian took the girl's hands in his—both her hands, in his—and urged her to sit down. Suddenly obedient, she sat: began to sob, pressing her forehead, which was damp but surprisingly cool, against the backs of his hands. He thought, She is Bianca's age; she is Glynnis's young friend. So long as he could think of Sigrid Hunt in those terms, in that specific equation, he believed he would be all right. His alarm, his excitement, even his acute sexual arousal, could be contained.

As Sigrid wept Ian told her, in a low, calm, unemphatic voice, as one might speak to a sick child, or an animal, that he could help her; he wanted to help her, if she would cooperate. He was not going to leave her, in any case. Not in the condition she was in. "What kind of drug have you been taking?" he asked.

"Nothing," she said. Then, "Just something to help me sleep."

"What is it?"

"I don't know."

"Of course you know."

"I want to *sleep* and I can't *sleep,* my head is filled with noises like breaking *glass*—"

"Sleeping pills? Barbiturates? How many?"

"—I want to die but I can't even *die.*"

Ian went into Sigrid's windowless cubbyhole of a bathroom, looked through the medicine cabinet, found nothing (apart from bottles of vitamins, calcium, aspirin, "stress tabs with zinc"); rummaged in a little wastebasket beneath the sink, where, holding his breath against the close, ammoniac smell, as of backed-up drains and soiled towels, he found, hidden beneath a wad of filthy Kleenex, an empty plastic pill container with a prescription label for the tranquilizer Librium.

"How many of these did you take?" Ian asked Sigrid.

And Sigrid, looking away, suddenly very tired, said, so softly he barely heard, "Not enough, I guess."

"How many?" he persisted.

"I don't *know,*" she said. She hid her face in her hands, elbows on her knees, knees apart, in an awkward, provocative posture: the insides of her thighs exposed, a patch of pubic hair. Ian stood over her, looking down at her so that he could not see.

He said, "Then I must call an ambulance."

"No, don't, really. It isn't necessary, really."

"But how do you feel?"

"I don't feel as if I'm going to die."

"How can you say that?"

"Other times, there've been other times—"

"Yes?"

"When I've taken a lot more."

Ian said, in sudden distaste, "Jesus."

He urged her to lie back on the sofa bed, on top of the crimson spread; he switched off the radio, stood sweating and panting above her, not knowing what to do. In the slanted mirror a flushed excited man regarded him covertly: glasses sliding down his nose, nostrils widened, flaring.

He said suddenly, as if he'd just now thought of it, "Your boyfriend, this Fermi—where is he?"

"Not here," Sigrid said.

"Then where?"

"Back up to Cambridge. He left last night."

"Did you have a fight, last night?"

"Nights. The night before too."

"And what came of it?"

"I'm going to have the baby. I said."

"You're going to have the baby?"

"The phone's off the hook, isn't it?"

Ian looked about, in the mess, for a telephone. Yes, the receiver was off the hook.

"I told him not to call me for a while, a day or two, but he might change his mind and call; and I can't talk to him now."

Sigrid was lying very still, surprisingly docile now, her bluish eyelids heavy and hooded but her voice quite clear. The disheveled braid poked out stiff and clublike above her head as if she, and it, had been frozen in mid-fall.

Ian said, "Have you seen a doctor about the pregnancy?"

"No."

"Would you like me to find a doctor for you? There is an excellent medical center in Hazelton."

"Thank you, but no."

"I'll be happy to; it's no trouble at all. And if you are concerned about payment—"

"It's really an abortion clinic I want."

"The doctor could refer you to one, couldn't he?"

"I want a woman doctor."

"It may be that there *is* a woman doctor."

Though Sigrid could not see him, Ian smiled, smiled in exasperation; their exchange reminded him of nothing so much as one of the typically, and maddeningly, circumlocutious exchanges he or Glynnis was likely to have with their daughter, in which undercurrents of will and desire contend, like literal currents beneath the surface of a body of water, tugging one now this way, now that, in response to no evident pattern. He said again, "Let me help you, though. You called me, after all."

"It isn't the baby's fault. That's the primary thing."

"I'm not sure that it's the 'primary' thing."

"Then what is?"

"Your health. Your well-being. Your—" And he paused, about to say, *Your future.* He said, "Simply your well-being. What you want to do, and not what another person wants you to do. Having a baby under such circumstances . . ."

Sigrid said, in a vague, rather wandering voice, "But I love him too. The father."

"I'm sure you do," Ian said. "Otherwise—" He laughed, but the sound was harsh, dry, and ungiving: the very sound of jealousy.

Sigrid's legs were not smooth-shaven but covered lightly, almost invisibly, with red-blond hairs. Ian felt an urge, an impulse, to kneel and touch, drawing a forefinger against the grain of the hairs . . . an urge, yet more powerful, to press his face, his hungry mouth, against her belly: against the wiry-soft mound of hair, red-gold too it would be, and curly, and warm, and damp, that most mysterious and secret of female hair, between her thighs.

And she was pregnant, too; and that too was secret.

He was thinking of, many years ago, his wife's fresh young body: its beauty that had seemed to him amazing, and amazing that it was in a sense *his*. He was thinking, his breath coming now quickly, the sweat breaking out more frankly beneath his arms, of how he'd made love to her, that first time; and the other "first" times: that summer in Italy and the subsequent winter in Cambridge, the long mornings when they'd deliberately stayed in bed, the long nights when they'd gone to bed early . . . before the baby was born, and their lives were irrevocably altered.

Yet their lives, it had always seemed to Ian, when he was in one of his brooding, involuted moods, had been irrevocably altered before Bianca's birth: Glynnis's very pregnancy and *her* moods, that so excluded him, that (and he was certain he did not imagine or invent) Glynnis willed might exclude him. For her exultation, her supremacy, in pregnancy, childbirth, nursing, had cut him out: made him feel not only irrelevant but, so often, in the way; his wife looked at him and felt the obligation of love, for of course she *did* love him, while another kind of love, sheerly physical, instinctual, as intimate as her own flesh, pulled at her. As hot, heavy, urgent, he guessed, as the milk in her breasts that gave pain if it was not released.

And she had insisted, both times, upon natural childbirth; the psychoprophylactic method, as the medical texts called it. And Ian too, of necessity, had been involved, had of course been involved: attending classes with her, going through her exercises with her, breathing with her, at first wholeheartedly and then with increasing concern and apprehension. For, both times, Glynnis's obstetricians had warned her and Ian against natural childbirth: the pregnancies were not quite right;

too much labor, too much pain, might be involved, a protracted strain on both the mother's and the babies' hearts. The obstetricians had issued their warnings; but Glynnis, being Glynnis, chose not to listen. She wanted, she said, to be fully conscious: to be in control of what was happening and not controlled by it. "Childbirth under anesthetic would be like making love under anesthetic," Glynnis had said half seriously. "I want at least to know that I'm alive."

So Ian had endured the labors with her, the first eleven hours, the second eighteen: unspeakably long hours of pain, unmitigated agony, poor Glynnis's screams so piercing Ian believed they must have penetrated the hospital walls. If he chose he could hear those screams still, those guttural cries with their note of sheer disbelief and astonishment, as if the sufferer could not quite believe that what was happening to her was really happening. At the height of labor he had assisted the obstetrician in a pelvic examination, each time, and had, each time, almost fainted: helping his wife (herself helpless, slick with sweat and flat on her back) fulfill herself as a woman. As if, he thought, she were a portal by which the invisible universe became visible . . . the inchoate God of mere spirit heaved into living flesh. Had not a mystic named Bousquet, of whom Ian McCullough had never heard, declared that mankind wants to be the soul of those forces that created him? So Glynnis said, and so Glynnis believed.

It was a miracle, and he bowed before it; it *was* a miracle, and he would not have denied it. But the hours of agony, and the hours of screams, and the tears, and the sweat, and the blood, and his wife's beautiful face contorted beyond recognition, like the face of a sinner in hell—in liquefied hell . . . like the face of one of the damned, the *anonymous* damned, on the ceiling of the Sistine Chapel—those hours had frightened him deeply, as if the marrow of his bones had been permanently chilled. And the second infant had died.

Ian had been impotent, intermittently, for months following both births. He had nightmares, sudden seizures of panic, dread, resentment, fury. He did not blame Glynnis for his own weaknesses, whether physical or emotional; nor did he, he was certain, blame her for the infant boy's death, for her loss after all had been greater than his. And yet, sexually aroused, he was likely to feel a contrary emotion, of something very close to visceral panic. For to enter another person in love is to violate the other in pain and bring about, at once, or in time, irrevocable loss.

He stood above Sigrid Hunt, who seemed to have fallen asleep, thinking these thoughts—indeed, being overcome by them—and could not have said, afterward, how long he stood there, his senses sharpened to the point of pain and his heart beating hard, angrily, as if in the presence of an adversary.

3.

He remained with Sigrid Hunt for most of that afternoon, at first watching over her while she slept (alert to alterations in her breathing that might mean she was slipping into a deeper and more dangerous sort of sleep), then reasoning with her (and Ian McCullough was at his most eloquent when "reason" came into play): persuading her finally that, in her special circumstances, terminating her pregnancy as quickly as possible was the only solution, a solution both humane and logical. Ian had perceived early on that of course the vain young woman did not really want to have a baby; but she did, no doubt, want the struggle, the *agon*, of wanting it and being denied it: or, rather, of being compelled (out of her own magnanimity, for instance) to sacrifice it to necessity. She was vain, but she was also tractable: far more tractable than Glynnis.

So, in the end, she acquiesced—"I suppose you're right; I see your point of view"—precisely as Ian had anticipated, as a gesture of submission to him. As if she could allow herself to go against her heart's desire, to be coerced into doing wrong, moral wrong, only at the urging of another.

By degrees Ian's eyes, which had been, since boyhood, abnormally sensitive to gradations of light—blinded in stark sunshine, weak in the dark—became accustomed to the attenuated light in Sigrid Hunt's flat; as, by degrees, he'd stopped hearing the barking dog in the adjacent yard. He had time, while Sigrid slept, to consider, in detail, his surroundings and to wonder, dispassionately now, why he was here; what urging, as of a hand pressed rudely against his back, had brought him here? With its low ceiling and exposed floorboards and crooked blinds and grimy windowsills, with its quarreling decorative "touches"—the orange, red, and parrot-green carpets, three Georgia O'Keeffe flower-abstraction reproductions on the walls, several aggressively ugly junk sculptures of the kind executed solely by friends—it seemed to him both squalid and intensely romantic; like the room in which he'd lived for a year, the most emotionally turbulent year of his life, in Ann Arbor, in 1959.

He had been a scared boy of twenty-two, skinny and round-shouldered and chronically perplexed, overworked in his graduate studies and exhausted by self-imposed deadlines and tyrannical dreams of perfection, prematurely weary of living, like a creature in whom spasms of life articulate themselves even as the creature sinks, ebbs, dies, like a pebble tossed carelessly into a pond: its very weight, its *quidditas*, dooming it to extinction. Ian McCullough had come to the University of Michigan on a fellowship, suffused with enthusiasm for the future, and within two months he had lapsed into depression, compulsive thoughts, a preoccupation with suicide: a preoccupation with the horror of realizing that, in his flesh, in his skin, in his very being, he was incapable of determining any connection with anything or anyone outside him. *Just as we lie alone in our graves, so indeed do we live alone,* he'd thought repeatedly, so hypnotized by these damning words that he'd long forgotten where he had first heard them. He had never told anyone, not even Glynnis, not even Denis Grinnell, of the visit he had once made to the most highly regarded professor in the Michigan philosophy department at that time, a former student of Wittgenstein, in order to confront the man with a proposition: "If there is no *logical,* no *necessary,* no *causal* connection between interior and exterior consciousness, shouldn't we all kill ourselves? What is the point of continuing?" The reasonableness with which these words were spoken quite belied the desperation behind them, but the man merely smiled at Ian, as at a son, and said, "You're undernourished, you've been neglecting your health, I know the symptoms: your blood sugar is down."

Not long afterward, in any case, Glynnis entered his life: and changed it forever.

Their meeting was sheerly accidental: Ian had been in a cafeteria, "behaving strangely," as Glynnis afterward said, as if he were dizzy, or walking in his sleep; suddenly his nose began to bleed, and he seemed helpless to deal with it: blood on his shirt, splotches on the floor, so very red, so suddenly and humiliatingly public. . . . Desperate, he'd searched his pockets for a tissue but found nothing. And a very attractive red-haired girl advanced upon him, asking matter-of-factly, "Can I help?"

Yes. Yes. Oh yes.

HE WAS SAYING, now, to Sigrid Hunt, in his most practical, fatherly tone, "This doesn't mean that you are cruel, or selfish, or vindictive—or 'unnatural.' It doesn't mean that you might not, at another time in your life, really want to have a baby." Sigrid listened, listened very hard. "And if it's a question of money. . . ."

She shook her head slowly, wiped her face with a towel soaked in cold water that Ian had given her. "I can't accept money from you," she said. "Even as a loan."

"Surely, as a loan?"

"I just don't think I can do that, Dr. McCullough."

"Are we back to 'Doctor'!"

Ian smiled, stared at her, thinking, Why am I so angry? I am in no way an angry man.

"But I think you had better do that, under the circumstances," he said gently. "Don't you?"

She stared at the floor, wriggled her bare, dirty toes. In moving she released a scent, an odor, of flesh upon which perspiration has newly dried, gummy, talcum-y, reminding Ian of those days, now long past, when he'd changed his infant daughter's diapers: the relief in tossing away the soiled diaper; the small cheery reliable pleasure of affixing the new into place; the comforting smell, now long forgotten, of baby powder.

Sigrid said, not meeting his eye, "But this is a loan, of course. I'll repay it as soon as"—and here her voice dropped, grew vague again—"as things fall into place in my life."

By chance Ian had forgotten to remove his checkbook from his overcoat pocket the day before, so it was no trouble to make out, to the order of Sigrid Hunt, a check on his personal account for the sum of $1,000. He had no idea of the cost of an abortion, nor did he want to know, even as he guessed that Sigrid's intention of repaying the loan would come to nothing.

She will pocket the difference and consider it money earned, he decided. And this thought for some reason pleased him.

Sigrid took the check from him and frowned at it, as if, even now, she might reconsider. But she said, "Thank you, Dr.—I mean Ian. Thank you so very much."

The pupils of her eyes were dilated, like a cat's, and their whites threaded with blood, rather yellowish, like smooth-worn coins; she was still "tranquilized" but determined now to behave with composure, dignity, even a belated social tact. She tied the sash of the terry-cloth robe more tightly around her waist, stuck her feet into slippers, smoothed her hair back from her face with a deft double movement of her hands. She asked, "May I make you some coffee? Though I'm afraid it isn't very fresh. Or would you like a—"

"Thank you, but no," Ian said. "I must leave."

"—a drink?"

"Thank you. No."

She helped him into his coat, handed him his smart green woolen scarf, his smart Astrakhan hat, and a fur-lined glove that had fallen out of one of his pockets. Repentant, shamed, or at the very least shamefaced, she followed him to the door: stood shivering at the top of the ill-smelling stairs, her braid loosened and askew down her back. "I'm so sorry," she said; "so damned *embarrassed*," she said, smiling suddenly and adding, "Will you come back another time, Ian, and allow me to be more hospitable?"

As if impulsively, she took up both his hands in hers and kissed them; looked up at him with such raw gratitude, such childlike undissembled hunger, Ian had to back off. "Thank you," she said softly, "—Ian."

But he was thinking, No.

IT SURPRISED HIM that, outside, the sun still shone, the day still continued; he'd been exhausted by his hours in Sigrid Hunt's flat. But the snowy glare was still strong enough to bring tears to his eyes.

A light snowfall had defined the trees and bushes around the garage more clearly, reminding him, yet more poignantly, of a Japanese watercolor or woodcut. Beauty in squalor, he thought. And how fitting, here.

It would go no further, of course. He would not allow it to go further. He had not once been unfaithful to his wife, in twenty-six years of marriage. Nor had he considered being unfaithful, except in rare vengeful fantasy. He wondered, not whether he should tell Glynnis about the visit, and the check—for of course he would tell her; it was inconceivable that he not tell her—but when he should do so; and in what manner. With Glynnis, sensitive as she was and startlingly quick, at times, to take offense, manner was crucial. *A very odd thing happened to me today. A very strange thing happened to me today. A very . . .*

Ian McCullough drove back to Hazelton-on-Hudson in a trance that was both erotic and rueful: guessing that what he'd done might be a mistake but quite satisfied with himself that, against the grain of his natural caution, he had done it. He thought of himself, that February afternoon—to be specific, the afternoon of February 20, 1987—with satisfaction and, even, a measure of pride, as a man crawling over a carved rock face whose lineaments he cannot see but which he has faith will be revealed to him in time. In time.

THE EVERGREENS' SNOWY BOUGHS

Two days later there was a heavy snowfall, and the temperature dropped overnight to −15 degrees F. and by 10 A.M. had risen to only 4 degrees. The air had a sharp Arctic taste that seemed to suit the day, which was Sunday; the earth's axis might have shifted, the sky was so blue, the sun so blazoning. Ian stood in the doorway staring, his breath turning thinly to steam. The freezing air eddied around him and Glynnis called from another room, "Ian? Is the front door open? Are you going out?"

He was. He was going out, dressed in a bulky down jacket frayed and grimy at the cuffs, a woolen ski cap on his head, his oldest pair of winter gloves. And boots: heavy snow boots the women of the household, Glynnis and Bianca, called his paratrooper's boots, their laces crusted with dried mud and left untied.

It was Ian's intention to shake the heavy clumps of snow from those branches of their many evergreen trees that were within reach. Yesterday, and during the night, about twelve inches of snow had fallen; some of the trees, particularly those on the windward side of the house, were bent nearly double. In bed that morning Ian had had a vision of them snapping under their terrible burden.

Glynnis came up close behind him, saying, shivering, "Why are you standing with the door open, Ian? Either go in or go out." She laid a hand on his sleeve. "Not that I'm urging you to go out in this cold."

"I don't mind the cold," Ian said, but since this wasn't altogether true, and Glynnis knew it, he smiled and added, "—certain kinds of cold."

He stepped outside into the knife-sharp air and Glynnis stood in the doorway in a long cardigan sweater, arms folded tightly beneath her breasts, a certain gaiety in her face and voice—she was by nature a happy person, and mornings were good times for her. "It's the sunshine, the pure air, like the Arctic," she said, drawing a deep breath. She spoke slowly, as if reading Ian's mind. "So beautiful. So *bracing.*" Midway across the snow-heaped courtyard (where, in milder weather, a profusion of roses bloomed, and English ivy snaked across the flagstones), Ian heard Glynnis call out, "Maybe I'll come out and join you; won't you need help?"

But Ian seemed not to have heard; he didn't pause or look back. Glynnis must have thought better of her impulsive offer and closed the door: carefully. The walls in which the heavy carved door was set were made entirely of glass and there was a danger, as the McCulloughs had been warned by the previous owner of the house, that, if the door should ever be slammed really hard, the plate glass might crack, or even shatter. Had that ever happened? the McCulloughs asked, concerned, and the man paused, as if thinking better of his warning, and said, smiling, evasive, Yes, I think it did happen, once—in the time of another owner.

CELEBRATION

1.

My house. My family. My life.

Midafternoon of the day of her husband's fiftieth birthday, Glynnis McCullough stands in the kitchen of their house at 338 Pearce Drive, Hazelton-on-Hudson, New York, her pulse pleasantly fast, her fingers chilled with anticipation: like an actress in the wings, awaiting her cue. It is April 7, 1987, a day merely checked on the McCulloughs' heavily annotated calendar, but a day of much plotting, calculation, expectation. That evening, there is to be a surprise birthday party in Ian's honor, to which only their closest dearest friends have been invited. Ian of course knows nothing about the celebration, suspects nothing; he is the most trusting of men, Glynnis says of him, amused yet respectful: he never asks questions about the household; he leaves that sort of thing to *me*.

The kitchen is warm with April sunshine, and warm with the odors of cooking, baking, activity. It is Glynnis's favorite room in the house though she does not think of it as merely a "room": rather as a place of retreat, sanctuary, unfailing consolation and pleasure. Many of the fixtures are new, or relatively new: the large, finely calibrated stove and microwave oven; the green refrigerator; the butcher-block table with its raw, clean, blond wood; the long horizontal glass window above the sink and counters, over which a dozen hanging plants have been set in ceramic pots. Crammed into shelves in the butcher-block table is a library of much-consulted cookbooks; overhead, hanging from hooks and positioned on the walls, are gleaming copper pans and molds, an assortment of wooden spoons, knives with shining blades, and whisks, and scoops, and carving boards, and bunches of garlic, dried herbs—mysterious dessicated things whose names and precise functions Glynnis McCullough can call up in an instant, should any visitor to her kitchen inquire. (And this is a Hazelton kitchen much visited.) Prominent atop the butcher-block table is a handsome new food processor; hidden away in cupboards are specialty utensils of various kinds—colanders, casserole dishes, gratin dishes, soufflé dishes, cast-iron skillets, a cast-aluminum crepe pan, woks and scone pans and egg poachers. In a corner of the kitchen is a round wooden table, several chairs, a Moroccan rug, a small portable television. Though the family eats breakfast at this table, the table is really Glynnis's; she answers mail here, does quick handwritten drafts of her writing—food articles and columns, cookbooks.

Glynnis's current project is a book tentatively titled *American Appetites: Regional American Cooking from Alaska to Hawaii*, at which she has been working, with varying degrees of inspiration and frustration, for the past year. Though Glynnis's first two books were praised by reviewers and have sold well, she prefers to think of herself as an amateur: an amateur writer, an amateur cook, an amateur "food person." (There is room for only one true professional in the McCullough family, Glynnis has told friends.) The first cookbook had seemed to Glynnis scarcely *written* at all, merely assembled, at the urging of Hazelton friends; the second was her publisher's idea; the third, though Glynnis's own idea, seems to her now overly ambitious, rather more professional in its background, research, notes than she would like. But with the passage of months the book has acquired its own idiosyncratic tone and its own erratic momentum. *American Appetites:* the title came to her, seemingly, in a dream, or in one of her kitchen reveries. In any case it is the first of Glynnis McCullough's cookbooks to be more than a mere assemblage of recipes; it is—thus the frustration, and the fear!—the first of her books to be really *written.*

Since the meal she plans to serve this evening is fairly demanding and involves an uncommon degree of time coordination, Glynnis has begun it hours, even days, beforehand—the seviche, for instance, to serve fifteen, has been marinating since yesterday morning in the refrigerator; the sourdough bread is even now in the oven, with twelve minutes yet to go; the preliminaries of the ballotine of chicken *à la Régence* are well under way—the several chickens properly boned, and the stock for the sauce simmering, and the *farce à quenelles à la panade* prepared, and the fine-chopped truffles, and the tongue (this delicacy gives Glynnis a curious sort of *frisson,* its mere touch—it took Ian years to acquire a taste for it). And the salad greens, in a large wooden bowl, are in the refrigerator, covered; and the tart, mustardy French dressing to accompany them has been mixed. Late last night, while Ian was in Philadelphia giving a lecture, Glynnis had made one of the desserts, with results that were encouraging: a sour-cream chocolate cake with thick rippled fudge frosting upon which, in crystalline vanilla frosting, she wrote HAPPY 50TH IAN! in childlike block letters. There is a delivery imminent from the wine and liquor store, and from the florist; and as soon as Marvis finishes with her housework, the two women will fit an extra leaf into the dining room table, to open it out for fifteen and to begin the task, which Glynnis always loves, of setting her table. We'll be a bit crowded at dinner, Glynnis apologized, when she called to invite her friends, but I hope you won't mind. Of course, Marvis is going to help every inch of the way.

(Knowing, of course, that no one in their circle would mind in the slightest; being crowded sociably together, for one of Glynnis Mc-Cullough's superb meals, has never troubled anyone in the past.)

Though Glynnis is an experienced cook and, most of the time, a quite confident hostess, tonight's party for her husband worries her: not so much the party itself, and the food—which will be tricky, but surely manageable—as the fact of its being a surprise, that most dubious of pleasures. "Do you think Ian might find it too much of a surprise?" she had asked their friend Denis Grinnell. "Coming into the house unprepared, preoccupied with his thoughts as he invariably is, and then finding all of you waiting?" "I think Ian will love it," Denis said. And then: "*I* would love it." (There is an old and not entirely resolved emotional issue between Glynnis McCullough and Denis Grinnell, to which, in the tacit understanding that has evolved between them, Denis may freely, yet never reproachfully, allude; while Glynnis is empowered to remain silent. Though Denis's allusions may sometimes annoy her, or make her feel guilty, they more often please her, with the knowledge that, though she and her husband's closest friend will never again make love, she is loved by him still; he remains faithful to her as any husband.) But Denis is not the point; Denis is no reliable measure, for he and Ian are quite distinct personalities, Glynnis thinks, and what the one might love, the other might not.

To another friend, a woman friend, Glynnis said, laughing, "Isn't it odd, I really don't know whether Ian will be happy with the party or furious with me afterward; whether a 'surprise' of this kind might be too extreme for him, or whether it's what he'd most like, in secret, for his fiftieth birthday. What do you think?"

The woman, Meika Cassity, like Glynnis the wife of a man prominent in his profession (in Vaughn Cassity's case, architecture), said, as if the question did not warrant much thought, "We must always do what *we* want to do and hope that it's what *they* will like, or, in any case, what they will accept as liking. Otherwise, you know, Glynnis," Meika said, dropping her voice in a sly pleased slide, "life in Hazelton would be quite dull."

"Yes, I suppose so," Glynnis said; and though ordinarily she would have liked very much to pursue the theme Meika had introduced—like Meika Cassity, Glynnis McCullough has a taste for adventure, and news of others' adventures—she persisted in her own theme; of limited interest to others, perhaps, it was of crucial interest to her. "Do you think it's odd, though—and please speak frankly, Meika—that after living with Ian for so many years, I really, at times, don't seem to know him at all and can't predict how he'll react to things? For instance—"

"Oh, they live in their own heads," Meika said, "our 'brilliant' husbands. They're happiest there, so we must learn to be happy here."

" 'Here'—?"

"Here."

Glynnis smiled; her friend's answer pleased her. They were speaking over the telephone, and Glynnis was in her snug corner of the kitchen, seated at the table, back to the wall, midmorning cigarette in hand; a mug of coffee, black and strong, before her. Spread across the table were notes and cards upon which recipes had been typed, and a miscellany of magazine and newspaper articles, columns, and clippings on the subject of food; a yet-unread section of that morning's *New York Times;* the April issue of *Gourmet,* in which Glynnis herself had an article. The dark-tiled kitchen floor shone; in the window opposite, several of the hanging plants, the Swedish geraniums, were in bloom; how quiet, how lovely, the house, my house, Glynnis thought, with Ian and Bianca gone. "Oh, yes," she told Meika. *"Here."*

And afterward thought, Why don't Meika and I feel more comfortable with each other? We are like sisters, really.

GLYNNIS WONDERED THEN, and wonders now, thinking ahead to the party, and to Ian's arrival, and the guests, and the food, and the small quick deft tasks she alone will have to do, to orchestrate the evening as she wishes, whether it is a terrible sort of vanity and selfishness, her contentment with such domestic matters: her happiness in them, and in making others, by way of them, happy. Food is such a simple thing, Glynnis's mother once said, perplexed—why is it so difficult? Yet Glynnis has never found it difficult; no more than she finds love, or at any rate lovemaking, difficult. "It helps not to think," she said. "Just *do*."

The evening's agenda is: Ian will remain at the Institute until his usual hour, around six o'clock, when he will drive to the Poughkeepsie airport to pick up Bianca (coming home from Connecticut for her father's birthday, presumably a small quiet affair involving only the three of them); he will arrive home, unsuspecting, between seven and seven-thirty, well in time for their usual dinner at eight. In the meantime, arriving between six-thirty and six-forty-five, their friends will gather in the guest room at the rear of the house, having parked their cars along Pearce Drive in a way calculated not to arouse Ian's suspicion. Bianca will lead her father into the house by a side door (the McCulloughs' long low modern multiroomed house has a half dozen entrances), a strategically safe distance from either the kitchen or the dining room. And Glynnis, her apricot chiffon dress more or less hidden by one of her oversized aprons, will go to greet them and behave as she normally would—assuming of course that Bianca is behaving as *she* normally would—and trusting to intuition and improvisation, Glynnis will lead Ian back into the guest room, where their friends await him. . . . But beyond that crucial moment she doesn't want to think; her heart beats too quickly.

The oven timer has begun to chime; Glynnis takes out the sourdough bread in three baking pans, sets them on the butcher-block table. But the heady delicious smell does not quite placate her. She thinks, What if it *is* a mistake? And our friends are embarrassed for us?

It is true, she'd given several surprise parties for Bianca when Bianca was a small child, and those parties, however meticulously planned and overseen, had not been unqualified successes: Glynnis recalls the house filled with laughing, screaming, galloping children; disappointment at the outcome of games and the inevitably "unfair" distribution of prizes; even outbursts of childish temper and tears; her own sudden fatigue, before the last of the children was taken away. Though she has long ago forgotten the woman's name (this was in Cambridge, while Ian still taught at Harvard), she will always remember another young mother saying to her, with a look of wonder and pity, "As the Irish say, Glynnis, 'Better you than me.'" But the good memories far outweigh the bad: a little boy pulling at Glynnis's sleeve to whisper, "You're pretty, Missus"; the gaiety, the high spirits, the laughter, the sheer silly fun of the children's games, and their excitement in playing them; the delight the children took in bringing Bianca presents, prettily wrapped by others, and watching her open them. And of course there was Bianca's excitement, Bianca's childish gratitude. In a pink party dress, eyes wide with pleasure, plump cheeks flushed, Glynnis's little girl clambering on her lap and throwing her arms around her: "Mommy I love love *love* you!"

Years ago.

The sourdough bread is perfect, Glynnis thinks. Crusty in precisely the way she'd wanted. It is Ian's favorite bread, of the numerous breads Glynnis bakes: a bread he himself tried to bake, in fact, a few years ago, under an odd short-lived inspiration, derived from a friend's enthusiasm about his own bread-baking experiences. (The man is Malcolm Oliver, a journalist and an adjunct fellow of the Institute, an old friend of the McCulloughs' and, like Ian, rather caught up in a world of abstraction: of words.) But Ian's kitchen adventures, amusing to relate to friends as anecdotes, were not entirely amusing at the time; and Glynnis did not much enjoy overseeing her husband so closely, forced of necessity—for of course she *was* forced—to correct him when he did things wrong, or was about to do things wrong. In Ian McCullough's world of dauntingly complex demographic studies, computer programs, *Journal of International Politics* business, and labyrinthine professional intrigues, his judgment and his authority are unquestioned; elsewhere, one might say (as Meika said) *here,* he seems so frequently at sea, well-intentioned but oddly clumsy, as if uncoordinated: as if there were some neurological lapse, or block, between word and act. In the kitchen, optimistic as he was, hands covered in flour and dough as he'd seemed rather to like them, he listened to instructions but did not hear; or, hearing, did not understand; or, understanding, did not want to understand. "You can't bear to take orders from another adult," Glynnis said, teasing, yet exasperated; and Ian countered, lightly and cleverly, as Ian McCullough invariably did, "Who then would I take orders from, Glynnis, if not 'another adult'?"

His questions so often strike her as riddles: Zen koans of a kind; though, in Ian's case, the questioner does not know the answer, and asks, it sometimes seems, in order to know. Yet there are no answers to such questions; that Glynnis knows.

She loves him; even in, sometimes, disliking him, raging at him, she loves him; for he seems to inhabit her, like an indwelling spirit that is both *other* and *herself:* a twin. If, over the stretch of their long marriage, Glynnis has been, now and then, unfaithful to Ian, she has rarely been unfaithful to him in the more spacious sense of the word; she has never loved another man as she loves him. Indeed, planning this birthday celebration and preparing, with such anticipation, the food, Glynnis feels her heart swell with love of him, and gratitude for him, that he is the source of so much happiness: a bounty of feeling that spills over onto their friends as well, for without friendship, without a circle of close friends, there can be no true celebration.

It is four-thirty. The delivery from the wine and liquor store arrives, and from the florist; Marvis finishes with her vacuuming, and she and Glynnis tug at the dining room table and pry the halves apart, after some effort (Ian evidently locked the table, without telling Glynnis, when they'd put it together last), and fit the extra leaf into place, and begin setting the table. Midway, Glynnis breaks off, to return to the kitchen, to the chicken and the *farce à quenelles à la panade:* working, as the afternoon wanes, in a bliss of concentration. For fifteen people Glynnis must in fact prepare three ballotines; going through the motions, dreamy yet deft, of sewing, rolling in waxed paper, then in a kitchen towel. Her fingers move with their own practiced intelligence; her skin warms as if lit from within; her eyes grow misty. Why is it Ian has never understood? Why does he imagine his world, because it is an abstract world, is naturally superior to hers, because it is physical, tactile . . . because it is food?

Glynnis moves from counter to stove to butcher-block table, from table to counter, counter to refrigerator, refrigerator to sink, sink to table to counter, counter to stove, stove to sink to refrigerator to counter to table, humming to herself, deeply absorbed, unthinking. From time to time she catches sight of her reflection in one of the kitchen's shiny surfaces; she likes best the floating, very nearly iconic face at eye level in the coppery undersides of her pans. This face is both Glynnis Mc-

Cullough's and that of an unknown woman; it reveals none of the small blemishes of middle age, the fine white lines bracketing eyes and mouth, the tiny dents, tucks, creases in the skin, the soft crepey look beneath the eyes, that ordinarily distress her. Glynnis is a beautiful woman still, she supposes; but, after all, she *is* forty-eight years old, and how much longer can beauty reasonably last? In her kitchen, however, where no true mirrors are allowed, reflecting surfaces are benign. Even Glynnis's hair, silver-streaked since girlhood, flames up a rich lustrous russet-red in this room.

Glynnis loves, too, her kitchen library: the shelf of cookbooks and food books. Many of their pages are torn and stained, the recipes annotated, modified: "corrected." In some margins there are stars, in others question marks, or exclamation points, or those curse symbols unique to cartoons. Leafing idly through certain of these books is like leafing through old diaries; the other evening, half seriously, she'd told Ian that, when they were both old, really old, elderly, they might read these entries aloud to each other; and certain meals, certain days in their lives and evenings with friends, entire pockets of lost time, might be returned to them: as in Proust. "Won't that be lovely?" Glynnis asked, struck by the notion; and Ian smiled, and ran a hand through his hair, and regarded her for so long in silence that Glynnis thought he must not have heard her question. Then he said, "Yes. It will. Lovely."

At five-twenty, when the table is nearly set and Glynnis is about to break off work and take a long restful restorative bath, the doorbell rings again; and it is another, and unexpected, floral delivery. This one, a half dozen pink rosebuds, filled out with those delicate lacy pale flowers—or are they in fact leaves that resemble flowers?—that florists use to such advantage, is unsigned, mysteriously unsigned: merely a small birthday card and the inscription *Happiness to both,* in what is very likely a florist's assistant's hand. Glynnis smiles, delighted as a child; puts the flowers in one of her cut-glass Waterford vases, inherited from her grandmother, thinking, Our celebration has begun.

2.

They were undressing for bed, one blowsy March night, when Ian said suddenly, in that way he had, though, since coming to Hazelton-on-Hudson, he spoke in this way less frequently, "Do you feel, Glynnis, that you have a soul?" Glynnis said quizzically, "Do I feel that I have a—?" "You know: a *soul*," Ian said. His smile was faint, and wistful; an expression in his face that Glynnis could not have named, except that it was so uniquely her husband's: a boyish look of sobriety and doubt, on the edge of anxiety; yet there was a readiness too to smile, and make a joke of it, if his mood was not matched by hers. (For, like all the men of Glynnis's acquaintance, like all Hazelton men, in any case, Ian most dreaded seeming naïve, or foolish: being made a fool.) He'd come to an absentminded stop in buttoning the shirt of his flannel pajamas; he had taken off his glasses, and his eyes looked inordinately round and exposed.

Glynnis slipped into bed; propped herself up against her pillows, arms behind her head; considered the question seriously, instead of making light of it, or outrightly mocking it, as she might, in other circumstances, have done. *Do* I have a soul? She said, after a moment, "I suppose I do."

"You have a soul?"

Glynnis smiled; and frowned; made an effort not to be annoyed by this old habit of Ian's, more pronounced in recent weeks, of repeating questions verbatim which had seemingly been answered. "I don't know," she said. "Do I? Is this a quiz, or a catechism?"

"You 'have' a soul?"

"Isn't that what you've asked me?"

Ian spoke slowly and gravely, as if transcribing his own words. "And your soul, you feel, is somehow distinct from you?"

"Distinct from me?"

"You say that you 'have' a soul, and you seem to be quite certain. But that means that the soul is something other than you, since you 'have' it. The way you have a foot, or a certain shade of hair, I mean. An object to your subject."

Glynnis saw in which direction Ian was headed, and laughed, and sighed; for really, if they were going to talk instead of sleeping, there were any number of practical things about which they might talk—household repairs, the problem of Bianca, a conflict of dates and appointments the following afternoon. She said, with an air of thoughtfulness, "It really couldn't be, could it?—I mean, distinct from me. I mean, if *it* is me. I'm sure you're right."

"What do you mean, 'right'?" Ian said, startled. "In what way am I 'right'?"

"That I can't have a soul distinct from me, if it is also me."

"Yet you speak of the phenomenon as 'it.' As something that must be distinct from you."

"Maybe it's a bad habit, a linguistic habit. Aren't questions like these—"

"Then do you think you might *be* a soul?—as distinct from 'having' one?"

Glynnis laid a forearm over her eyes, shielding them from the bedside lamp. For all her sense of herself as a person of nearboundless energy, the envy of her friends, she felt, many nights, very tired; tiredness, sheer physical tiredness, pulsed from her knees, ankles, feet. "Oh Ian, could we talk about this another time? *Haven't* we talked about it already? It's nearly one in the morning," she said, disliking both the practicality of her tone and its familiarity, "and we'll be getting up at seven. We have to figure out what to do about tomorrow. If the Honda is going to be serviced first thing in the morning, and if you want to drive to—"

"Just tell me, please," Ian said, with a peculiar sort of urgency. "It's important to me to know what you think."

"But that isn't what you asked a minute ago."

"What?"

Glynnis took pleasure of her own in such needle-sharp rebuttals. "You asked what did I *feel.*"

"Of course. Of course I did. Yes, I want to know, not what you think, but what you feel."

"I *feel . . .*" But suddenly, with, almost, a stab of fear, she did not know what she felt; or even, with Ian standing there, staring toward her, so unnervingly intense, what she thought. She said, less patiently, "Oh, Christ, honey, I'm perfectly happy to *be* a soul or to *have* a soul; whatever suits you."

Ian said, hurt, "You really do think me a fool, don't you."

"Of course I don't. I love you."

"Is that a refutation?"

"A what?"

She saw he was smiling at her, trying too to joke, even clowning a bit, mugging. He rubbed his head with both hands energetically, like a cartoon character. "At least, if one is neither a soul nor possesses a soul," he said, "one can't *lose* his soul. That's a cheerful proposition."

"Come to bed," Glynnis, laughing. "Make love."

"Which would prove—?"

"*Dis*prove."

Though Glynnis hadn't been serious—the hour was alarmingly late; she and Ian were both very tired, and were, in any case, no longer in the habit of making love with much frequency, and never at such odd, impromptu times—she began to feel, as Ian approached, a warm dark pool of desire, rather blurred, amorphous, both desire and the memory of desire, pulsing in her loins; and felt a moment's anguish, as at a loss undiscovered until now.

Ian said practically, as he slipped into bed, cool-limbed, coltish, always taking up more room than Glynnis anticipated, "It's too late for love."

IN HER BATH, Glynnis recalls that night; and other nights, since then, when Ian has behaved not oddly, or even disagreeably, but not as "himself"; even when making love, or attempting love, with her. At such times his thoughts are clearly elsewhere, careening and darting and plunging: elsewhere. Glynnis thinks, He doesn't love me in the old way. She thinks, hurt, angry, baffled, yet hopeful, Things will be better in a few months. (A political situation is brewing at the Institute: Dr. Kreizer will be retiring in the fall of 1988, and his successor must be named within the next six months. Though Ian has not cared to talk about it, Glynnis knows, from Denis, that Ian is Max's favored choice to take over the directorship. And Ian does not know, is in an anguish of not knowing, if he wants the honor, and the work, and the responsibility; or if, in fact, he wants to cut back on his professional commitments, with the hope of taking a year off fairly soon and working on an old project of his—political theory? historical theory?—set aside when the McCulloughs moved from Cambridge to Hazelton.)

Now that Bianca is away at college and Glynnis and Ian are alone together, for the first time in nineteen years, it seems to Glynnis that their relations are more tentative: at times more romantic, yet nervously so, as if something were not quite settled between them. There is relief, certainly, in Bianca's absence, since the strain between mother and daughter has been, these past two or three years, considerable, yet not the kind of relief Glynnis might have anticipated. If, for instance, she touches Ian, in affection or playfully, he is slow to respond: and then responds as if by rote. In sleep, he no longer responds at all, as if sleep were a counterworld, into which he disappears, and Glynnis cannot follow.

She thinks, How far he has come since that morning in Ann Arbor. In the cafeteria, stricken by nosebleed.

Stricken. Helpless.

He misses Bianca, of course; misses that other, if unpredictable, corner of their triangle. Misses, in Bianca, a part of his youth. (As Glynnis understands she does too; it's pointless not to acknowledge the fact.) When Glynnis telephoned Bianca at Wesleyan, to tell her about the birthday celebration and to invite her, Bianca had been guarded at first, as if suspecting that Glynnis wanted something from her, or of her; then she became enthusiastic, almost excessively so, as if the idea had been her own. "Of course I want to be included," she said. "It isn't every day Daddy has his *fif*tieth birthday." During their ten-minute conversation Bianca returned to the subject of Ian's age several times, as if the fact were a surprise to her; as if, like those countless statistical facts with which her father conjured in his demographic studies, it had to be interpreted in a social and not merely a personal context. "Well, fifty isn't really old any longer, is it?" Bianca said. Then, "For a man, I mean."

You little bitch, Glynnis thought.

But said, only, laughing, "Honey, it isn't old at *all*."

It is in her bath, conscious of her breasts buoyant and warmly lifting, as if caressed from beneath, that Glynnis is likely to recall her pregnancy, her pregnancies: thinking, rather unfairly, of Bianca as she is now in terms of Bianca as she'd been before her actual birth . . . those many hours, those terrible hours, of labor. How true it is: bringing forth a child is labor; bringing forth *that* child was labor! Glynnis had worked to give birth to Bianca, and Bianca, it seemed, had resisted, as if not wanting to be born; one body, pain-racked, had expelled another body from it, in order that both might live. We have never quite forgiven each other, Glynnis thinks.

Though in fact Glynnis has forgotten the pain, mostly. As she has forgotten, except as a minor stab of a loss, Bianca's infant brother, to be named Jonathan, who died aged three days. It is a few minutes after six. Glynnis dresses with care, regarding herself critically in the largest of the bedroom mirrors; feels an urge, quickly suppressed, to get herself a glass of wine and sip from it as she dresses, a habit of some years ago. (When the affair with Denis—begun, really, as play, quite innocent play, on Glynnis's part—became something rather more serious than either had intended.) Like most extremely attractive women, at least during the period of their lives when their attractiveness is incontestable, Glynnis has always enjoyed dressing for special occasions: takes delight in making herself up, fashioning her hair, painting her nails, wearing jewelry, perfume. There is something about the ritual that is reassuring, Glynnis thinks, though with the passage of time one will not want to look *too* closely in the mirror.

She has chosen a chiffon dress, not new but allegedly Ian's favorite: a soft, romantic apricot shade, with numerous narrow rippling pleats and a low-cut beaded neckline, that shows her breasts to advantage. Her shoulders and arms too are partly exposed; bare, and rosy from the bath, they suggest the boneless yet resilient flesh of a woman in a Renoir painting. She stares at herself as if hypnotized. Is this the person, the face and body, others see? But who *is* it, they see?

The telephone begins ringing. She hears Marvis answer it, in a distant room.

And the celebration, so long anticipated, cannot be more successful: at the outset, at least.

Ian, with Bianca, arrives home just after seven-thirty; and it is immediately evident, from their faces, that Bianca has told him nothing, and that Ian—ah, Ian!—suspects nothing. He hangs his trench coat in the closet, retires briefly to his bathroom, and, when he emerges, having washed his face and combed his hair, Glynnis, under the pretext of serving him a before-dinner drink, leads him back to the semidarkened room where their friends are waiting, as easily, she will say afterward, as a lamb is led to slaughter. How could he follow her so trustingly? so unquestioningly? Hadn't he noticed her chiffon dress beneath the apron? Her hair, her perfume? The pearls around her neck, the pearls screwed into her earlobes?

But no: he is taken totally by surprise. *Happy birthday, Ian! Congratulations, Ian!* He is moved, quite deeply moved, by his friends' greetings: their handshakes, embraces, kisses; the warmth and obvious love they feel for him. And Bianca, who throws her arms extravagantly around his neck: *Happy birthday, Daddy!* For a minute or two Glynnis sees that he is rather disoriented: adjusting his glasses, smiling, blinking, peering at faces, looking around, as if for someone not there. (But surely Glynnis has invited their closest dearest friends? Is there someone Ian would have added?) One of the men fixes a drink for him, and Malcolm Oliver takes a series of quick flashing shots with his Polaroid camera, and Glynnis links her arm through his and leads him into a quieter corner of the room and says, "Ian? You aren't angry with me, are you? Is it too much of a surprise?"

Ian kisses her, and says, "Of course not; why would I be angry with you? I'm delighted. I am absolutely delighted. It is worth it, almost, after all, to be fifty years old in America."

BUT NO ONE will acknowledge the pink roses.

Glynnis makes inquiries; Glynnis is curious and perplexed and, of course, flattered—for the anonymous sender was thoughtful enough to say *Happiness to both*—but no one will acknowledge the roses. The Kuhns had had delivered, that afternoon, a rather regal floral display, too large, in fact, for Glynnis to use as a centerpiece; and Glynnis herself had ordered flowers, as she always does for a party, when flowers from her own garden are not available; and Leonard Oppenheim and Paul Owen brought, in hand, an assortment of red roses and carnations. "But who sent us these?" Glynnis asks, holding the cut-glass vase aloft. "Who is so sweet, and so teasing?"

They tell her, "Maybe you have an unknown admirer, Glynnis," but Glynnis says, "No, the card says 'Happiness to both.' It must be one of you," she says, looking at them half pleadingly—at Denis and Roberta, at Malcolm and June, at the Kuhns, at the Cassitys, at the Hawleys, at Leonard and Paul. But no: no one will acknowledge the pink roses.

Later in the evening Glynnis whispers, in Denis's ear, "*Did* you send them? Please tell me if you did." And Denis says, guiltily, "Darling, I wish I *had*."

THE SURPRISE PART of the party is an unqualified success, Glynnis sees. Her husband is in as high spirits, as boyish, as flush-faced, as eloquent and witty and tender, as she has seen him in a very long time. And the appetizers are excellent, as Glynnis McCullough's appetizers invariably are; Beluga caviar, and two kinds of pâté, and a fastidiously prepared vegetable platter. "But don't serve them too much," Glynnis instructs Marvis. "After all, there is dinner yet to come."

Leonard Oppenheim and Paul Owen, who have lived together in

one of the old "historic" houses in Hazelton for nearly twenty years, have brought the McCulloughs a half dozen bottles of champagne, and a stunning champagne it is—Taittinger Blanc de Blancs 1976. ("Is this as good as it tastes?" Malcolm Oliver asks the room, holding his champagne glass aloft.) Others have brought bottles of Scotch, brandy, liqueur, candied fruits, chocolates; Ian's fellow squash players—Denis, Malcolm, Vaughn, Vincent—have chipped in to buy him a "custom-sculpted" milk chocolate squash racquet, from the Hazelton Gourmet. There are birthday cards, most of them comical, one or two quite blackly comic, turning upon the theme of being fifty years old. ("I was really quite surprised, browsing through gift shops," Roberta Grinnell confides in Glynnis. "The extraordinary number of joke cards, in *very* bad taste, that have to do with men turning fifty." "Men, and not women?" Glynnis asks. "Men, and not women," Roberta says. "Why, do you suppose?" Glynnis asks, frowning. "Wouldn't the other kind sell?") Glynnis had virtually pleaded with their friends *not* to buy Ian presents, *not* to be extravagant, but of course they ignored her, for what is a birthday celebration without presents, they protested, and, before dinner, seated in a high-backed chair rather like a throne, Ian McCullough unwraps these gifts, taking care, as Glynnis cautions him, *not to rip the beautiful wrapping paper.* And some of these presents are indeed more extravagant than Glynnis might have wished: a wheat-colored Shetland sweater, for instance, from Meika and Vaughn, bought at Hazelton's notoriously overpriced Scotch Wool Shop; an enormous art book, from the Olivers—*Treasures of the Etruscans;* and, of course, the costly liquors, the gourmet shop items. And then there are the funny gifts, the gifts that make Ian laugh, an ebony and brass dress cane, for instance, from the Hawleys, with a rolled-up backgammon set (board, chips, and dice) inside; an elegant silk tie in the shape of a stylized but aggressively ugly fish, from a friend, Leo Reinhart, who couldn't be with them tonight; a gigantic roll of athletic support tape, also from Ian's squash buddies—says Ian solemnly, brandishing the tape aloft, "This *is* just what I need." And Glynnis's present to Ian, fussily wrapped in tissue paper of all colors of the rainbow, is a ten-speed Schwinn racing bicycle: hardly an extraordinary surprise, since Glynnis and Bianca have been after Ian for years to replace his battered old three-speed bicycle with something newer and more à la mode; but Ian seems genuinely taken with it, and thanks her, and kisses her, and makes as if to ride the bicycle out the door. And there is a good deal of laughter, and more drinks are poured. Glynnis hears another of the Blanc de Blancs being uncorked.

And this leaves Bianca, who had, pleading exhaustion from the flight and the general busyness of the day—"I had classes this morning, Mother, you seem to forget"—slipped away from the party after the initial toasts.

But now, dramatically, as if on cue—for Glynnis is about to summon her guests to dinner; it is almost nine-thirty—Bianca reappears, in theatrical attire: a black cutaway coat and trousers, starched white shirt, black derby jauntily aslant on her head. The McCulloughs' friends turn to her, make way for her—*What on earth, Bianca! Ah, look at Bianca!* Glynnis and Ian merely stare at their daughter, so suddenly the center of attention; they are taken totally by surprise. They know that Bianca has been involved in theater, dance, and "performance arts" at college; but they are not prepared, ah, they are *not* prepared, for this.

Bianca's face is powdered a deathly white, like a geisha's; her lips are a luscious bee-stung red; her eyebrows and lashes are blackened as if with soot. Her cottony fawn-colored hair has been pinned back under the hat, and dangling rhinestone earrings gleam in her ears. And she wears spike-heeled black patent leather shoes! Glynnis thinks, This is not like Bianca at all. This is not Bianca, at all.

A space is quickly cleared at the far end of the room and a spotlight of sorts set up. Bianca has brought a tape deck and sets it going; tinny, discordant, cutely lurid music begins—a "symphonic poem" by a contemporary American composer of whom no one in the room has heard. ("Turn down the volume at least," Glynnis pleads; "we'll be *deafened*.") With no word of explanation and no acknowledgment of her audience, Bianca begins her dance on a percussive note, strutting so heavily the carpeted floor shakes; she plays with her hat Charlie Chaplin style: dropping it, kicking it up with a foot, squashing it down hard on her head. She high-steps; she blows moist kisses at the audience; rolls her eyes, winks, smirks, leers; provokes her startled audience into laughter—though why they are laughing, Glynnis does not know. The makeup itself is comical, on a young girl with Bianca's open, fresh, girlish face; it makes her look both innocent and depraved, like a performer out of *Cabaret*.

Then, to Glynnis's horror, Bianca begins to dance more suggestively, as the music itself shifts to another key. She throws her head back until the cords in her pale neck stand out; she moves her rather plump, fleshy body against the beat and the grain of the cacophonous music. In her demonic exuberance she collides with a chair and seems not to notice, gives the fireplace screen a glancing kick, nearly loses her derby hat when its elastic band breaks. She is mocking, funny, defiant, in her heavy-footed strut: swinging her hips clumsily, going through a routine of tics, twitches, salutes, winks, shrugs, and shudders, and a simulation of kisses aimed at her audience. As Glynnis and Ian stare in disbelief, Bianca begins to strip: throwing off the cutaway coat, tossing aside the hat, slowly and provocatively unbuttoning the starched white shirt, all the while smiling, smirking, winking at her audience of middle-aged men and women, most of whom are no longer laughing. For *this* is not funny, is it?

But under the shirt Bianca is wearing another shirt, identical to the first; and under her trousers—no wonder they were so bulky!—another pair of trousers, identical to the first. And under her second shirt there is a third; and under the second pair of trousers—not a third pair, but a black leotard. The adults laugh, most of them, and applaud loudly, seeing that the joke is on them, on their lewd expectations. (Glynnis's eyes have filmed over with moisture. She tries not to see how tight Bianca's leotard is, how revealingly snug against the fatty quivering buttocks, the crotch, the bas relief of pubic hair . . . for this is not parody, or even metaphor, but the real thing, the stark defenseless unmediated flesh of an overgrown child, at which one should not look except in love.)

The performance is over: the dissonant music comes, thank God, to an abrupt end; Bianca, flushed and exuberant, undoes her hair, which falls down past her shoulders, unglamorously yet sensuously, and bows low toward her father, who manages to clap as if he means it and to say, "Bianca, you astonish us!" as if astonishment were a good thing. Bowing low to the rest, Bianca backs out of the room, amid applause and seemingly sincere cries of "Encore! Encore!"

And in the doorway, as if she too is on cue, stands Marvis, in her purplish-black velvety skin and her white maid's dress, hors d'oeuvres tray in hand, staring baffled and unsmiling, uncertain of what she sees: is this funny, or is it not so funny? Bianca McCullough, nineteen years old, exhibiting herself, scarcely clothed, before a room of her parents' friends on her father's fiftieth birthday? Bianca nearly collides with Marvis on her way out, unintentionally provoking another outburst of laughter.

Meika Cassity, meaning to be kind, lays a hand on Glynnis's arm and says, "I never realized your daughter was so *talented*."

Glynnis laughs, and wipes her eyes, and says, "I don't think Ian and I realized either."

"I CAN'T STAY for the actual dinner, Mother—I'm sure I told you that."

Bianca is out of breath from her performance: staring, not at Glynnis, but at her reflection in her dressing table mirror as, with quick, rough, impatient swipes of a Kleenex, she removes the lurid white makeup and the inky black mascara and the red lipstick. She is still wearing the black leotard; her hair hangs in her face; she is barefoot, crouched, the shirt damp and clinging against her back. She leans so close to the mirror that its surface steams faintly.

Glynnis is hurt, and Glynnis is angry; but she says, calmly, " 'Can't'? But why not? You know I've set a place for you."

Bianca shrugs guiltily, assumes another angle at the mirror. She plies the tissue against her skin as if she were scouring herself.

"Beside your father," Glynnis says. "I've set a place for you beside your father."

"But I thought I'd explained," Bianca says, evasively, "that last time we spoke on the phone? Last Thursday? Kim has invited me over, and Greg O'Connor is going to drop by; he's home from MIT for the week, and Scott will probably be in town too, you know, Scotty Simon—"

"Can't you go over to Kim's after dinner? I'm sure your friends will understand."

"Mother, we've made these *plans*."

"But, honey, *when* did you make them?"

There is an edge to Glynnis's voice which she has not intended; Bianca, tossing down the wad of filthy Kleenex, gives her a guilty sullen sidelong look. "*When* did I make them? I don't know, for Christ's sake. Is this an interrogation or something?"

Glynnis says, as if this were the issue, "You do have to eat, don't you?" and Bianca says, shrugging, embarrassed, "Mother, I'll *eat*." And within seconds, though Glynnis has vowed not to be drawn into a quarrel that evening—has vowed not to lose her temper with Bianca, no matter how the girl tempts her—they are quarreling: their old quarrel of years, in a new or, in truth, not so new guise, turning upon Bianca's thoughtlessness, her forgetfulness, her surely *deliberate* selfishness. "You want to spoil the evening, don't you," Glynnis says, her eyes filling with tears. "You want to spoil your father's birthday, and all my plans."

Bianca says meanly, "Mother, the universe does not turn upon you and *all your plans.*"

She seems to be daring Glynnis to slap her: to slap her in the face as she deserves to be slapped; as, not so very long ago, mother slapped daughter, not often, not with any regularity, but often enough.

I hate you, daughter would then scream. As if a lever had been thrown, a lock clicked into place. *I wish I was dead, and I wish you were dead.*

Glynnis says now, carefully, "I'm sorry you feel that way, Bianca." She leaves her daughter's room, closes the door, her heart beating quickly and her hands trembling, as if she has narrowly escaped danger. From the other end of the house comes laughter and raised voices, that familiar, gratifying, so very consoling sound of friends: friends enjoying themselves at one of the McCulloughs' parties. It is always the same party, Glynnis thinks, happily; from even so short a distance as this, always the same. And, *pace* Bianca, the universe does turn upon it.

In the kitchen, she sips from what remains of her glass of champagne. She must begin her last-minute sleight of hand; she and Marvis planned to serve the first course before nine-thirty, and now it is nearly ten.

4.

It would turn out to be three-thirty in the morning, a Sunday morning, the previous September, hardly a week after Bianca had left for college (though there was no relationship between the events, of course), that the McCulloughs were wakened from their sleep by a knocking: more than a knocking, as they'd afterward describe it, a violent hammering, at the front door. What in God's name? Ian said, and Glynnis, terrified, clutching at his arm, whispered, We can't answer it! Don't let them see us!

The McCulloughs' house, designed by a prominent local architect, was set back from the road, even more reclusively than most houses in this part of Hazelton; it had a good deal of glass—plate-glass windows, sliding doors, skylights. It consisted of eight units, four of which were built around an open atrium; one entered the atrium to approach the front door. The bedrooms, the "private" quarters, were of course hidden from the others yet not, in terms of distance, so very far from them. The terrible hammering at the front door was probably not more than thirty feet from where the McCulloughs, now fully wakened, were sitting up in bed, not knowing what to do: for what, in such circumstances, such frightening and wholly unprecedented circumstances, *should* one do?

Glynnis wanted to call the police; Ian thought he should go to see who it was; Glynnis begged him no, no—Then they'll see you; they'll know we are here. Ian said, practically, fumbling for his glasses, But they *know* we are here; the cars are in the driveway. (The hammering had stopped; then began again, as if with renewed ferocity.) The McCulloughs were on their feet now, Glynnis with the telephone receiver in hand, pleading with Ian not to leave the bedroom. It could be kids, she said, half sobbing, kids on dope; we could be murdered, she said, but Ian was at the bedroom door, Ian had opened the door. Call the police, he said, and lock the door after me; I refuse to hide in my own house, for Christ's sake.

So Glynnis locked the door after him and dialed the police emergency number; and Ian inched along the corridor until he was in a position, himself unseen, to see through the glass walls that two—or was it three?—men were standing on the doorstep, and that they had unusually strong flashlights, which they were beaming into the house. Could the men be police? Hazelton police? *Their* police? But why? Why at this hour? And why such furious pounding, as if they wanted to break down the door?

As Ian would afterward recount, in his numerous telephone calls and letters of complaint, he had wanted to call out, "Who is it?"—but the words stuck in his throat. For Glynnis was in the house, and vulnerable; and *he* was vulnerable, God knows, an unarmed middle-aged man whose vision was poor without glasses, lithe and sometimes fairly impressive on the squash court but not, otherwise, in extraordinary physical condition: no match, in any case, for two or three able-bodied men. (And, though he could only make out their approximate shapes, the men on his doorstep certainly did appear to be able-bodied.) Though the men hammered on his door they did not identify themselves in any way.

While Glynnis was speaking with police headquarters and being told, in a mysteriously circumlocutious manner, that the situation was "under control," Ian watched the men in the courtyard: now prowling about, shining their flashlights rudely into the living room and into the dining room; one of them rapped on the kitchen door; then, for no apparent reason, as abruptly as they arrived, they decided to leave. They backed their car out of the driveway so carelessly, Glynnis discovered in the morning, that there were tire tread marks in the wildflower garden bordering the driveway.

It turned out, however improbably—for Hazelton-on-Hudson is hardly the Bronx—that the intruders *were* police, not Hazelton police but state police, investigating, at this late and surely unnecessary hour, a "reported act of vandalism" on Pearce Drive. They would claim to have mistaken 338 Pearce for 388, where, allegedly, a sixteen-year-old boy lived who had been involved in acts of vandalism in the past. They would claim that no harassment of the McCulloughs had been intended; there was "absolutely no connection" between the episode and the McCulloughs' involvement in a recent American Civil Liberties Union case charging police brutality against two young men. (The Thiel-Edwards case, it was called: both Glynnis and Ian had signed a petition, and Ian had helped Malcolm Oliver, an officer in the local branch of the ACLU, organize a protest hearing at the Cattaraugus County courthouse the previous spring.)

At the time, though, the McCulloughs had been quite baffled by the incident and badly shaken. Glynnis wept in relief, in Ian's arms, when the men left. For what, after all, weaponless, unprepared, merely the two of them—and Ian, for all his well-intentioned courage, was hardly a physically imposing man—could they have done, had the three men chosen to break in? *Our house is made of glass,* Glynnis thought, *and our lives are made of glass; and there is nothing we can do to protect ourselves.*

NOW GLYNNIS SAYS, half to herself, "Must we talk about this again? It will only upset us all."

They are at the dinner table, midway in the chicken ballotine; and in a general and quite animated discussion of crime, violence, false arrests, and police corruption—for Malcolm Oliver is researching an article on one or another or all of these subjects—the episode of September 21, 1986, is renewed. The "McCulloughs' harassment," it is called; for naturally their friends know all about it in detail. (Ian in particular was outraged by the incident and talked of little else for days. He made numberless telephone calls, demanded a formal explanation and apology from the state commissioner of police, enlisted the aid and advice of friends in the ACLU about whether he should file charges. For, after all, as he argued, his and Glynnis's civil rights had been violated.) Glynnis would rather talk about something else but knows the subject must be allowed to run its course. Malcolm has much to say, most of it new and quite interesting; Vaughn tells an anecdote, buttressed by Meika, which Glynnis does not remember having heard before; Denis, an old, fiery SDS radical of the sixties, speaks with vehemence of the "encroaching police state"; Ian has something to add, of course; and Amos Kuhn; and the others. Glynnis listens, or half listens; warmed by drink and gratified by the success of her dinner thus far—the seviche, the chicken, the vegetables, the sourdough bread, the Bernkasteler Doktor Auslese 1982 and the equally superb Château Mouton-Rothschild 1976—she allows her thoughts, for very pleasure, to drift. The table is elegantly set, beautifully set: with her finest tablecloth, white embroidered Irish linen-lace, and the pair of pewter candelabra inherited from her grandmother, and the lovely pink roses in the Waterford vase, in the center. Because they are Ian's favorites, Glynnis set the table with the Italian earthenware plates they had brought back years ago from Florence. And the fine-stemmed crystal wineglasses and goblets bought a few weeks ago at Neiman-Marcus's post-Christmas sale. And the beautiful thick Tunisian napkins, a gift from the Grinnells. And, for fun, Glynnis's great-grandmother's gold-plate service . . . really quite beautiful, if a bit, as Glynnis always says, *much.*

Everything appears to be going well; apart from Bianca's behavior, her rudeness both in public and in private, everything is going, Glynnis thinks, wonderfully well.

At his first taste of the ballotine of chicken, Leonard Oppenheim laid down his fork and said, "Glynnis, you've outdone even yourself, this time." And raised his glass to her.

And Glynnis tasted it too, and thought, Yes, it's good, thank God it's good; my effort has paid off.

She has not, she thinks, seen Ian so happy in any social gathering in quite a while.

Nor has she, she thinks, seen her friends so . . . attractively and attentively happy, so harmonious together; no matter if, even with Bianca's place removed, they are a bit crowded around the table.

Denis is talking about an incident that happened to him the other day, in New York City. A near mugging, as he describes it. Glynnis listens to him, as always, with immense interest, watches him admiringly, feels a surge of affection for the man, her husband's closest friend, her closest friend's husband, that is still deeply erotic: yet perhaps more companionable, as if she and Denis had in fact been married, instead of deciding that they must not push things beyond a certain point . . . must not destroy the delicate fabric of their domestic lives. Denis, an economist, like Ian a senior fellow at the Hazelton Institute, is a year or two older than Ian: a thick-shouldered, thick-necked man of moderate height, with a head that might have been painted, in its shrewd peasant solidity, by Brueghel. A bulldog face, Glynnis thinks, but a handsome one. In the candlelight, Denis's somewhat coarse skin is softened and the sharp quizzical frown lines between his eyes have vanished.

Glynnis has seated Denis on her left and, at these close quarters, is led to consider the brief eight months of her affair with him: the "physical" affair, that intense, rather unnervingly intense, parenthesis within the long romance of their friendship. (Has it been fifteen years since the McCulloughs came to Hazelton? It seems impossible.) The affair had begun innocently enough when, in Ian's absence, Denis drove Glynnis home from a party. A kiss, then kisses, and she'd invited him in for a drink; and, next morning, as she'd known he would do, Denis called. *You know I love you, Glynnis. I haven't slept all night. Please let me see you. You must let me see you.* In all, Glynnis supposes they made love, in the fullest sense of the word, less than a dozen times, charged with adolescent fervor and an adulterous sense of guilt. She remembers, dreamily, one vertiginous summer day when, at the zenith of the affair, she made love with Denis in his air-conditioned office at the Institute, on his couch, and reappeared no more than fifteen minutes later, in Ian's company, to have lunch with him and Denis and one or two of their Institute colleagues, on the outdoor terrace of the dining room. And later that afternoon she'd dropped by the Grinnells' house to see Roberta, at that time, as now, Glynnis's closest woman friend. How high she'd been, those days, on her own bravado, her own daring, her astonishment at such behavior. *Am I really doing these things? Is it I, Glynnis, who is capable of such duplicity?*

She had known, then, that absolute trust in another human being is an error. We believe, not what is true, but what we wish to perceive as true.

But the affair ended, as precipitously and emotionally as it had begun. And Glynnis was the one to break it off, thus retaining, in both her imagination and Denis's, a certain measure of advantage.

The discussion of crime, violence, police, et cetera, still continues; Glynnis hears herself say, quite feelingly, in response to a question, "Yes, I still have nightmares about it. I don't know if what they did was really harassment or, as they insisted, a mistake"—"Of course it was harassment," Malcolm says—"but it made me realize how vulnerable we are, how helpless, in a house like this—in any of our houses, I suppose— people like us who don't own weapons, and don't want to own weapons. I suppose you could say," Glynnis continues, pleased at her own eloquence at this table of articulate and assertive people, who frequently interrupt one another in their eagerness to speak, "that, in an equation in which others are assailants, people like us are inevitably victims."

This provokes Vincent Hawley and Meika Cassity, who do not, they declare, want to be victims; what does Glynnis mean, *people like us?* But Roberta agrees with Glynnis; and so does, perhaps too somberly, white-haired Elizabeth Kuhn, who says that there must inevitably be situations, in human society—"in decent civilized society"—in which one simply cannot fight back, even to save one's life; one cannot match evil with evil. And Amos, her husband, rather pointedly disagrees with her; and Denis supports Amos's position; and Meika Cassity interjects a remark or two, closing her pretty beringed hands into fists and raising them aloft: "*I* intend to resist to the death." And they laugh, but the subject, even then, is not, to Glynnis's annoyance, dropped; for Elizabeth, dogged in her Quaker idealism, has more to say; and Sonia Hawley, it turns out, was once, as a child, molested—"And not by a relative, either: by an older boy at school"—and Leonard Oppenheim, and Paul Owen, whose luggage was stolen on a recent trip to India, have a great deal to say; and Ian can be passionate on the subject. And so it goes.

At what she calculates to be the proper moment, Glynnis lays down her napkin and goes out into the kitchen, returns with Marvis at her elbow, the two women bearing warm heavy plates. "Will you all have a little more?" Glynnis asks.

It's odd, how, at her age, mature as she is and surely gifted with a healthy sense of humor, she asks that question with such apprehension; as if her very worth—or is it her very life?—were being proffered.

5.

In addition to the chocolate cake there is a crepe dessert prepared by Glynnis at the table; a light, delicious, orange- and raspberry-flavored crepe, new to most of the company, made with Chartreuse. How lovely, Glynnis thinks, as the crepes flame up: that low bluish-purple flame, a child's sort of magic, and the aroma of alcohol and sugar; how lovely, how sad, things coming to an end. Both desserts are great successes, and Glynnis is pleased that everyone wants a bit of both. Flushed with pleasure and wine and feeling at last that she can relax, she *has* come through, she accepts her friends' compliments with thanks. Praise, particularly at such close quarters, embarrasses her; though its absence, as she well knows, would certainly wound her.

Deflecting attention from herself and onto Ian, she says, "Thank *him*. He has been the inspiration for everything."

Ian, absorbed in conversation at his end of the table, does not quite hear what Glynnis has said but smiles down the length of the table at her, the lenses of his glasses winking in the candlelight. On the plate before him are the remains of his dessert, partly eaten.

AT GLYNNIS'S END of the table, over coffee and liqueur, they are talking of food: of whether, in civilized societies, among the affluent classes at least, food can be said to exist *in esse;* or does it, as Amos Kuhn suggests, always stand for something that is not food. "Who among us, after all, eats merely to live?" Amos asks. "Who eats food of the kind you prepared for us tonight, Glynnis, merely to—eat?"

Glynnis says, "It's just food. After all."

"No. It is material, and you make of it art."

Amos Kuhn, the anthropologist, the Institute's most distinguished elder, is an uncommonly tall, snowy-haired, well-spoken gentleman in his sixties with a fair, handsome, lapidary face: a protégé of Gregory Bateson and Margaret Mead whose reputation, if not popular fame, now equals theirs. He did his earliest fieldwork in Borneo and can tell remarkable tales—many of which, of course, Glynnis and her friends have heard before—that turn upon the mysterious nature of mankind's obsession with food. It is, Amos says, both the most fundamental and the most abstract of issues: "You can study the subject for a lifetime; you can amass a staggering quantity of data and come away with contradictory theories.

"The very concept of 'taboo,' for instance—why some foods are taboo in certain cultures and not in others; why, within a single culture, some foods are taboo and others not; and why 'taboo' itself can shift from season to season. In any number of aboriginal cultures, for instance, a too-close proximity to death—that is, to dead bodies—violates taboo; and when one is in violation of taboo he can't eat certain foods, nor can he feed himself; he must eat from the ground, without using his hands, or be fed by hand by another. Even more perversely"—Amos pauses, as if suddenly aware of his voice, which has steadily risen; and Glynnis sees how, sensitive as the man is, and mildly impaired in his hearing, he quickly gauges that, yes, others at the table are now listening, the entire table in fact is now listening, he is therefore empowered to continue—"in cultures in which food is always scarce, and consequently a source of anxiety, food is ceremonially wasted—offered up to gods, totem animals, even dead enemies. Before head-hunting was suppressed in, for instance, Borneo, Melanesia, West Africa, and elsewhere, head-hunting tribes used to insert delicacies in the mouths of their victims' shrunken heads, accompanied by the most exaggerated, absurd, yet, it seems, altogether sincere endearments! I've witnessed the ceremonies; they're really quite astonishing, not so much in their grisliness—you soon get accustomed to the idea of the shrunken head, as a sort of artifact—as in their sincerity. And, of course, in obedience to divine will, or the cycle of the moon, primitive peoples, as we like to call them, are in the habit of gorging themselves to the point of serious illness or starving themselves literally to death. Feasting, fasting—it's apt that the words sound so much alike. Food is codified," Amos says, concluding, with a smile, "but who among us has cracked the code?"

So they talk of feasting and of fasting, of bulimia and of anorexia; and Malcolm, who is in fact one of the leanest of the company, strokes his stomach above his belt and says, "Food is love, no more and no less"; and Denis says, "But is love *food*? That's the crucial question." And Ian, just rising from the table, says, with smiling husbandly courtliness, "If it is nourishing, it is."

Ian excuses himself from the company and disappears into the rear of the house, to use his bathroom perhaps; in his absence they talk of Institute politics, and Vincent Hawley, a senior sociologist involved in the National Health Service project, asks Glynnis pointedly if Ian "has yet been approached" by the search committee for the new director; and Glynnis says, annoyed, "You'll have to ask him" but immediately adds, "But please don't: it's all, as you know, confidential."

"Oh, as to that: 'confidentiality,' " Vincent says, smiling. "What place has it ever had, among friends?"

But the subject is quickly suppressed, for such talk is premature, and they revert to their previous subject, food: talking variously of ritual cannibalism and of Catholic communion; of several passionately recalled meals in three-star French restaurants—the Hawleys, leaving soon for a year in Provence, are instructed by Leonard Oppenheim about precisely where to go, and when, and what they must order; of fad diets and real diets; and food obsessions, childhood and adult. June Oliver confesses to an appetite for cheap rock candy, the kind sold in dime stores, "all stuck together in a sort of obscenity, like Laocoön"; and Roberta Grinnell confesses to an appetite—"it would be insatiable, if I gave in to it"—for peanut butter spread thick on Saltine crackers. And Paul Owen, that most fastidious of men, the editor of a prominent art and antiques journal, has a weakness for popcorn: cheap, greasy, salty, even rather stale, with a faint taste of the cardboard box in which it comes, "and a smell overall of the disinfectant used in movie theaters in the 1950s." And Leonard Oppenheim, the connoisseur among them of good wine, confesses to a "corrupt" fascination for junk cookies of all varieties: chocolate chip, Oreos, peanut butter, marshmallow sprinkled with pink-dyed coconut—"When I was depressed, in my twenties, I used to buy a big bag of them at a Seven-Eleven Store and eat myself into oblivion." Malcolm Oliver, a resident, in the mid-1960s, of the Zen center at Tassajara in California and a food purist of sorts even now, admits that he too likes junk candy, and cookies, and potato chips, and pizza, and onion rings—"The greasier the better." Elizabeth Kuhn confesses to a craving for oatmeal so thick she can barely manage a spoon in it, with lots of cream and sugar: a remnant of her upbringing, otherwise rather bleak, by a Scots grandmother. Amos Kuhn, eating, still, his second helping of cake, says, "Chocolate. But it must be very *good* chocolate, like this." Denis, and the Hawleys, and Vaughn Cassity, as well as Glynnis, admit to being obsessed with ice cream; Denis jokingly wonders if, in his case, it has to do with infantile trauma at the breast, and subsequent traumas, at subsequent breasts? By this time Glynnis is aware of Ian's absence as palpable and deliberate; she wonders if he is ill—he *must* be ill—yet laughs at her friends, who vie with one another in naming their favorite ice creams, their favorite flavors: Baskin-Robbins, Häagen-Dazs, Abbotts, Breyers, Old Philadelphia, Frusen Glädjé . . . marshmallow mint, peach-strawberry ripple, lemon-cherry whirl, chocolate fudge, chocolate chip, chocolate walnut, chocolate rum, and classic vanilla, of course—"the purest, the most ethereal of tastes," in Leonard Oppenheim's solemn words. Though she is distracted by Ian's absence—he is either ill, in his bathroom, or being unaccountably rude—Glynnis springs to her feet, hurries out into the kitchen, and returns, gaily, with an armful of quart containers of ice cream, seven dramatically different flavors: tosses down spoons, tells her friends to taste, to sample, to pass the containers around—"We needn't bother with bowls."

"What of Ian?" someone asks.

"Ian will have to fend for himself," Glynnis says.

So, like children, they pass the containers around: protesting, some of them, that they cannot eat another mouthful of anything, yet spooning up the ice cream nonetheless; like children. A cigarette burns in Glynnis's fingers, though she cannot recall having lit it; and she has finished her second tiny glass of crème de menthe; and her eyes water, after a spasm of laughter; and she licks banana-ripple ice cream from a spoon held by Vaughn Cassity and wonders where Ian is, and where Bianca is. And why, now, when the party has crested, and all that might have gone wrong with the meal has not gone wrong, and their friends are so clearly enjoying themselves, warmed, mellowed, agreeably intoxicated with food and drink, why, she wonders, should she feel, in secret, so melancholy, as after love, after the expenditure of love in passion; so leaden, behind her party vivacity; so susceptible to tears? She thinks, too, even as she laughs in a fit of helplessness at a funny remark of his, that Denis and she have had relatively little to say to each other tonight; he has been more keenly attuned, in fact, to Meika, and Meika to him: Meika Cassity, with her stylish streaked ash-blond hair, her so very French so very feminine laughter, looking, aged forty-three or -four, a decade younger, and ravenous for men. . . .

"IAN? IS SOMETHING wrong?"

Glynnis has opened the door to Ian's study, without knocking, and there he sits, in the dark, at his desk, the telephone before him, his head in his hands. When the light from the hall falls onto him he looks up, blinking and guilty. Seeing him without his glasses always arouses, in Glynnis, conflicting emotions of tenderness and impatience. She guesses, at such times, that he can barely make out the expression on her face.

"Who are you calling?" Glynnis asks, frightened. "*Is* something wrong?"

Ian gets quickly to his feet, puts on his glasses, says, apologetically, "Nothing is wrong, Glynnis, I'm sorry to have . . ." and there is a long pause, as, it seems, he cannot think of what he means to say. Glynnis is puzzled; she is hurt and angry, asking why on earth he has to make a telephone call now, doesn't he know their friends are about to leave, isn't he aware of having been away from the table for a very long time, of having been rude, when everyone has been so wonderful to him, when the evening has gone so well?

"I'm sorry," Ian says. "I hadn't realized I was away very long. I seem to have lost track of . . ."

"Ian, how could you!"

His hair is disheveled, his necktie loosened; there is an unpleasant dampish odor about him, commingled with a sweet wine smell. A guilty man, Glynnis thinks. An adulterer.

She says, calmly, "Something is wrong, isn't it? Who did you call?"

"I *tried* to call Stanley Brisbane . . . but no one answered. I've been trying to get through to him most of the day."

"Who is Stanley Brisbane?"

"My co-chairman for the Budapest conference in October . . . he and I are organizing the world population symposium . . . we have to get speakers, panels. There is a minor crisis, a budget problem; I've been trying to reach him in Chicago for two days, actually, with no—"

Glynnis cries, "Ian, please do not speak of that *now.*"

When they return to the dining room, it is to discover, to Glynnis's chagrin, that several of their guests are on their feet, ready to leave; and Ian apologizes, not without a certain measure of charm, explaining about the telephone call, his futile attempts to reach Stanley Brisbane, the political scientist, of Chicago, the problems he has been having with Brisbane overall, in organizing their part of the conference, and so on and so forth, glossing over the awkward moment and making everything all right, or nearly. Denis, in whom drink arouses belligerence and a curious stubborn loyalty to friends, says, "You should know better than to get involved with Stanley: the man is spoiled rotten." Denis proceeds then to tell one of his convoluted and, in this instance, not entirely coherent tales, and the Hawleys and the Kuhns, though prepared to leave, linger; and everyone laughs at the posturings and pretensions of Stanley Brisbane, of Chicago, of whom, until now, Glynnis has never heard. But she laughs, with the others. And pours herself another tiny glass of crème de menthe. So lethal, and so delicious.

BY THE TIME the taxi comes for Marvis it is 1:20 A.M. Glynnis, switching off the lights in the kitchen, dining room, living room, sips a glass of leftover Bernkasteler Doktor Auslese 1982, swaying, in her stockinged feet, with exhaustion and exhilaration: for Ian McCullough's fiftieth birthday has been a great success . . . a memorable evening, as everyone said . . . the food superb . . . no one quite like Glynnis. Ian, helping clear the dining room table, swaying too on his feet, was apologetic, contrite, speaking slowly, enunciating each syllable, his way when he has had too much to drink and doesn't know it. Saying for the third or fourth time, "I am sorry, I hadn't realized, I didn't mean to be rude, I seem to have lost track of. . . ."

And then Bianca comes home; and Glynnis feels compelled to speak with her, if only to show her, the hurtful little bitch, how little her absence meant: how little, in truth, her mother *had* been hurt by her selfish behavior. "And did you enjoy yourself, with—who was it, Kim?" Glynnis begins.

And Bianca says quickly, "Yes. Kim. And, yes, I did"—peeling off her sweater—"and how was Daddy's party here?"

"Daddy's party was fine," Glynnis says, betraying no irony, no anger, not even reproach, as, all but ignoring her, Bianca stretches, and yawns, and shakes her head as a dog shakes its head, a handsome young woman whose vision of herself, so far as Glynnis can determine, is deliberately crude, flat-footed, clumsy, the obverse of her mother's style, it might be said, and in defiance of it. "Where did you eat finally?" Glynnis asks.

And Bianca says, shrugging, "Nowhere special."

Glynnis says, "Yes, but where?"

And Bianca turns away, bored, sullen, belching beer. "One of the usual places."

Why do you hate me? Glynnis thinks. Why, when I love you, when I would love you, except for your opposition?

Mother and daughter are standing just outside the door to Bianca's room. It is twenty to two; Ian has gone to bed; beyond them, the house, emptied of its guests, seems deafeningly silent, a mysterious becalmed ship at dock in a nighttime sea. Glynnis stares at Bianca, who will not look at her, wanting to take the girl's face in her hands, to squeeze, to frame, to define; thinking, And shall we quarrel, or shall we kiss each other good night? Or shall we, accustomed as we are of giving and taking hurt, simply say good night, and turn away, and let things as they are.

Bianca says, "Well—"

Glynnis says, "Well." And then, turning away, softly, "Good night."

IAN, ON HIS back, lies with a forearm slung over his eyes, to shield them from the bedside lamp. His breath is audible, rasping; he appears to be asleep, unmoving, his long legs outstretched, perfectly still, like a stone figure atop a sarcophagus.

Glynnis slips on a nightgown; out of old habit draws her hands up, and over, her breasts, cupping them for an instant, feeling an instant's perplexity and regret. They say of course that it is the body that betrays; the self, the soul, remains inviolate; thus you are twenty years old so abruptly, so rudely, in a fifty-year-old body. And your journey has only now begun.

I cannot bear it, Glynnis thinks.

Something will happen and it will happen soon and it will happen without my volition or responsibility: but what?

She thinks of Ian, surprised in his study in the dark, having made, or having attempted to make, or having contemplated making, a telephone call. A professional call, and why not believe it, why not? For after all (Glynnis begins to think, heartened) it is not the first time Ian, or one or another of his colleagues, like Vincent, like Denis, above all Amos, has acted similarly. . . . Social life does not mean to men what it means to women, Elizabeth Kuhn once remarked. That is a fact we must always remember.

But an old memory, an old perplexity, intrudes: in January, Ian went to a professional conference in Boston at which he, or the *Journal*, received an award; but when Glynnis telephoned, on Saturday afternoon, she was informed that Ian had already checked out of the hotel. The conference was scheduled to disband on Sunday afternoon; Ian had told her he would be home Sunday evening; where was he? She thought, I will resist the impulse to call one of his friends. I will resist the impulse to hunt him down.

And when, Sunday evening, Ian returned home, tired, irritable, vague, telling Glynnis that the conference had not gone "perfectly"—there was a conservative faction gathering power among his colleagues, a sort of political-sociobiological element he found incipiently racist and in other ways distasteful—Glynnis said only, "What about your award; aren't you pleased with that?" And Ian said, "Oh, yes, yes, of course," as if he'd only then remembered it; and to placate her, as a child might placate his mother, he showed her the gilt-stamped document from the National Association of Political Scientists and the check for $1,500. Glynnis had determined she would not ask him about the hotel but heard herself nonetheless ask, casually, "When did you leave Boston?" Ian said, with no apparent hesitation, "Today. This afternoon. The conference lasted until this afternoon." Still casually, Glynnis said, "But I telephoned you yesterday and they told me you'd checked out, a day ahead of time," adding, lest it seem she was accusing him—for she was hardly, after all, accusing him—"There must have been a mistake at the desk." By this time Ian had turned away, was walking away, said only, over his shoulder, "Yes, that's right—I mean, that is probably right. A mistake at the desk."

And Glynnis wanted to scream after him, to rush at him, striking with her fists, hitting, hurting, demanding: Are you lying to me? Are you deceiving me? Don't you know there will be consequences?

NOW SHE SLIPS into bed, not wanting to disturb him, switches off the bedside lamp, turns to him, as, usually, reflexively, he turns to her; and she kisses him, sleepily; and he wakes, and kisses her, yet very sleepily; and they ease apart. Glynnis customarily sleeps facing the edge of the bed, on her right, partly hugging herself: a childhood habit never outgrown. Except for infrequent restless nights and more frequent bouts of nighttime sweating, she is a quiet, even inert sleeper:

heavy-seeming, in sleep, as a dark quivering pool rises to meet her and enclose her, her breath oddly quickening as a cascade of images, primarily faces, rush at her . . . some of them recognizable, the faces of her friends (though distorted, distended, as in a fun-house mirror) but most of them the faces of strangers (yet so striking in their vivid, hallucinatory detail, she cannot believe they are but mere fictions of her unstoppered imagination): rush at her like a speeding landscape in which she is passive, frozen, an uncomprehending witness. Yet it is not nightmare, nor does it ever lead to nightmare; simply a sleep of exhaustion steeped in alcohol . . . through which she makes her way, drifting, dropping, sinking, an element dense and porous as water that yields, always abruptly, another place . . . ah, but she is barefoot, and the floorboards are cold, and an odor as of stale food permeates the air, and drink . . . someone has spilled wine on the tablecloth, Ian said, a pity, do you think it will come out, our beautiful tablecloth, Ian said, but the brass chandelier shines and the candelabra with their tall grace-ful candles, the afterimages of the flames reflected in the mirror above the sideboard and in the glass walls and sliding door, and in the kitchen the bottoms of the copper pans shine like miniature moons and the hanging plants in the window quiver spiderlike with their own secret life and why, Glynnis thinks, why is Marvis so barely civil to her the latter part of the evening, unsmiling and unresponsive and Glynnis has always been so nice to her, generous at Christmas, careful not to be, not even to seem, condescending, what do they want, these black women, the women as mysterious finally as the men, what do they want from us we seem incapable of giving? . . . but Glynnis and Ian are at the door saying good night to their friends, Glynnis's warm cheek is being kissed, and she kisses in return, happily, greedily, Denis's liquorish breath in her face, and she laughs, and winces, and pushes him away, or is it another man, a stranger, she pushes away, as a woman she does not recognize stands on her tiptoes and kisses Ian good night, no, it is Roberta, or is it Meika, it *is* Roberta, but her hand is skeletal and cold so that in fright Glynnis drops it but shows no alarm, her facial skin tight as a mask showing no alarm, I love you both, I love love love you both, I drown in all of you.

AND THE DOOR is closed, with care, in the glass wall.

It's an instinct now, with the McCulloughs.

Living in a glass house, after all.

On her bare drifting feet Glynnis traverses the many rooms of her house, these rooms that, though some of them appear unknown to her, are nonetheless hers, and her responsibility; in one of them, cave-like, cavernous, she discovers her daughter sleeping or the child they assured her was hers sleeping a baby's intense trembling sleep so deep she cannot be wakened; and how am *I* responsible, Glynnis protests, what am *I* to do? And in another room, in which the walls come together at a peculiar slant and the ceiling presses low and the air is humid, as in a greenhouse, there are Ian and Glynnis, the McCulloughs, in bed, beneath familiar covers, turned from each other in the privacy and lone-liness of sleep and their bodies curled inward, coiled, like the bodies of soft creatures whose shells have been prized off them; and each is the other's twin, though turned resolutely away from the other, in the pri-vacy and loneliness of sleep. And Glynnis is suddenly angry with them, and impatient, yawning a swift savage jaw-aching yawn like the one that overcame her in the kitchen, the bright lights on and Marvis at the sink noisily rinsing dishes, noisily setting them in the dishwasher except for those too delicate to entrust to the washer which will have to be done by hand: surely you know which ones, Marvis, after all our years together? At the far end of the beautifully set table sits a tall pale stranger eating her food drinking her wine baring his teeth in a wide white grin; but the candlelight is blinding, Glynnis cannot make out his face.

But now the house is empty. And the silence is deafening. A becalmed ship, drifting out to sea. Her bare feet have brought her to that spot at which the dining room opens out onto the living room, perpendicularly, the farthest wall, which Glynnis, though her eyes are good, can barely see; dissolving into mere night, the plate-glass walls and windows and sliding doors dissolving to mere night, no words and no language, and Glynnis thinks in triumph, My house. My family. My life. Mine.

GLASS

1.

The end came swiftly and irrevocably. And surely without premeditation.

It was April 23, and unseasonably warm; and when Ian returned from the Institute, at dusk, it was, still, warm as an evening in summer; the air smelled both flowery and crystalline: an evening, Ian thought, to break one's heart. The sensation of vertigo, of being rudderless, adrift, suspended, that had plagued him for so many weeks—or had it been, now, months?—seemed the more intensified tonight, as if the very air had altered. He would not be able to breathe, he thought; he would suffocate, entering his house.

He parked the Honda in the graveled drive, in its usual position; noted that Glynnis's station wagon was in the carport, in its usual position; had a vague recollection of having seen something out of place, or amiss, out front . . . though he would not realize what it was until the next day: an oblong package, by the size and shape of it a shipment from the Musical Heritage Society containing a record Glynnis had ordered, signaling the curious fact that the mail had not been brought in, as it always was, when Glynnis's car was in the drive; when Glynnis was home. On days when Glynnis was out and returned after Ian did, he sometimes wandered about the house, looking vaguely for something he could not have named, feeling that it should be on the kitchen table, where Glynnis usually sorted the mail, though sensing too that, whatever it was, it might also be waiting for him on his desk; for Glynnis sometimes brought his mail there. If he made a particular effort to figure out what was missing, he would remember; often, of course, he simply pushed the vexing thought away, and forgot, and to Glynnis's amusement, or annoyance, failed to bring it in at all. "You leave everything for me to do," Glynnis would say, half seriously; and though the accusation was surely unjust, Ian could offer no refutation. He lived in a world of his own thoughts and had done so since boyhood. And, of late, it seemed to be getting worse.

That morning, Ian had been at his desk, at the Institute, at seven-forty-five. There was a problem with one of the computer programs they were using for the Health Service project, and there was a problem, made the more nettlesome by distance, about the exact day when Ian was scheduled to give his paper at the Second Annual International Conference on "Hunger and the 'First World'" in Frankfurt, West Germany, in late May. (The paper itself, for which Ian had high hopes, was not yet written: consisting, at this time, of mere scribbled notes and pages of computer printouts, which, when Ian stared at them, refused to crystallize into the formal, impeccable logic characteristic of Ian McCullough's best efforts. I will sleep on it, Ian told himself. I will give myself a few more days before I begin to get desperate.) There was, at his office, the usual daunting wash of mail, including, these spring mornings, a number of those dispiriting, because so frequent, requests from former students, former colleagues, former friends, for letters of recommendation (for university positions, Guggenheim, Rockeller, National Endowment fellowships, and the rest). Sometimes I think I dare not die, Denis said, for fear my ducklings would expire. Through the day the telephone rang, and rang, and rang, and some of these calls Ian took in his capacity as editor of *The Journal of International Politics,* and some of these calls he took in his capacity as the head of the demographic research team; and some he took as, merely, Ian McCullough. When he was gone from his desk for any period of time—he played squash, late mornings, five days a week, then had lunch, most days, in the Institute dining room, with his friends—he would return to find a tidy little pile of pink slips awaiting him, with notations from Mrs. Fairchild, his secretary. *A message from. Please call.* Always, he looked through the pink slips quickly, with both anticipation and dread. Would she have called him? No? Yes? Today? But why *not* today? She called at unpredictable times.

He did not like to telephone her; though, of course, he sometimes did, having long ago memorized the Poughkeepsie number, which he could punch out as rapidly as his forefinger moved; a sort of stylized tic it had become, requiring little conscious thought. At the other end in the paid-for but so rarely, these days, occupied apartment, Sigrid Hunt's telephone rang and rang and rang; and Ian McCullough, gripping the receiver, would think, Yes, good, no one is home. Good.

But most of the time he was working, of course. At his desk or in the computer room or in the Institute library, a handsome vaulted plushly carpeted space in which the individual was dwarfed, not in size (for the highly specialized library was not large as libraries go) but in significance: amid the neatly arranged stacks of books, books to the floor and books to the ceiling; amid the hieratic portraits of great men, Hobbes, Comte, Bentham, Mill, Marx, Engels, Spencer, Durkheim, William James, John Dewey; amid glass-encased exhibits of such items as newly acquired antique or rare or simply very expensive books like the leatherbound gilt-embroidered *Iliad* opened to the early speech of Achilles when the hero tells the doomed Lyacon, who has begged him for mercy, *Now there is not one who can escape death, if the gods send / him against my hands in front of Ilion, not one / of all the Trojans, and beyond others the children of Priam. / So, friend, you die also. Why all this clamor about it? / Patroklos also is dead, who was better by far than you are. / Do you not see what a man I am, how huge, how splendid / and born of a great father, and the mother who bore me immortal? / Yet even I have also my death and my strong destiny, and there shall be a dawn or an afternoon or a noontime / when some man in the fighting will take the life from me also* . . . words which, beyond the curving glare of the glass case, stirred in Ian so profound yet so inexplicable a sense of his own extinction that he had to leave the library at once and return to his office, to the little lavatory adjoining his office, that no one might be a witness to his agitation.

But most of the time he was at his desk: quite visibly and, it seemed, happily working. His young assistants joked behind his back of being terrorized by Ian McCullough: not by the man himself—"he's really wonderful, so easy to talk to, actually sweet, and unpretentious"—but by the professional standards of integrity, industry, singlemindedness of which he was a model.

Ian would not have wanted them, or anyone, to know how he plunged into his work these mornings as a swimmer plunges into the wave that sweeps toward him and will engulf him. There is no way but forward, after all.

THE NIGHT BEFORE, it had happened again; or, rather, had *not* happened again; and Glynnis with her instinct for self-hurt murmured, You don't love me, you are indifferent to me, is that it, isn't that it, do you love another woman, is *that* it?—and Ian could do nothing but protest, for he too was hurt, and perplexed, and anxious, and resentful, yes, and angry as well, saying of course he loved her of course of course he loved her, why didn't they let the matter rest?

It was not precisely a new issue in their marriage, in any case. Over the trajectory of twenty-six years and even, as Ian vaguely recalled, intermittently at the very start, he had sometimes been impotent in their lovemaking—if "impotent" was the right, the not too cruelly clinical term—not, as Glynnis believed, out of indifference to her, and certainly not, as she was beginning to believe, out of rejection of her, but simply because it happened that way. And did not happen the other way.

Glynnis called him "abstracted," when she was in a mood to forgive, and "cold-blooded" when she was not.

From time to time they had discussed the possibility of going to a marriage counselor, or to "some sort of therapist"—not in Hazelton where everyone knew everyone else but in New York City, of course; but the problem never seemed quite serious enough, really chronic enough, to warrant such desperate action. And they were both too busy. And they weren't the kind of people who did such things: no one in their circle was. (With the notable exceptions of Leonard Oppenheim and Paul Owen, who had both undergone psychoanalysis, as young men; but then Leonard and Paul were gay and presumably less adjusted to the quotidian.) Glynnis's pride would never have allowed her to spill her guts, as she inelegantly called it, to a stranger; and poor Ian would not have known the first thing to say. Should one apologize? Stammer out a sort of defense? Plead one's own inviolate and evidently intransigent nature?

What was new, mysteriously new, since, in fact, the night of Ian's birthday party, was Glynnis's emotional response, her so very emotional response; the startling and, Ian thought, wholly uncharacteristic bitterness she voiced, as if it were a bitterness long withheld out of charity to him. *That* was the surprise—the insult! For years the problem had come and gone, waxed and waned, held to its own unreadable cycles, a consequence of so many factors in their shared lives, such a snarl of domestic, social, and professional contingencies, it would have required the subtlety of a demographic study to diagnose causes, assign blame. Glynnis had been, most of the time, really quite sympathetic—Ian's "abstractedness" had not yet shaded into "cold-bloodedness." But now the hurt, the childish contorted face, the shifting of the eyes that held in them, so far as Ian could see, no love of him, not even pity of, or aware-ness of, *him*—these scenes, enacted for the most part in embarrassed silence, seemed, for no reason Ian could name (except the reason he could not name), to be worsening.

On the very day following Ian's birthday he and Glynnis had had a quarrel of an indeterminate sort, over a trifle, yet protracted for much of an evening; and quite spoiling that evening, which, with Bianca home, was supposed to have been rather special. And a few days later they clashed again, and quarreled again, over another trifle: their emotions flaring up, and raging, like a grass fire in a dry season.

"I suppose it was a miscalculation," Glynnis said; "a surprise party for you." She spoke quietly, yet there was a mild emphasis on *you* that fell harshly on Ian's ears.

But he naturally protested, insisting that her party had been a great idea, and brilliantly executed; everyone had enjoyed it; *he* had enjoyed it; what more was there to say? "We certainly all look happy enough here," he said, indicating the dozen or more Polaroid snapshots tacked on Glynnis's bulletin board. "I look in fact transcendentally happy," he said, though his lean narrow face, surprised in the camera's glare, was bleached out and curiously distended, and his smile looked too emphatic to be genuine. "And look at you: radiant."

(For Glynnis, long practiced in being photographed, and naturally photogenic, seemed to know how precisely to smile for a camera: a forced pose that became transmogrified, on film, into utter ease and spontaneity.)

Still Glynnis would not let the matter rest, seemingly could not let it rest, alluding yet again to his "air of distraction" and the lengthy telephone call he'd made "that might have waited until morning." Ian said irritably, "I didn't make a telephone call, in fact. I *tried* to make it and couldn't get through." "Ah, I see," Glynnis said, lighting up a cigarette and eyeing him frankly. "Was that how it was." Ian walked out of the room, his heart beating hard; paused, thought better of his retreat, and came back; and told Glynnis that, since she asked, since she pressed the point, he supposed he *was* distracted much of the evening . . . by Bianca's behavior, for one thing, but also by—how to express it?—his uneasy sense that there was something shrill and self-congratulatory about the party. "Us celebrating us," he said.

Immediately, even as the words were uttered, Ian knew they were terrible words, words never to be unsaid; yet, plunging head on, as something heated and constricted in Glynnis's face seemed to bid him to do, he said, "I just felt, I suppose, that the occasion was somehow . . . excessive."

"But it was your fiftieth birthday," Glynnis said, in a faint, hurt voice, as if he had struck her. "We've gone to other parties . . . like that."

"I don't give a damn about my fiftieth birthday," Ian said, trying, now, to make a joke of it, "or any of my birthdays. That, surely, you understand?"

"But I love you," Glynnis said, stubbornly, as if that were a refutation.

So, repentant, Ian tried to temper what he'd said, for he had not meant it, exactly; but Glynnis was wounded, and struck out in bewilderment and rage; and within minutes, again, they were speaking angrily, in clumsy raised voices. And again Ian left the room, pain beginning between his eyes and his heart beating suffocatingly hard; and Glynnis shouted after him, in a fury, "Then go! Just—go! Go to hell!"

(Ironically—or was it, by Hazelton's anecdotal standards, comically?—Ian fled into town on the marvelous Schwinn racer Glynnis had given him for his birthday. He would not have trusted himself, in such circumstances, in such agitation, to drive a car.)

In a telephone booth he'd called one of the numbers Sigrid Hunt had given him, a Manhattan number, and after many rings a woman answered; no, Sigrid wasn't there and no she didn't know where Sigrid was and no she couldn't take a message—sorry. Her own life, she said, with a hint of malice, was complicated enough.

Ian, embarrassed, tried to explain that he was a friend of Sigrid's from upstate; his name Ian. He wanted very badly to speak with her, or, failing that, simply to know how she was—"How is her health, for instance?" There was a pause, a murmurous sound of voices in the background; perhaps Sigrid was there after all and would speak with him; but the woman said, "*Her* health is fine, mister," and the sound, as of muffled laughter, increased; "how is *yours?*"

A cruel, gratuitous remark; and now the dial tone hummed derisively in Ian's ear. His cheeks burned as if he had been slapped. He thought, This is nothing less than you deserve.

2.

Some weeks before, in March, Ian had woken with the conviction that something had happened to Sigrid Hunt; for he had not heard from her in weeks; had seen her only once, briefly, in Manhattan, since the abortion. (Which she had had in the city, without telling Fermi; or so Ian gathered. It was all rather disconcertingly ambiguous, Sigrid Hunt's relationship with the man she called her fiancé.)

He thought of the apartment over the garage, that place of romance: the young woman's attempts to decorate, to create her own space and style, in a derelict rain-rotted building whose first floor was used for storage. The scene of the crime, he thought it. If anything has happened to her, it has happened there.

Instead of going to his office, Ian drove that morning down to Poughkeepsie, to 119 Tice, and persuaded the caretaker of the building that there was the possibility, a remote possibility but a real one, that something might have happened to the young woman who rented the apartment above the garage; and that they should unlock the door and see. "I have telephoned her any number of times," Ian said nervously. "At this number, and at others she has given me. She is supposed to be here . . . but no one answers."

The caretaker, a man of Ian's approximate age but curiously wizened and lethargic, with a sharp, shrewd, squinty eye, hesitated awhile, then did as Ian requested, without, as Ian had feared, asking who Ian was: without asking questions of any kind. He said only that he had not seen her (he referred to Sigrid Hunt solely as "her" or "she") in a while but that he didn't take much notice of tenants, kept his nose clean—"Which you soon learn to do, in a place like this."

But Sigrid Hunt was not in the apartment; the apartment was quite empty and rather stale-smelling and disordered, as Ian recalled. He felt a shock of relief, yet also of disappointment. How reduced, how diminished, how inconsequential this setting, without Sigrid Hunt's presence. . . . Simply Ian McCullough, trembling, in the company of a stranger who appeared, to the casual eye, to be in some way misshapen, and whose oddly audible breath suggested derision.

No young woman's partly clothed dead body, no signs of struggle, no evidence to suggest that Ian's concern was anything less than intrusive. He was not a relative of hers after all; he was not even a lover. He said, apologetically, "Well. I'm sorry to have troubled you."

There, the sofa bed with its crimson quilt hastily drawn over rumpled sheets; there, the dressmaker's mirror at its careless slant, reflecting, now, merely a wall. The little woven carpets seemed less colorful, and more soiled, than Ian recalled; the Georgia O'Keeffe abstractions less coolly elegant, and rather more like magazine illustration, than he recalled. In the tiny kitchen a fly buzzed languidly, wakened from its long winter sleep; there were plates and several scummy glasses in the sink, which Ian had an urge to wash, to scrub and put away. He would have liked, were he alone and unobserved, to prowl about . . . to look through her closet and her bureau drawers. But he did no more than peek in the bathroom, which, of course, was empty. Again he said, glancing at the caretaker, whose name he did not know, "Well—I'm sorry."

The man was lounging in the doorway, arms folded, watching Ian. His left eyelid twitched as if in irrepressible mirth. "What's to be sorry about, mister?" he said slyly. "She ain't been killed like you was worried."

On the way out Ian, deeply ashamed, gave the man $25 for his trouble; and wondered, driving home, if $25 was enough.

But how much, in these circumstances so very new and strange to me, would be enough?

SOME YEARS BEFORE, Denis had told Ian obliquely, with a good deal of embarrassment, that he and Roberta were "going through a difficult time" in their marriage: that, in fact, there was the possibility of divorce—"It's entirely Roberta's decision, now." Ian had stared at Denis in disbelief, not knowing what to say. Such confidences, such sudden revelations, were not Ian McCullough's forte; nor were they Denis Grinnell's. Ian stammered a response of some kind, must have asked a few questions, clumsy, wondering, "But you seem so happy, both of you, as happy as ever, it all seems so"—and he paused, without the vaguest idea of what he was saying, or meant to say—"seamless."

They were in Denis's office, going through page proofs for the next issue of the *Journal;* it was late in the afternoon; most of the secretarial staff was gone. Denis had been fidgety and distracted for some time, but Ian had not, in truth, taken much note, and now he wondered too about Roberta; when was the last time he'd seen Roberta, and didn't Glynnis see her, or speak with her on the telephone, virtually every day? . . . "Yes, right," Denis said, startled by Ian's oddly chosen word, "that's Hazelton-on-Hudson's ideal: the seamless façade."

Denis told Ian that it was his fault, essentially; no, it was his fault entirely; he'd become involved with another woman. "A woman I know professionally, she lives in La Jolla, we met at a conference, most of our meetings in fact were at conferences; she is no one you know," Denis said carefully; "you, or Glynnis." Now he was deeply embarrassed; his ears reddened; he could not quite look Ian in the eye. "I made a fool of myself, I think. It was a reckless sort of thing I couldn't then undo; I didn't want to hurt the woman, and I *was* attracted to her—Jesus, I shouldn't minimize this, I was very attracted to her, sort of obsessed, you might say . . . for a while. I tried to make Roberta understand that it was essentially a mistake, an error, on my part; I tried to make her understand that it had nothing to do with her . . . and I think she finally understands. I think."

Ian said, "What would happen if you and Roberta were divorced?"

"What do you mean? In terms of my career? I'd probably move away."

"Move away? From Hazelton? But where?"

"I don't know; Christ, I don't want to think of that yet. As I said, it's up to Roberta. I *think* we'll be all right. . . ."

Ian was hurt, resentful; in that moment, it seemed to him that Denis Grinnell had betrayed him, as he had betrayed Roberta. Were they not close friends?—close as brothers?—as, at the very least, the sentimental idea, among the brotherless, of brothers? He said, "I don't think, Denis, I could bear it around here, the Institute, the *Journal,* without you." (Though this was an extraordinary thing to say and not, on the face of it, wholly probable.) Denis, unnerved now by the turn the conversation had taken and wanting only to end it, said, "Well—I feel the same way about you."

And the subject was dropped; and never again taken up.

And, to Ian's infinite relief, the Grinnells remained married, their union as seamless as any in Hazelton.

LIKE ANY LOVER—THOUGH of course he was not a lover—Ian Mc-Cullough believed he saw Sigrid Hunt sometimes, in places as unlikely as the local shopping center, or the dining room of the Institute; he saw, or seemed to see, her long glimmering rippled-red hair, her slender shoulders, her profile as it turned from him; but knew enough not to call her name, still less to cry out. It was not love he felt for her but—how could he define it?—an intense concern, a sympathy: a preoccupation, if such be possible, of an ethical nature. For all that he knew of the young woman's life suggested a randomness both slovenly and stylized, a mode of being for which he felt an intense moral disapproval.

And he loved Glynnis, of course.

Even in sometimes resisting her, disliking her, raging against her, he loved her: that was absolute, final.

For he could not conceive of his life, his very self, apart from her.

She had saved his life when he had come close, at least in desire, to throwing his life away; and she continued to save it, Ian did not doubt, every day.

Yet he spoke with Sigrid on the telephone, now and then: gave her advice, to which she listened or, flattering him, seemed to listen. After the abortion, she had stayed for a while with friends in Manhattan, in a loft on Vandam Street, below Houston; they'd met, for drinks, in a restaurant on Seventh Avenue, and Ian, in the city for the day, had wanted to take her to dinner as well; but Sigrid wasn't free. My life is so complicated now, she said, with genuine, or genuine-seeming, regret; and Ian had laughed and said, When has your life *not* been complicated? He could not determine whether, in some way, she was still connected with Fermi Sabri or whether there was another man, or men, in her life. He was jealous, but only in the abstract. Ah, only in the abstract.

The very night of his birthday party, Ian had tried to telephone Sigrid Hunt, for no particular reason other than, simply, to speak with her: to hear her voice. He had been enjoying the party enormously; he'd had a good deal to drink and was, in fact, deeply touched by his friends' affection for him, and Glynnis's extraordinary effort—the Château Mouton-Rothschild, for instance, was the first really good wine the McCulloughs had been able to afford, on the occasion of, was it, their fifth anniversary?—and of course she had remembered and served it with their main course. And then there was the Schwinn racer, which Ian would never have gotten around to buying for himself. . . . He'd been enjoying the party, certainly, after having overcome his initial surprise and disorientation; then, suddenly, perhaps because he'd had, simply, too much to eat and drink, a wave of disgust came over him, self-disgust, primarily; and he'd felt, sitting at his end of the table, being feted for his age, like a sacrificial victim of an archaic kind, one of those totemic demigods or luckless kings written up in anthropologists' studies. Delicacies placed in the mouth of the victim's (shrunken) head.

I cannot breathe here, Ian thought, rising from the table.

So he'd slipped inconspicuously away, into his study, assuming no one would miss him; for, at this point in the long, leisurely meal, one or two others had similarly excused themselves, to use the bathroom. He supposed it was a foolish thing to do, yes of course it was foolish, very possibly it was desperate, and, punching out the glowing numerals on his phone, he'd consoled himself by thinking, Of course she won't answer: her life is not contiguous with mine. Hearing the voices and laughter in the other part of the house, washing wavelike, and distant.

3.

Now, as then, Glynnis was saying, rather sharply, "Ian, what *is* wrong with you? For Christ's sake, what is *wrong?*"

Her voice was slurred; she was drunk. And very angry.

Ian had been standing in the courtyard, for how long he didn't know: simply standing there, staring . . . at the evergreen shrubs he'd planted fifteen years ago; their names, which were very likely melodic, long since forgotten, as so much in his life, melodic, lyric, tender, precious, was forgotten. They were evergreens with low-sweeping boughs, bluish-green acicular needles, sharp as the thorns of roses. A sharp odor, too, but one Ian liked: a beautiful smell, if smells could be said to be beautiful.

As if he had been thinking, all along, of such practical matters, Ian said quickly, "I was noticing that some of the evergreens are dying. I should clip them back, I suppose." He paused, scarcely daring to look up; for surely Glynnis had been watching him for a while, had caught him out in one of his reveries.

When he looked up, however, the doorway was empty. The door yawned wide.

So he entered uneasily, called her name; the atmosphere was still, brittle—or so in his apprehension he thought it. "Glynnis? Is something wrong?" he said. He looked for her in the kitchen and in the guest room at the rear of the house; rapped on her bathroom door; found her in their bedroom, lying on top of the bed, in the dark. A smell that might have been medicinal, but was surely alcoholic, wafted toward him. "Honey? Is something wrong?"

After a pause Glynnis said, "I have a headache. Why don't you let me alone."

Ian said, "Is it a migraine? Can I do anything for you?"

"Just a headache," Glynnis said, her voice low, indistinct. "Please just leave me *alone*."

Ian stood hesitantly in the doorway, knowing Glynnis was angry with him, yet not knowing, not daring to guess, why. (Had she been brooding all day about last night's abortive lovemaking? That was not like her, surely.) He said, "But isn't there anything I can do?"

"Let me sleep."

"I'll make dinner tonight," Ian said. "You'll want to eat, won't you? It's already past seven."

Glynnis said, quietly, "I'll make dinner, later, myself. Please just leave me alone *now*. I want to sleep for a while, *now*."

So Ian closed the door and went away, got a beer from the refrigerator, took off his coat and his tie, and went to his study to work. His hands were shaking slightly. *She knows,* he thought. *But what does she know?*

Ian had not, to his shame, spoken to Glynnis of Sigrid Hunt, though he'd meant to, had fully intended to, months ago. Somehow the occasion never arose; the right words never came. For what was there to say, really? To confess? He had not so much as touched the girl; it was not that kind of relationship. (Though she'd offered herself, he supposed. If pressed, he would have had to admit that.)

But: *Once something is said in a marriage it cannot be unsaid.* Those were Amos Kuhn's cautionary words, and Ian had never forgotten them. (Though he could not now remember what had provoked the remark. Had Amos been in love with a woman other than Elizabeth? Ian seemed to recall rumors to that effect.)

Once something is said. It cannot be unsaid.

You inherited that chilly disposition of yours from your parents, Glynnis once said.

Not accusing him, exactly.

I didn't realize I had a chilly disposition, Ian said.

Didn't you?

Do I?

Do you?

He finished his beer and went to get another; the house was unnervingly silent; he wondered if Glynnis was actually asleep or simply lying there, in the dark. Why was she angry with him? Why did she reproach him? He had apologized for his ill-considered remarks about the birthday party; he had apologized for everything. Of course I love you. You know I love you. He wondered how Denis had summoned up the strength to confess to Roberta: what words he had used; what emotions were aroused; how poor Roberta—among their circle, the sweetest, the most sensitive of them all—had reacted. He felt a pang of disapproval; again, of hurt. Perhaps he should have spoken to Roberta about it, should have offered her consolation: commiseration. If Denis is capable of lying to you, he is capable of lying to us all.

The telephone rang, in all, three times that evening. Each time, at his desk, Ian picked it up on the first ring, not wanting Glynnis to be disturbed. (The phone would also be ringing in the bedroom.) The first call was for Glynnis, from a woman named Stacey, of whom he'd never heard; the second call was from Leo Reinhart's new woman friend, inviting the McCulloughs to brunch, in New York City, a week from next Sunday—an invitation Ian tentatively accepted, seeing that, on his calendar, the date seemed to be open; the third call was from Homer Taylor, an elder colleague of Ian's, inviting him to lunch the next day— there were crucial matters to be talked of, concerning the "future of the Institute" after Dr. Max's retirement. (Though he had misgivings, Ian accepted the invitation almost eagerly; it would provide a pleasant bit of news to share with Glynnis. It was she, rather than Ian, who hoped that the directorship might be offered him.) After that, Ian left the receiver off the hook.

SHORTLY AFTER TEN, Glynnis knocked on his door and told him, without opening the door, that dinner was ready. "Not a very formal dinner," she said, "but the best I could do tonight."

Ian rose at once from his desk, as if he'd been released from a prison cell. Though he had drunk several cans of beer he was very hungry.

He supposed they would be eating, tonight, in the kitchen, and that he would set the table, as, on such nights, he usually did; so he was surprised to find the dining room table set, and covered, even, with a tablecloth, and candles burning. This was hardly Glynnis's practice when they dined alone.

A bottle of good white Italian wine had been uncorked, and a glass already poured, at Ian's place. "Sit down," Glynnis said. "Please."

Ian smiled at her, uneasily. "Shouldn't I help? Isn't there anything for me to do?" he said.

Glynnis said, "It's late, we'd better start. You must be hungry." She spoke with an air of mild reproach.

So, hesitantly, Ian sat; and Glynnis brought in their food from the kitchen, setting his plate before him in silence. She moved with care, rather stiffly, for of course she was still drunk and was drinking again. He said, "Glynnis? Have you been taking aspirin, for your headache?"—meaning, Should you be drinking wine now?—but Glynnis seemed not to hear.

"You'd better start," she said. "I'm afraid it's already rather dry."

They were having salmon steaks, one of Ian's favorite meals, which both touched him and worried him. Yet he was hungry, and ate hungrily, with an appetite that surprised him. Glynnis ate slowly—indeed, with increasing slowness—until finally she laid her fork down and sipped wine, replenishing her glass before it was entirely empty. She stared at him contemplatively. She lit a cigarette and stared. Ian said, "Please tell me what's wrong."

Glynnis shrugged, and said, "You know me—remarkable powers of recuperation."

"What?"

"My headache." She smiled and continued to stare at him. She did not appear angry so much as bemused. "How is the salmon? You haven't said a word. I'm afraid I grilled it a little too long. And there are bones, unfortunately. Watch out for the bones."

"The salmon is fine," Ian said, smiling. "My favorite—"

"Yes, I know. Watch out for the bones."

Indeed there were bones, a curving backbone of bones, saw-notched and cartilaginous. Ian picked them carefully out of the cooked flesh and off the tip of his tongue. The asparagus and small red potatoes Glynnis had prepared were overcooked; the salmon itself, dry as if baked, had rapidly cooled.

"It's delicious, actually."

"*Is* it." Glynnis's smile, stretching her lips, rapidly vanished when released.

Ian, eating, saw that Glynnis's cigarette trembled in her fingers and that, in the glass of the sliding door behind her, the entire table—the candle flames in particular—seemed to be trembling. The outdoor lights above the terrace had not been switched on, as they always were in the evening, so that the plate-glass windows reflected only the interior of the room against an opaque background of night. Ian thought, Someone should switch on the lights. But he made no move.

Nonetheless he smiled and tried to eat, finished a glass of wine and poured himself another, thanked Glynnis for having prepared a meal, so delicious a meal, when she hadn't been feeling well and probably should have gone to bed for the night. "It's too dry," Glynnis said flatly. "And there are bones." She was adjusting one of the candles, which had begun to tilt in its silver holder, and hot wax ran down her fingers, unnoticed. She said, "I forgot to slice lemon. There are lemons in the refrigerator, and I forgot to slice them."

Ian said quickly, "That's all right, Glynnis."

"No," Glynnis said, rising from the table, but taking her wineglass with her, "I don't at all mind."

When she returned she set a plate of lemon quarters before Ian. "There may be seeds," she said. "Watch the seeds." Ian thanked her, offered to squeeze lemon juice on what remained of her salmon, as well as on his own, and Glynnis laughed without smiling and said, "But do watch the seeds." In her distracted state she had brought the knife with which she'd sliced the lemons to the table with her and seemed not to know where to place it: a steak knife, one of the new set from Bloomingdale's, perhaps ten inches long, gleaming. She laid it down beside the plate of lemons.

Glynnis said, belatedly, "I'm afraid it will only make the salmon colder. The lemon."

Ian said, almost eagerly, "No. It's fine. But you don't seem to be eating, much, yourself."

"When I'm alone, sometimes, in the kitchen, working on a recipe, I eat a good deal," Glynnis said slowly. "When I'm—you know—alone."

She laughed, again without smiling, and ran a hand through her uncombed hair.

She was wearing a rumpled bathrobe and, over it, an apron, an old gift from Leonard Oppenheim, Beethoven's face imprinted on its front. The face was somber yet tinged with cartoon mania, the hair lifting in wild tufts. Glynnis's own hair, disheveled from sleep, lifted in wild tufts; her face, denuded of makeup, looked pale, puffy, flaccid, as if incompletely formed. She said, "I found the check."

Ian did not hear: or, hearing, vaguely assumed that Glynnis was referring to a household matter about which he was supposed to know but had forgotten. He remembered to tell her about the invitation to the brunch in New York City—"I accepted, tentatively; I hope that's all right with you?"

He had thought this might cheer Glynnis, as under ordinary circumstances it would, for Glynnis thrived on social invitations and did not mind, as Ian surely did, driving all the way into Manhattan for a meal. But she took it in silence, then said, "You could always go alone."

"Go alone? Why? Why should I go alone?" Ian asked.

"Leo is your buddy, not mine," Glynnis said, replenishing her wineglass with an unsteady hand. "We are not shackled together by leg irons after all."

"Why do you say that?" Ian asked. "That's a rather odd thing to say."

"Nonetheless it is true," Glynnis said.

She rose abruptly from the table, went into the kitchen, returned with a tossed green salad and a fresh bottle of wine. Ian, who had thought the meal was over, saw to his surprise that the wine was French and quite expensive, one of the birthday gifts brought by their friends. He said, indicating the bottle, "Do you really think we should? Tonight?"

Glynnis said indifferently, "*You* don't, of course, if you don't want to. We are not shackled together by leg irons after all."

The salad, which consisted of coarse Romaine leaves, some of them spotted with brown, was rather warm; the dressing was both vinegary and oleaginous. The first bite brought tears to Ian's eyes but he said nothing. Glynnis had given up all pretense of eating.

Ian asked again about her headache; she dismissed the question with a negligent wave of her hand. He asked if something was wrong, if perhaps she'd heard from Bianca that day; again, the negligent wave of her hand. He remembered that she had agreed to do several articles, in conjunction with her new regional cookbook, for the food section of *The New York Times,* but he could not remember if she had completed the articles; he could not remember, even, if they had already appeared in the paper . . . and dared not risk her anger by inquiring. She would say, You pay no attention to *me,* you do not take *me* seriously; and what reasonable defense would he have?

He'd laughed hard when, once, at the periphery of a typically ambitious multi-course Hazelton dinner party, a like-minded fellow had murmured in Ian's ear, "When I hear the word 'cuisine' I reach for my revolver." Yes, Ian thought, it is so. He would not hurt Glynnis's feelings for the world but, in truth, everything that had to do with food elitism, gourmet philosophizing, "the science of cuisine," and the like struck him as utterly, utterly trivial.

Guiltily, as if fearing that Glynnis might read his thoughts, Ian told her about the invitation to lunch at the Institute, thinking that *this* surely would not fail to please her; but she confounded him by saying, coldly, "As long as I'm not expected to be there."

"Of course you're not expected to be there," Ian said, hurt. "It will be just—"

"You and your colleagues."

"*Some* of my colleagues."

"Well," Glynnis said, with a conspicuous effort not to slur her words, "if you take the job, we can always use the extra money."

Ian's own hands were trembling. He recalled—not many days ago, when had it been?—a return flight from Washington in a small twelve-passenger plane and they had had a good deal of what pilots call "turbulence," and though Ian's hands shook and his handwriting on his yellow legal-sized pad was virtually illegible, he'd continued working nonetheless, jotting down notes for this paper he must give, this "seminal" paper he must concoct, for the damned Frankfurt conference. Ian McCullough had become a world-renowned figure in charting the courses of populations, in many cases of countries he had never visited, populations he'd never seen; thus any paper delivered by him must be "seminal," if not "definitive" or "ground-breaking." Outside the airplane's rather smeared windows there were clouds gusting about, and patches of blue bright and terrible as fissures in the skull. If the plane does not crash I will have done my work, Ian told himself, with his usual pragmatic equanimity. If it crashes, it will not matter.

That day, the plane had not crashed. He had been returned safely to Hazelton-on-Hudson, New York.

Glynnis said again, in her tight, careful voice, and this time Ian could not fail to know what she meant, "I found the check."

"The check?"

"For one thousand dollars. Made out to 'Sigrid Hunt.' "

Ian felt cold; tasted cold; could not, in the face of his wife's accusatory silence, speak. Finally he managed to say, weakly, "It isn't what you think, Glynnis."

"Isn't it?"

"It was a—"

"How do you know what I think?"

"—a loan. She asked for a—"

"I found it in your desk. The canceled check. I was looking for something else, and I found the check. *Pay to the order of. One thousand dollars. February 20, 1987*—a long time ago." Glynnis spoke slowly and thoughtfully, regarding him with bright, narrowed eyes. Ian did not think he had ever seen those eyes, quite those eyes, before.

He began to speak, and she cut him off. "How do you know what I think?" she said. "*What* is it you think I think?"

"She asked for a loan. She was in need of money."

"Money from you? *Us?*"

Ian put his hand to his forehead in a sudden gesture of pain. Was he telling the truth? Was he lying? He could not remember clearly: was he lying? "She seemed to be in desperate need of money," he said, beginning to stammer, "and I lent it to her, and I'd meant to tell you, and—"

"Your lover Sigrid. Sigrid *Hunt*," Glynnis said, as if the name amused her. "And you thought I would not know. *You* thought I would not know."

"She isn't my lover, Glynnis; don't be absurd," Ian said. "You know as well as I—"

"*You* thought I would not know. Could not guess."

"It was just a loan, and—"

"What a fool you are. Your mistake was not providing her with cash." Glynnis smiled and stubbed out her cigarette in her salad plate, crudely, amid the Romaine lettuce leaves. "*You* thought I would not know—as if I were an idiot. A fool like you. As if I could not guess."

Ian said quickly, "But it isn't what you think, Glynnis. I scarcely know her; she was your friend—"

"Who is 'she'? 'Her'? Are you afraid to say her name?"

"—and somehow I met up with her, with Sigrid, after that party here—when you introduced us—"

"*That's* important, isn't it—a bit of evidence for the record—that *I* introduced you?"

"—and I don't know how or why, for the life of me, Glynnis, I don't really remember the sequence, when she called me, or how it developed," Ian said, stumbling over his words. "One day she telephoned me at the Institute and seemed to be—hinted that—wanted me to see her, to help her in some way. And I—I didn't think I could—I couldn't say *no*. She seemed so desperate and so—"

"Your lover. Sigrid *Hunt*."

Glynnis spoke in a tone of supreme yet amused disgust. If she was drunk, as Ian guessed, quite seriously drunk, as he suspected, and as he himself, rather helplessly, was beginning to be, nonetheless she maintained a really quite extraordinary control: might almost have been giving—granting?—one of the frequent interviews she had begun to give, in recent years, since the unexpected development of her public "career." And Ian too began to speak assertively, emphatically, as if for the record. "The woman is not my lover. Sigrid Hunt is not my lover. I do not have a lover, I have a wife. I scarcely know her—"

"Who is 'her'? The lover, or the wife?"

"I said: I do not have a lover."

"Why cannot you say her name? Sigrid *Hunt*."

"I've told you, I scarcely know her."

"Yet you love her. You fuck her. *You*—and *her*."

Ian stared at her, shocked.

"Glynnis, that's absurd."

"*You*—and *her*," Glynnis said. "That diseased little *tramp*."

She lit up another cigarette, and tossed down her matches, and exhaled smoke from both nostrils, and said, fixing him with a look of rather theatrical contempt, "Did you think there would be no consequences? *You*—and *her?*"

Ian laughed angrily. "You've been drinking and you're in no state to discuss this. I tell you there is nothing between Sigrid Hunt and me; there has been nothing; I scarcely know her—really. I think we'd better save this for another time."

"But did you really think there would be no consequences?"

"There *are* no consequences."

"Except that, by accident, though possibly it wasn't entirely an accident, I found the check," Glynnis said. "One thousand dollars. Payable to Sigrid Hunt. Signed, Ian McCullough." She too laughed, with a strange joyous violence. "*In Ian McCullough's inimitable hand.*"

"She was in desperate need, I told you, of—"

"What was the money for? An abortion?"

"—It was a loan, Glynnis, not a gift. I'll have Sigrid explain—"

"Was it for an abortion?"

Calmly he said, "You don't really believe I would be unfaithful to you, do you? When you know, you absolutely must know, that I love you. That I could not live without you."

"*That* I believe," Glynnis said, laughing. "But it doesn't follow from it that you love me. Still less, that you haven't been unfaithful to me."

"Glynnis, this is all so absurd. In the morning—"

"That diseased little tramp. Sigrid *Hunt*."

Ian winced. "Why do you say that? Why say such a thing? Diseased? Why? How?"

"Are you worried? You *do* look worried!"

"Sigrid was your friend, not—"

"As if I wouldn't know. Wouldn't guess. *Sense.*"

"She was your friend, not mine. She came into my life by way of—"

"And do you really fuck her? *You?* Ian McCullough so very suddenly the *lover?*"

"I've told you there is nothing between us. There was nothing. Damn you," Ian whispered. "It isn't what you think—I swear."

"How many times have you fucked her? Or *have* you—at all?"

"Glynnis, please stop. This is ugly, this is absurd, you are saying things you'll regret—"

"*I* am ugly, *I* am absurd, because *I* have ferreted out the truth, is that it?"

"I swear—"

"Swear on a stack of Bibles!"

Glynnis's face glowed in mockery. She was making an allusion—an unforgivable allusion, Ian thought it—to an incident of many years back: while at Harvard, the McCulloughs had befriended a young man in Ian's department, like Ian an assistant professor without tenure; and this young man, by the name of Scobie, "borrowed" heavily from an article of Ian's he had read in manuscript and hurriedly published his borrowings in the prestigious journal *World Politics*—with no reference to Ian McCullough, of course. He claimed that the ideas were his own, and not Ian's; they had come to him quite independently of Ian; who could prove they had not? Certain ideas circulated in the air, in the very atmosphere; who could prove they did not? "I would never steal from you or from anyone," Scobie had said indignantly. "I swear on a stack of Bibles." Though really quite angered by their friend's betrayal, and, at the time, deeply hurt, the McCulloughs had managed finally to laugh together over Scobie's rhetoric: for would not, as Glynnis pointed out, a single Bible have been enough for Scobie's purposes? Why a stack?

"You're drunk," Ian said.

"*You're* a liar," Glynnis said.

"We'll talk about it in the morning," Ian said. "Morning is soon enough."

"Where are you going tonight?"

"Going—?"

"I want you out of here. Tonight."

"Glynnis, for Christ's sake—"

"Go to *her*, go quickly to telephone *her*. Why sit here with *me*?"

"Glynnis, please. You must know—"

"I know too much."

"You are exaggerating this. There was absolutely nothing—"

"Swear on a stack of Bibles!"

"Goddamn you, that isn't funny. In the morning—"

"There isn't going to be any morning."

"I am not leaving this house. This is my house, and I am not leaving it."

"Ah, but did you, *do* you, really fuck her? *You*—and *her*?"

"Shut up!"

"I find that a novel idea, really. I find that—*novel*."

"Why are you doing this? Making it so vulgar and—"

"You of all people: Ian McCullough the *lover*," Glynnis said, laughing. "I find that *novel*."

"—so vulgar and degrading—"

"And not ro*mantic*? I'm so sorry."

"It isn't like you. In the morning—"

"And it isn't like *you?* Lying to me, and deceiving me, and making a fool of me, and—"

"*There was nothing between Sigrid Hunt and me.* I've said—"

"Don't shout at me, goddamn you. Who do you think you are, goddamn you? I found the check, and you weren't going to tell me about it, were you, ever: you and *her,* imagine you fucking her, Sigrid *Hunt, you,* Ian McCullough, impotent half the time, three quarters of the time, goddamn you don't you look at me like that, I won't tolerate that, you pack your goddamn things and get out of the house tonight, I don't have to tolerate you, or her, bringing that woman into our lives, that bitch, that cunt, into our bed, how many 'sexual partners' do you think a woman like that has had in her lifetime, and how many have each of those 'sexual partners' had, goddamn you, I'm talking to *you,* bringing disease into our lives, bringing death, for all I know bringing *death*—"

Glynnis's voice rose precipitously. Her eyes were wild, now, and bright with tears. Ian tried to take her hand, to calm her, but she drew away; he said, "But Glynnis, you haven't listened. I am not Sigrid Hunt's lover—as I've tried to tell you. All that might be said of me, or of our relations, is that we are friends of a kind. Vague, undefined—"

"Ah, yes, 'vague'! 'Undefined'!"

"But I am not her lover: I have not ever made love to her. You might speak with her, if—"

Glynnis gave a little scream and brought her fists down hard on the table. "Speak to her yourself—go and sneak away and telephone her yourself. That little conniving *bitch.*"

Ian's temples throbbed, his gut was awash with nausea. He could not bear this terrible scene, yet he knew he must; he must think of it as a game, a codified game, not unlike similar games Glynnis had forced him to play in the past: his humiliation, her self-righteous triumph. For he was to be humbled and surely deserved to be humbled; she had right on her side, was therefore righteous: deserved, however rough the passage, triumph. He could not bear it, yet he must. He said, "But I love *you*, Glynnis—you must know that."

Glynnis said angrily, "I don't know the first thing about you."

At this point Ian rose to embrace her, meaning to comfort her; but, as if perversely, Glynnis misunderstood the gesture, gave a little scream and shrank back, and the table shook, and one of the candles toppled from its holder. Before Ian could pinch out the flame with his fingers the tablecloth was scorched. Ian thought, Something terrible is going to happen.

Yet he did not walk away, did not, as instinct urged, flee the house and Glynnis. He sat down again at his place, heavily, as if fated: staring at this woman with the wild hurt eyes and disheveled hair with a new fascination, as if he had never really seen her before, had not, before tonight, really known her. And Glynnis in her turn stared at him. "Just don't you *touch* me," she whispered.

IAN WOULD RECALL afterward, to the degree to which he recalled the next hour and a half at all, that much of the time he and Glynnis had not seemed to be quarreling; were merely talking, talking earnestly, if heatedly, their voices slightly raised and slightly careening as if from side to side, like roller-coaster cars. Again and again, with numbing persistence, Glynnis returned to the matter of the check, to Ian's deception, as she saw it; and Ian defended himself, telling her—or trying, through her interruptions, to tell her—what had happened between him and Sigrid Hunt, what had not happened between him and Sigrid Hunt. If Glynnis listened she did not hear, seemed incapable of hearing. It is her self-hatred with which I am contending, Ian thought, and the thought astonished him. He had not known, had not guessed.

There was the matter of Sigrid Hunt, but there was also the matter, as it developed, of Bianca: Bianca's love, the loss of which Glynnis blamed on Ian, with a cold, reasoned passion that quite astonished him. And there was the matter, yet again, yet now more embittered, of Ian's "chronic impotence"—his withdrawal, as Glynnis saw it, from her and from their marriage.

And there was the matter, revealed with unnerving candor, of the affairs Glynnis herself claimed to have had: intermittently, as she said, throughout their marriage.

Affairs? Glynnis? Throughout their marriage?

Seeing Ian's look of utter disbelief Glynnis said, "Of course, *you* would never have guessed." She smiled at him, angrily. "*You*—wrapped in your own little world—would never have guessed."

Ian thought, I must get out of here; I can't breathe.

Glynnis said, "Wouldn't you even like to know who they were? The men? Aren't you at least curious?"

Ian shook his head mutely. He really could not believe what he'd heard; stared at Glynnis, as if in appeal.

"One of them I really did love—I love him, as a matter of fact, even now," Glynnis said, her voice breaking. "Gave him up for *you*, hurt his feelings, hurt myself—for *you*."

"Glynnis, you are saying things you—"

"And all for what? For *you*."

"For God's sake—"

"For *you*, for *you*. And now you're too cowardly even to ask his name."

Again Ian shook his head. His heart was knocking against his ribs.

He said, "Who was it?"

"*Is* it."

"Who is it?"

Now that she had roused him to anger, Glynnis smiled at him bitterly and shrugged. "What difference does it make? It's over now."

"Who is it? Someone I know?"

"Too late! All over! Because of you!"

"Someone in Hazelton?"

"Yes, it's someone in Hazelton," Glynnis said indifferently, pouring herself another glass of wine. Her hands were very unsteady now. "A prominent man, a much talked-of man, in Hazelton. A friend of yours, in fact. And I gave him up, and that was a mistake; Christ, was that ever a mistake, *wasn't* it. And now you, *you*, lying to me about *her*, you hypocrite, you bastard—thinking you could deceive *me*—"

"Glynnis, you must listen to me—"

"As if I can believe anything you say!"

Then, with no warning, Glynnis was on her feet, sobbing uncontrollably, screaming at Ian to get out of the house. Ian leapt up and tried to restrain her, for she'd become, in that instant, hysterical; and she shoved him away, screaming, as if fearful he meant to hurt her. Though he had not seen her snatch it up, she was holding the steak knife in her right hand; brandishing it, in fact, in an extravagant gesture, that at another time would have reduced them both to tears of laughter. Ian reached blindly for the knife, closing his fingers around the blade, and Glynnis, screaming, struck him on the head and on the nose, bloodying his nose; and in their desperate struggle the table was overturned, and everything went flying and crashed to the floor—china, food, candles, bottles. Ian had no awareness of his fingers bleeding but he knew his nose was bleeding and still Glynnis continued in her fury, striking wild blows against his head, his chest, taunting him with that terrible word *you, you, you* as if it were the foulest of obscenities. He seized her shoulders and began to shake her, pleading with her to stop, to stop this madness, damn you oh goddamn you, *stop;* and still she struggled, demonically strong, and would not stop screaming, her eyes wild and her forehead gleaming with sweat and her hair charged as if with static electricity. Ian thought of Medusa: that monstrous being at whom the hero Perseus could not look directly, out of terror of being turned to stone. Ian thought, She wants my heart; nothing less will appease her.

He ducked to avoid her crazed flailing blows and shoved her from him, with all his strength; and Glynnis stumbled, and tripped, and fell with great force, backward, against one of the plate-glass windows— and through it, the wall of glass shattering instantly, amid her terrified screams. Shards and splinters flew into Ian's face like stinging insects.

The noise of the breaking glass was deafening, yet it died away at once; as Glynnis's screaming, so terrible in his ears, died away at once: almost at once.

She was lying on the flagstone terrace beneath the window, one of her legs still caught in the window. Ian stepped through to help her and almost fell on top of her, his ankle suddenly livid with pain—he'd cut it on a jagged fragment of glass still in the window frame. He called her name repeatedly, crouching over her, trying, in nightmare panic, to lift her. There was, suddenly, glass everywhere: in Glynnis's hair and in Ian's, in their clothing, on the flagstones. A net of blood began to spread over Glynnis's face; she did not seem to have lost consciousness yet was incoherent, insensible, writhing and moaning, her eyelids fluttering, her body a dead weight in his arms. Ian knew he must run to the telephone to call an ambulance, to get help for her, but for some seconds, for what seemed a very long time, he squatted there, paralyzed, simply unable to move; unable to lay Glynnis back down on the terrace, amid the shattered glass and the blood, and leave her.

TWO

THE VIGIL

1.

On an evening of the previous year, in another lifetime, it now seemed, Ian McCullough entered a crowded, buzzing room—was it in fact his own living room? in his own house?—and paused for a moment on the threshold and stared, overcome by a sudden sense of confronting, not the men and women who were his friends, but a gathering of souls.

How strange we are to one another, he thought.

Each soul was encased in flesh, bound by an envelope of skin, turned inward, immersed in silence. The soul was light, or flame—its heat small, ephemeral, easily extinguished. Ian stared and felt afraid: yet felt, in that instant, an uncanny happiness. He saw himself so brotherly, so deeply kindred to them all—these souls, these separate beings, whom he did not know.

And then Meika Cassity came up to him, and slipped her arm through his, and said, "What a lovely party, Ian!" as if she had never said those words before.

And Ian said, "Is it? We're so glad."

AT THE HAZELTON Medical Center, waiting for Glynnis to be returned to him, waiting out the long hours—there would be nearly seven—during which she was in surgery, Ian was overcome by this same strangeness: a certitude that we are all in disguise from one another and from ourselves, souls glimmering like phosphorescent fire, hidden in the opacity of flesh. He stared at the faces of strangers as if he knew them and was in dread of their knowing him. If Glynnis should die? If he should never speak with her again? The thought opened before him like a chasm, the far side of which he could not contemplate, let alone see. He was bathed in terror as in a cold slick sweat.

He himself had been treated, efficiently and sympathetically, in an open area of the emergency room: his erratic heartbeat monitored; his lacerated right hand cleaned, stitched, and bandaged; the cuts on his forearms and ankle attended to; his bloodied face washed. The police had requested that he take a Breathalyser test, and Ian had, shamefaced, acquiesced; it would have seemed very wrong of him not to. (And what were the results? A blood alcohol level of .14, when anything above .10 constituted legal intoxication.) He could have wept, to be so exposed and humiliated. He and Glynnis both, a matter now of public record.

"Did you and your wife have a struggle of some kind, Mr. Mc-Cullough?" the doctor asked, in a rather too casual voice.

And Ian said, shutting his eyes, "I don't know, I really don't know, everything happened too quickly. . . ."

He had telephoned for an ambulance at 11:40 P.M., and the ambulance had arrived at 11:44 P.M. Within five swift minutes both he and Glynnis were admitted to the Medical Center, and by midnight the decision was made to operate on Glynnis as quickly as possible. With a hand that shook so badly he could barely hold a pen, Ian managed to sign papers, papers in triplicate: yes he had medical coverage yes he was on the faculty at the Institute yes he had a local doctor yes he would gladly sign this form and that form and all forms, if only they would save Glynnis. "Do anything you can," he begged; "anything, everything." He must have said many extravagant things before witnesses, as he doubtless had in the ambulance being brought from that scene of shame and ignominy—the smashed window, the glass crackling underfoot like laughter, in the dining room a havoc of china, cutlery, glasses, bottles, food. Could it be possible such a nightmare had happened? And had happened to the McCulloughs?

How swiftly his drunkenness faded. He'd been rendered sober, he thought, as if by a sledgehammer blow to the head.

A NEUROSURGEON OF local reputation, Dr. Morris Flax, was called in, and by 12:35 A.M. of April 24, Glynnis was undergoing emergency neurosurgery to repair arterial damage in the brain: to the degree to which, as Ian was told, it could be repaired. Glynnis had suffered some subarachnoid hemorrhaging as a consequence of multiple fractures to the skull, and without immediate surgery, brain damage, paralysis, even death were "imminent."

The operation lasted until 6:45 A.M., during which time Ian waited in the visitors' lounge, sitting, and standing, and pacing about, and sitting again, his head in his hands. His bandaged right hand was stiff as a club and throbbed with pain, but the powerful drug with which he'd been injected, to ease the acceleration of his heartbeat, made him lethargic, heavy-headed. All that had happened was rapidly fading, like a bad dream; he could think only of Glynnis, on the operating table, her skull sawed open . . . for wasn't the skull sawed open, for brain surgery? And what were her chances, her real chances, of recovery? Of survival?

Ian would recall, vaguely, wrapping his bleeding hand in a kitchen towel; but it was in fact one of the young police officers who had wrapped it for him, seeing how he bled, how he stood helpless and staring, like a man wakened from a dream. And his nose and mouth were bloodied too. Take care, mister, the young man said, you're hurt too.

And the other police officer asked, What happened to your hand?

A Hazelton police patrol car had swung into the driveway almost immediately after the ambulance's arrival; two youngish police officers had entered the house, as boldly as if they had been summoned, and moved upon the scene, seemed indeed to move into the scene, with an authority Ian would have found outrageous under other circumstances. For what right had they to enter a private residence? What right to intrude, to interfere, to ask their blunt and unanswerable question: *What happened here, mister?*—staring at the wreckage, the unconscious woman being lifted onto a stretcher. Ian's initial thought was that they were the same police officers who had come to his door last September, under the pretext of mistaking his house for another. The very men about whom he had filed a formal complaint and written a half dozen letters.

Two ambulance attendants were strapping Glynnis to the stretcher, and then they were lifting her, glass crackling underfoot. The precision of their movements, their practiced coordination, reminded Ian of a crewing team plying oars in perfect unhesitating rhythm. They bore Glynnis out to the ambulance and Ian hurried panting beside them, pleading with them to hurry, to hurry, to hurry.

One of the police officers was saying, Just a minute, mister, how'd all this happen? How'd she go through that window?

An accident. We've had an accident.

What kind of accident, mister?

The window—

Yes, mister?

The window broke—

Yes? By itself, the window broke?

—and my wife fell, and—

Fell? How?

—fell, and hit the ground—

Fell, mister? Or was pushed?

They were escorting Ian to the ambulance though he had no need of their assistance. His legs were strangely elastic and seemed distant from him, yet under his control. His head was ringing and buzzing but all his thoughts were clear, lucid . . . logical. He was thinking that Glynnis's kitchen knives were all finely honed for she could not bear a dull knife; no serious cook can bear a dull knife; he had bought her a knife sharpener for Christmas a dozen years ago when Bianca was a child, and Bianca had begged to sharpen her mommy's knives for her . . . that whirring grinding noise, and the faint aromatic smell that arose from it . . . how captivated the child had been! And if the knife in Glynnis's hand had been razor sharp, and if Ian had closed his fingers around it to wrench it from her, and if he'd shoved her from him violently, to free himself of her, and if she'd fallen against the window, and if the window had shattered, and if she was badly hurt, if, even, she were to die . . . none of this had any bearing upon what had really happened. It had no bearing at all upon either of them.

STILL, THE BLADE had been sharp; the cuts went deep. Ian wondered indifferently if he had severed nerves, bone; if his hand, already stiff as a claw, would ever mend.

He waited, waited for news: watching the slow red second hand of the clock high on the wall, sitting for as long as he could bear it and then standing, and walking about the lounge, and out into the corridor, several times out of the hospital altogether, into the night, which smelled of something like asphalt . . . cold, damp, brackish. They had offered him a cot in the emergency room, empty at this hour of the morning, but he preferred the waiting room, preferred the anxiety of his vigil. By degrees the sedative was wearing off. His heart began to leap again, to kick against his ribs.

And how many times that night he hurried to the lavatory . . . needing suddenly, with no warning, to urinate, as if his bladder were pinched. And afterward, his discomfort at being unable to wash his hands, running hot water over his left hand alone. He was thinking of Bianca: the time she'd fallen on the playground at school and broken three fingers. Had it been the left hand or the right? Poor baby; poor love. A plump-cheeked pretty child with startled-looking eyes, slate blue for a while, then shading, like his own, to gray. As a little girl she'd been intelligent enough but sometimes maddeningly clumsy, graceless, rather loud, eager to please yet, if not pleasing, just as inclined to be sullen; with a look, as Glynnis said, teasing, of having swallowed a toad. They'd been happiest, though, in those years; Glynnis had thrived on motherhood, had loved not only her little girl but her little girl's friends, a bedlam of little girls at times, really quite amazing. Ian would return in the late afternoon to a kitchen full of them, and a smell of baking cookies—chocolate chip, peanut butter, oatmeal, gingerbread—and Glynnis smiling flush-faced and beautiful in their midst: Look what we've made. Now Glynnis resented it that Bianca seemed to prefer her father, and that Ian was "undemanding" of Bianca; it was an old quarrel, an old charge: his attitude was a form of male condescension, she said, if not scorn. And Ian protested; you're being unfair, you're being absurd. I love Bianca as she is.

And Glynnis said, Yes. That's the problem.

Toward morning he went to stand for a while in the parking lot, staring at the sky as if waiting for a revelation. The long night was ending, dissolving, an orangish-pink light radiating from the horizon like something spilled, Ian thought, in water.

He seemed then to know that Glynnis would be all right; for was it not inconceivable, after all, that she *not* be . . . ? Years ago, in Cambridge, driving their feisty little red Volkswagen, she had banged her head on the windshield in a minor accident, and naturally they had worried but nothing came of it except, a day or two later, one of her mysterious migraine headaches, the kind that left her exhausted, sweating, eyes streaming tears. The accident had been an ambiguous one: the driver ahead of Glynnis had braked his car suddenly and Glynnis collided with it, damaging its rear and the front of her own car; blame lay with Glynnis for tailgating, though it would seem to have been as much the other driver's fault. There had been some unpleasantness, but the insurance company finally paid and the matter was settled. And Glynnis said, chastened, I've learned my lesson: I must keep my distance from the car in front of me, and I must wear my seat belt.

WHEN DR. FLAX IN his surgeon's green gown came to speak with him, Ian woke, groggy and fearful, having fallen asleep only minutes before on a chair in the waiting room. He struggled to his feet, anxious yet outwardly composed, and began nodding as Flax spoke, in that quick, vague way of his that often annoyed Glynnis, for it seemed to suggest that he wasn't listening carefully. Flax told him that, so far as he could judge, the operation had gone well; they had every reason to be optimistic. There had been considerable trauma to the brain, exacerbated by the amount of alcohol Glynnis had ingested, but the arterial damage turned out to be less severe than the CAT-scan had indicated. "Your wife is unconscious now, of course, but she will probably begin waking by mid- or late morning. You should be able to see her then."

Ian stared at Flax, wondered if there was something more he should be told. Or something he should ask.

He said, "Do you think she will make a full recovery?"

Flax hesitated only a fraction of a moment, then said, "Frankly, I don't know. We won't know for a while. Why don't we just hope for the best?"

"Yes," Ian said numbly. "We'll hope for the best."

He was advised then to go home, to sleep for two or three hours before returning to the hospital; but Ian did not want to go home and did not want to think about why he did not want to go home. Now that it was fully morning, past seven o'clock, he had telephone calls he must make . . . to Bianca at Wesleyan and to Glynnis's sister, Kate, who could, if she thought it necessary, telephone relatives of Glynnis's. And he would call the Grinnells, and the Kuhns, and the Olivers, and Martha Fairchild, who would tell people at the Institute and cancel Ian's appointments for the next several days.

And one of the calls would be to the glass and mirror shop on Charter Street, the one that did emergency repairs. He would have a new plate-glass window installed, Ian thought, that very day: well in advance of Glynnis's return home.

3.

In her high bed in the intensive care ward, a translucent tube snaking up into her left nostril and others attached to the soft flesh of her inner arms, Glynnis lay immobile except for her breath, which was hoarse, labored, and arrhythmic. Her heartbeat was monitored; her shaved head and much of her face were swathed in bandages tight as a nun's wimple. Had Ian not been shown to her bedside he might have stumbled past her, unrecognizing. He drew a deep sharp breath, astounded. Glynnis? That woman? Within a space of hours she appeared to have aged years.

So, at her bedside, he waited, waited patiently, holding her hand in his, whispering her name. He had read that absolute unconsciousness does not exist; the anesthetized patient on the operating table hears, and absorbs, what is said within earshot, while being unable of course to respond. When he whispered, "Glynnis?" it seemed to him that, from time to time, her fingers twitched in response; her eyelids fluttered. He had the impression that she wanted to wake, to speak to him; she was keenly aware of his presence, yet separated from him by a sort of veil, impossible to penetrate. Consciousness was the surface of a body of water of incalculable depth; and unconsciousness was that depth; and Glynnis, a swimmer trapped beneath the surface, was struggling valiantly to rise, but was pulled back, and again struggled to rise, and was again pulled back.

Yet each time it seemed to Ian that she rose higher and fell back less, that by degrees, by a supreme effort of will, she was making her way to the surface. He spoke her name like an incantation, repeatedly, tirelessly, his eyes fixed upon her face with such concentration that he no longer knew where he was, or even why he was here, what unspeakable turn of destiny had brought them to this: this hospital bed in an intensive care ward that, against one's natural expectations, was a place of much irreverent bustle and noise. Ian tried not to look toward other beds, at other visitors holding lifeless hands, speaking urgent incantatory words to unhearing ears. He thought, My love will pull her back.

Shortly after two o'clock, Bianca arrived, breathless and frightened, and sat beside Ian, close by the bed. "My God, my God," she said in a weak voice, staring at Glynnis, "I just can't believe this, I just can't *believe* this—" until Ian told her to please be still; Glynnis could hear every word.

It was late afternoon when, at last, Glynnis opened her eyes.

She looked directly at Ian and squeezed his fingers, or seemed to, in an effort to speak. Her eyes were bloodshot and not altogether in focus yet she seemed to recognize him, he would swear to it that she recognized him. He said excitedly, "Glynnis? Darling? Can you hear me?" Again she squeezed his fingers; the cords in her neck tensed; she stared at him, or toward him, the pupil of the right eye much blacker than that of the left. Bianca sat silent, as if transfixed; Ian was saying, in a low, urgent, crooning voice, "I'm here, I'll take care of you, don't be frightened, I'm here and I will never go away. I will never go away." He stood over her, gripping both her hands in his, promising, pleading, begging. It seemed to him that Glynnis heard and understood, yet could not speak. Ah, could not!

And finally she closed her eyes. And Bianca, released, burst into tears.

GLYNNIS DID NOT regain consciousness again that day, or the next, though Ian and Bianca waited expectantly, always hopefully. Then they began to spell each other, a five-hour vigil for Ian, a three-hour vigil for Bianca. It seemed to them that, at any instant, Glynnis would again open her eyes and rouse herself forcibly from the stupor that had settled upon her limbs: would, this time, speak their names; *see* them.

But the hours passed, and the days. And it did not, so very mysteriously, happen.

Ian spoke with Flax, for Flax was the man, clearly, with whom to speak. He asked, "Is Glynnis in a coma? Is that what this condition is—a *coma?*"

Flax, frowning, seemed to say yes, unless Flax said no; it was not altogether clear what Flax said, still less what he meant. He spoke slowly and at length, explaining the details of the operation, letting fall remarks that might be interpreted as cautiously optimistic, unless they were guarded or frankly evasive. Ian gathered that Flax was waiting for the return of his partner Pois, a neurologist, who was returning to Hazelton that very day.

Bianca said of Flax, "If he knew Mommy he'd *care* more."

Ian said, "We have to believe that the man is doing the best he can."

SO THE DAYS passed, and they waited and kept their faithful vigil; like several others at bedsides in the intensive care ward, whose sad stories they soon learned but did not consider in terms of their own situation. For Glynnis was younger after all than these luckless (and clearly moribund) patients; her heart and her other vital organs were said to be strong. The changes in her condition that took place were nearly all internal, monitored by machines of exquisite precision and meticulously recorded, in a script and a vocabulary unreadable save to the initiate. The more public terms *critical list* and *coma* came to be uttered, but never their precise explanation, still less their cause. Having witnessed Glynnis's awakening once, Ian and Bianca were certain that they would witness it again. "My wife is a fighter," Ian said, though this was not a thought he had ever had before in his life, still less uttered; and Bianca agreed, as passionately as if the point had been contested. "Mommy isn't the kind of woman to just give *up.*"

To their friends they said, "Things are more or less the same" or

"Things are more or less stable." It would have made a powerful impression upon Ian, had he the time and the emotional energy to consider it, that so many people in Hazelton, including a number whom he scarcely knew, came forward to offer their services. He understood that Glynnis had many women friends and acquaintances, but he could never have guessed that there were so many, or that, hearing of Glynnis's condition, they would react with such sympathy and alarm. Tell us what we can do, tell us how we can help, they said, and Ian's mind went blank, so confronted. The plainest truth was that what anyone could do for him he hardly cared enough to want done.

He sensed that there was much speculation in Hazelton about what had happened to Glynnis; it was a community in which everyone knew everyone else, or knew *of* everyone else, and was never loath to know a little more. By way of Denis Grinnell, though without Denis's seeming to know Ian had not known, he learned that the police officers who had come to the house had not accompanied the ambulance but had in fact been called by their neighbors the Dewalds, who reported having heard screams. "They must have exaggerated it," Denis said; "—what they heard, I mean."

"I suppose so," Ian said slowly. He was stricken with shame and alarm. Had Glynnis screamed? Had *he* screamed? He could not remember.

IN THE INTERSTICES of visiting hours at the hospital, Ian fell into the pattern of seeking out Flax, when Flax was there to be sought out. He saw the neurosurgeon as a counterpart of himself, a highly bred professional man, nervously attuned to his public reputation, outwardly affable, amiable, yet made of a steely substance that might be made to bend if confronted with a like substance in another man. Ian surprised himself, and, no doubt, Flax, by the audacity with which he hounded the man, surrendering, as the days so bafflingly passed and there was no change in Glynnis's condition, all vestiges of pride, tact, diplomacy, and even honor: as if Flax stood between him and his wife's recovery. He reminded himself of those men, and some women, who courted Ian McCullough with the hope of appropriating from him some degree of his power; as if, by a mere gesture of generosity on his part, he could grant them the means of altering their lives. He acquired medical books, neurological books, back issues of the *New England Journal of Medicine* from a neighbor of his who was an obstetrician, and with the manic intensity that had characterized his work in graduate school, but rarely since, he became an amateur expert, though very amateur, of brain anatomy and pathology and the latest microsurgical techniques. He came to believe that Glynnis should be operated on another time and did not like it that Flax resisted; told Ian, in fact quite bluntly, that another operation would be pointless. "I can't accept that," Ian said. Flax said, not unkindly, "You will."

At his most desperate, Ian McCullough was likely to be his most cerebral and abstract. If Flax would not, or could not, talk helpfully of Glynnis, he would ask of him questions of a philosophical nature: "Where, Doctor, does the soul reside? Is it generated by the brain, or filtered through the brain, or *is* it the brain?" And: "I have not read Plato in years, but isn't it in the *Phaedo* that proof is offered of the immortality of the soul? What do you think of Plato's proof, Doctor? Is it just fantasy, or is there something to it?" At such times, waylaying Flax in a corridor or in the parking lot behind the Center, Ian made an effort to hide the fact that his eyes brimmed with feeling and his hands shook.

Flax had nothing to say about the soul but offered to write Ian a prescription for the tranquilizer Librium, which, in the extremity of his need, Ian accepted. He'd heard that the tranquilizer should not be taken beyond two weeks, since it was quickly habit forming, but he reasoned that by that time Glynnis would have recovered or begun to recover. By that time he'd have no need of Librium, or of Flax, apart from settling the bill.

BIANCA SAID QUIETLY, "You just want to protect him."

Ian said, "What on earth are you talking about?"

Her eyes appeared oddly lashless, naked and exposed. Her face looked as if it had been scrubbed with steel wool.

Bianca said, "You men, you men who run the world, you stick together."

"And what on earth does *that* mean?"

Bianca made an airy gesture with her hand, a gesture in such mimicry of Glynnis, Ian thought for a mad instant that she was mocking her mother. But, to the contrary, she was altogether serious. She said, regarding Ian levelly across the cafeteria table—they ate many of their meals here, in the pleasantly crowded basement cafeteria of the Hazelton Medical Center—"You cover up for one another's crimes."

The words so took Ian by surprise, he could not reply, and stared at his daughter with a look of hurt, chagrin, dismay. Though Bianca was nineteen years old and physically mature, though she had always received superlative grades in school and was commended by certain of her teachers for her "leadership qualities," she had always shown a different face, struck a different note, at home. Ian said, gently, "What do you mean, Bianca, by 'crimes'? Are you suggesting malpractice?"

"I mean 'crimes' in a generic sense," Bianca said. "The crimes of the patriarchy, which are immeasurable, because they have always been identified as virtues."

Ian laughed. "Bianca, really."

"The other side of a blessing is a curse, after all," she said. "Like the Greek word *ara*, which means prayer but also a curse: The Greeks realized that a curse is after all just a prayer against one's enemies."

"But I don't quite see," Ian said, "how this applies to us. To Dr. Flax and us."

Bianca looked at him levelly, unblinkingly. He had a moment's panic: Does she think I purposefully injured Glynnis? Tried to kill her? Bianca said, "No, you wouldn't."

Ian rose blindly from the table, thinking of escape. He would run out into the street, clear his head, breathe. That this sullen young woman in the gunmetal-gray sweatshirt and well-worn jeans, hair straggling in her face, was his daughter, and therefore *his*, struck him, for the instant, as a fact of melancholy irony, a fact that his life had brought him to, as it had brought him to the comatose woman in the hospital bed seven floors above. They were women entrusted to his care, whom he loved desperately, but of what good was his love to them?

He walked away but did not leave the cafeteria; his legs simply could not take him out the door. Instead he bought two more cups of coffee, Styrofoam cups of bitter hot coffee, and brought them back to the table.

Where, now, Bianca sat crying, tears glistening thinly on her cheeks. "It's just—you know, Daddy, the way it has turned out, I mean the way Mother woke up as she did, clearly conscious, and looking right at us and recognizing us . . . it's just—" She broke off, baffled, unable to complete her sentence. "It's just . . . something I can't accept."

Ian shivered and said, "Yes."

LIKE IAN, BIANCA was careful always to refer to what had happened to Glynnis as an accident.

When Ian had telephoned her at college she'd been upset, emotional, asking Ian several times what had happened, and how, my God *how;* but once she arrived home she asked no further questions. Ian had shown her the window that had been broken—that is to say, the new window that had replaced the broken window—but, subdued, she'd made no comment beyond remarking with a shudder that plate-glass windows and doors are notoriously dangerous, like children's playgrounds . . . did he know that the statistics were really quite shocking, involving playground accidents?

Nor did she inquire about whether they had been drinking that night. Or even whether they had been quarreling.

She did, however, ask about Ian's hand, his sixty-five stitches. "Was it trying to save Mommy?"

Ian, staring at the hand as if it constituted a riddle, said slowly, "Yes, I suppose that was it . . . trying to save Mommy when the window broke. But I failed."

It was the first time since Bianca had passed the age of four or five that, in addressing her, Ian referred to Glynnis as "Mommy." The word reverberated oddly between them.

WHEN FATHER AND daughter had a rare meal at home they did not eat in the dining room, of course, but in the kitchen at the table in the corner, round and wooden-spoked and rather cozy there beside Glynnis's cork bulletin board. One side of the table was still heaped with Glynnis's things—notebooks, recipe cards, magazine and newspaper articles, cookbooks—which Bianca organized into tidier piles but did not remove from the table. She had taken to saving items from *The New York Times* that might, she thought, be of interest to her mother: food-related articles and recipes.

The dozens of spice jars in their racks; the shiny copper utensils; the crammed bookshelves; the cork bulletin board with its strata of postcards, snapshots, clippings, invitations; the hanging plants in the southern window (Ian was not certain how frequently they should be watered, and how much: the Swedish geraniums seemed to be dying); the handsome butcher-block table, and the gleaming surfaces of the stove and refrigerator—all bespoke Glynnis: her taste, her tireless effort. "I love this part of the house," Bianca said. "When I first went away to school, the kitchen was the room I remembered. I have such nice memories of it." "Yes," Ian said, smiling. "I do too."

Ian did not know if what his daughter said was true; he did not even know if what he said was true. But he knew what must be said.

Now they were alone together so much, and so intensely, they fell into a pattern of Bianca talking and Ian listening—except for those times, and these were, Ian guessed, rather consciously cultivated times, when Bianca asked Ian about his work. She was most interested, not in demographics, but in biostatistics, a fairly new and innovative field, contiguous with Ian's but essentially very different. Since her mother's accident, Bianca spoke yearningly, and, it almost seemed, calculatingly, of wanting "to do good in the world—to *try* to do good."

At other times, she simply talked, her voice bright and nervous as water cascading down a mountain stream: all flash, motion, little depth. Ian perceived that she was terrified of the house's silence; not even the radio, its dial seemingly fixed at Glynnis's favorite station, could fill this silence. Ian listened to her, and nodded, and responded, and allowed his thoughts to drift. It seemed to him that at any moment Glynnis would come through a doorway, or the telephone would ring and he would hear Glynnis answering it, in another room.

Instead, when it rang, Bianca answered it. Rather too quickly, eagerly. Ian overheard her saying, to an unknown party, "Oh, Mother is still the same, her condition is more or less stable, they say it takes a long time to recover from an operation like that, such a major operation, she was on the operating table almost seven hours. . . ." Another time, when Glynnis's condition had further deteriorated, "Oh, Mother is on a respirator now, it makes breathing easier; breathing, you know, is a purely mechanical activity, it's just something that is *done*. . . . But her condition is stable. More or less."

Ian thought of Glynnis at all hours of the day, both when he was at her bedside and when he was elsewhere. Unconscious, steadily losing weight, she acquired, in his imagination, a powerful presence, as if he were, in a sense, pregnant with her; as if the responsibility for keeping her alive lay with him: *in* him. He had let his work at the Institute slide, had spread his authority about, like, he thought, a gardener tossing manure from a pitchfork, among his energetic young assistants.

Nor were his friends, who telephoned often and invited him and Bianca to dinner often, very real to him. I could live without any of them, he thought.

And that young red-haired woman, the dancer, whom Glynnis had mistaken for something other than what she was: Ian had not heard from her in weeks and hoped he never would hear from her again.

THE TELEPHONE RANG a few inches from his head, and Ian, seated at his desk in his study, having dropped off to sleep with his head on his arms, fumbled to pick it up, and it was, with dreamlike abruptness, his friend Leonard Oppenheim . . . calling to ask about Glynnis and about what Leonard called, with some embarrassment, Ian's financial resources. "We dread interfering but we are somewhat concerned, Paul and I, whether, you know, Ian, you're going to be hard pressed. I know what medical bills of that kind are like—neurosurgery, intensive care—twelve hundred dollars a day it was, at Columbia Presbyterian, when my poor father . . ." And Ian, sleep-dazed and puzzled, found himself listening to his friend speak at considerable length of his eighty-nine-year-old father, moribund for months after a brain tumor operation and kept alive by high-tech miracle machines and the antiquated, and inhuman, New York State legal code "protecting" patients from euthanasia.

Euthanasia!

Ian, feeling faint, gripped the phone receiver so tightly the blood drained out of his fingers. He did not listen—did not listen—and when at last Leonard finished, he said politely, "Thank you for your kindness, Leonard, but I doubt I will need to borrow money; I think our insurance policy will cover most of it, thank you very much."

Leonard said quickly, "I have this trust fund, as you might know, and Paul too . . . Paul asks me to tell you that he would like to help too, if, for instance, you wanted to bring in another doctor or surgeon." Leonard paused; Ian said nothing. "I would never intrude upon you if I weren't so terribly concerned about Glynnis. It's such a shock to us all. It happened so *suddenly* . . . as of course these things do. There have been such disconcerting rumors. . . . But enough of this; I won't keep you. I simply wanted you to know, Ian, that should finances be a problem, we would like very much to help: in secret, of course. No one need know but ourselves." There was another pause. "Ian? Are you there?"

Ian had not been listening, but he said politely, "Yes."

"I hope I haven't offended you . . . ?"

Ian said, "Not at all, of course not; I'm grateful for your concern."

"Truly: you aren't offended?"

Ian murmured an ambiguous reply and hung up. He was very upset but could not, after only a few minutes, remember exactly why.

It was the end of April, and then it was early May, and still Glynnis McCullough lay trapped in her stony sleep, impervious to all appeal. The machine that breathed for her breathed with perfect regularity, yet cruelly. Ian was certain that it must give pain. And the IV fluid that dripped constantly into her veins, and the wires that monitored her heartbeat, her sweat rate, the shimmering pulsations of her brain, turning them into waves on a green computer screen, and the suction devices that drained toxic fluids from her organs . . . all must give pain. Ian thought, as if in wonder, And I feel none of it.

But he too had lost weight; his clothes felt pleasantly loose on him, like a stranger's. The feeling seemed to him penitential and therefore beneficent.

In the highly specialized medical literature he was reading, out of an unexamined conviction that somewhere, duly recorded as medical history, Glynnis's very case had been transcribed and its mysteries decoded, Ian discovered any number of remarkable things: accounts of comatose patients who sleep for years and then wake to full consciousness and (presumed) normality, like time travelers propelled into the future, yet bereft of a segment of their own lives. (And what did they remember of their years of sleep? "A sort of blur," one woman said.) There were casualties of combat, accidents, crimes; surgical and anesthetic mishaps; mysterious brain-attacking diseases; there were men, women, children who simply failed to wake from their ordinary sleep . . . as if under a fairy-tale enchantment. But then, for as little reason, they *did* awake. Sometimes.

At Glynnis's bedside, a book or medical journal opened on his knees, Ian often fell into a waking dream, his eyes open but fixed upon Glynnis as she'd been, years ago, a girl, hair red-gold and glossy over her shoulders, approaching him with her bold query: Is something wrong?

Can I help? Daring to reach out and touch his sleeve. Later, when they were lovers, she climbed the stairs to his room and knocked on his door, Ian? Ian? Open up, let me in, it's Glynnis, let me *in*. She undressed herself and him, laughed her high-pitched delicious laugh, squirmed in his arms, ran her fingers up and down his sides, teasing him for his thinness—I could play your ribs like an *xy*lophone. Ian had never made love to a girl like this before, never in any sociable, protracted, emotional manner; he was an amateur, a baby, endearingly clumsy, so excited by her touch that he ejaculated before he could enter her, to her exasperation and disappointment. Now we'll have to wait, Glynnis said, sighing, kissing him, and try again. She was twenty years old, an undergraduate arts major, with an interest in so many subjects, so many possible careers—acting, art history, photography, working "in some capacity" at the United Nations, social work, foreign service work—Ian could scarcely keep up with her. She was, she confessed, not a very dedicated student, as such—"Mostly I just want to live."

Her face was moon-shaped and beautiful, her body paralyzingly beautiful: breasts like balloons filled with something soft and giving, like water, belly softly rounded, the hips, thighs, solid columnar legs— Ian could not believe his good fortune, for he knew he did not deserve it and played, sometimes, at losing it: "I can't see what you see in *me*. I can't see why on earth you would love *me*." He hoped to quarrel with her, to see that, as he suspected, she didn't seriously want him; yet he held her tight, tight as if she were life itself, in terror of losing her.

Lying in his lumpy bed in Ann Arbor, Michigan, 1960, Glynnis in his arms, warm and silky in his arms, and so quickly asleep, her mouth wetly open and her breath deep and intense as a child's, Ian felt his heart race; he loved her, adored her, wanted to marry her—for how otherwise could he keep her?—yet he feared her, for the very spaciousness of her spirit, all that she promised or threatened, of a life complex beyond his reckoning: a normal life, the life of the species, yet uniquely American. Marriage, children, a job, a position, property to be acquired and protected, and, in time, a place in a community: a reputation. Ian McCullough had wanted to be lost, unnamed, a Kierkegaardian casualty of faith, an existential being-in-the-making, a doomed hero of Camus, a maniac martyr like John Brown. He had studied American political history as if reading a long, lurid, clamorous novel in which self-proclaiming figures contended, each isolated from the other yet citizens of the same enormous landscape. The American continent was large enough to absorb all, yet not so large not to be domesticated. Marry me, Ian begged, and save me.

He was ravished by the extraordinary hunger she aroused in him. And her own intense pleasure in what they did together, which was a revelation to him: that any girl might feel such things, let alone express them, let alone show gratitude for them. Oh, Jesus, Glynnis wept. Oh, sweet Jesus. And in the morning she would stretch her young body before him, peer at him playfully through her spread fingers. She let the window shade fly up to the ceiling and laughed, unrepentant at what she'd done.

Ian adored her and was overwhelmed by her. Dreamily she teased, Do you think I'll get pregnant? Do you think, after last night, I *am* pregnant? She asked about his mother, and his father, but scarcely listened; she did not care for melancholy tales, however true. She collected his stale, soiled clothes, hauling them out of the closet where he'd hidden them, stuffing them—socks, undershirts, cotton jockey shorts—into a pillowcase, to be carried to the laundromat. She folded towels and sheets atop the machines, loving, she said, the smell of freshly cleaned laundry, burying her face in a bath towel as, with no warning, she'd bury her face in his neck and tickle him with her tongue, Oh love love I'm crazy about you, I don't give a good goddamn what happens. (She meant: If my father doesn't want me to want you.) She told him she would rearrange his life, and she meant it; he was made for success and prestige: needed new glasses, his teeth examined, some new clothes, new shoes, a haircut, a different place to live. She examined his bookshelves: political theory, classical philosophy, European history, American history, Marx and Engels, Spengler, Toynbee, Bertrand Russell, John Dewey, whom one of his professors in the graduate school revered. Glynnis opened the *Essays in Experimental Logic* to a much-annotated page and read, " 'Not to know the world but to control it; and remake it. . . . ' " She crinkled her nose in distaste and tossed the book away. "So much for John Dewey," she said, wiping her hands. Ian regarded her with amazement and smiled. So much for John Dewey.

Dewey had also made the cryptic remark that complete adaptation to environment means death. But Ian hadn't quite understood his meaning, at the time.

IT WAS IAN'S new practice to nap at odd times during the day, if he could, since sleeping at night had become problematic. He had come to dread the bedroom, the bed: that profound sense of imbalance as he lay, stretched to his full, somehow unnatural length, without Glynnis beside him. Waking in the night he knew that something was wrong but did not always know what it was, how to give it a name. Then he might say aloud, "Oh, my God. Oh, sweet Christ." His tone at such times was marveling, awestruck. Was Glynnis really in the hospital? Had she really had emergency neurosurgery; was she really in a coma? He understood that these things were true, yet by night, flat on his back, open-eyed and blind in the dark, he could not believe them.

He worked to imagine the words with which, one day, the imperturbable Flax might greet him. *Mr. McCullough, I have some good news for you this morning. Mr. McCullough, there has been an improvement in your wife. Mr. McCullough, I think you will be pleased to hear. . . .* The exact phraseology eluded him; he felt like a dull-witted schoolboy, stymied by words. He knew what he wanted to hear, but he could not, even in fantasy, hear it.

Mornings, Glynnis's absence took on a different quality. Ian dressed as quickly as he could, avoiding mirrors, out of a fear of seeing his wife's reflection behind him. In his bathroom, running water or showering, he heard, or believed he heard, her voice on the other side of the door; it was a habit of Glynnis's to speak to him at such times, when he could not properly hear her.

Whether he had slept fitfully or had not slept at all, he got up each morning at 6 A.M.; he was eager, even hopeful, to begin the day. Unless it was raining hard he went for a run of some two or three miles along the unpaved residential roads and in the woods down behind Pearce Drive, desperate to get in motion, to work off the wire-tight tension in his limbs. Like an aging athlete he prepared for the long, the incalculably long and dangerous day, in which anything might happen for the simple reason that it could not be prevented from happening.

On the morning of May 12 he rose at his usual time, and put on the soiled clothes he'd worn the morning before, and went out to run along the route he'd run the morning before: filling his lungs with air; working his heart up into a fast percussive beat; taking no interest in where he ran, or over what familiar scene his eyes passed; aware of, but indifferent to, the pains darting through his feet, calves, thighs, back, and the taste of something black and tarry at the back of his mouth. Once he began his run nothing mattered but the beat: keeping to the beat, making no allowance for pain or shortness of breath. He recalled the tragic case, for so it was locally called, of a younger Institute colleague, an urban studies specialist, who, in the habit of jogging for an hour each morning on the Institute grounds, and seemingly in excellent physical condition, was found dead one morning a few years ago on the reservoir embankment. Probable cause of death was cardiac failure, coronary thrombosis: a shock to the community, since the victim had been no more than forty years old.

In a fairy tale, Ian thought, he might be allowed to exchange his life for Glynnis's. But the somber logic of this world held no such recourse.

That morning he ran a little farther than usual, drawn, in fact, to the grassy, uneven path that circled the reservoir, though running here was tricky, hard on one's feet and ankles. The water's surface was placid, as always, mirroring a cloudy, mottled sky, that look of density in a single flat plane; Ian stared at it, willing himself to be consoled, transformed. When Glynnis was recovered . . . he would be a better man. When Glynnis came home from the hospital . . . when she was recovered . . . they would travel, to Italy perhaps. It was a decade at least since they had taken a trip not related to—indeed, centered upon—a professional commitment of Ian's.

He left the reservoir, headed home, running up the long slow incline back to Pearce Drive, the rhythm of his stride slightly broken, his back and sides drenched with sweat. Midway along a narrow curving street called Lombardy one of Ian's neighbors drove by and might have waved a tentative hand in greeting, but Ian stared resolutely at the ground before him and did not acknowledge it.

It gave him pain to remember, as, at such times, he could not help remembering, that their neighbors the Dewalds had called the police . . . and that the entire neighborhood must know. All of Hazelton must know. Glynnis would be furious, her pride greatly wounded.

How dare the Dewalds, who were not even friends of theirs, poke their noses into a private quarrel; how dare they go so far as to telephone the police? Glynnis had always distrusted Audrey Dewald's intermittent attempts at friendship: the way, uninvited, the woman dropped by the house at an inconvenient hour with a question for Glynnis or a favor to beg of her; it maddened Glynnis that she borrowed cookbooks and was careless about returning them. Jackson Dewald, her husband, a man of Ian's approximate age, was a highly successful stock market analyst who seemed to have taken an obscure offense at a casual remark of Ian's made at a cocktail party years ago, to the effect that Ian hadn't time to think about money; he hardly even had time to think about things that *mattered*. Really, Dewald had said stiffly, it must be lovely to be so superior to us all. Ian had laughed, taking the exchange as a joke, and said, Why, yes, it *is*.

Ian's heart beat hard in dislike. Goddamn them: I will never forgive them.

IT HAD BEEN eighteen days thus far; today would be the nineteenth.

At the house he would shower, shave, dress, make coffee—not fresh, of course: that was Glynnis's province—unless Bianca had already done so. He would get in the Honda and drive the familiar route to the hospital and park in the familiar high-rise garage and take his place at Glynnis's bedside and resume his vigil. How long can you keep this up? one of the nurses had asked, meaning, Ian was sure, no harm, but Ian was stung and said curtly, As long as my wife needs me.

Ian turned up the graveled drive to his house, running rather sluggishly now, his legs aching and eyes stinging with sweat. He had gone out at 6:10 and was returning at 6:55, slower than yesterday's time: an ordeal to no specific purpose, like so many, now, in his life, but one that must be done. He saw Bianca waiting for him, in the driveway, and knew that something was wrong. Standing there, barefoot, in the gravel, in jeans pulled up over her nightgown (it appeared) and a shirt carelessly buttoned. Something was wrong, for why otherwise would the girl's hair be so disheveled, and tears shine on her face, with a look of anger?

THE POLICE

1.

Bianca wept in a fury of hurt: "I didn't say goodbye to her, Daddy! I didn't say goodbye to her!"

As if, she seemed to be thinking, he had. There came then the logic of what must be done, and what would be done, whether he wished it to be done or not, whether he was capable of doing it himself or not. And of course Ian McCullough was capable: assuming the role in their household that would in ordinary circumstances be Glynnis's . . . dealing with an emergency situation that required numerous telephone calls, and calm in the face of others' emotion, and decisions made without much, or any, deliberation; for there was no time for such a luxury now. The old habit of deliberation, of Ian McCullough's former life.

A. J. Braun & Sons, Funeral Directors, came highly recommended by those friends who knew about such things, and so Ian telephoned A. J. Braun & Sons and made the preliminary arrangements. (A $300 deposit would be sufficient, payable by check.) Then there was the task of securing a plot in the Hazelton Memorial Cemetery, which abutted on the fifty-acre Institute woods. (Another modest deposit was required, and, yes, Ian readily agreed, it would be practical to buy a family-sized plot of course.) Next he located the "last will and testament" of Glynnis McCullough, crammed inside a bloated file labeled, in Glynnis's precise hand, HOUSEHOLD RECORDS—that somber document Glynnis confessed to having signed without reading thoroughly. (Yet it was Ian's will that depressed her more. She could not bear to think that she would probably outlive him and end her life as a widow—"Isn't that the usual story? the statistically fated story?"—remembering their happiness together, and even their bouts of unhappiness, as the absolute core of her life, her life's very meaning.)

Friend after friend spoke of arranging for a memorial service for Glynnis, and of course Ian agreed, bemused at how immediately that prospect, so communal, so celebratory, came to the fore, as if to deflect them from the rawness of grief; as if a memorial service, weeks after the funeral, had the power of keeping Glynnis from completely dying, or from being declared dead.

(Roberta Grinnell and June Oliver volunteered to make the arrangements, with, of course, Ian's approval. This meant a consultation about dates, not unlike the circle's frequent consultation about dates for social occasions, and Ian found himself, as Ian often did, staring at the much-annotated calendar tacked to Glynnis's bulletin board in the kitchen. This document unnerved Ian with its suggestion of countless future commitments, its appearance, which the most superficial glance could not fail to absorb, of being a domestic variant of Spinoza's fully determined universe, in which free will could not possibly exist, even as a speculative luxury. Though Glynnis's accident had occurred before the month had even begun, the majority of its days were taken, some with two- and even three-tiered obligations: mornings, afternoons, evenings, initials and abbreviations, some notations in ballpoint ink, others in

pencil, with question marks; the final weekend was marked, simply, BET-
TER HOMES & GARDENS—the deadline, Ian assumed, for one of Glynnis's
food articles. His instinct was to tell Roberta and June that there was
no room in Glynnis's schedule for the memorial service, but he caught
himself in time. The thirtieth, he said, looked fine.)

IT WAS NOT Ian McCullough's own grief that frightened him but his
daughter's.

His own, secreted inside him like a tumorous growth, he believed he could contain; there would be time for the thing to take root,
to flourish, to dig down deep into the marrow of his bone, to seed
itself throughout him: plenty of time. But Bianca's emotion was so
immediate, so violent, so frenzied—she oscillated between periods of
relative calm and sudden manic outbursts that seemed to take her, no
less than her father, by surprise: throwing herself around the room,
screaming, screaming at the top of her lungs, *No no no no no*, pounding
at her thighs with her fists, tearing at her hair, at her clothes, *No no no
no no!* Ian had to constrain her, hug her tight, tight, tight; he would not
have thought he had more tears but tears sprang nonetheless from his
eyes, and his face contorted, like Bianca's, in the rage of infantile grief:
No no no no no.

She might lock herself in her bathroom, she might lock herself
in her bedroom, or, repentant, apologize for "going crazy—I just don't
know what comes over me." She might drift about the house, or wash
her hair, or stand in Glynnis's closet burying her face in Glynnis's
things, or open a can of beer and swig it out of the can like a man, or
run the vacuum cleaner until Ian's teeth grated, or make a quick telephone call to one of her friends, speaking in a low rapid undertone Ian
had no urge to overhear. After one of her worst bouts of hysteria, when

Ian feared she too might go crashing through a plate-glass window, the telephone rang and Bianca volunteered to answer it, panting, swollen-faced, disheveled, yet with enough presence of mind to speak clearly and even courteously—in Glynnis's very voice, in fact. "Yes, thank you. . . . Yes, we are, and yes, that's right, it's set for tomorrow morning, eleven o'clock . . . the Unitarian church on South Main, just past the square. . . . Yes, that's the one."

IAN DRESSED HIMSELF with slow dreamy fingers in his old pin-striped suit, the darkest suit he owned: Glynnis's choice and once quite handsome, though now the lapels were of an unfashionable width and the shoulder pads were bulkier than he recalled. A long-sleeved white cotton shirt that required cuff links, a dull darkly shiny tie; and as he stood before the mirror trying to knot the tie he saw Glynnis's shadowy figure behind him and steeled himself for her voice, raised more in surprise than in censure: Ian, are you serious? Why on earth are you wearing *that?*

Her death was now publicly official: an obituary had appeared that morning in *The New York Times,* accompanied by a photograph Ian did not immediately recognize. Glynnis Ann McCullough, writer of popular cookbooks. Cause of death, complications following surgery. Married to the political scientist Ian J. McCullough, of the Institute for Independent Research in the Social Sciences, Hazelton-on-Hudson, New York. Survived by husband, daughter, sister.

Bianca carefully clipped the obituary. She said, with her short breathless laugh, "Mommy looks so beautiful here, doesn't she? Thank God."

There had been nothing in the *Times* about a police investigation, which did not mean of course that there was no investigation, or would be none, only that the information had not been given. Ian thought, They will arrest me in the cemetery; that's the proper place.

Bianca's mourning costume, as she called it, consisted of a black silk shell and a matching jacket, quilted, with slightly puffed sleeves and tight cuffs, and a skirt of many ambiguous layers, black cotton, not altogether free of wrinkles, that fell unevenly to midcalf. The silk had belonged to Glynnis; the cotton was Bianca's own. She had brushed her long hair so harshly and flatly against her head it seemed devoid of color, and fastened it behind her ears with gold clips that struck Ian as familiar—hadn't he bought them for Glynnis, many years ago, when Glynnis had worn her hair to the waist? Marching in student antiwar demonstrations, picketing Dow Chemical? Bianca said, "What are you staring at, Daddy? Is something wrong?" Then, with a shift of direction very like her mother's, she said, "Daddy, what's that on your jaw? Did you cut yourself shaving?"

He had, he had. Tiny nicks in the flesh that emitted a few drops of blood and merely stung.

He went away and dabbed at his face with a wadded tissue, and when he returned some minutes later Bianca was still at the mirror in the front hall, still regarding herself critically. Her face was carefully made up, powdered, with a pale oysterish powder, and her eyes were outlined in black; her lips seemed fuller than usual, and thicker, an eerie frosted scarlet. Ian was startled, as he so often was, by what the popular press might call the miracle of cosmetics, strategically applied: no one could guess how his daughter had looked only the night before, red-eyed, puffy-faced, defiantly ugly. She had transformed herself into a good-looking, if rather hard-looking, woman in her early thirties.

As soon as Ian reappeared she said loudly, "One thing about a funeral in the morning—the rest of the day is likely to improve." She laughed and leaned closer to the mirror, running a finger along the lower rim of an eye. If she caught her father's disapproving gaze, his look of hurt, she gave no sign; she wasn't that sort of daughter.

OF GLYNNIS'S FAMILY so few remained extant, to use the expression Glynnis was in the habit of using, that notifying them of her death, and of the funeral, involved only a few telephone calls and a second telegram sent to the Tokyo Hilton, where, Ian had been given to understand, Glynnis's older sister, Kate, and her husband, Richard, were staying. Richard Kirkpatrick was an official with the World Bank, and the trip to Japan was primarily for business purposes, though, as it turned out, he and Katherine had already left for Kyoto; by the time they returned to Tokyo, discovered the first telegram, and made arrangements to fly home, Glynnis was already dead. If it arrived at all, the second telegram arrived after their departure.

Katherine, whom Ian had not known well, and with whom Glynnis had not been close, was greatly upset by Glynnis's death, came close to breaking down when she viewed the body, and, with her husband, had a good many questions to ask, both of Ian and of the hospital authorities, about what had happened to her. An accident involving a plate-glass window, emergency neurosurgery, the patient's regaining consciousness only to lapse into a coma and die within nineteen days— Katherine said repeatedly that she did not believe it, simply could not believe it: could not accept it. In private Richard Kirkpatrick asked Ian if his sister-in-law had been drinking, and Ian hesitated so long before replying that he said, curtly, "Never mind—I can find out from the medical report."

In all, only six members of Glynnis's family made the trip to Hazelton: the Kirkpatricks, a woman cousin of Glynnis's whom Ian had never met before, and a sad trio of elderly aunts. Ian invited them to stay

with him and Bianca—he would happily sleep on a couch in his study—
but they preferred accommodations in a Holiday Inn near the Thruway.
At such a time he couldn't possibly want houseguests, Katherine said.

She knows, thought Ian.

IAN AND BIANCA McCullough and the Kirkpatrick contingent were
driven to the First Unitarian Church on South Main, and then to Hazelton Memorial Park, in two hired cars: "stretch limos" as they were
known in the trade, elegantly black of course, and smartly gleaming of
course, with darkly tinted windows, to match the hearse. Ian had spoken of driving his own car but Bianca had objected strenuously. "You
know Mommy would want things done in style," she said. Once in the
limousine Ian had been grateful enough for it: for being spared the effort, in this instance a public effort, of driving his own car; grateful for
the tinted windows, which spared his eyes from the achingly bright
spring sunshine, and for the space that allowed him room to stretch his
long, rather stiff legs. The limousine was surely empowered by gasoline
yet made virtually no sound; it passed by familiar sights as if effortlessly,
like a car in a dream. Bianca said, striking the cushioned seat beside her
with a fist, "This is the life!"

Their driver wore a uniform and a visored black cap with a military
look; had it been royalty he bore along Hazelton's streets he could not
have been more deferential. He introduced himself to the McCulloughs:
"Poins is my name." Ian smiled in surprise but could not, for the life of
him, figure out why.

THE FIRST UNITARIAN Church of Hazelton-on-Hudson, one of the
village's officially designated historic buildings, was plain, even spartan,

both outside and in; wood-frame and foursquare and painted a shade of white so subdued as to resemble pearly gray. The windows were tall and narrow and emitted light that too seemed subdued. All was sobriety, a sort of cerebral calm: the pews were oak and comfortingly hard, the minister's pulpit no more despotic than a lecturer's podium. Ian, who had never stepped inside the church before and had, until the other day, never exchanged with Reverend Ebenbach, or, as he wished to be called, Hank Ebenbach, more than a dozen casual words, felt both relief and disappointment: if the church did not embarrass, neither did it excite. Ian thought it sad and perplexing that, drawn to Christianity as she was, in resistance to the genial humanism-atheism of her community, Glynnis should have chosen this church; should have chosen Hank Ebenbach, who might have been a colleague of Ian's at the Institute, rather diffident, scholarly in manner, earnest and self-effacing, over other possibilities. Did a Unitarian minister, Ian wondered, conceive of himself as a man of God, or was such a notion simply too extravagant and histrionic to be taken seriously? Ebenbach seemed to say, Trust me; I will never lie to you.

But there was the terrible casket bearing Glynnis's body, and here was the family of the deceased, and here, filing into the church, filling up the pews, the many friends and acquaintances who had come to mourn: half of Hazelton-on-Hudson, it almost seemed. Surely, Ian thought, they required more than simply not to be lied to. . . . Once, speaking impulsively, Glynnis had told a gathering of friends, I don't believe in God as such and I don't want to believe if it requires the usual anthropomorphic crap, but I want some sense of there being, you know—and here her voice trailed off self-consciously, defensively—a little more than just *us*: just *here*.

She had not, however, attended church regularly or even, in a sense, irregularly; her own family had been nominally Episcopalian and she'd seemed to retain, like Ian, few haunting memories to contend with of a specifically religious nature: no familial sense of obligation or duty. When Bianca had been a small and therefore tractable child, Glynnis had sometimes taken her, but this custom was eventually discontinued; Glynnis had once or twice invited Ian to join them, but never, it seemed to Ian, sincerely—as if churchgoing, so against the grain of Hazelton-on-Hudson and, in a sense, of Glynnis's own nature, were too private a matter to be shared with another adult. In recent years Glynnis had probably not attended Sunday morning services with Reverend Ebenbach more than a dozen times, but, to Ian's considerable relief, this seemed not to have offended the man in the slightest. "Even when I hadn't seen your wife in months I always thought of her as a member of the congregation," Ebenbach said, "and I'm reasonably sure she thought of herself in those terms too."

Ian stared at Ebenbach, struck by the notion—of course it was absurd, and instantly dismissed—that this man had been Glynnis's lover. But he said only, quietly, "Yes."

At eleven-fifteen, though most of the pews were filled and Reverend Ebenbach was waiting to begin, people were still crowding into the church. Ian felt a moment's anxiety, that he had made a mistake; it might have been better to have kept the ceremony private and small. He had not quite considered Glynnis's local popularity and her measure of local fame, nor had it occurred to him that most of his Institute colleagues and their wives would turn out, as if in a solid phalanx of sympathy. That it must have been sympathy for him, and not for Glynnis, whom some of his colleagues scarcely knew, pierced him to the heart.

And there were, too, surely, the merely curious, the morbid minded: those who had an instinct, however infrequently gratified in Hazelton, for local scandal.

Reverend Ebenbach began the service by calling upon them to

pray. Ian meant to concentrate on all that took place, to memorize, if possible, the man's elegiac words; but within minutes his thoughts drifted compulsively, his gaze, like Bianca's, drawn to the casket only a few yards away—that fiercely polished object, a work of art, a work of mystification, appearing, in the narrow space at the front of the church, so much larger and heavier than it needed to be. It was for all its beauty somehow rude and barbaric: the very cynosure of interest, beside which Ebenbach's earnest words quickly faded. To think that Glynnis was inside it—contained inside it! Dear sweet Jesus, Ian thought, paralyzed by a wave of terror, can such things be?

The service lasted less than an hour, and there followed then the ride, slow, even languorous, to the cemetery . . . the sense, more pronounced now than earlier, of floating through a dream, being borne, helpless and unresisting, to a horrific end. From the sidewalk people looked after them; children stared; Ian recalled the funeral processions of his childhood, and how they had filled him with dread. The very slowness of the vehicles had seemed unnatural. He could not remember when he had learned about death, its unspeakable finality; he wondered if, in the vanity of his absentmindedness, he had ever learned. His father had died when Ian was twelve but had been so long separated from the family, living in a distant state, the death had seemed belated; nominal; not even, though a suicide, particularly shocking. His mother had died when Ian was seventeen, of lymphatic cancer, so suddenly diagnosed, and so suddenly lethal, it had seemed hardly more real.

Bianca said uneasily, "Aunt Katherine doesn't seem very friendly, does she. I think she blames us for . . . what happened."

"What? For what?"

"Oh, you know. It's an unconscious sort of thing. Like we didn't protect her or something. Mommy. Like we didn't get the best doctor for her or something. The way people are when they're upset . . . sort of primitive." She paused. She said, "Aunt Katherine was always jealous of Mommy, you know. At least that was what I gathered from some things Mommy said. I guess a lot of people were jealous of her—women, I mean."

Ian, who was staring out the window, did not want to think of his sister-in-law, Katherine, still less of her tall stern husband, Richard. He did not want to think of what the vehicle in front of this vehicle held, its rear doors opening as the ambulance doors had opened: receiving its cargo, relinquishing it.

Fell, mister?—or was pushed?

In the Hazelton Memorial Cemetery, on stiff yet shaky legs, Ian and Bianca walked a short distance, most of it uphill, to the plot Ian had contracted to buy only the other day. The air smelled of green and of damp, of fresh unambiguous earth. There was no marker for Glynnis's grave, but the grave, which is to say the rectangular gash in the earth, had been dug; was there: a category of being to which no helpful name could be assigned. For surely "hole" was inadequate.

The pallbearers bore their heavy burden up the grassy incline, moving carefully: very carefully. Ian felt his shoulder muscles twinge in sympathy. It struck him as a matter of immense significance that the casket, containing, as it did, a human being, one of their party, should be so calmly surrendered to the earth, that no one was going to object, or think it queer.

Without the scrim of the limousine's dark glass the cemetery looked subtly different: the sunshine was rawer; the grass thickly threaded with dandelions; numerous birch trees, their roots cruelly exposed, appeared to be slated for demolition. The faces of Ian's friends too looked raw, and less attractive than he recalled: aging, if not frankly aged; on the edge of being old. The pallbearers panted from their effort; Denis Grinnell wiped his forehead with a handkerchief.

Ian realized something, suddenly . . . an elated stab, as of supreme wisdom. But he could not think what it was.

Something he wanted to tell his friends?

During the brief burial ceremony, so much more valedictory than the ceremony in the church, Ian had to resist the impulse, at times nearly physical, of looking around for Glynnis.

He found himself looking at feet: at the women's high-heeled shoes, at the men's polished shoes; at legs, stockinged, trousered; at his own trouser cuffs, his shoes. His? He noticed that Bianca wore no stockings: was bare-legged, startlingly white-legged, in beat-up old shoes about which her mother would lament, How could you, Bianca?—at such a time?

Glynnis's coffin was being lowered into the grave: a sheerly mechanical process that aroused interest in the onlookers, as such processes usually do. Would it work, or would it break down at the crucial moment? The motorized whirring reminded Ian of the machines of incalculable precision that had kept Glynnis alive for so many days; for he saw now, and wondered at the opacity of his thinking, that of course she had been dead during much of the time he'd sat by her side, a deluded suitor. Had he really thought she would be returned to him and their life would continue as always?—as if nothing had happened?—seizing her shoulders as he had, in a paroxysm of murderous rage, and throwing her backward, helplessly backward, into death: into a sheet of glass. He had not known what he'd done but he had (and this was the paradox) intended it; he had not intended it (and this *was* the paradox) but he'd known what he did. There was something about a knife, a knife that had gone flying, and he'd cut his silly fingers on it, the sort of mad self-hurting thing one spouse does to get a point or two up on the other: You want to hurt me, yes fine hurt me, yes like this, I will help you goddamn you, like *this*. Afterward he'd come home to the devastation and soberly cleaned it up, looked for but did not at first find the knife: someone had carried it out into the kitchen, laid it on a counter. Who? One of the police officers? Ian himself? He could not recall, did not care, washed the dried smears of blood off the knife, returned it to its magnetized rack from Bloomingdale's.

Now the fingers and palm of his right hand were numb, as if with Novocain. *You see, Ian told Glynnis, what you have done to me.*

Ebenbach was concluding his little talk. *I loved him, I love him now, I gave him up for you*—were such words possible, in terms of Ebenbach?

If not Ebenbach, and Ian was beginning to doubt Ebenbach (for the man, though appealing, looked scarcely more virile than the inadequate husband), then, Ian wondered, who? For surely the man was present, would not have stayed away. *A friend of yours, in fact.* Ian looked covertly about but was distracted by Bianca leaning against him, rather heavily, and Roberta's silent weeping, and the rivulets of tears on Meika's powdered, rather too rouged cheeks; by the way the lower part of Denis's face was stiffening, as if with a muscular spasm—and Denis's tears too, which Ian did not want to see; and there was Vaughn Cassity's fresh haircut, which was too short and unflattering to the man's large, rather regal head. There was, however, Malcolm, handsome Malcolm, the stiff springy dark hair, the thick brows, the "sculpted" mouth— Malcolm Oliver. *I loved him, I love him now, I gave him up for you.* Malcolm *was* plausible: more plausible than Ebenbach.

But there was Leo Reinhart, who had divorced his wife long ago and showed no interest in remarrying: handsome puckish Leo with his Italian-made clothes that fitted him tightly, but not too tightly. And there was Vincent Hawley. And Vaughn Cassity. And, not least, Amos Kuhn. *A prominent man, a much talked-of man. I gave him up for you.*

In its snug grave the coffin was slightly tilted; one of the attendants deftly straightened it; the ceremony seemed to have ended. Was anything next? What was next? They were to be spared the literal burial, the dumping of earth upon the gleaming artifact, for which thank God; such a sight might do permanent damage to already strained nerves. Now that Ebenbach had relinquished his mild authority over the assemblage, things were coming loose, as if unglued; the day was revealed as an ordinary day, just as a holiday, awaited eagerly by children and extended beyond its significance, is only an ordinary day after all; though fraught with danger. Ian tasted panic: what was there to say, where was there to go, what was there to do?—he looked around for Glynnis and could not find her.

On their return to the graveled drive where their cars were parked, strung out, numerous and seemingly festive, as at a party, Ian realized what it was he wanted to tell their friends. It was a clear, simple thought, so simple it might be overlooked. He raised his voice to speak; he said, "Wait: do you know what this is?" They were walking in a loose informal group, speaking as if conversationally of the morning's weather, and of Hazelton Memorial Cemetery, which was such an attractive place, and of the brunch planned at the Cassitys'—a variation of a funeral breakfast to which in a weak moment Ian seemed to have agreed, though now he doubted he could force himself to attend—and, since Reverend Ebenbach was not in their group and could not reasonably be expected to overhear, they spoke approvingly of him, and of the Unitarian service, which had been so tasteful and so moving—exactly what Glynnis would have wanted. "Wait: do you know what this is?" Ian interrupted. "Do you know what this is?" When he had their attention, and the attention of several others close by, he said excitedly, "This is our first death."

SO IT WOULD be repeated afterward, the words radiating outward in rough concentric circles from their core. Ian McCullough, the husband of, the one involved in, yes but what was it, what exactly was it, a woman walking through a plate-glass window blind drunk, or falling through a plate-glass window blind drunk, or had she been pushed, had they been fighting and had she been pushed, or had he killed her outright? . . . Yes but you must expect them to lie.

He foresaw that even a posthumous being would not be possible.

2.

There began now an interlude of clockless days: soft time, Ian Mc-Cullough thought it. Time spilling beyond its natural boundaries of day, night . . . daylight, dark . . . wakefulness and the stupor of sleep.

They had not taken him into custody at the cemetery: nor were they waiting for him back at the house, when he and his daughter returned.

He thought, They respect death.

He thought, They are waiting for me to go to them.

He thought, Of course, my own death would be easier.

"DO YOU KNOW what the Bardo state is?" Bianca asked. "The forty-nine days following death?"

Drifting restlessly about the house as if, without the weight and stolidity of her mother's presence, it was a house new to her, and dangerous with secrets, Bianca had discovered an aged paperback copy of *The Tibetan Book of the Dead* in a remote bookcase. The book, which had belonged to Glynnis in the 1960s, was faithfully annotated through two thirds of its length; then untouched, as if unread. The section called "Bardo of *Karmic* Illusions" was most meticulously marked.

"The Bardo state," Bianca read aloud, "is forty-nine days following death, during which time the soul is trapped in a dream-state, suffering from *karmic* illusions and nightmares. These images distract the soul from the purity of consciousness that means liberation from the cycle of birth and death so it's necessary for the holy book of the *Bardo Thodol* to be recited by a *lama* in the presence of the corpse. . . ." She looked up from the book and stared into a corner of the room. Her voice had been halting, uncertain; though she'd meant simply to share this arcane knowledge with Ian (the bright curious daughter, the scholarly father), she seemed to have become rather intimidated by it.

She wondered why the soul could not make its own way after death, why it required a guide. Why reincarnation—returning to the phenomenal world, getting born again, and again—must always be hell. "That isn't a very encouraging vision of life, is it," she said.

She wondered aloud, "Why forty-nine days? Why not fifty, or forty-eight?"

She sniggered, drawing the edge of her hand roughly beneath her nose. "Imagine sitting there and reciting to a corpse! All those days!"

Ian said, "No. I can't imagine."

She put away the book and talked of other things; bicycled to the cemetery, though she and Ian had been there only that afternoon; planned to go out with her friends; but returned early, at dusk, and sought out Ian in his study, where, with little success, he was making an attempt to work. (Though he would not be attending the Frankfurt conference and had no need to do so, he was revising his paper: "perfecting" it, as he liked to think.) *The Tibetan Book of the Dead* again in hand, Bianca insisted upon reading to him passages on the Chikhai Bardo, "the primary clear light seen at the moment of death"; and the Chonyid Bardo, "when the *karmic* apparitions appear"; and the Dharma-Kaya, "the state of perfect enlightenment."

She leaned in Ian's doorway, her pale skin glowing with a fervor he could not interpret. "This is how it begins, this is what the lama recites to the dying person at the very moment of death," she said. *"O nobly born: listen. Now thou art experiencing the Radiance of the Clear Light of Pure Reality. Recognize it, O nobly born, thy present intellect, in real nature void, not formed into anything as regards characteristics or color, naturally void, is the very Reality, the All-Good. . . ."* She read as if the words gave her difficulty, as if she were translating them as she went along. "What is hardest for me to understand, unless I don't understand it right, is that the Buddhists believe that our moment of greatest lucidity is at death . . . at the very instant of death. And afterward, as the days pass, we sink back into illusion again, these *karmic* remnants, and things gradually degenerate, get crazier and crazier, as we approach physical rebirth." She regarded Ian with her rather flat gray eyes, contemplatively yet urgently, as if this were a snarl of a problem which, together, they might unravel. "Of course you have to believe in reincarnation to believe in any of it, don't you," she said. "That's a stumbling block to people like us."

Ian said, "Unless you read it as metaphor."

"Metaphor for what?" Bianca said suspiciously. Then: "I don't want *metaphor*, I want the real thing."

Ian laughed and said, "Well."

Bianca stared at him and did not reply. She was leaning in the doorway, her forehead puckered; Ian saw, with a father's attentive eye—or was it, Glynnis being gone, a mother's attentive eye?—that she would soon wear out her face, her very youth, with such severe frowning. "Did Mother take this stuff seriously?" she asked.

Ian considered the question. Glynnis had gone through phases of belief and commitment and skepticism, as they all had, though perhaps with more passion than most, in those terrible years of war abroad and assassinations at home; he could recall her immersion of some months in Buddhism, both Mahayana and Zen; her *zazen* meditation, in the company of other devotees, in the University of Michigan arboretum;

her conversation, her reading, her . . . passion. "We tended to believe things while we were caught up in them," he said. He paused, hoping Bianca would not misunderstand. "Then, afterward, we forgot."

"You moved on."

"We moved on."

YET BIANCA COULD not, it seemed, let the matter rest; began to frighten herself, and Ian, by wondering if Glynnis were truly dead.

After all, you know. What if?

Those ancient beliefs, those strange religions "people like us" dismiss as superstition: What if?

One evening Bianca embarrassed Ian, not to say Roberta and Denis Grinnell, who had dropped by the house for a drink, by deflecting their questions (about her first year at Wesleyan, the friends she'd made, the final exams that still lay before her) and talking instead of *The Tibetan Book of the Dead* and Mahayana Buddhism; how little people know of such things in the West; how little they want to know.

"It forces you to think, doesn't it," Bianca said passionately. "I mean, it scares you half to death, the possibility that these beliefs might be right, and ours wrong. Reincarnation, for instance . . . being trapped in what they call the cycle of *karmic* illusion . . . being born again, and again, and again . . . and no escape."

Though Bianca seemed to be making an effort to speak in the usual measured cadences of Hazelton-on-Hudson, like any bright young person hoping to impress her elders even as she learns from them, or, indeed, challenges them, they could see a thin film of moisture on her upper lip, and they could hear her breath. She panted as if she had run to them with urgent and incomprehensible news, to seek them out where they sat, drinks in hand, on the flagstone terrace overlooking the lawn.

"They believe that the soul is still in the body after death. Forty-nine days after death. My God! Think of it!" She shook her head forcibly, as if to clear it. Her eyes were wide, staring, protuberant. "I know it's impossible, but I keep thinking . . . what if she woke up somehow? Mother, I mean. Mommy. In that coffin. In that *box*? That we let them put her in? I know it's crazy and of course it could never be but—well, what if it *is* true?"

The adults stirred in discomfort. Ian made a faint sound as of pain. After a moment Denis said, "I don't see any reason for you to torture yourself like that, Bianca," in a father's reproving tone, and Roberta said softly, "After all, dear—it *is* impossible."

"Yes," Bianca said coldly. "I know."

Roberta went on to say—for Roberta Grinnell, Glynnis's friend of fifteen years, her closest and dearest woman friend, may have felt something of Glynnis's authority, here, at this moment, giving counsel to Glynnis's daughter, and in any case she was a former psychiatric social worker—"The Oriental religions, Buddhism, Hinduism, aren't they fundamentally life-negating? not life-affirming? Don't they take the position that life is suffering, and that—"

Bianca said sharply, and with surprising dignity, "That's the usual bullshit, reducing systems of complex psychological and epistemological thought to some damn old jargon term. Life-affirming, life-negating. I mean, my God."

"*Bianca*," Ian said, wincing.

"I mean, it's just so much more com*plex* than that."

"But hardly a reason to be rude."

"I didn't mean to be rude," Bianca said, with a perfunctory glance toward Roberta. "I'm sorry if it came out that way." She said again, as if someone had challenged her, "It's all so much more com*plex* than that, that's all I meant."

So they talked at length, but disjointedly, Bianca's attention focused exclusively on the men, as if poor Roberta did not exist or were invisible. Oriental religion and Western religion: "organized systems of belief," "sociopolitical-economic transpositions of interior 'mystical' states" (to use Denis's clinical terminology), the immortality of the soul, and of course "reincarnation"—whatever the word meant.

Denis thought the concept sheerly nonsense, since it was contrary to all scientific evidence; Ian thought it might be interpreted in two ways—as literal or as metaphorical. ("Not metaphorical! Not again!" Bianca said, laughing. "It's reality we want, Daddy.") "If literal," he said, "it *is* illogical and should be rejected out of hand; if metaphorical, and what is meant is genetic inheritance, with all that that signifies of the will's curtailed freedom, then it makes a kind of sense. A kind of tragic sense." He heard, and loathed, his own voice. Who was he, to speak such words, to make such judgments, and in so pontifical and melancholy a tone, as if knowledge heavily weighed upon his shoulders? . . . Seeing his daughter's disbelieving look he said, "It's a legitimate way of talking about something so mysterious we can't in fact talk about it. Something so terrible we can't in fact . . ." And his voice trailed off, weak, faltering, for he seemed not to know what he meant to say (Ian had of late fallen into his old habit of failing to complete sentences, a mannerism of speech from which Glynnis had presumably weaned him, an infuriating habit, he knew, for it left his listeners waiting expectantly, never quite certain if he meant to continue or if, in fact, he had stopped) ". . . can't in fact comprehend it. Except as metaphor."

Bianca said sharply, "Look, Daddy: 'reincarnation' is really beside the point and you know it. What I'm trying to talk about, and what you won't let me talk about, is the living soul in the dead body in the coffin in the ground." Her eyes were red-rimmed and quick-darting, her mouth damp; she sat on the edge of one of the heavy wrought-iron chairs Ian had painted white the previous summer, leaning far forward, hands squeezed between her bare knees, bare shoulders hunched. Ian saw belatedly that she was wearing a batik wraparound skirt that had once belonged to Glynnis: orange, green, yellow, brightly tropical in its colors. Her sandaled feet, long, narrow, bare, white, were set flat upon the flagstones with a look of enormous tension.

Ian began to protest, "The living soul *in—?*" but Bianca cut him off, in an ironic voice, as if conceding a point.

"Of course she *was* embalmed, wasn't she, that's what you are all thinking. That makes it all clean, blank, neutral, final. So sanitary," she said. She looked at him like a bright, arrogant student finally confronting her teacher: playing a bit to the audience. "I mean, it couldn't be the case, if she died—I mean of course she *did* die, but I mean it couldn't be the case that she is somehow still alive, in that Bardo state. Suffering nightmares and hallucinations, remnants of her past life, or some sort of collective unconscious of the past—that kind of thing." She paused, staring at Ian. "It couldn't be the case, except: what if it *is?*"

Ian said, "What are you talking about, Bianca? Of course Glynnis was embalmed. The body was embalmed."

" 'The body'! 'The remains'!" Bianca said contemptuously. "You think it's finished then, don't you. People like you. All so fucking sanitary." She looked from Ian to Denis, Denis to Ian, her eyes widened in derision. "You think it's *over.*"

"Bianca, honey—"

"Bianca, *shit.*"

Then, with no transition, Bianca was talking about the past, past centuries, when people in comas were surely buried alive, the kind of comas in which breathing and heartbeat can't be detected and skin temperature is low: Lazarus, for instance; Lazarus is the obvious example, Lazarus raised from the dead. . . . "Just think of what it would be like," she said, shivering, "to wake up and find yourself *buried*. How you'd scream for help, and push at the coffin lid, and scratch and claw at it, how *horrible!* You would know immediately what had happened, where you were. You would know that people you trusted had abandoned you. It must have happened all the time. . . ."

Roberta was shaking her head, and Denis murmured, "Surely not all the time," but Ian, transfixed by his daughter's words, sat silent; knowing what would come next—such lucidity, and madness.

"What if Mommy *is* in that situation? Right now? Buried alive? And there's only us to save her? Like, she wasn't really dead in the hospital, but the machines couldn't detect life. The soul shrunk to something small, like a pea. In hiding. In a kind of shock." She paused and smiled. "At the same time, I know it's crazy to think this way. It's hopeless. Because for one thing she'd have suffocated by now—they all must have suffocated fairly soon, people buried alive—and also there's the—what was it, the other thing?—embalming. *Embalmed.*" She smiled again and shook her head vigorously, as if to clear it. "The fact, of course, that she was embalmed."

These words of acquiescence did not signify a conclusion, only a sort of end stop. Ian thought, She does not know what she is saying or even what she means to say.

Though it was not yet fully dark, fireflies had begun to appear in the shadows of the McCulloughs' backyard. Stray, wayward, isolated, as if improvised: tiny pinpricks of light, like pulse beats, or the beating of one's thoughts. To what purpose, Ian wondered, other than the self's stubborn assertion: I am here, if only for an instant; *I* am here, if so shortly gone. The first sighting of fireflies in the early summer, like the first sighting of red-winged blackbirds in the early spring, had never failed to give Glynnis pleasure. Look, Glynnis would say, and Ian would look, and say, Yes? What?—ah, fireflies!

Now Roberta said, "Look at the fireflies," and they all looked, even Bianca, and took pleasure in the moment; or seemed to.

Denis said, "At our house, last year, they were really quite remarkable—one night I had to get out of bed to look out the window, it had seemed the night was luminescent, I'd been afraid it was some sort of cataclysm in the sky; do you remember that, Roberta?"

Roberta laughed and said, "No, I think that was starlight, Denis. That night. Not fireflies."

"I'm sure it was fireflies," Denis said.

"*Star*light, Denis."

"You know how you're half asleep and half awake and your thinking is both muddled and logical? I remember thinking, What if it's the end of the world? And I have so much work to do tomorrow."

They laughed, even Bianca laughed, and Roberta said, "But I'm afraid it was *star*light, not fireflies."

Ian was thinking, Glynnis must be dead, because she isn't here. If she were not dead she would be here.

Bianca said good night and left the adults on the terrace, as night came on. Damp, fragrance, fireflies, night. What would they say of Bianca? What could be said? Denis murmured a few words, and Roberta murmured a few words: commiseration, consolation, the usual, meaning only to give comfort; and, yes, to some small degree they did give comfort, for which Ian was grateful. He said clumsily, "Well—it's hard," as if he had not said these words not long before to the same people. "It's all so new and raw to her—"

Though Ian understood that his friends were eager to go home, he heard himself ask nonetheless, in a perfectly casual, shameless voice, would they join him in another drink?—for he certainly intended to have one.

And how, being his and Glynnis's closest friends, could they refuse?

THAT NIGHT, IAN believed he heard Bianca crying in her room. He had not been sleeping, yet the sound, dim, vague, muffled, had roused him from sleep.

Without switching on the hall light he went to her door and touched the knob, but did not turn it, remembering that his daughter was a young woman now, and not his child: or not his child only. He rapped gently on the door instead. "Bianca? Are you all right, honey?"

There was silence, perhaps abashed silence; then words Ian couldn't distinguish. He opened the door an inch or so but did not look in. (A dim light was burning. Bianca must have been reading in bed.) "Are you all right, honey? I thought I heard a sound."

"Yes, Father. Of course."

He stood indecisive, as if rebuffed. The word "Father" struck an odd formal note. "I was just wondering," he said. "Good night, then."

Still he lingered, his heart beating hard. Had he been asleep? Imagining himself, these nights, sleepless? Woken with rude abruptness yet unable to recall being woken, dazed as if by a purely physical blow. . . . He swallowed; his mouth was dry, parched dry, the consequence of too much alcohol that night, several drinks after Roberta and Denis had finally managed to slip away. ("I must fix Ronnie's supper," Roberta said, apologetic, embarrassed. "Ronnie will be wondering where we are.") And now in his cotton pajamas, barefoot, leaning his head against the door of his daughter's room, politely rebuffed, yet not quite comprehending. What day was this, what year? Glynnis's death might not yet have happened.

Bianca said, raising her voice, "Good night, Father," but added, "I guess I'll be going back to school soon."

"Yes? How soon?"

"Maybe tomorrow."

"Tomorrow?"

"If I can get an afternoon flight."

Ian nodded, though Bianca could not see him. He murmured good night another time and returned to his room, thinking, It is impossible to imagine our lives without Glynnis between us.

3.

Roberta Grinnell telephoned, to ask if she might drop by. She had some plates of Glynnis's to return, she said—"I forgot to bring them over the other evening"—and something she felt she must tell Ian.

Couldn't she tell him over the phone? he asked.

It might be better, she said, if she told him in person.

"Yes," Ian said quietly. "I see." He understood that Roberta would be bringing him bad news, even as he understood that no news, however bad, could make the slightest difference to him now.

So Roberta Grinnell came to Ian McCullough, surreptitiously, he guessed, without having told Denis, or anyone, uneasy and self-conscious in his presence, as if fearful of him, or of being alone in the house with him—for which, after all, he could not reasonably blame her. In the more than fifteen years of their acquaintance they had never been so explicitly alone together as this.

And in a house, Ian thought, from which his own wife was absent.

Roberta had brought him not only the borrowed plates but an enormous seafood casserole, which Ian did not doubt would feed him for days. "Thank you," he said. "You're all so kind." (And they were:

since Glynnis's death, a number of women friends had brought him food, primarily casseroles; Roberta herself had prepared several meals.) She said, smiling, nervous, "I can't imagine why I forgot these plates when we came over the other evening; I seem to be forgetting so much these days. . . . The irony is, because of Glynnis, I called off the party: postponed it indefinitely. It was to be for some economists and their wives, a dinner Denis has been wanting us to do for some time, we *owe* so many people, I mean people like that . . . professional colleagues, mainly . . . nice enough but not really friends. I don't even want to think about it now. And Denis too, Denis has said . . ."

Ian, bemused, lifted one of the plates out of the Neiman-Marcus box and weighed it in his hand. It was about the size of a salad plate, milky white, with a border of purple and lacy green, and two shallow circles, the larger in the center, the smaller, and deeper, near the rim. "These are beautiful pieces of china," he said, "but what are they? I could swear I've never seen them before."

"Artichoke plates," Roberta said.

"*What* kind of plates?"

"Artichoke."

Ian laughed and set the plate carefully back in the box. He felt, for the moment, really quite light-headed. What a world: artichoke plates! A set of twelve! And his dead wife's friend was dutifully returning them without having had the opportunity to use them.

Roberta laughed too, as if in embarrassment. "Yes, Glynnis is the only one of us, *was* the only one, who would have had a set of anything so . . . specialized. This indentation is for the artichoke, see, and this is for the dressing. It's really quite ingenious." She paused, looked up at Ian as if in appeal. There was, between them, even now, that air of light, quicksilver, rather insistent banter cultivated at social gatherings in Hazelton-on-Hudson: a heightening of the rhythms and cadences of ordinary speech itself. "I'm sure you've eaten off these plates, Ian, even if you don't remember."

"I have never liked artichokes," Ian said.

"Denis has trouble eating them too."

"I have never *liked* them."

Ian shut the top of the box, as if he could not bear to look inside, and carried it to a high shelf in one of the cupboards.

Before Roberta's arrival he had been sitting at the kitchen table, not so much sorting through old snapshots as simply looking through them, seeking his wife's shifting image amid the daunting, ill-organized accumulation of years; we must sit down one day and put these things in order, Glynnis had warned, before it becomes impossible. But they had not, of course, and now the task *was* impossible: hundreds of loose snapshots, formal photographs, newspaper clippings (badly yellowed, curled, torn) . . . the mementos of nearly three decades. Glynnis had filed everything away in manila envelopes crammed into boxes and stored in a closet of the guest room.

"Ah! I see what you're doing," Roberta said. When Ian made no reply but stood stiffly aside, clearly not wanting her to look at the snapshots, she said, as if apologetically, "I was the same way . . . my mother, my sisters, and I . . . after my father's death. Looking through photograph albums for hours. . . ."

Ian said, though it was hardly true, "I'm trying to put things in order."

"It's amazing how important pictures are, after a death. Any pictures. At any age. How precious. . . ."

"Yes," Ian said, wanting to change the subject. "Shall we sit in the other room? Would you like a drink?"

Roberta did not want a drink, not even a glass of chilled white

wine, for it was early in the day, not yet three o'clock; but, being Roberta, sensitive as she was to others' feelings, whether these feelings
were articulated or not, or consciously acknowledged or not, she naturally acquiesced—"But only one."

Ian said, as if reprimanded, "Only one."

He led her into the living room, thinking, as he so frequently
thought, of late, that this more public part of their house was ill-suited
for mourning: flooded with sunshine as it was and so beautifully furnished, in Glynnis's impeccable taste. The sun, through the glass walls,
had the effect of a subtle magnification, or intensification, of color,
texture, weight; there were, seemingly, no shadows, no interstices for
thought, recollection, grief, to take substantial root. There were stacks
of glossy magazines on the tables, *Art & Antiques, Country Life, House &
Garden;* there were hardcover and paperback books, most of them in
bright, stylish jackets; wall hangings in colorful fabrics; potted rubber
plants; the dwarf orange tree a friend had given Glynnis, which had to
be nursed with a good deal of care, that it might, as it now did, yield
oranges tiny and perfect as ornaments. Ian felt an impulse to apologize
but in the act of beginning to speak could not remember what he meant
to say.

Roberta was admiring, as she'd admired, a thousand times, what
she called the house's unique architecture—"Vaughn says it's Korean-
inspired; it *is* exotic"—and the landscape beyond the windows, a wooded
area, dense with foliage and partly wild, inherited, in its complex if almost overpowering beauty, from the house's previous owners, who had
spent thousands of dollars on trees, shrubs, plantings. And there was
Glynnis's little rose garden, in the courtyard. "The peach-colored, with
the white, that sort of watercolorlike rose . . . those are my favorites. Do
you know what they are?"

Ian stared blankly. "Are—?"

"What they're called," Roberta said. "Is it Double Delight?"

But Ian didn't know, of course. He was very tired suddenly.

So he sat down, not really wanting to sit down, for he knew his fatigue would deepen if he sat, but it seemed that Roberta Grinnell, his guest, was sitting down, despite his rudeness in failing to invite her, and the floor tilted precariously, and he was trying to think why this woman was here, in his living room with him, at midday: this friend, this wife of a friend, someone to whom he was obliged to speak, to smile, to be gracious, charming, kind, hospitable; why Glynnis was not here to happily shift the burden of conversation from him to herself, as he'd always depended upon her to do; ah, he was desperate for her to do!

He shut his eyes, but only for an instant. He opened them, and saw Roberta looking at him with an unreadable expression—pity? sympathy? apprehension? alarm?—as if from a great distance. She wore a white jersey blouse that fitted her loosely, and a denim skirt; she was bare-legged, in sandals: a small-boned, slender woman, dark-haired, graying, yet with a strand of dark gold at her left temple, a look of stray and unintended beauty. Her eyes were a pale, washed blue, set wide in her rather small face; her skin was still smooth, and relatively unlined, with a fragrance (but was Ian remembering now, or pointedly dreaming?) like almonds. His dear friend's wife. His friend's dear wife. Why, Ian wondered, had he not *looked* at her in so long . . . it must have been years. . . .

Now, in her mid-forties, Roberta was perceptibly past her bloom: wore no makeup, or very little; did nothing with her hair except to have it cut, cropped short; wore clothes Glynnis might describe, if she meant to be kind, as serviceable. She was the mother of two near-grown sons, of Bianca's approximate age, boys Ian had liked, had perhaps even coveted, at least in theory; he had spied upon them once in the village, mother, sons, some years ago, by accident really, seeing the three of them in the parking lot behind the public library: Roberta Grinnell, Ronnie, Greg, in their mid-teens at the time, considerably taller than their mother but unmistakably her sons. Ian thought, My own boy is dead, but the statement was clear and factual and bare of all emotion, even the denial of emotion, for it was really the Grinnells in whom he was interested, so oddly, intensely, interested, for what were they talking about so earnestly? What made Ronnie laugh, and grin, and shake his head? Why did Roberta give him a little push with her hand, as Glynnis sometimes did to Ian, a gesture of mock-repulsion, mock-exasperation, a love so intimate it might have been one flesh, one single motion?—but this was not erotic love, not married love, but the love of a mother for her son. Ian, who spent out of necessity most of the hours of his days in an interior world of his own tyrannical devising, felt, watching the Grinnells, an inexplicable yearning, a wholly unarticulated, inchoate yearning: as if they were strangers to him, and not the wife and sons of his closest friend. He thought, There they are.

He had kept out of the way and had not greeted them.

From time to time Ian recalled the conversation he'd had with Denis, of some months ago, that startling and upsetting conversation when, for no reason Ian could guess, Denis had told him—had confessed to him?—about having been unfaithful to Roberta. And he had not known how to respond, simply had not known. So happily married were Roberta and Denis Grinnell, so much an ideal couple in the community—as, indeed, the McCulloughs had always been (or seemed)—Ian would have found the disclosure hard to believe, had not Denis told him directly. Who was the woman, no one Ian or Glynnis knew, no one in Hazelton, a professional contact, hadn't Denis said? And Ian translated that to mean a young woman, a graduate student perhaps, an assistant professor perhaps; that was the usual story. (Ian had never told Glynnis about the revelation and wondered if she had known. Surely she had?—surely Roberta had told her?—but *he* had not told.)

He could not imagine how Roberta Grinnell, sensitive as she was, wholly undeserving as she was, had borne Denis's revelation: the knowledge forced upon her; the fact, appalling in its simplicity, that infidelity is a physical event—two bodies joined together, in love or in love's mimicry, joined together that the rest of the world might be excluded. Had she cried? Had she been angry? furious? Like Glynnis, had she lashed out against her husband with the intention to wound?

Ian stared at Roberta, thinking of these things. And thinking, as if peripherally, as one "thinks" of a physical discomfort or pain grown familiar with the passage of time, of Glynnis's infidelity: a hurt lodged so deep it might have shaded into his very sense of life's injustice, its willful and haphazard evil, as if the revelation, personal and private, had become a fact of brute nature itself.

He did not mean to, but surely he was, frightening his visitor, who sipped at her unwanted wine and crossed and uncrossed her legs, taking up a book on the coffee table before her and examining it, asking Ian about it—as if he'd read it, or remembered reading it—and putting it down, and picking up another, books of Glynnis's in their smart colorful jackets; one of my vices is buying hardcover books, Glynnis said, apologetically yet with an air (for who could deny it, Glynnis had these airs) of supreme self-congratulation. She had liked novels—contemporary novels, by both well-known writers and unknown writers—if "like" was not too mild a term for the voracity with which she read them, and responded to them, a passion Ian could not imagine in himself . . . who read fiction, when he had time to read fiction, with the air of a scientist or an anthropologist—so this is how these people live? and *this?*—not believing for a moment that his own life, still less his own soul, might be examined by way of any book, held up to a moral scrutiny as intense and unremitting as his own.

So Ian smiled and said, "I miss Denis; I miss my old schedule, in the gym."

And Roberta said, as if on cue, "Denis misses *you*, but he isn't sure if he should call you or not; he knows how busy you are"—"Not busy exactly," Ian said—". . . how difficult it is for you, right now," Roberta said. And that subject was exhausted.

Ian, dry-mouthed yet smiling, was reminded of those taxing interviews he had with prospective junior fellows at the Institute, in which apprehension yielded to paralysis, and in the face of another's timidity Ian McCullough found himself obliged to be bold. He smiled again, and hooked his fingers about the knee of his crossed leg, and said, with a jauntiness that rang horribly false. "Well. What news have you brought me, Roberta, that you couldn't have told me in front of Denis?"

"Not news exactly," Roberta said shyly. "More along the lines of . . . something you should know. Information."

"Yes? About . . . ?"

". . . a conversation I had, with Glynnis. Just before . . . I mean, earlier on the day of . . . when it happened. The accident."

Ian nodded, as if, knowing nothing, he knew everything. His heart had begun almost literally to hammer, in an instant he was flooded with dread, cold, fear.

He thought, I don't want to hear this, I cannot bear to hear this, I will get up and walk away; but of course he remained where he was, seated, smiling his ghastly smile, as if in encouragement. (For Roberta was as tense as Ian had ever seen her, in their many years of friendship; her hands so shook, she clasped them together, and her face, drained of blood, had taken on the stiffness of a mask.)

"First of all, Ian, I want you to know that I haven't told Denis . . . or anyone. If the police . . . I mean, I've heard that . . . there is a possibility . . . but . . . I have not told anyone, not even Denis, out of a respect for . . . you and Glynnis . . . for you both. Because I really don't know how to interpret what she told me, and I don't think it is my prerogative or my right to interpret it. . . . I mean," Roberta said, confused, not meeting Ian's eye, "I don't really want to interpret it. There is a sense in which, now Glynnis is dead and I miss her so, that I don't want to think about it. . . . I simply don't want to think about any of it."

Ian nodded, transfixed. He was listening with enormous concentration but had heard only part of what Roberta said.

"It happened really by chance, I mean the conversation, at that time. . . . At about two in the afternoon . . . I called Glynnis because she was supposed to have dropped something off at the house that morning, and she hadn't, and it wasn't like her to forget, you know, even such minor, trivial things . . . so I called her, and when she picked up the phone she seemed very upset; I'd never heard her quite so . . . upset . . . as if," Roberta said hesitantly, "she'd been drinking . . . I mean quite heavily drinking . . . as Glynnis never did. She asked me point-blank what I knew of you and . . . a young woman, Sigrid Hunt. Did I remember Sigrid Hunt? she asked; did I know whether you and Sigrid Hunt were having an affair; had I ever seen the two of you together; was Denis in on the secret . . . ?

"I was astonished; I'd never heard of such a thing, and I told her so; but it was difficult to talk to her; she was so enormously upset. 'Don't lie to me, please, Roberta,' she said, 'don't lie to *me*,' she said several times, and I told her I wasn't lying; why on earth would I lie? 'To protect him,' she said, 'to humor me,' she said, and I insisted that I'd not only never heard of you and Sigrid Hunt having an affair but I found it impossible to believe . . . and she said, '*I* find it impossible to believe but it happens to be true.' She asked about Denis, certainly Denis knew, why hadn't Denis told her if he knew, why was she being shielded, did all of Hazelton know, was she being talked about, laughed at, pitied, behind her back? She couldn't bear it, she said, she wasn't the kind of wife who could bear it. . . ."

Ian thought calmly, I can still walk away; I can get up and walk away. He said, "I see."

"In any case I told Glynnis I knew nothing about any affair. I told her several times. But she didn't seem to believe me, hardly listened to me. She had proof, she said; something about a canceled check, money you had given the girl . . . I think it was a thousand dollars. I mean, I think that's the sum Glynnis mentioned. I told her I knew nothing, and I was certain that Denis knew nothing, and she got rather nasty at that point, for the life of me I don't know why; she said, '*Your* husband, do you think he has been faithful to *you?*' and I asked what did she mean, I was getting upset myself now, I couldn't believe the turn this had taken, or Glynnis's anger . . . really a kind of rage . . . I'd never seen in her before. I knew she had a quick temper, of course, we all did, but this was really quite . . . alarming. So I said I was going to hang up, and Glynnis said, 'Yes, do, goodbye, the hell with you all,' and slammed down the receiver. And I . . . I was so shocked . . . I sat there with the phone in my hand and could scarcely believe what had happened. . . .

"I thought, There must be some mistake, some terrible misunderstanding. I dialed Glynnis back but the phone was busy . . . I tried a number of times before giving up, but she must have had the receiver off the hook. In retrospect I see that I should have driven over here immediately, but at the time I suppose I was rather hurt, and upset, and a little frightened of her . . . of her recklessness . . . of things she might say that could not be unsaid. I wasn't a very good or loyal friend, was I, Ian?—letting it go like that, assuming it would be cleared up in a few days. And in the morning Malcolm called us with the news about Glynnis's accident, and the emergency operation, and . . . the rest."

Ian said again, blankly, stupidly, "I see."

Roberta said, "Oh, Ian, I wasn't a good friend to Glynnis, was I? When she needed me? I keep thinking that I might have prevented it, somehow; I might have saved her. Calmed her down, stopped her from drinking more, *talked* to her. I knew, I simply knew, that her suspicions were unfounded . . . I knew it was all a terrible misunderstanding. . . ."

Roberta's eyes were suddenly brimming with tears; her voice had gone hoarse. Ian stared at her helplessly, in dread of what she would say next.

"I told her I knew nothing, and she would not believe me. Would not hear me. As if she wanted to think the worst, wanted to torture herself. She spoke of asking you to leave, demanding a divorce. . . . It was all so sudden, so intemperate. I *told* her, and she would not listen. . . . This Sigrid Hunt, this girl, red-haired, a dancer or former dancer, teaching at Vassar, I think; Glynnis was the one who'd introduced me to her . . . introduced several of us to her . . . at a luncheon last fall . . . a women's luncheon at the tennis club. And then she was at a party in this house, wasn't she? I didn't speak with her that night but I seem to remember her. A striking face, but there was something strange about it, about her, something sickly, like a pre-Raphaelite painting she was, those obsessive portraits of the young red-haired woman Rossetti was in love with, the woman he eventually married, and she committed suicide, and didn't he bury a packet of his poems with her corpse, and afterward exhume it to retrieve them . . . ? Those dreadful people and their dreadful deathly loves! Well, Sigrid Hunt made me think of such things. She was Glynnis's friend, of course, for a while, a short intense while, one of Glynnis's new young 'interesting' friends; she had these . . . passionate friendships, as you know . . . taking people up, inviting them into her life, and then, for no very clear reason, dropping them. I always thought it might be that we, Glynnis's closest friends, her 'real' friends, were not enough for her, not enough for her imagination to seize upon. Did it seem to you that way? Did you think about it at all?" She was speaking rapidly now, her eyes dangerously bright with tears. "Of course, I realize I'm probably jealous . . . I was probably jealous . . . though Glynnis always came back to us in the end, never left us, really, of course, at all. After I'd hung up the phone I was frightened that our friendship might be endangered; I was fearful of losing her . . . but also of the things she might say to me, lashing out against me, and Denis, things she hadn't any right to speak of or even to know, I really don't know *how* she knew, because it is true that Denis and I . . . that Denis . . . some years ago . . . but that had nothing to do with . . . with Glynnis, or with anyone in Hazelton. So I thought, I can't face her! She's drunk, she isn't herself! I can't face her! I had the terrifying idea I didn't even know her. . . ."

She broke down suddenly, hid her face in her hands, began to cry. Ian thought, So Glynnis spilled her guts after all.

"You must not blame yourself, Roberta. Of course you must not blame yourself. . . ." He remained sitting, stiffly, his legs crossed, fingers hooked about a knee, in a posture of paralysis, speaking in a slow dull stunned voice. "Please, Roberta. You must not blame . . ." I will not defend myself, he thought. He had heard clearly enough but could not believe: Sigrid Hunt's name known, Glynnis's mad accusation known, their unspeakable quarrel made public.

His eyes too brimmed with tears. Not of grief or even of regret but of hurt, humiliation, outrage! For Glynnis had betrayed him doubly: had betrayed their marriage and had in effect willed her own death, for which he was not to blame yet would be blamed. I will not defend myself, he thought.

The hell with you all.

ROBERTA GAVE HERSELF up to the luxury of grief: a specifically female luxury, Ian thought it, in envy. And then she rose to leave, wiping her face with a tissue, clumsy, apologetic, deeply embarrassed, and, yes, fearful of him—for it was so very explicit, his failure or refusal to speak: to deny Sigrid Hunt, and Glynnis; to proclaim, like any guilty man, his innocence.

He walked with her to the door, clumsily too, tall and stork-legged and blundering, walked with her into the courtyard, which was fragrant with the heavy scent of wisteria, that scent, Ian thought it, of desire: of utterly inchoate, undifferentiated, unnamed desire. She was wiping her face with a tissue, her eyes, which were bloodshot, and her cheeks, which looked tender, even chafed, streaked with tears. How close to the surface of our lives are tears, Ian thought, recalling his daughter's childhood, her babyhood in particular, when Bianca wept so easily, and stopped weeping so easily, and a while later wept again, a depthless reservoir of tears, it seemed; and you must endure another's pain, attempt to alleviate another's pain, protect, embrace, caress, shield with love or love's mimicry—so he found himself touching Roberta, his dear friend's wife, his arm about her shoulders, his face against her hair, murmuring words of comfort that were in truth words of desperation: Please don't blame yourself, don't blame yourself in any of this, it was a dreadful thing an unspeakable thing an accident that might have been prevented had we only known. . . .

She stood very still, did not turn to him, yet did not step away from him or push his arms away; did not repulse him. Ian felt a wave of sheerly sexual desire that hit him like a blow; a concentration of blood, yearning, need; a crisis as of a sudden terrible density. . . .

He said, "Don't go," begged, "*Don't* go," now weeping himself, hoarse and guttural, yet childlike, helpless. "Roberta, don't leave me, don't go, I'm so afraid."

They were in the courtyard, in the open air, stumbling together like drunken lovers, Ian's arms around Roberta as if he were drowning and she might save him, the very buoyancy, warmth, and life of her body might save him, and Roberta, so much shorter than he, shorter than Glynnis, was swaying on her feet, taken by surprise yet not resisting him; nor acquiescing. What words she managed to say, what confused comfort she proffered, what gestures of womanly, motherly, spontaneous, and unwilled solicitude, he would not afterward recall, any more than he would recall his own anxious words: only that, knowing Ian's desire for her, knowing his ravenous need, she nonetheless detached herself from it and refused it. "I can't stay. You know I can't stay. Don't ask me. Let me go. Please. I can't stay. I must leave—" And Ian, suddenly repentant and deeply ashamed, let her go.

At her car he heard himself speak in a nearly normal voice, and Roberta, a former psychiatric nurse after all, replied in a nearly normal voice. "Of course," Ian was saying, and, for some reason, "I know, I understand"; and Roberta was saying, "Please come to dinner with us soon, now that Bianca is gone," and squeezed his hand. "It isn't good for you to be alone." Ian opened her car door for her, and shut it; stood back, smiling at her, dazed, stricken with desire, something beating behind his eyes, yet—and how astonishing this was, how his pride would batten on it!—speaking calmly, even affably: would she say hello to Denis, and would she tell Denis he'd like very much to resume their squash games soon, perhaps next Monday; by then things should be more under control; he'd been going over to the Institute for a few hours a day and bringing work home with him; the correspondence was piling up, "It's this time of year, God knows why everything comes to a crisis now." They made a tentative date for dinner, Thursday evening: day after tomorrow.

As Roberta backed her car carefully out of the drive, Ian thought again how easy it would be for him to say, You know of course that I am not that young woman's lover, I have never been that young woman's lover; how easy for him to follow after her, to defend himself, to say, In that, Glynnis was mistaken, poor Glynnis whom I loved so much but who did not trust me—how easy, yet how impossible; something bitter and resolute in him would not allow it. He might have said, Glynnis died out of pride; he might have said, Please forgive me: I allowed my wife to die out of pride; but of course he said nothing, simply stood in the driveway, like any host seeing off a visitor, waving goodbye, farewell, come again soon please, a man observing the rudiments of social protocol though disheveled, flush-faced, sweaty, absurd as any rejected suitor.

HE WENT BACK into the house and, in the kitchen, poured himself an inch or two of Scotch and drank it down, not as Ian McCullough would do but as another man might do, practical-minded, tough, willing to face facts: And if the police questioned her? and if she told, as she must tell, the truth?

He thought, staring at the snapshots scattered across the kitchen table, the sympathy cards in piles on the windowsill, But I am a posthumous man, am I not?

He smiled, thinking, What can they do to *me?*

Glynnis died: and was buried. But her death, in a sense, was only now beginning.

In compliance with state law, the Hazelton Medical Center had reported the death to the Cattaraugus County Department of Health. The chief medical examiner for the county, a physician named Boesak, found nothing with which to fault the Medical Center itself, either in its surgical or its postsurgical procedures, but did rule that the circumstances surrounding the death were suspicious: enough to justify turning the case over to the county prosecutor's office with a "strong recommendation" that a criminal investigation be made. It did not appear, on the basis of X rays taken upon admission to the hospital, that the subject had walked into the plate-glass window, or even, in all probability, that she had fallen against it; her injuries were to the back of the head primarily, and not to the front, and of sufficient severity to suggest she had been pushed, with considerable force, against the glass. Which might indicate, under the New York State statute, charges ranging from second-degree murder to voluntary or involuntary manslaughter.

It was early, not yet eight o'clock in the morning of May 27, the day following Roberta Grinnell's visit, when two Hazelton police detectives, Wentz and Holleran as they introduced themselves, came to the house to ask Ian a few questions and to take a look, if Ian did not mind, at the scene of the accident. Though at this time Ian knew nothing about the medical examiner's report, and certainly nothing about a formal police investigation, he asked the detectives at once, and simply, "Am I under arrest?" And they said, "No, no, Dr. McCullough, you are not under arrest"—politely, even a bit deferentially—"but we do have a few questions; may we come in?"

"Yes," Ian said. "Of course."

He had been waiting for this for so long, so very long, the crucial telephone call, the knock at the door, the hour of accounting. Now that it had arrived, however, he realized he had not been prepared for it at all—for its effect upon him was immediate, and visceral, and surely transparent. He must have looked like a man who has been kicked hard in the belly.

In a haze of pain he let the police detectives in, led them in. "This is the dining room," he heard himself say, surely unnecessarily, "and this is the window that shattered . . . this is the window that shattered." There was a brief pause during which time the three of them stared at the window; and, beyond it, at the splendid morning sunshine, and the flagstone terrace with its white wrought-iron furniture, its pots of now rather desiccated geraniums—plants that Glynnis had wintered over, and someone, not Ian so it must have been Marvis or Bianca, had set outside. "Of course, as you can see, I had it replaced," Ian said. "The window."

"When did you have it replaced, Dr. McCullough?" Wentz asked, notebook in hand, unless it was Holleran who asked, for Ian could not remember which man was which, or even whether he had heard the names correctly. At the door they had shown him their IDs and their smart polished badges, not unlike television actors impersonating police officers, but Ian hadn't seen; hadn't somehow heard. He knew only that the men were strangers to him, not friends, though with an edge of friendliness—unless he imagined it: no taller than he but large, stocky, physically imposing, within seconds using up too much oxygen in the room, so that, despite the most strenuous efforts of his will, he became dangerously light-headed; indeed, he was suddenly on the verge of fainting and was obliged, to his embarrassment, to lean forward against the dining room table, both hands flat on the table, his head lowered, until the spell passed. Replaced? When had he had what replaced . . . ?

They asked was he all right, would he like to sit down, and Ian seemed not to hear, trying very hard to answer the question he knew he'd been asked. "The window," he said. "The day after the accident, I had it replaced, that glass installation and repair store on Charter Street in the village; the receipt is in my desk drawer if you'd like to see it." It pleased him that he could proffer these men—so reassuringly professional in their suits, white shirts, neckties; the elder of the two even wore horn-rimmed glasses that resembled Ian's own—this small nugget of information, this most factual of facts.

"Are you all right, Dr. McCullough? You're looking a little pale."

"Not at all. No. I am fine."

"Do you mind—?"

"What? Oh, no. Of course."

They unlocked the plate-glass door and pushed it carefully open; went outside to examine the terrace beneath the window; spoke in an undertone to each other, which Ian could not hear and did not wish to hear. As soon as he'd come home from the Medical Center that day he had done his best to clean up on the terrace—he'd swept away the broken glass, scrubbed away the bloodstains. There had been blood in the gravel directly beneath the window, too, and this gravel Ian had carefully raked up, and tossed away in the woods behind the house, and replaced with fresh gravel from the driveway. He had performed his terrible task slowly and even dreamily and had forgotten it immediately afterward; now, as he watched the detectives squatting outside the window, poking in the gravel, he remembered; felt physically sick, remembering; for he'd known at the time that, later, at this time—he hadn't any doubt this time would arrive—he would remember having done these things, with the understanding that of course he was a murderer, whether Glynnis died or lived.

Wentz, or was it Holleran, lifted a sliver of glass between his fingers, and examined it briefly, and let it fall. When the men stood they brushed their hands against their heavy thighs, and Ian thought of how they were kindly men, men who wished him no personal harm, yet his enemies, as Glynnis was becoming his enemy, against the grain of all he desired: in opposition to all he knew of himself, of the fundamental decency of his soul.

The men came back into the house, staring hard, it seemed, at Ian, as if something had been decided. It was Wentz (if Wentz was the one with the glasses) who had the police report, the young officers' report, made on the night of the twenty-third of April, regarding the circumstances of the accident as it had been told to them, the condition of the dining room, evidence of struggle, and so on and so forth, reading aloud, skimming, too quickly for Ian to entirely grasp. He was stunned to realize that a police report existed; he remembered only dimly the young police officers in his house, summoned, for reasons of inexplicable and unforgivable malice, by their neighbors the Dewalds. One of the officers had wrapped Ian's bleeding hand in a towel, had helped him walk out to the ambulance. Careful, mister. *Careful.*

They had had no right to enter his house. He'd made an irrevocable error to have allowed it.

Wentz and Holleran were examining the dining room table, the chairs, the rug, the parquet floor . . . though there was nothing to examine, nothing to see. What was there to see? Ian had put everything to rights long ago, Marvis had done a general housecleaning; what was there to see? They went into the kitchen, commented on the attractiveness of the kitchen; they'd heard, they said, that Ian's late wife—the words "late wife" hung oddly in the air—was a well-known writer of cookbooks, and Ian said yes, yes, that's true.

Had he not feared they might think him boastful, he would have showed them Glynnis's books in their bright cheery wrappers.

Wentz and Holleran took note, though without comment, of the snapshots on the kitchen table and of the bulletin board, whose numerous items Ian had not touched and did not intend to touch. In the kitchen, the men seemed yet larger and fleshier than before, their expressions graver. Wentz pointed to the magnetized knife rack on the wall and said, as if casually, "Which is the knife the officer found on the floor? Is it one of these?"

"Knife? What knife?"

" 'Steak knife, ten inches, bloodstained.' Is it one of these here?"

"I don't remember any knife," Ian said carefully. "There wasn't any knife."

"According to the officers' report there was a knife, and your hand was cut from the knife; it was bleeding pretty badly from the knife, wasn't it?"

"From the glass," Ian said. "The broken glass."

"Wasn't there a knife?"

"I don't remember any knife."

"Don't remember any knife?"

"There wasn't any knife."

"And how did you cut your hand so severely?"

"It wasn't cut severely," Ian said. He held out his hand for the detectives to examine, should they wish to examine it: the stitches had been taken out; the cuts were healing nicely. "I cut it on the window," he said. "On pieces of glass in the window."

He was trembling violently, absurdly. His teeth were nearly chattering in his head.

"I didn't know what I was doing, I was so upset. When Glynnis fell. I tried to catch her, I think—I nearly fell through the window with her. I reached out and grabbed hold of something and it was glass—"

"What exactly happened between you and your wife, Dr. McCullough? Could you tell us, in as much detail as possible?"

They led Ian back into the dining room, as onto a stage. Ian was sweating inside his clothes, badly confused, unable to judge if the detectives were respectful of him or mocking. Did they know? But what did they know?

"Where were you standing, approximately, Dr. McCullough, when your wife 'fell' through the window? Where was she standing?"

"I don't know . . . I really can't remember."

"Assuming she was standing where I am, with her back to the window, where were you standing? Why were you standing, the two of you? Hadn't you been sitting, at the table?"

Ian said, "I've explained so many times . . . it was an accident. I truly don't know how it happened." He removed his glasses and rubbed his eyes, his eyes that were raw with pain, unable to bear the men staring at him, so casually yet so frankly, with their air of knowing that he lied even as he inwardly protested he did not lie. "It was an accident," he said. "A tragic accident. An accident that grew out of a misunderstanding."

"Yes? A misunderstanding?"

"A misunderstanding."

"A misunderstanding about what?"

But Ian, try as he could, could not remember.

"Finances, marital problems, another woman? You weren't seeing another woman, Dr. McCullough, were you?"

Ian shook his head angrily. He said, "My wife and I were happily married."

BY THIS TIME Ian's legs were so shaky he had to sit down. Invited the detectives into the living room, to sit down. Thank you, Dr. Mc-

Cullough, they murmured. Wentz, Holleran: his enemies. His and Glynnis's.

He recalled the state police officers, last September, pounding on his door. The terrifying authority of the police, of raw physical power. These men, for all that they wore suits, ties, decently polished shoes, Wentz with his horn-rimmed glasses and Holleran with his affable pot-belly, nonetheless carried revolvers on their persons. Should Ian make a sudden, desperate move, should he in any way threaten them with "bodily harm," they had the authority to shoot him down; even to kill. He wondered how easily that might happen . . . so lurid, improbable, yet rather tantalizing a scenario. Suppose he'd opened the door to the policemen that night, in a mimicry of rage, shouting for them to get off his property, threatening them with his fists—or, better yet, a knife, a gun—they would certainly have shot him down on his very doorstep and been considered justified in doing so. In such ways, Ian thought, we *do* control our destinies.

They continued to ask him questions, and he continued to an-swer, in his vague, halting, suspicious manner: a man still in shock, it seemed; stunned, still, by the fact of his wife's death. And indeed the fact of it was to Ian, and would be for weeks to come, if not months, like a sound so explosively deafening it could not be heard, only felt.

The subject now was the McCulloughs' drinking on the night of the accident, the high alcoholic content in their blood, and Ian, deeply embarrassed, said yes, yes, they'd both been drinking, more than they were accustomed to, wine mainly, wine at dinner, a protracted dinner, a mistake. Why was it a mistake? Wentz asked. Because they weren't really drinkers, weren't really accustomed to drinking, Ian said. And why was that? Holleran asked, frowning the way a friend might frown, purse-lipped, thoughtful, wanting to know the truth; but Ian was silent,

Ian was mute, not knowing the truth or not knowing how to speak it. He sat with his hands clasped in his lap, long bony fingers they seemed to him, their backs covered with pale hairs, as his forearms, his legs, his chest was covered in pale, fine, baby-fine hairs, which Glynnis used to stroke: so long ago, when they were first lovers, and each small discovery in the other's body had the force of revelation. What were they asking him? What was the mistake? Ian lifted his face blindly to his interrogators and said, with dignity, "I tell you, I don't know."

Wentz was seated on one end of the sofa, Ian on the other, Holleran in a lime-green velvet chair whose small, spare frame looked inadequate to bear his bulk. Ian watched the chair's curved legs nervously. Once, many years ago, when they were all new to Hazelton, Vaughn Cassity, having had a few too many drinks, had sat down hard in an antique chair at someone's house, and the chair had comically buckled. Holleran must have weighed two hundred thirty pounds and had a disconcerting habit of leaning forward, then settling backward, readjusting his buttocks in the seat.

The detectives circled about the idea—the theme, it might have been—of the McCulloughs' mysterious misunderstanding. Did it escalate into a quarrel? Did the quarrel escalate into a pushing and shoving match? Were there weapons of any kind involved . . . candlestick holders, bottles, a knife? Ian shook his head mutely, stubbornly. He knew he must say nothing further, must not incriminate himself, or poor Glynnis, further. He would not make of his wife whom he loved a drunken frenzied knife-wielding woman, to save his own skin.

Casually, or with a pretense of casualness, Wentz informed Ian that it had not been only the Dewalds who'd heard screaming on the night of April twenty-third; the twelve-year-old son of their other neighbors, the Weschlers, had heard something too but hadn't been certain, thinking it might have been a television set turned up loud. The boy told police he'd heard shouts or screams for a long time, an hour maybe. Did Ian have any comment on that?

Ian stared at the floor at his feet: one of Glynnis's inherited Oriental rugs, beautiful colors, serpentine patterns, arabesques. He said, "The boy is lying." He said quickly, "I mean—he's exaggerating."

Again, quite casually, Wentz mentioned that they'd heard, from residents in the neighborhood and in Hazelton generally, that the Mc-Culloughs belonged to a circle of unusually social people; that they were in the habit of giving parties frequently, going to parties frequently . . . was that true? Reluctantly, Ian said, "Yes," still staring at the floor, "it's more or less true, we seem to have been caught up in social life more than I wanted. . . ."

"This looks like a great house for a party," Holleran said. "You could fit how many people in here, fifty? Sixty?"

Ian said, as if in rebuke, "But we weren't in the habit of drinking heavily."

"Why, then, Dr. McCullough, on the night of the twenty-third, were the two of you drinking 'heavily'?" Wentz asked.

His tone was matter-of-fact, in no way aggressive; as if, Ian thought, the three of them were uniformly engaged in the pursuit of an elusive but not ineluctable truth. Yet Ian spoke with surprising anger. "How many times must I tell you! *I don't know.*"

Wentz regarded him quizzically. "Don't know *why* you were drinking? Why that night was something out of the ordinary? You told us—"

"*I don't know.*"

It was nearly ten o'clock. The detectives had been questioning him for two hours.

Ian got abruptly to his feet, told Wentz and Holleran that he couldn't speak with them any longer; he had an appointment (it was true: he had an appointment) at the Institute, at ten o'clock. And he couldn't speak with them in any case, any longer, without an attorney.

So, affably enough, they put away their notebooks and thanked Ian for his trouble; and, at the door, which Ian opened for them, Wentz, unless it was Holleran, the one with the horn-rimmed glasses, shook Ian's hand, and smiled, and said, "You won't be leaving town of course; you'll be staying in this area, Dr. McCullough, for the foreseeable future, won't you."

And Ian said, furiously, "I'll go anywhere I damned want to go; in fact I am going to a conference in Frankfurt very soon"—though the Frankfurt conference was past; he'd missed it of course, had never even completed his paper.

"Well," Wentz said, still smiling, "I wouldn't, Dr. McCullough. If I were you."

HE'D KNOWN AT the time that he was making one blunder after another in talking to the detectives as he had: with so little premeditation or calculation; with such emotion, such a hope of making them see his innocence, even as he lied. His initial mistake, of course, was letting them into the house without a warrant.

Yet, as he was to tell his attorney, would an innocent man refuse to talk to the police? *Why* would an innocent man refuse to talk to the police?

"Because he's an amateur," Ian's attorney said. "And they are professionals."

5.

After May 27 things happened swiftly.

As if a dike were unlocked, a great flood of water unleashed.

And there is no stopping it now, Ian thought.

He hired Nicholas Ottinger to represent him, upon the advise of his friends, for suddenly, within a space of twenty-four hours, it was obvious he would need representation; might even need, in time, "defense." Ottinger spoke cautiously yet optimistically; he thought the Hazelton police were probably just harassing Ian, trying to intimidate him with the possibility of pressing charges against him in Glynnis's death: involuntary manslaughter was the most they could try for, and that, without witnesses, would be very difficult to prove. There was no motive, for instance. There was no prior history of arrest, no criminal record. And Ian's position in the community, his professional reputation . . . all above reproach.

"It might be that the police have a grudge against you because of our ACLU campaign a few years ago," Ottinger said speculatively. "You remember: Thiel and Edwards. You and Glynnis were involved in the protest, weren't you?"

Ian was astonished and hurt. His political beliefs were so intimately allied with his sense of personal integrity—and his activism in such matters, in fact, so rare—it struck him as profoundly unjust that he should be punished for them. "They would harass me, make me the object of a criminal investigation, a suspect in the death of my own wife, because of . . . that?"

Ottinger said, in mild rebuke, "Of course, Ian. This is the real world, now. This isn't the Institute for Independent Research."

Nicholas Ottinger, a friendly acquaintance of the McCulloughs, though not in the strictest terms a friend, was a criminal lawyer with an excellent local reputation. A slender sinewy man in his mid-forties with a thin olive-pale skin and wiry black hair, quick, shrewd, inclined to impatience—Ian had admired his squash game over the years but would never have wanted to play with him—Ottinger had narrow opalescent eyes that looked as if they might shine in the dark. He was a graduate of Harvard Law who had, according to Ian's friends, distinguished himself in several criminal cases in recent years; he'd been involved since the 1960s in liberal-activist causes and in the American Civil Liberties Union; he knew, in the jargon of the trade, where the bodies were buried. Thus it should not have surprised Ian that he did not come cheaply. His fee was $200 an hour . . . for time out of court.

"And in court?" Ian asked.

"This will never go to trial," Ottinger said. "It will never get past a grand jury."

"But if it does?"

"A retainer of, say, thirty thousand against the two hundred dollars out of court, and three hundred and fifty an hour for time in. The balance to be returned if the jury doesn't indict." Ottinger spoke casually, as if he and Ian were discussing something quite innocuous. "But, as I say, this will never go to trial. They're just bluffing."

FROM ALL SIDES, so very suddenly, Ian began to hear of the police "making inquiries" of people: his friends, his neighbors, his associates at the Institute, even the secretarial staff, even his young assistants. What shame! What mortification! Like Glynnis, Ian found it painful to tolerate the very idea that other people were talking of him, forming opinions and judgments of him, enclosing him, it might be said, in a cocoon of words, a communal adjudication in which he had no role. Denis spoke with him, worriedly, and Amos Kuhn, and Dr. Max (who struck Ian as rather more embarrassed than sympathetic), and Malcolm Oliver, who warned him against incriminating himself in any way—"Don't give those bastards a crumb." Meika Cassity assured him, with a vehemence he found both touching and alarming, that she would "never give the police the slightest grounds for suspicion of *anything.*"

He wondered if they had contacted Bianca, but the thought filled him with such sick dread he pushed it out of his mind at once.

He wondered what were the questions they asked. *Tell us what you know of Ian McCullough. Tell us what you know about his relationship with his wife. Tell us what you know about his character.*

He wondered what were the answers they were given.

ON MAY 29 Ian was summoned to police headquarters for further questioning, as it was judiciously phrased: this time, of course, in the presence of "counsel." Entering the building, Ottinger beside him, passing through the revolving door—and stumbling as he maneuvered it, out of sheer nerves—Ian understood with a dreamy resignation that he was crossing the threshold into a new realm of being; had he any residual innocence, it was now to be shorn from him, as a sheep's clotted and soiled wool is shorn from it, to lie in tatters on the ground.

Awaiting Ian at headquarters, in a room resembling a seminar room, were Wentz and Holleran, old friends turned informants, and another detective, an older man, white-haired, ruddy-faced, with glacial blue eyes and a look of professional impatience, whose name Ian clearly heard and immediately forgot. The questions put to Ian were numbingly familiar: how had the "fatal" accident occurred . . . how could it have been an "accident," given the nature of Mrs. McCullough's skull fractures . . . had Ian and his wife been quarreling . . . what would account for the screams, "over a considerable period of time," reported by neighbors . . . why, if the McCulloughs were not, by Ian's own testimony, drinkers, had they been drinking on the night of the twenty-third of April . . . ?

"I don't know," Ian said, frequently.

Or: "I'm afraid I don't remember."

Nick Ottinger had coached Ian on how to respond to the detectives' questions, had assured him he need not answer any questions he didn't want to: or, indeed, any questions at all. If Ian did not know, he did not know; if he did not remember, he did not remember. He had after all freely confessed to having been drinking heavily . . . which the hospital report substantiated. ("Of course," Ottinger said, in warning, "you must know how residents in the area feel about people associated with the Institute," and Ian was moved to ask, naïvely and with dread, "No, how do they feel?" "Resentment, hostility, generally," Ottinger said. "You might say 'grudging admiration' if you wanted to stretch things a bit.")

Ian saw it now: resentment, hostility, thinly disguised contempt— the appellation "Dr." quickly acquired a certain mocking tone, as did "McCullough"—and, if admiration, very grudging indeed. It hurt him, and bewildered him, that he, of whom everyone was so fond, should be disliked generically; and that Wentz, whom Ian had thought an ally of a kind, stared at him with a peculiar intensity, as if he were a rare species of creature, like the unicorn, to be netted, entangled, trapped, brought down, his sides pierced with spears. . . . You are smart, Wentz seemed to be saying, but we are smarter.

It was not Wentz, however, but the older detective who, in the second hour, at about the time Ian thought the session might be ending, suddenly asked if the name "Sigrid Hunt" meant anything to him. The dramatic abruptness with which the question was posed, the misleading sense Ian had had of the session's coming to an end, suggested contrivance of a particularly clumsy and malevolent sort.

Quickly he said, "No," and then, his face heating, like a child caught in an obvious lie, "Yes. The name."

"But only the name, Dr. McCullough?"

Again Ian said, without quite thinking, as if, by answering so quickly, seemingly so spontaneously, he might deflect further questions of this kind, "Yes. She was a friend of my wife's."

" 'Was'?"

"My wife is no longer living."

"But Miss Hunt wasn't, or isn't, a friend of yours?"

Ian was staring at the tabletop, at its dull, scarified surface. For a long moment he could not speak. He felt physically ill yet dared give no sign; they were watching him too closely. "I loved my wife," he said.

"Excuse me, Dr. McCullough? What?"

"Nothing."

"What did you say?"

He sat mute, sick, sullen, staring at the tabletop. He thought, I will never forgive Glynnis for what she has done to me.

"Your name has been linked with a young woman named Sigrid Hunt," the detective said, with a schoolmasterly sternness, "yet you claim not to know her?"

Ian shook his head as if the question gave him pain.

"A young woman who resides in Poughkeepsie, a former dance instructor at Vassar College, her current whereabouts unknown. . . . Are you aware, Dr. McCullough, that Miss Hunt is missing, that a male friend of hers has reported her missing, and that the last time he spoke with her was on the very day of Mrs. McCullough's death?"

Ian looked up. "How is she missing? What do you mean?"

"Do you know her?"

"I . . . know of her," Ian said.

"Were you having an affair with her?"

"Where is she? What happened to her?"

"Were you having an affair with her, Dr. McCullough?"

"Excuse me," Ottinger interrupted, laying a restraining hand on Ian's arm. "My client has nothing further to say on the subject."

He cast Ian a fierce sidelong look; Ian had told him nothing about Sigrid Hunt.

Ian removed his glasses and rubbed, hard, at his eyes; he could not now recall a time when his eyes were not sore and when their soreness, with its acidic feel, did not give a kind of pleasure. The satisfaction of the penitent: I have cried my eyes out, what more do you want of me? While Ottinger and the white-haired detective spoke together, interrupting each other, two practiced professionals whose quarrel, Ian thought, did not interest him in the slightest, he thought of Sigrid, of how, so very oddly, he had not been thinking of her, in weeks: had not dared to think of her.

And so she was missing? And had her lover murdered her? And would Ian be blamed, too, for that?

He said quietly, "Sigrid Hunt was my wife's friend before she was my friend. I knew her, yes, but I didn't know her well. . . . I was not having a love affair with her." He paused, put his glasses back on, did not meet the detective's ironic look. "I was not having a love affair with her. And that's all I have to say on the subject."

"You have no idea, Dr. McCullough, where Miss Hunt is? You aren't concerned?"

Ottinger said sharply, "My client has nothing more to say on the subject."

THOUGH IN HIS own estimation Ian had betrayed himself, provoked to agitation before witnesses, and for the record—the interrogation, of course, had been taped—the police did not arrest him that morning. He and Ottinger left the station shortly before noon. In sheer nervous reaction Ian skipped down the steps and laughed. "I'm a free man!"

Ottinger said grimly, "You'd better tell me about this woman."

Ian, who had not yet eaten that day, drew a slow, deep, tremulous breath. It puzzled him that traffic passing in the street had the look of objects seen through water. He laughed again, and amended, "Temporarily. I'm a free man temporarily."

In as neutral a tone as possible, with exquisite tact, Nicholas Ottinger asked, "This woman, Sigrid Hunt—*is* she your lover?"

Ian said, "I have no lover."

"You'll have to tell me, you'll have to be frank with me," Ottinger said.

Ian said quietly, "I have no lover. I have not seen Sigrid Hunt in months. I know nothing of her being missing, and I know nothing of where she might be, and I know nothing of *her,* I assure you. Beyond that, it's really none of your business."

Ottinger said, "I see."

"My private life is none of your business, any more than it's their business, the goddamned police," Ian said, less quietly, beginning to get excited. "Intruding into our lives, putting us on public display. Poor Glynnis: she never meant all this! Never, never would she have meant all this!"

He could not bear another minute, another second, of Nicholas Ottinger's company; so shook hands with the man and walked off. The sunlight was dazzling: blinding. He was thinking he must call Bianca to warn her: Your father is being investigated in your mother's death. He must call Roberta Grinnell, whom he had not meant to frighten. And Sigrid Hunt, what of Sigrid Hunt? . . . He never wanted to see the woman again, or even speak with her, but he must know if something had happened to her; he must know where she was.

He went into a pub on South Street, sat at the bar, ordered a sandwich, beer, another beer, feeling, so very oddly, a measure of elation: he was free for the remainder of the day; hours opened up before him. He was free as anyone in Hazelton was free; that fact impressed him profoundly. He told himself, in Ottinger's well-chosen words, that the investigation was not serious, was merely a form of harassment, would come to nothing in the end: no one could prove it was not an accident. For there were no witnesses, and there was no motive. There were no witnesses, and there was no motive.

He told himself, swallowing down the last of his beer, *Of course you are guilty; and of course you will be punished.*

6.

They arrested Ian on the morning of May 30, eighteen days after Glynnis's death. And informed him, in words that had the solemn ring of antiquity, that anything he said "can and will be used against you."

THE FORMAL CHARGE was second-degree murder, not manslaughter as he and Ottinger had expected.

Preposterous, Ottinger said.

The grand jury will never indict, Ottinger said. He seemed to take the arrest as a personal insult; as, perhaps, it was intended.

Ian was served the warrant not in his home, or at the Institute—where, if they meant to be cruel, they might have surprised him—but in the Cattaraugus County courthouse, where Ottinger had arranged to "surrender" him privately: see him through the arraignment, post his bail bond, and get him released in a matter of minutes. Ottinger's strategy was to bring his client into the courthouse by way of a rear dock used for loading and unloading prisoners, that Ian might be spared a more public entry, and take him out, take him *quickly* out, the same way. As Ottinger told Ian, "You never know what sort of gauntlet you might have to run, in a case like this."

"Like this?"

"So much local publicity, rumors."

"Ah," said Ian humbly, with the air of a man who has a great deal to learn, "I hadn't known."

Before the arraignment, Ottinger telephoned the justice of the peace who had issued the arrest warrant, objecting strenuously to the $75,000 bonding fee, which he saw to be both excessive and insulting—"My client is hardly a man who would run away"; but the fee remained $75,000. Ian said, "Does it matter? Why does it matter?" The great shock was the charge itself, *murder,* that astonishing accusation *murder,* what did the rest of it matter? He had no difficulty meeting the 10 percent bail; $7,500 seemed a fair sum to him; after all, they were accusing him of having murdered his own wife.

Ottinger looked at his client, as he would, in the months to come, so frequently look at him: with patience, pity, some measure of sympathy, yet a measure too of contempt. You fool, he seemed to be saying. You asshole. "Of course it matters, everything matters; you must know you're fighting for your life," he said.

Startled, Ian laughed and said, "*My* life? Surely not."

THREE

THE GAME

How could he give it up, for even penitential reasons? The squash court was quite simply one of his sacred places.

He warned Denis, when they resumed playing again, that he was badly out of condition but did not want to be humored. "*My* pleasure," Denis said happily. The men, near evenly matched, though Ian was by nature a methodical player given to spurts of sudden inspiration and Denis an impulsive, aggressive, even at times rather manic player, given to inexplicable lapses of skill and attention, had been playing together, or with others, for a decade: to think of squash, for Ian, was to think of Denis Grinnell.

For a season, years ago, their wives had tried to play too but soon gave it up; they much preferred tennis. Glynnis objected that squash is noisy, nervous, claustrophobic, and surely conducive to paranoia; what on earth attracts people to it? And Ian, or was it Denis, naturally replied, The fact that it is noisy, nervous, claustrophobic, and conducive to paranoia. Of course.

It *was* an unremittingly fast game, leaving little time for thinking, let alone reflection, always, in Ian's imagination, a shadowless game, performed at high velocity within a space so brightly, if artificially, lit it resembled an overexposed photograph. It was even, to a degree, a dangerous game, the ball flying against the walls and sometimes, though it was out of bounds, the very ceiling, spinning, ricocheting, rebounding, a small dark sphere that seemed to carry a luminous life within it, rock hard and malevolent. And the racquets, foreshortened, wicked, swinging past one's head, grazing an ear, clipping a forehead, crashing into an eye—one memorable time Ian lunged for a tricky shot and struck Denis on the bridge of his nose, nearly breaking it and causing a good deal of bleeding; another time Denis in a desperate swing had sent Ian's glasses flying twenty feet to crack against a wall: "Oh shit!" Denis screamed. "Look what you made me do!"

It was the frenetic pace, the heart's acceleration, the pitiless present tense that so drew Ian to the sport, erratic player as he was and, by even local standards, hardly more than average; he liked risking hurt, even injury, at the hands of a friend. He liked, of course, winning: that stab of childlike triumph in the face of another's defeat; yet he liked, in a way, losing too, in such quarters, among friends, abashed, embarrassed, temporarily angered, having only (and surely this was crucial?) himself to blame.

If another man is the vehicle of my defeat, Ian thought, bemused, I am its cause. On the squash court at least.

He also liked the game because it was a game, and not life: it had a beginning, and an end; it was played in a specific place, as on a game board large enough to accommodate human beings; it had its rules, regulations, and customs, and even, should one be interested, its history. (Ian McCullough was not, much. The epistemology of games was not his field.) Its dimensions were so scaled down, its skills so specialized, one could not speak of it as a metaphor for life . . . unless everything in which human beings involve themselves with an unreasoned intensity is a metaphor for life.

Approaching the squash courts, hearing their percussive, breathless sounds, smelling their characteristic smells, Ian felt his heart lift in expectation and in hope. It was June 22: for the next hour he would not be obliged to think of the fact that he had been arrested and charged with his wife's murder; that newspaper headlines and articles and photographs (of a man identified as "Ian McCullough" and a woman identified as "Glynnis McCullough") had luridly yet, in a sense, quite properly publicized the fact; that, despite his attorney's protestations and what might be called community support, organized by certain of his friends and colleagues, the county prosecutor had decided to take the charges before the Cattaraugus County grand jury, which was now in its June session; that fifteen men and women, strangers to Ian, were, even now, as he and Denis took their places on the squash court and began their practice volleys, considering evidence in the case of *People of the State of New York v. Ian J. McCullough.* The grand jury's sessions were closed, its procedures confidential. One day soon there would be a public announcement and further headlines: an indictment would be handed down or would not be handed down, and Ian McCullough would or would not be arraigned to stand trial for the murder of Glynnis McCullough. It was that simple. His fate existed outside him.

That morning Denis played his usual fiery, impulsive game, hard-breathing and sweaty and crowding Ian rather more than Ian liked, winning points one after another, winning the first game, and the second, and, not quite so readily, the third. Ian played as he usually did, holding back, cautious, then throwing himself into inspired or, more usually, abortive outbursts of effort—it was true he was badly out of condition, breathing through his mouth after ten minutes, his heart hammering, his reflexes slow. But with each game he gained in confidence and made Denis, who had a tendency to wind down sharply after his initial expenditure of energy, work harder and harder for his points. Denis was a noisy, happy, gregarious player, bounding about, laughing at his own and others' blunders, as fiercely competitive, Ian well knew, on the squash court as off, yet wonderfully boyish and direct. "Good shot!" he cried. Or: "*Damn* you, McCullough!" Denis's face was as animated as his stocky muscular body, smiling, grinning, grimacing; his eyes shone with sheer pleasure, the frizzy crown of brown-gray hair above his forehead lifting like a rooster's comb. Beside him Ian felt thin, leggy, uncoordinated, though his shoulder and arm muscles were well developed and his right wrist, like Denis's, from years of squash, was perceptibly thicker than his left. After that accidental blow to Denis's nose Denis had frequently teased Ian about being a dangerous man, often to others—"This is a man who can kill you with one swing of his racquet: be forewarned"—but since Glynnis's death such teasing had abruptly stopped; of course it had abruptly stopped. That Ian McCullough was dead forever.

But Ian sensed that, for all his joking, Denis did fear him, less, in fact, here on the squash court than when they found themselves alone together, or spoke on the telephone; as if there was something unarticulated between them that had to do of course with Glynnis's death, for what in Ian's life did not, now, have to do with Glynnis's death? . . . Ian wondered: Had Denis been Glynnis's lover, the man she'd loved here in Hazelton and claimed to have given up for Ian? One night when he had had enough to drink and felt he'd debased himself sufficiently to undertake such a task, violating a dead woman's privacy as he'd never have dared—indeed, desired—to violate it while she was alive, Ian had made a quick anxious search of Glynnis's things and found nothing; or, rather, he'd found everything: hundreds of letters, hundreds of postcards, Christmas cards and birthday cards and valentines and cards that exclaimed *Congratulations!* and anniversary cards *To My Beloved Wife.* . . . Some of these were signed with names Ian knew, or was fairly certain he knew; others were signed with the names of strangers. Of course Denis was there, Denis and Roberta both, and there may have been notes signed with the initial *D.*, as there were notes signed with other initials, or mysteriously not signed at all. . . . In one of Glynnis's disordered desk drawers there were numerous memos that appeared to be in her own hand, or in slovenly variants of it, notes to herself or codified transcriptions of telephone conversations, most of them illegible. Ian read them with fascination and a slowly intensifying sense of horror, thinking that the person who had written down these messages (with their air of urgency!) was not only, now, "dead" but no longer existed, in any sense; and the hours in which she'd lived, those hours through which they had all lived, were "dead" as well: had passed completely out of existence. Time was a sea in which a single enormous wave moved relentlessly forward, not bearing men and women along but simply passing through them.

Ian gave up the search within an hour. Glynnis's things in her absence had become—mere things. Her lover was hidden among them, faceless in a crowd.

It was the final game of the final set, and Ian, belatedly rousing himself, began to play with more accuracy and ferocity; and Denis lost a point, laughed in surprise, and murmured, "*You're* hot," and lost another point. In a flurry of desperation, panting through his mouth, sweating, exhausted, bent at the knee, head lowered, a spectacle, he didn't doubt, of a comical sort, Ian somehow managed to win the final game: his only win of the morning.

He laughed, happy, seeing Denis's face, that look of surprise and momentary disappointment, self-disgust, that in another instant would break into a congratulatory smile: only one game but it was the final game, and a significant game, and both men knew it. Denis wiped the sweat out of his eyes, and shook Ian's hand warmly and hard, and said, "Well. I guess you're back."

A posthumous victory . . . but so sweet.

ON THE SQUASH court he sweated as nowhere else on earth.

His pores exuded sweat like tears: rivulets of sweat down his sides and, stinging, in his eyes; the bridge of his nose so slippery with sweat that his glasses (though secured to his head by an elastic band) began to slide. *Sweat, sweating:* the very words gave satisfaction of a kind. *Sweating like a pig;* though less like a pig than Denis, who was heavier than he by at least fifteen pounds, soft flaccid flesh around the waist, ham-sized thighs not fat but compact, solid, a true heft to Denis's swinging stride: the kind of man who, walking, gives the impression of always knowing his destination and of how to get there.

On the court he sweated; in the shower he washed the sweat away.

The very purposelessness of such actions, such contrary motions, gave him pleasure of a kind. He would not have wished to admit it, but the shower too, at the gym as at home, was rapidly becoming another of his sacred places.

Under the shower, its nozzle emitting the needle-fine stinging spray that Ian preferred and the water as hot as he could bear, he shut his eyes and saw, fragmented as hypnagogic images, and no less graceful and unwilled, highlights of the triumphant game just played: Ian's serves, Ian's returns, Ian's lucky shots, Denis's misses. And fragments of other games came to him: tricky serves of Denis's he'd managed to return, to Denis's surprise; a protracted exchange, early on, Ian would have won had not the damned ball, struck at an unintended angle, sailed to the very top of the wall and hit the ceiling—"Fuck it!" Ian said. And there was that crucial moment in, had it been the second set, when he'd swung his racquet blindly but managed to connect with the ball, and hard, really hard, and Denis had nearly fallen on his face rushing to make the return. . . .

How you men love your games, Glynnis had said. Your games that exclude women.

Your games that are about being men together, excluding women.

And it was true, though Ian had naturally denied it, that he felt his maleness, such as it was, most keenly in the presence of other men: in games of competition or their social equivalents. Since boyhood it had seemed to him that maleness was determined not by women but by other men. . . . What was the Greek heroes' code? To help one's friends, to harm one's enemies. Maleness. A game. Its parameters shifting, its center always the same. Oh yes.

He stood with his face lifted to the shower, hair plastered over his forehead. Hot water streamed over his body, and then, with a twist of the faucets, cold water, bracingly cold water: as if to stroke his flesh into oblivion.

A shower is the very place, Ian thought, in which to slash one's wrists. The blood would drain away immediately, since it is always present tense.

But it was not a serious thought.

He was thinking of a dream he'd had the night before . . . one of a number of thin, stray, wayward dreams, the product not of a deep and profound sleep but of a sleep contaminated by consciousness and memory: a dream of sexual desire and sexual frustration, acute as an adolescent's. Glynnis stood naked before him, not as she'd been at the time of her death but as she'd been when they were first lovers, yet taunting and mocking him as she'd never done in life; and shifting, even as he reached desperately for her, into another woman . . . was it Sigrid Hunt? . . . a female body, female being, faceless, abstract, unnamed. How Ian had wanted to bury himself in her, nameless as she was—bury his blood-swollen penis in her—but more than his penis: his very soul!

But he woke, and the dream abruptly faded. His rodlike penis throbbed with desire, shameful to him, like an old remnant of a lost self: this too, rapidly fading. Self-loathing washed over him; its sourness coated the inside of his mouth.

The needle-thin spray had gone very cold. Ian's teeth began to chatter; his genitals withered, retracted; gooseflesh dimpled his body. He turned off the shower, dried himself roughly, entered the crowded locker room with a towel around his waist. Without his glasses he blinked myopically and innocently, under no obligation to recognize anyone or to note that others seemed not to recognize him.

At such times he had always felt uneasy, absurdly exposed and vulnerable; since boyhood it had seemed to him (and seemed so still) that others, boys and men, inhabited their bodies in a way that he did not. And now of course that the scandal had so publicly broken around him, this "Ian McCullough" that was both him and not him, he knew that other men regarded him with special interest, with curiosity if not frank repugnance: even those who had always liked him; even, he supposed, those who thought the charges against him unjustified. He moved among them as if he were one of them—note the bare feet, the dripping hair, the towel tucked adroitly around the lean waist—but he knew himself a terminally ill man to whom individuals felt themselves obliged to be kind, but not at all obliged to seek out.

How Glynnis would be hurt, and incensed, at this diminution of my popularity, Ian thought. For of course it reflects upon her as well.

Dressing hurriedly, yet with unusual clumsiness, Ian listened to Denis on the other side of the row of lockers: the deep-chested baritone voice, the explosive laughter. . . . To whom was he talking? Ian did not recognize the other man's voice. Denis was enormously well liked in Hazelton, at least by men in no way his professional rivals, primarily because he was so easily amused, so ready to laugh: taking and giving pleasure by way of his laughter. No one quite like Denis! Glynnis used to say with an enigmatic smile. She had been fond of Denis, and he had certainly been fond of her: very likely attracted to her, sexually, romantically. That could scarcely have been avoided. But had the two of them been lovers? Would they have dared . . . ? Ian envisioned his friend's broad hairy body lowering itself over his wife, the woman who was his wife; and that woman reaching up playfully, greedily, as she had so often with Ian, to draw him down to her. Yes. Good. *Hurry*. Like *this*.

Ian writhed in excited revulsion. It was impossible to believe, he thought, yet, in his mind's eye, so brutally vivid.

HAD HE NOT seen Glynnis, once, years ago, talking earnestly with Denis, in the vestibule of someone's house . . . and had not Denis's characteristic expression of sociable mirth and expectancy been gone, in its place a look of hapless worry: a look, Ian had almost thought, of husbandly anxiety? Seeing Ian, Glynnis had smiled a quick radiant smile and made a gesture, extending a beringed hand to him, opening her arm in a semblance of an embrace, as if to say *Yes, you too, I want you both*, and the awkward moment passed: passed over, if Ian remembered correctly, into good-natured bantering. They had all had a fair amount to drink, Denis in particular; for some reason he'd come alone to the party. . . . Unless that had been another evening, another party. There had been so many, after all.

I love you anyway, Ian thought. Both of you. I don't care what has passed between you.

AS THEY HAD done numberless times in the past, they ate lunch in the Institute dining room, Ian McCullough and Denis Grinnell, and Malcolm Oliver came to join them, and the conversation was brisk, unforced, pleasantly general: Institute matters, Hazelton news, talk of mutual friends, acquaintances, colleagues, plans for the future. Malcolm was leaving for a two-week tour of Argentina to do a piece for *Life*, and Denis was leaving the next day for a week in Zaire: he was an economic consultant for the State Department and had some connection, perhaps not entirely official, with the Arhardt Center for Strategic and International Studies. "I don't subscribe to their politics, of course," Denis said defensively, "but this is such an excellent opportunity for research, I really can't pass it by." Ian listened to his friends' plans—which, like all plans that involve flying to distant parts of the earth, had a happy, celebratory tone—and felt only the mildest stirring of envy, or hurt. He had been one of them, once. Now he was posthumous; his life contained no future.

Eventually, for such questions could not reasonably be avoided, Denis and Malcolm inquired after Bianca, and Ian told them that his daughter was well: not adding, for of course it would only sound self-pitying, that she was as well as might be expected under the circumstances. (In fact Bianca had returned from Wesleyan exhausted and undernourished, so obsessed with taking examinations and writing final papers she'd forgotten, she said, to eat and simply hadn't time for sleep; which hardly mattered, did it? since she'd done so unexpectedly well: all her grades A or A-minus.) They talked for a while of Denis's sons, both away with summer jobs; and of Malcolm Oliver's seventeen-year-old son; and Ian made an effort to listen, but his thoughts drifted onto Bianca: at home now for the summer, living so strangely alone with him, the two of them in that house, that house of absence, each of the rooms defined, it seemed, by absence, by the fact that a presence had vanished from it . . . as if the old folk superstition of "hauntedness" really meant "absence."

Bianca had not been seriously ill, she'd insisted, only "worn out"; now recovered, or nearly, working at a summer job with the local YM-YWCA. Ian told his friends about the summer job but did not tell them that Bianca, once so happily combative, so, in Glynnis's words, prickly spirited, was now quiet, subdued, even submissive: spending her spare time reading Buddhist literature and talking, God knew how seriously, of making, some day, a "pilgrimage" to Kyoto. (Glynnis had had the identical notion, years ago. Glynnis and certain of her Zen-minded friends. But nothing had come of it of course and, when, eventually, the McCulloughs had traveled to Japan for an academic conference, they'd stayed for two days at the Kyoto Hilton, made quick visits to the shrines. Beautiful, Glynnis had said passionately; so peaceful! And that was all.)

Ian glanced up. Dr. Max and three other men were passing by their table without acknowledging them; without, it seemed, seeing them. The director's ruddy face was crinkled in mirth; the men were laughing about something; it was remarkable, Ian thought, how much laughter one heard, in the Institute dining room, at such designated times. One of the men was Homer Taylor, the older colleague of Ian's who had called, the evening of Glynnis's accident, to invite him to lunch.

Of course, since Glynnis's death, all talk of Ian McCullough as the next director of the Institute had stopped. In that too he knew himself posthumous.

It was not yet twelve-thirty but Ian and his companions were finished with their lunches; men eating alone together, without women, eat notoriously fast. Let's have three more beers, Denis suggested. And Malcolm agreed, and Ian said yes, good, why not? Now that the anxious malaise of his life had settled over him like a low-lying mist, in which even familiar objects are obscured or given a malevolent cast, he set more store than he would have wished to acknowledge on precisely such occasions: casual, improvised, spontaneous.

As if he had only now thought of it, and brought the subject up with some reluctance, Malcolm asked Ian how "the case," as he called it, was developing. So rarely was Ian asked this question, particularly in so point-blank a way, he hardly knew how to answer: the grand jury's hearings were closed, after all; it was primarily, for the defense, a matter of waiting.

Malcolm said, glancing at Denis, who indicated by his downward gaze that he was out of the conversation or wanted nothing of it, that he'd been hearing various things about the prosecution's approach: no more than rumors, of course, nothing substantial. "You know," he said, with a twitch of a smile, "what Hazelton is like."

Do I? Ian wondered. "What sorts of things have you heard? Or shouldn't I ask?"

"Well. About the girl, for one thing," Malcolm said uncomfortably. "All this emphasis they intend to place on the girl."

"The girl?"

"The young woman, I should say. Sigrid Hunt."

Ian drank beer, stiffening: thinking—or rather, not thinking, for his response was sheerly physical, emotional—I will say nothing about her; I will not even deny her.

Malcolm said, "I met her, you know, just briefly, that evening at your house. That large party back in . . . I forget when. Last fall. And June seems to have met her at some sort of luncheon Glynnis arranged. My initial impression of her—that is, my only impression—was that there was something desperate about her, even then. In her face. Her eyes. But something certainly attractive. And, Christ, that man she was with, that 'Egyptian fiancé,' as he's described in the papers: he was looking at me as if it wouldn't have taken much for him to attack me . . . and

I wasn't doing anything but talking to her. I remember him as clearly as I remember her."

Denis said, "Cut the crap, Mal. Did you ever call her?"

"Of course I never called her," Malcolm said. He looked at Denis, smiling. "Did you?"

Denis laughed. "In fact, no."

"Did you want to?"

"Did you?"

There was a sudden wild silence. Ian said quietly, "When one is happily married one doesn't do such things."

"Exactly," Denis said.

"That's the point," Malcolm said, raising his bottle to his mouth. "The entire point. One *doesn't.*"

"And now, in any case, she seems to have vanished," Denis said. His face was still flushed from their game, and his hair, parted low and combed conspicuously over the crown of his head, was still damp. He did not look at Ian, though he seemed to be addressing him. "As the media has it, 'without a trace.' "

It was true, sadly, grotesquely true: in mimicry of Ian McCullough's dead wife the young woman with whom he was generally believed to have had "relations" had become, too, an absence.

Ian shrugged his shoulders, said carelessly, "I suppose, eventually, I will be blamed for her death too."

"Don't talk like that," Denis said, shocked. "For Christ's sake, Ian!"

"Why not?" Ian said. "Do you think I would mind?"

AS THEY LEFT the dining room Malcolm reverted to the subject of the grand jury: the rumors he'd been hearing from his lawyer friends. He was acquainted with the county prosecutor, Lederer, Samuel S. Lederer: had had a nasty confrontation with the man five or six years ago, over a case taken up by the ACLU. "The bastard is shrewd, manipulative, opportunistic, yet—and this is the worst part of it—sincere. A Republican, and conservative, anxious to placate his constituency, so far undistinguished in office—this is his first term, I suppose you know—and casting about for something or someone to make a public issue of. To erect a mission around." Malcolm looked at Ian frankly. "That makes him a dangerous adversary, given the power he has as prosecutor. But I suppose Nick Ottinger has filled you in on all this?"

"Yes," Ian said, wanting to change the subject. "I suppose he has."

"Lederer will probably stack his case against you with an undercurrent of populist sentiment, if he can get away with it," Malcolm said. "Playing off the jurors' supposed resentment of people, in Hazelton, like us."

"Like us?" Ian asked mildly.

"Playing off the notion that we are not indigenous to this part of the country but are intruders, of a kind . . . that we constitute, or even think of ourselves as, a sort of elite, a class of our own." Malcolm made a gesture, at once extravagant and dismissive, that took in the Institute dining room with its high vaulted ceiling and tall leaded windows and gleaming parquet floor, the numerous tables at which their colleagues, most of them men, were sitting. His nostrils widened darkly in contempt: to Malcolm Oliver, the Hazelton faculty was hardly a homogeneous community, nor was it one with which he felt an identifying kinship. "That we live *in* Hazelton but aren't *of* Hazelton. That sort of thing. I don't really know who the jurors are on the grand jury but, God forbid, if there is to be an actual trial . . ."

Malcolm's voice trailed off in embarrassment; clearly, he had not meant to say all he'd said.

Denis said, "I'd let Ottinger worry about it; it's his job, after all. *I* wouldn't worry." He laid a consoling hand on Ian's shoulder and said, in a kind, vague, falsely hearty voice, "*I* wouldn't."

MALCOLM LEFT THE building, and Ian and Denis climbed the stairway to the fourth floor. Instead of turning in the direction of his own office, however, Ian walked with Denis to his. He had not meant to do so, yet, evidently, he was doing so; the gesture took both men by surprise.

Denis asked if something were wrong, casting Ian a worried sidelong glance, and Ian said, no, of course nothing was wrong, but he'd like to speak with Denis for a moment, if he could. In private. Just for a moment.

"Of course," Denis said.

As soon as Denis closed the door behind him and they were alone together in his office, Ian began to speak. Afterward, recollecting this strange scene, Ian would think it extraordinary that, until the moment of crossing the threshold into Denis's office—a long, narrow, crowded space the approximate size of Ian's own office—he had not known he meant to say such things: meant to speak so freely. Even his voice, higher-pitched than usual, was not one he might have recognized. "There is no one else I've told this, Denis," he said, "but, that night, the night she died—I mean the night she injured herself— Glynnis told me something . . . unexpected. Something I haven't been able to forget."

"Yes? Did she? What was that?"

"She said she'd been . . . that she had had . . . a lover. Lovers. That there was a man in Hazelton whom she loved . . . and had given up, she said, for me."

Denis regarded Ian with a look of absolute and seemingly unfeigned astonishment. He said in a whisper, "Really! Really!" Then, "Are you sure you want to tell me this, Ian? Under the circumstances . . ."

Ian said quickly, "I must tell someone."

". . . considering that Glynnis is dead."

"I *must* tell someone."

It seemed to him that Denis was frightened of him; as, so very suddenly, he'd become frightened of Denis.

He was standing close by a window, in a humid patch of sunshine. Below was the Institute pond, its rippleless sky-mirroring surface, and, beyond, a spectacular stand of birch trees. They were the same trees Ian saw, at a slant, from his own office window, and he recalled having thought, as a boy, a city boy, that birch trees were too elegantly beautiful to be real. "Those trees," he said.

"Yes? What?"

"They look artificial."

"Artificial?"

"If you didn't know better, wouldn't you think they'd been painted? By hand?"

Denis stared at him as if he had said something incomprehensible.

"They look flat, too," Ian continued. "But then, I suppose, if you look at objects hard enough, people as well, they begin to go flat. Into two dimensions."

"Would you like to sit down, Ian? You're looking a little tired."

"It's just that she was unfaithful to me, you know. And then she died. I mean, she was injured: there was the accident; she recovered consciousness only for a few minutes, without speaking to me; then she died. It happened," Ian said, frowning, "so damned quickly. And irreversibly."

"Please sit down, why don't you."

"I'm not at all tired. I feel in fact as if I've just woken up. That last game of ours . . ."

Denis said, "If Glynnis was upset when she told you . . . what you say she told you . . . I don't really think you can take it seriously." He chose his words carefully, as if they were being recorded. "We all know that Glynnis sometimes said things without thinking: things meant to surprise, or to wound. She was a passionate woman, and—"

Ian looked searchingly at him. " 'To surprise, or to wound,' " he repeated. "But that doesn't mean she wasn't telling the truth, does it."

"Look, I don't care what she said, or what you remember her saying," Denis said quickly, "the fact is she loved you. That was obvious. Everyone knows that. Whatever she said, whatever she wanted you to believe . . . I don't think you should believe. Or repeat: to me, or anyone. Under the circumstances."

"Because it casts me in an unfortunate light?"

"An unfortunate light?"

"Because it suggests we were quarreling?"

Denis made an impatient gesture. It was clear to Ian that he was greatly agitated, yet making an effort to appear calm: as on the squash court, when the play was unexpectedly accelerated. In the jaunty V of his sport shirt, unbuttoned at the throat, some twists of chest hair—curly, kinky, gunmetal-gray—seemed to glisten with an electric, kinetic alarm.

Ian smiled, staring. "Because it suggests we were quarreling, before the accident?"

"Because we all know Glynnis," Denis said. "We know how emotional she could be. Not that, to a degree, we all aren't emotional, even Roberta. To a degree. Saying things we don't mean, lashing out at people we love. And if she was, as you've said, drinking . . ."

"We were both drinking."

". . . all the more reason not to take it seriously. Any of it."

"Wouldn't you take it seriously, if your wife told you what mine did? Or if Glynnis herself had told you?"

"I don't consider it any of my business," Denis said. Though he spoke calmly enough, he'd begun to pace about his office, not quite meeting Ian's eye: all but pressing his hands, in desperation, against his ears. "As I said, I don't think you should be telling me this. I think our conversation should stop right here. Out of respect for poor Glynnis, and for . . ."

". . . the cuckolded husband?"

"No matter what she said, Glynnis loved you. You must know that."

"But she was unfaithful to me. Not once but, by her own account, numerous times."

"I don't believe that," Denis said. "Nor do I want to hear about it."

"Don't you?"

Denis said, recklessly, "Look: I could believe it of a few women of our acquaintance, of Meika Cassity for instance, but in truth, Ian, and I mean this seriously, I can't believe it of Glynnis; she wasn't the type."

Ian looked at him, considering. "You have such confidence in her!"

"I know Glynnis, and I know you."

"You *knew* Glynnis. Glynnis is no longer living."

"And I know you."

"Really? Do you?" Ian removed his glasses and rubbed his eyes hard, stood motionless in the patch of sunshine: content, for the moment, simply to stand there, as if his friend's indignation were a kind of protection. "Such confidence! It's remarkable. It does you credit. I've lost that sort of feeling, myself: the luxury of it. Glynnis killed it in me. She has killed everything in me."

"Don't be ridiculous," Denis said nervously. "You're upset. And I'm upset. This isn't the time or the place to talk about such things."

"Where would be the place, and when would be the time?"

"It's all so close, so raw. . . . I'm still having trouble grasping the fact that she's dead." Denis wiped at his face with a wadded tissue. His eyes brimmed with moisture, and his cheeks were reddened as if they'd been slapped. "And this thing that has happened, is happening, to you. . . ."

Ian said, "Were you the man?"

"Who? What?"

"Glynnis's lover? Her lover, here in Hazelton?"

Denis stared at him, appalled.

"Just tell me the truth, Denis," Ian said. "Yes or no."

Denis said, "I would think you knew me better than that, Ian. To even ask such a question."

"Yes or no?"

"No."

"You weren't her lover?"

"No. I was not your wife's lover."

"Then do you know who was?"

"Certainly not. I don't believe, as I've said, that she had a lover."

"At any time?" Ian asked skeptically. "At *any* time?"

"Judging from what I knew of her, and of you, of your marriage—yes, at any time."

"I see," Ian said.

He felt light-headed suddenly, as if with exhaustion. The conversation was over! He was free to leave!

At the door he thanked Denis for the squash game and for having lunch with him: for allowing him to speak so frankly about so personal a matter. "It's just that I seem to have no one else," he said with his slow sweet perplexed smile. "If you can forget what I've said, please forget it. I won't embarrass you again."

Denis said, "Of course."

"Will you? Forget it?"

"Of course."

"I suppose," Ian said, "I had wanted to think it was you. Of the men I know, and Glynnis knew . . . I had wanted to think it was you."

Denis laid a tentative hand on Ian's shoulder. He said, softly, as if in an undertone, "I'm sorry to disappoint you, Ian."

THE INDICTMENT

1.

A nd then he was indicted, after all: Ian McCullough, who had wanted to believe that his destiny, legal and otherwise, was determined for him not by mere men, mortal like himself, and fallible—if not "shrewd," "manipulative," "opportunistic"—but by inhuman processes beautifully abstract as the rising and falling of the tides, the clockwork orbiting of planets, the ghostly trajectory of starlight across the void. But of course such thinking was, in the crude but accurate vernacular, bullshit. For the six women and nine men of the Cattaraugus County grand jury, June session, had simply voted to support Samuel S. Lederer's case against Ian McCullough: had found his narrative account of Glynnis McCullough's death persuasive. It was that, and nothing more.

And they had voted to indict not on lesser charges of manslaughter, criminally negligent homicide, but on charges of second-degree murder: had signed their names to the "true bill" of indictment, which charged that

On the night of April 23 of this year, within the venue of Cattaraugus County, New York,

Ian J. McCullough,

defendant herein, did commit murder in the second degree in that he caused with force the death of Glynnis McCullough, his wife, thereby taking the life of the aforementioned Glynnis McCullough:
In violation of Section 125:25 of the New York State Statutes.

And so he was arraigned in the Cattaraugus County courthouse another time, before another judge, his case to be sent to the docket of one Chief Superior Court Judge Benedict Harmon, of whom he had never heard, for motions and trial. The defense had fourteen days to file motions and the prosecution fourteen days in which to respond, at which point a date for the trial would be set, very likely in the fall. When Ian McCullough would have, as it's said, his day in court; when he might be exonerated of the crime lodged against him. When he might be publicly eviscerated, gutted like a fish.

Ian asked the assemblage, "If I were to plead guilty now, would this all come to an end?"

And they looked at him, to a man, as if he were mad. And Ottinger took him hastily aside and spoke with him: *What are you saying what on earth do you mean don't you understand have you no idea for Christ's sake Ian I'm not even open to pretrial conference for purposes of plea bargaining don't you know they have no case against you don't you understand a jury will never vote to convict,* and Ian sighed and acquiesced, or must have acquiesced, since the procedure, the talk, legal quibbling, paperwork, continued. It was lengthy and exhausting. His jaws ached from yawning. He thought, How could Glynnis have done this to me! I will grow to hate her, yet.

He thought, If I am guilty, I am guilty.

He thought, I will not lift a finger to defend myself. I will not play their contemptible game.

THIS TIME THEY were waiting for him; this time he could not contrive to elude them, reporters, photographers, "media" people with hand-held cameras and microphones jostling close, shouting questions at him: *Dr. McCullough? Dr. McCullough? Ian? How did you plead? What is your defense? When is the trial?* A crowd of thirty or more, men, women, all of them strangers, a proverbial pack, they seemed to him, like hyenas: yet with such enthusiasm for the hunt and, for the moment, for him, he stared at them with interest. *Dr. McCullough? Over here! Could you say a few words to our viewers—*

The contentious little crowd followed him to the sidewalk, where one of Ottinger's young assistants was waiting with a car; like any guilty man Ian ducked his head, shielded his face. He felt his sleeve plucked, a blow of sorts against his shoulder, heard Ottinger's raised voice, the startling fury of Ottinger's raised voice.

"I seem to be becoming a celebrity," Ian said, as they drove away, "without quite remembering what I did, still less why I did it."

Ottinger was not amused. "Just don't talk to those people," he said. "Any of them. *Any*one."

Ian, still cringing, nonetheless looked back at the crowd. It had grown alarmingly, within a few minutes, and was growing still. Women shoppers, men in business suits, boys on bicycles who slowed, stopped, straddled their bicycles, asking what was going on; who was in the Cadillac Seville as it sped away from the curb, why the cameras? In his rumpled seersucker suit, a tie of drab neutral colors knotted loosely about his throat, the object of the crowd's excited scrutiny looked like no murderer of distinction; certainly like no celebrity. Ian said shakily, but smiling, "It seems so easy, somehow."

"So easy? What is?" Ottinger asked. He was beginning to regard his client with a look of professional caution.

"Crossing over."

"Crossing over—?"

"To what's on the other side."

Ian was driven by a roundabout way to the Sheraton Motor Hotel by the Thruway, some six miles north of Hazelton-on-Hudson, a ten-story structure so new it was surrounded not by a carpet of perfectly trimmed green grass but by jagged rutted raw earth that gave it a startling, improvised look: the very place, Ian thought, for a murderer incognito. Ottinger had made a reservation for Ian and Bianca there under the pseudonymous identities of "Jonathan Hamilton" and his daughter "Veronica" until such time—it might be a few days, it might be two weeks—it was believed to be safe for them to return to 338 Pearce. If it would ever be safe.

WHEN, ON THE morning of July 2, Nick Ottinger telephoned Ian to tell him the grand jury's decision—"Ian, I'm so sorry, I'm afraid I have bad news, preposterous bad news"—Ian felt a spasm of physical chill that left him weak and breathless. He had to grope for a place to sit down, telephone cord comically twisted around his legs, glasses skidding down his nose.

So extreme was his reaction, so stunned was he for hours afterward, like a steer struck a sledgehammer blow to the head, Ian realized that, yes, he had come to believe the grand jury would not indict; he had listened to Ottinger and his friends, had believed what they'd said. Not only that the grand jury would not indict but that it would not dare. I must have been desperate to believe, Ian thought. Even as I tried to convince myself I felt nothing.

Even as I tried to convince myself I am already a dead man.

Of course, capital punishment was not a possibility. The charge of murder in the first degree had been reserved in New York State for cases involving the killing of police officers or prison guards, but it was recently declared unconstitutional. Second-degree murder, as Ottinger explained, was a fairly general category, with which prosecutors might do as they wished; it yielded to three subcategories, which blurred and overlapped—"intentional" murder, "felony" murder, and "depraved indifference to human life." Such homicides ran the gamut from coolly premeditated gangland murders to crimes of passion to acts of self-defense, overzealously prosecuted. And there were those "murders" that were, at best, types of manslaughter or criminally negligent homicide.

"If I am convicted," Ian said, "what would be my sentence, and where?"

Ottinger winced. "You aren't going to be convicted, Ian. Lederer's case is so weak, I'm reasonably sure Harmon might dismiss it. I intend to—"

"Yes, of course," Ian said, "but if he doesn't, and if there is a trial, and if—?"

"It's impossible to say. The charges will probably be dropped to manslaughter-one or -two, for one thing. And there is the fourth degree of homicide, 'criminally negligent.' Which, at the discretion of the judge, could mean probation and no prison sentence at all. You have no prior record, your character witnesses will be impressive, your professional standing is extraordinary . . . and so forth. When you take the witness stand—"

"I'm not going to take the witness stand," Ian said.

Ottinger very carefully did not look at him. "That is your prerogative, of course."

"I have nothing to say in my 'defense.' It was an accident, and I don't remember its details. It was not my fault, nor was it Glynnis's fault, no one can prove it was not an accident, and I have nothing more to say." Ian paused. His voice had become high-pitched and defiant.

"As you like, Ian."

"Except for me, Glynnis would be alive today. I know that, and you know that; it is the single incontestable fact."

"Yes, perhaps. But—"

"If it had not been for me, for the very fact of me, not even taking into account any of my actions," Ian said, "my wife would be alive today."

"Perhaps. But you must not say such things."

"I will say such things," Ian said excitedly, "as I want to say. And I will not say such things as I do not want to say."

Again Ottinger spoke carefully, and tactfully. "You must understand, Ian, that the law is incapable of calibrating anything so subtle as metaphysical distinctions. It tries to measure intent, but it cannot measure what one might call the swerve, or the inclination, of the soul. . . . If you retain me as your defense attorney you will have to allow me to defend you as if I were defending—which indeed I am—an action, and not, in the most abstract terms, a man. Do you understand?"

Ian shrugged impatiently. "I'm not sure I want to understand."

"The law under which we operate, and cooperate, is adversarial in structure, as you know. It's a game of a kind, but unlike most games its boundaries are somewhat hazy. For instance, if the jury, however improbably, were to vote for conviction—"

"Yes, if the jury *were* to vote for conviction?"

"We would naturally appeal to the state supreme court. And there, of course, the game is radically altered: no jurors, for one thing; no emotion, or not much. I have had good luck," Ottinger said modestly, or was it in fact reluctantly—an acknowledgment of past success being simultaneously, in this instance, an acknowledgment of past failure— "with the state supreme court as it's presently constituted. But I won't go into that now. The point is—"

"But if I *am* convicted," Ian interrupted, "and if the supreme court upholds the conviction, what then? How long might I be sentenced to prison, and where?"

Ottinger said, almost irritably—how the man disliked being driven into a corner!—"It's difficult to answer, since sentencing is at the discretion of the judge. Murder-two, with which you're charged, carries with it a mandatory minimum of fifteen years; the maximum is twenty-five years of life. By minimum I mean that you would serve fifteen years before being eligible for parole."

"Fifteen years. That doesn't seem very long."

Ottinger stared at Ian as if he had said something not only mad but incomprehensible. He said, "In one of our state prison facilities, for instance at Sing Sing, a man like you—given your background, your profession, your temperament, your physical type, and, not least, the color of your skin—might discover that a single week is very long. A single day. A single hour. What *is* your field exactly? Demographics? It might be difficult to explain that to some of your fellow inmates."

"They would not like me, would they," Ian said slowly.

"They would not like you quite as you are accustomed to being liked."

"As, perhaps, I have not deserved being liked."

"*That* has nothing to do with the law," Ottinger said. "Very few of us are liked, still less loved, to the degree we imagine we deserve. The point is, Ian, for the sake of everyone in your life, particularly, I'd think, for your daughter's sake, you want to keep out of prison. Being physically humiliated, beaten, terrorized, sodomized, whatever, might have its theoretical appeal—"

"You think, then, it is only theory?"

"—but you are not a criminal in any reasonable sense of the word, and it's ridiculous to acquiesce to charges that you are. Keep in mind that 'Samuel S. Lederer' is no principle of wrathful justice but a run-of-the-mill backwoods prosecutor who went to a third-rate law school, hides his envy of more successful men inside a pose of moral rectitude, and would railroad his own grandmother into prison if it could help his faltering career. If you don't want to testify in your own behalf that is your decision; you can't be forced, and I won't try to coerce you, though I should say it's possible, in mid-trial, when you hear some of the prosecution's witnesses, you'll be moved to change your mind."

"I will never change my mind," Ian said. His voice was flat, icily uninflected. "There is no power on earth that can make me change my mind."

"Well. You make it a challenge, then," Ottinger said, smiling, "to defend you."

"Would you like me to find another attorney?"

"Of course not!" Ottinger said happily. "As I said, it's a challenge. *You* are a challenge."

"But if the trial drags on, if there's an appeal," Ian said thoughtfully, "there may be some problem about paying you. My finances are limited. My resources. With Bianca's college tuition and bills, and if I am forced to resign from the Institute—"

"You are not going to be forced to resign from the Institute," Ottinger said. "Put that thought out of your mind immediately."

"—and I'm not going to sell the house, because, you know, it was always, from the first, Glynnis's house; she loved it so, did so much to improve it, furnished it with such imagination, decorated it—well, you know. I would be killing her a second time if I sold the house . . . and for such a petty expediency, defending my*self.*" Ian paused, looking at his hands. He spoke in the same flat dull dead voice, but his hands had begun to tremble. "I won't do it."

"Of course not," Ottinger said.

"I *won't* do it. She's so much more there, in the house, than she is at the cemetery . . . that's the main thing."

"You won't have to sell the house."

"Even as I know it's ridiculous to talk like that, as if a dead person 'were' anywhere at all, except in the memories of the living. Like the illustrious dead, our great mentors and ancestors—our fathers, you might say, if not, strictly speaking, *our* fathers. . . ." He paused; touched the back of a hand to his forehead, as if confused. "Still the house may, in time, be sold anyway," he said, "as my estate. If something happens to me, and Bianca inherits. Bianca *will* inherit, won't she, even if she is not yet twenty-one?"

"Don't think about the house, please," Ottinger said.

"You would help Bianca, wouldn't you, if something happened to me?"

"Of course," Ottinger said, managing, still, to smile, "but what are we talking about, exactly?"

Ian said, "The future."

"It might be better for you to leave the future to me," Ottinger said. "And not to think about the house, or your daughter, or going to prison, or—whatever. After all, you have indicated your faith in me, haven't you?" Ottinger's kindly, practical, eminently reasonable voice was so finely modulated as to suggest control achieved at some cost; he was regarding Ian as—was it Denis Grinnell, or Malcolm Oliver, or another of his friends?—had looked at him recently: a look of sympathy, pity, mild fear. Ian noticed for the first time a scattering of tiny scars around Ottinger's eyes, near-invisible, like stitches in the skin: an expression of perpetual squinting, and perpetual and intense thought. Had he had an accident? Slammed his head through a pane of glass?

Ottinger talked as Ottinger so brilliantly, and not inexpensively, did; and Ian nodded, as if knowing himself rebuked, chastised. He saw that his attorney was, as usual, handsomely dressed, in a powder-gray sharkskin suit with a silk polka-dot tie and matching silk handkerchief in his lapel pocket, dark polished shoes, white shirt, cuff links, clean close-trimmed nails. Of course he was smoothly shaven and gave off a subtle astringent odor, the very fragrance of sincerity. Beside him, or, rather, facing him—they were in Ottinger's inner office, a walnut-paneled and beautifully furnished room with a large disordered antique-looking desk behind which Ottinger sat erect and alert—Ian felt like a poor relation, an embarrassment: not yet shaven that day, or even showered, and dressed in clothes he'd pulled out of drawers and closets, groggy from another night's uneasy sleep. He was coatless, tieless, in a shirt and trousers surely in need of laundering, rundown and entirely too comfortable "moccasins," one frayed navy blue sock not quite the mate of the other. Help me, he thought.

Had Nick Ottinger been Glynnis's lover?—improbable, yet not impossible; not even, if one thought hard about it, improbable. Adulterous affairs were a matter (Ian gathered) of propinquity and opportunity; you drove out, if you were a woman, with the intention of shopping at the A & P, and *did* in fact shop at the A & P, but after a deftly orchestrated hour or so with your lover—in his office perhaps, if his office was private, or reasonably so; or in (this, upon reflection, more practical, and certainly more decorous) a room rented for that purpose, a motel room perhaps, miles away, the farther away the better (except of course for the logistics of time: marital life is bound together by a perpetual logic of time), one of the new Holiday Inns, Ramada Inns, Hilton Inns, Sheratons. Or one of those cheap, sleazy, *film noir* motels, older, grittier, possibly more evocative of sexual excess, sexual shame. Ian could not have said, the thought being so fresh and consequently so unnerving, whether he preferred Nick Ottinger to Denis Grinnell as Glynnis's lover: the one admittedly more stylish and attractive, the other frankly warmer, sweeter, more . . . fun. Did adulterous lovers have fun with each other's bodies, as, it might be presumed, married lovers often did not? Married lovers with a history of knowing too much, and too intimately, about each other's bodies? She'd scorned him for his impotence and of course it had been so, in his memory now, blurred as an underwater scene, decades of impotence, one after another episode of sexual failure and humiliation, the limp penis, the too-erect too-excitable too-quickly-ejaculating penis, so many ways of failing, like so many avenues of entropy, and so few of succeeding: a principle of the physical universe, as of civilization, that there was but one ideal standard of order beside which, falling away from which, all others were disorder. Ian tried to recall that year or two, so condensed in retrospect, when the Ottingers' daughter Rachel had been a friend of Bianca's, had drifted in and out of the McCulloughs' house in a pattern of tides, like most of Bianca's high school friends—*H'lo, Mrs. McCullough; H'lo, Dr. McCullough!*—pretty, smart, flirtatious, as brainy girls are flirtatious, all ironic nuances and ellipses, as difficult to interpret as a miniature poem of Emily Dickinson's. With her father's darkly bright eyes and his lawyerly interrogative manner, Rachel had been a favorite of Glynnis's, if Ian remembered correctly: a contrast, if not a rebuke, to their own daughter's less subtle style. Unless Ian had imagined it, he'd noticed the girl's level gaze sometimes lingering on him . . . unless he had imagined it. Oddly, his memory of Rachel's mother was less vivid, though the McCulloughs and the Ottingers, at one time new to Hazelton-on-Hudson, had been social acquaintances for a while: on the brink, one might have thought, of being friends. Each couple had entertained the other in their homes; for a while each had included the other in fairly small dinner parties; then, in obeisance to the law of tides of social life, of which Ian McCullough knew increasingly less with the passage of time, they had drifted apart. . . . Ian could not remember the last time he had been in the Ottingers' house; could not remember, in fact, the house itself. He wondered if Nick Ottinger was more familiar with his own.

All this while Ottinger had been talking, in that voice—of Ottinger's several voices—Ian thought teacherly, even avuncular: explaining to his client the differences, which seemed to Ian very difficult to grasp, between gradations of guilt, under the state statute. Why was "depraved indifference to human life" a murder-two charge instead of a manslaughter-one, or -two, or . . . Ian, who was not listening to much of this, interrupted—oddly, it must have seemed—to ask, "How is Stephanie these days? I don't think I've seen her in a long time."

"Stephanie? She's fine." Ottinger paused just long enough to allow Ian to know, as Ian perhaps did not quite know, that his question was both rude and inappropriate. "You may have heard," he said, "we've been divorced for about two years."

"No," Ian said, surprised. "I hadn't heard."

Ottinger, staring at papers before him, on the desk, said, "Well— I might have mentioned it to you, in fact, a while back; but there's no reason for you to remember."

Ian said, awkwardly, "You and Stephanie always struck me as such a . . . well-matched couple. And your daughter. Rachel. She always struck me as . . ." But why was he speaking of these people as if they were no longer living? "Is Stephanie in Hazelton? Or—?"

"No. Neither my wife nor my daughter is in Hazelton at the present time."

"I'm terribly sorry to hear it."

"*I'm* sorry," Ottinger said, coolly. "But, as you must know, these things happen."

"These things," Ian said sadly. "Or others."

With the precision of a finely calibrated machine, Ottinger reverted to his subject, to the exact sentence Ian had interrupted; but, now, nerved up as he was, oppressed by a new heaviness, as of a thickening of the air itself, Ian could not listen at all. Divorced! So that was it! He began to see, with hallucinatory vividness, Nick Ottinger (the vigorous hairy muscle-legged Nick Ottinger of the squash court, the locker room, the shower) making love to Glynnis, in the McCulloughs' very bedroom, luridly reflected by the several mirrors with which Glynnis had decorated the room. Their love affair would account for the atrophying of the McCulloughs' and the Ottingers' friendship; it would account for the Ottingers' divorce.

Ian wondered if there was, hidden away inside Ottinger's rather pretentiously impractical desk, in a folder at which no one but he was ever privileged to look, a sheaf of letters, cards, notes in Glynnis's handwriting.

Though, being a lawyer, the man would have them locked away. In a safety deposit box, perhaps.

Or would he, being a lawyer, have destroyed them systematically. . . .

Ian said, rather bluntly, "I never quite understood, Nick, why the four of us—that is, Glynnis and me, and you and Stephanie—didn't continue to see one another, as we were doing at one time. It was always something of a riddle to me"—though in truth, over the years, he'd only given the Ottingers a thought, and that fleeting, when he encountered them at Hazelton parties or ran into Nick at the gym—"our drifting apart."

"Well," Ottinger said reluctantly, clearly annoyed, or alarmed, at the turn their conversation was taking, "—these things happen too."

"Even our daughters, I think, aren't as close as they once were?"

"I wouldn't know."

"Glynnis, I'm sure, was very fond of you. Of you and Stephanie. I really can't understand—"

"Why don't we talk about this another time?"

"Another time?"

"*This* isn't, after all, the most felicitous time."

Ottinger smiled, to lessen the sharpness with which he'd spoken.

"Because I'm paying you two hundred dollars an hour, is that it?" Ian said, smiling too. He thought, You bastard.

And then, with no warning, he began to cry; tears astonished him, spilling hot and stinging from his eyes. He leapt to his feet and hid his face in his hands. "Christ, I'm sorry," he said. "I'd better leave."

Ottinger too was on his feet, as if outbursts of this sort, and his professional intervention, did not entirely surprise him. He said, "No. Don't leave. Use my lavatory, Ian, until you feel better."

So Ian used Ottinger's lavatory: a white-tiled, rather too coldly air-conditioned little room, with a light switch that tripped a waspish rattling fan. He ran water, washed his face, could not stop crying, angrily, helplessly, thinking that Nick Ottinger was the logical man to have been Glynnis's phantom lover, and that of course he had not been her lover; the idea was absurd. I am losing my mind, he thought. I must stop thinking of these things.

Beyond the noisy splash of the water in the bowl he heard a telephone ring in Ottinger's outer office, heard Ottinger's secretary put the call through to him, heard, through the wall, Ottinger's voice, a voice brotherly yet distant: close, familiar, intimate, yet muffled and indistinct. He felt a thrill of something very like passion, to realize that, at another time but in that room and at that desk, Nicholas Ottinger might have been speaking with Ian's own wife over the phone; while Ian McCullough, in blissful ignorance of being cuckolded, was at the Institute, knowing nothing of what they planned, what they did, with no recourse to him. How it fascinated him, even as it horrified him: the appetite and happiness of the lovers' lovemaking, the play of their bodies, without conscience or sentiment, mouths hungry for each other, hands grasping, clutching. . . . He remembered Glynnis's legs locked about his hips, her ankles snugly crossed; the quick tight hard rhythms of her body; the heat of her flesh: breasts, belly, thighs, vagina. At the peak of orgasm her body arched, convulsed, tightened frantically about him, racking him with pleasure so intense he could not bear it.

Yet he'd borne it; of course he'd borne it, so far as he could, in manly silence. Glynnis had screamed and screamed, but Ian had not.

On those occasions, that is, when he hadn't been impotent. When Glynnis had not turned aside from him, in hurt, or disappointment, or unarticulated rage.

OTTINGER WAS PROMISING Ian that he would get him through the arraignment in the morning as swiftly and as painlessly as possible. "Then Graham and I"—Graham was one of Ottinger's assistants, a young Harvard Law graduate—"will check you and Bianca in at the Sheraton. I'll put it on my Visa card; I'll take care of everything. Including a guard at your house, to protect your property." He walked Ian to the door, brisk, spirited, smiling, as if nothing out of the ordinary had happened a few minutes before; as if Ian had not suddenly broken down. He said, cheerfully, "It's expensive, of course, but it's worth it. Believe me, it's well worth it."

As if reluctant to give Ian up just yet, or doubtful of his ability to get down the stairs, Ottinger accompanied him out into the street. In the midday sun the smartly restored Georgian townhouse, muted red-brick, with black shutters and black wrought-iron grillwork, was striking as a stage set. Ian could not have said, staring at perfectly budded wax begonias in the window boxes and at the mica glint of the brick façade, why, on this warm midsummer day, he was here, on Chase Street, in the company of a man whom he did not much like; whom he'd always, for no reason he could name, distrusted.

"May I give you some final advice, Ian?" Ottinger asked. "At the risk of seeming presumptive? I would not, if I were you, try to contact that young woman, Sigrid Hunt, however tempting it might seem to do so. You have told me several times that you don't know where she is, that you have not spoken with her in months, and I believe you. But, still, it's crucial that you understand you'd be making a serious error if you try to contact her, or succeed in contacting her, and the prosecution finds out. They will subpoena the telephone company for your toll calls from your home or office, as I'm sure they already have, for past calls. Keep that in mind. If Lederer fails to locate Hunt to serve her a subpoena, we will hire a private investigator to see if *we* can't find her. But leave her to me!"

"Yes. Fine," Ian said indifferently. But thinking: Toll calls! The telephone company! Subpoena!

"And try not to become obsessed with your case, as, so often, men of your temperament do—*our* temperament, I should say; perfectionists, I mean: men who are accustomed to controlling their lives, not to being controlled. Remember that as your attorney I am going to 'defend' you; that is not your responsibility. My defense is an utterly simple one: no crime occurred, the death was an accident, purely and clearly an accident, as you have told me. So far as it's humanly possible, you should try to continue with your life and your work. You should *not* resign from the Institute. If you do so, that will be a victory for Lederer. *Mors tua, vita mea*—as the Romans said. 'Your death, my life.' "

"Yes," said Ian. "I know the Latin."

"But do you know the sentiment?"

Ottinger had the lawyer's instinctive habit of counterpunching: with him, you would never get the last word.

"The case, you know, may go on for a considerable period of time. It's in our interest to delay, until the excitement has quieted down. This inane Hazelton *notoriety*," Ottinger said.

He was smiling and squinting in the bright sunny air. The tiny scars around his eyes were clearly visible now: like stitches, thorns. The trauma to his head, Ian thought, and the bleeding must have been considerable.

"The fundamental thing is not to despair," Ottinger said. He shook Ian's hand, hard. "Not in private, and not in public."

As Ian turned away, he added, "Especially not in public."

2.

HAZELTON-ON-HUDSON SCHOLAR INDICTED IN WIFE'S
DEATH. INSTITUTE FELLOW TO STAND TRIAL
SECOND-DEGREE MURDER CHARGE

AWARD-WINNING HAZELTON SCHOLAR
INDICTED IN WIFE'S DEATH
Ian McCullough, 50, to Be Tried for Second-Degree Murder

Some were loose clippings; others were complete newspapers, spread out, with care, on the table in the hotel suite: gathered by Bianca for reasons, as she said, of "personal history." The *Hazelton Packet,* and the *Cattaraugus Monitor,* and the *Poughkeepsie Journal;* the *Newburgh Times,* and the *White Plains Herald;* the *Hudson Valley Shopper;* the *New York City Tribune;* even, its article prominent on the front page of the Metropolitan section, *The New York Times* . . . that brooding conscience, or consciousness, of the region from which there could be no escape short of death. ("Since academic and professional reputations cannot be made outside the pages of *The New York Times* it does seem just, and surely poetically just, that reputations are unmade there too," Ian told Bianca in a bemused voice.)

It was the tabloid *New York Post* that headlined the terrible words BATTERING DEATH and provided, in stark unequivocal print, the name "Sigrid Hunt": describing the "flame-haired dancer and model" as a "mystery woman" in her late twenties whose "current fiancé" knew nothing of her whereabouts, "not even whether she is living or dead." In the accompanying photograph, which had the sleek synthetic look of a publicity still, Sigrid Hunt faced the camera with her hands on her hips, torso slightly turned, hair dramatically, if not quite convincingly, windblown; she looked about twenty years old, if not younger: wearing no glasses of course, her makeup stylish and bold, particularly around the eyes.

The photographs of Glynnis most frequently used by the press were those taken for the jackets of her cookbooks, in which, too, she looked much younger than she'd been at the time of her death. The photograph of Ian most frequently used was the one taken by the *Boston Globe,* in Cambridge, Massachusetts, in January, on the occasion of his award from the National Association of Social Scientists; in it, Ian smiled uneasily at the camera, his eyes narrowed against its incandescent flash. He was a tall lean-jawed man of indeterminate age, youthful but assuredly not young, with dark-rimmed glasses and fair, filmy hair and a murderer's mock-innocent face.

A few days later the *Post* printed a lengthier feature, SCANDAL AND TRAGEDY IN "THINK TANK" PARADISE, with numerous photographs, not only of Ian, Glynnis, and Sigrid Hunt but of former Hazelton-on-Hudson residents who had brought shame, ignominy, or, at the very least, unwanted public attention to the Institute. These included the "world-renowned specialist in European economic policy" who had been charged with child molestation in 1959 and had duly resigned his post; the former assistant to the director of the Institute who had been suspected, if not formally charged, of embezzlement, in 1965 and was discharged from his post; and the "chronically depressed" wife of one of the senior fellows who had committed suicide, in a spectacular manner—driving her car into the Hudson River in a November snowstorm—in 1971. Hazelton residents who "asked not to be named" gave their candid opinions of the Institute, which was viewed with a good deal of suspicion as a tax dodge, a "Communist stronghold," and a harboring place for cranks, nuts, and the occasional genius ("who thinks he's above the law"); and of Ian McCullough, who was said to belong to a "prominent social circle" notorious in Hazelton for its parties, its alcoholism, its adulteries and promiscuities and divorces.

"It is all happening to other people," Ian said, appalled, fascinated, "but those other people are us."

Bianca said quietly, "They are killing you and Mother. Again and again. And there is no way to stop them."

WHAT WAS THE name of the Greek goddess of shame?

Ian McCullough tried to recall, but could not. Where that name had been—teasing, tantalizing; wasn't it something like Aurelia, Aurora, Aviva?—there was nothing: an image, if an image suggested itself, of only his own face.

They were "Jonathan Hamilton" and his daughter "Veronica," staying, for an indeterminate number of days, though not less than a week, in a top-floor suite at the Sheraton Motor Hotel. A bedroom for each, a bathroom for each, a rather spacious and handsomely appointed parlor; a miniature refrigerator and a miniature bar; three full-sized television sets; a view, in perspective resembling a Dutch landscape, of the Hudson River to the south, beyond the steady streams of traffic on the Thruway. The Hamiltons, who valued privacy, ate most of their meals in their suite and rarely used the hotel's facilities, except, at odd hours, when few other guests were likely to be around, the swimming pool. "It's surprisingly nice here," Ian said, as if he'd expected something very different, and Bianca said, "That's because, Daddy, in a place like this, you can't notice the usual texture of how unreal things are. Here, everything is unreal." She spoke not in rebuke but gently, in approbation, as she invariably spoke now. She alternated her reading, which was intense, as fiercely concentrated as if her life depended upon it, between the newspaper articles and the *Bhagavad Gita*.

For the first three or four days, Ian spent a good deal of time lying in, or on, his enormous bed. It was king-sized, of course; so wide he could, if he wished, stretch his arms out on it crucifixion-style. His fingers groped in vain for the edges. The drapes at all the windows were drawn and, being green velvet, gave to the room's shadows a queer viridescent cast, as if Ian were floating beneath the surface of the sea; the room's unfamiliar proportions were hazy, like those of an inadequately imagined dream. In this state Ian did not sleep, but neither was he awake, in the usual sense of the word. Nor did he, strictly speaking, think; it seemed rather more that thoughts ran through him—disjointed, staccato, accelerated, or in slow motion—like currents of electricity.

He spoke with virtually no one except Bianca, who, rising to the emergency, with something of the intrepid goodwill of Glynnis herself, saw to such routine but exhausting tasks as ordering meals from room service, making purchases in the hotel drugstore, dealing with the hotel staff. It was she who answered the telephone when calls came from Ottinger, or his office. (The Grinnells knew where Ian and Bianca were staying, but did not know their incognito.) Bianca had chosen the name "Veronica" because, she said, it was both exotic and saintly; and, as "Veronica," she made it a point to be courteous, mild-mannered, patient, and uncritical: so self-effacing as to seem, at times, scarcely there. Ian interpreted her behavior as a complicated form of hysteria with which he had not the slightest inclination, at least at the present time, to interfere.

He had, of course, brought along work to do: a dozen books to read, weeks of unanswered correspondence. Months ago he'd been invited to write an omnibus review of several newly published books in his field for *The Times Literary Supplement*, to which, from time to time, he contributed, and he hoped to work on that essay, or at least to take notes on it, without wanting to consider whether the editor had written him off and reassigned the books to another reviewer: whether the entire topic might now be dead. But he could not concentrate on anything for more than a few minutes at a time and often found himself, with a zombie's affable calm, standing at one or another window, staring toward the bluish-gray river to the south. What was its name? He had to think hard, to remember.

At dusk, he and Bianca drove out into the fragrant countryside and walked briskly, or jogged, in silence, along deserted country roads. What peace! What solitude! Ian went first, Bianca a discreet second, for father and daughter had nothing to say to each other at such times and wished only to forget each other's existence. After a few days, Ian agreed to come down to the hotel pool, where, to his relief, under no one's particular scrutiny, he swam slow meditative laps in lovely turquoise water that smelled of chlorine like mouthwash and reminded him of younger, presumably more innocent and happier days. If I die now, he thought, smiling myopically into the sun-splotched water, executing his Australian crawl as, long ago, in high school, he'd been taught, I die happy.

BIANCA BOUGHT FOR him, in the hotel drugstore, a pair of plastic clip-on lenses, dark green, to affix to his glasses. To give substance to the incognito. Following her suggestion, offered rather more in play than in seriousness—unless more in seriousness, than in play—Ian began to part his hair a bit differently and comb it a bit differently, slightly downward, toward instead of away from his rather high forehead. A subtle transformation but a transformation nonetheless. "Jonathan Hamilton," businessman, of Boston, Massachusetts.

Why not a mustache? A beard? Ian had never worn either. Seeing him, no one would know his identity. In which case no one would see "him" at all.

(ONE OF GLYNNIS'S probable lovers, back in Cambridge, had had a beard: a pirate's rakish black beard. Gerry Michaels his name, black Irish, a hotshot young economist who would not, as the relentless drama of their lives, careers, fates, unfolded, make it at Harvard. Gerry had been a friend of Ian's too, or so Ian had thought at the time. The young men had respected each other's work, and each other. So Ian had thought, at the time.

Where was Gerry now? Ian wondered. Had he and Glynnis completely lost touch, or had they, from time to time, for sentiment's sake or, more expediently, for love or lust's sake, contacted each other?

I will never know.

And there had been at least one other probable bearded lover, back in the early 1970s. . . .

And had not, for a while, Denis himself worn a beard, a goatee . . . ?

Reverend Ebenbach. Did he wear a beard? Ian could not, for the life of him, remember, and asked Bianca, who could not remember either. I've blanked out that entire day, Bianca said.)

THE "HAMILTONS," FATHER and daughter, stayed at the Sheraton Motor Hotel for nine days in all, until such time as Ian could not bear his exile any longer. Yet, in that time—it must have been the mysterious influence of "Jonathan"—Ian discovered in himself a keener interest in other people, an anticipation of the unguarded, unself-conscious ways in which they might, to a stranger's unjudging, often admiring eye, reveal themselves. Reentering the world, by cautious, even timid degrees, swimming in the pool and afterward sitting in the sun, daring to linger in the sun, which seemed so public, hence so forbidden to one of his notoriety, Ian took note, covertly, of those hotel guests who, during the slack hours of the afternoon when most travelers are on the road, stayed behind to swim in the pool, to oversee the play of children, to give themselves up, eyes trustingly closed, skin oiled, to the sun. The children were particularly appealing, Ian thought. Rowdy, noisy, splashing, beautiful. He did not even feel compelled to think of his own child (now grown, swimming in this very pool), or of his own fatherhood, in that other lifetime he could envision now only with an effort of the imagination, as if it had happened to another man, lost to this man in his fallen, contemptible state. He watched the children, and their parents, sporting in the water, laughing, flailing about, playing with miniature life vests and colorful floating toys: yellow ducks, emerald-green frogs, purple alligators. When Bianca was a small child surely Ian had taught her to swim, had frolicked with her, as (for instance) that skinny young father was frolicking with his tiny daughter?—the young mother looking on from a beach chair at the pool's edge, pretty, in fact very pretty, brunette, curly haired, warmly tanned, in her stylishly abbreviated two-piece bathing suit that had a satin sheen, cupping her breasts tight as a man's hands might grip them, in desperation or in love. The young father stooped above his daughter and guided her through the water as she "swam" with frenzied arms and legs, kicking wildly and squealing with pleasure, as, a few yards away, another child, no relation, went through the arm motions of swimming, his feet firm on the pool's bottom. Ian felt a stab of sheer pleasure, in watching. And in the innocence of watching: for no one knew who he was and what he had done. No one noticed him at all.

Ian was thinking, surely he'd played with Bianca like that; surely he had not, in his concentration upon his work and the ceaseless rumination of his mind, abrogated such play, such effortless and unmitigated delight, to Glynnis.

He thought of Spinoza's enigmatic remark: *The first and chief endeavor of the mind is to affirm the existence of the body.*

Come off it, friend. The body is all that's there.

AND SUDDENLY, IN the middle of the night, he remembered the goddess's name: Aidos.

Aidos: goddess of shame.

And her twin, and perennial ally: Nemesis.

ON THEIR LAST morning in the hotel, at breakfast, Bianca said thoughtfully, "I'll miss 'Veronica'; she hadn't any soul to contend with."

"It *is* easier, isn't it," Ian said. "Without."

These many days, he had waited for Bianca to ask about Sigrid Hunt; but she had not asked. This too, he supposed, was a form of hysteria.

He said now, embarrassed, "About this young woman, Sigrid, that the newspapers are making so much of—we were friends, but only friends. She was your mother's friend initially, and then Glynnis introduced her to me." (But was this true? Had Glynnis introduced them? Ian suddenly could not remember ever having met Sigrid Hunt for the first time.) "Believe me, Bianca, it has all been insanely distorted, misrepresented—"

As soon as Sigrid Hunt's name was mentioned, Bianca's face seemed to have gone shut; her eyes narrowed, with a look of being blind. She said, quietly, "Never mind, Daddy. I take your word for it."

"The prosecution is building its case around a—"

"I believe you. I take your word for it."

"—a chimera."

"Yes. I know. I understand."

"*Do* you know?" Ian asked, perplexed. "But how can you?"

"Daddy," Bianca said, laughing, "I know *you*. And I know how much you and Mommy loved each other. I *know*. I don't have to be *told*."

Ian stared at his daughter: who did not, clearly, want him to say another word about Sigrid Hunt, even to deny her. She trusted him absolutely, did she? Or did she, in her newly acquired mystical fatalism, trust no one at all?

"Well," he said, lamely, "I thought I should make it clear. In case, you know, you were wondering."

"I wasn't wondering," Bianca said.

They finished their breakfast in silence. Ian said, after the waiter had come, to wheel the trolley away, "I will miss it here, won't you?—our oasis of unreality."

AND AGAIN, THAT last afternoon, at the pool, Ian said, "I *will* miss it here. The people we almost were."

Bianca laughed, as if gaily, and executed a near-perfect dive into the pool.

Ian did not dive after her but sat on the tiled edge of the pool and slipped off prudently, yet with a kind of childish anticipation, into the water. He was accustomed now to its chlorine sting and the glimmering ghostly white of its underwater tiles, made the more hazy in his vision since he swam without glasses. This would be their final swim at the Sheraton; the day before, Ian had dived, for the first time, from the diving board, God knows why, and had struck the water at an awkward angle, smacking his chest and stomach hard. For a moment he'd thought he might drown, or might come close to drowning, bringing embarrassment to Bianca and to himself. Flailing to keep afloat, managing to surface, he'd heard the young lifeguard call out to him—calling him "sir"—and waved a brave restraining hand and called back, "I'm all right! Just swallowed a little"—swallowing another mouthful. But he regained control and, under the watchful eyes of both the lifeguard and his daughter, swam several laps, at his usual pace; and when he climbed out he'd felt vindicated. Winded, out of condition, feeling his age, but vindicated.

Today he felt stronger, optimistic, for there was something redemptive about swimming, even in the close confines of a pool. You are weightless, you are without sin. As his shoulder and arm muscles began pleasantly to ache, and his scarred hand began to lose its stiffness, he thought of how, returning to his life, which is to say his grotesquely altered life, he might bring with him something of what he'd learned here at the hotel: an attentiveness to others, a quietness and stillness, a humility, perhaps, in the face of others' being. If he might empty his despoiled soul of himself, and allow it to be filled with . . .

He recalled his impromptu drive to Bridgeport, in January. Checking out from the elegant Boston hotel, a day earlier than he'd planned, and driving, for no reason, to the city of his birth . . . which he had not visited for twenty years. A story of some kind, inchoate, teasing, was telling itself to him, as he drove; as, a few weeks later (but surely there was no connection), "Sigrid Hunt" would be a story told to him. He could not have said why he'd felt the need to escape the conference, why the desperation to flee that happy milling gregarious place where his hand was shaken at every turn, and warm wishes and congratulations heaped upon him: the fruition of his dream as a young ambitious scholar, hungry for advancement, praise, the adulation of his peers. But he'd felt impatient, restless, his nerves abraded by the sound of his own name: particularly in the mouths of strangers. It seemed to him that his life was being stolen from him, his blood drained from him drop by drop, and in its place . . . "Ian McCullough."

So he checked out of the hotel on Saturday and drove to Bridgeport and, there, made his way aimlessly, yet with increasing excitement, along the streets of his childhood, through the old neighborhood, taking note not of what was new (and distracting) but what was old: the few remaining landmarks, St. Timothy's at the foot of Bridge Street, the old elementary school, the old junior high school (with its new addition, that looked as if it were made of Plexiglas). A winter day of no distinction, sky like soiled ashes, air damp and thick, with a chemical aftertaste; and there, suddenly, like a visitation, the old house on Ninth Street. Ian swallowed hard, seeing it, remembering, or, rather, trying to remember—for was not the very process of "remembering," in such instances, a fraud?—the many years he'd lived there, the child of the household, watchful, quiet, subdued, hiding his anger and his hurt, biding his time. The house was a duplex, probably still a rental, on a street of undistinguished if not frankly shabby houses; someone had painted it robin's-egg blue so that it stood out, brave, festive, foolish, among its drabber neighbors.

He thought, seeing it, I want my life back.

But drove on, aimless, inquisitive, up another street, past the sturdy begrimed brick house, scarcely changed, in which a friend, a classmate, had lived . . . a boy Ian had not heard of, or thought of, in thirty-five years. There was a romance of some kind in these streets of wood-frame houses built painfully close to the curb, these streets of warehouses and boarded-up buildings, the sun on the steely water. It seemed to him the very atmosphere of loss: yet what was it he'd lost that he would have wanted restored to him? What was it that had been drained from him drop by drop?—seeing now the old park and the wading pool, so much smaller than he would have thought, covered in dirty snow. Children were playing in the park, but they were no children Ian McCullough would have known: for one thing, they were black.

"ATTRACTIVE YOUNG WOMAN, *isn't* she."

Startled, having thought himself alone, Ian glanced up from his book. He was reading in the sun and, despite his dark lenses, the glimmering afterimage of the white page danced in his eyes.

"Great swimmer too. You don't expect it, somehow."

For a moment Ian could hardly make out the face of the man who had silently, and it seemed almost invisibly, seated himself in the canvas chair beside him. Then it shifted into focus, the smiling face of a stranger, a man in his mid- or late fifties with a florid, ruddy skin, like an overripe tomato, heavy-lidded eyes, and tufted eyebrows: a handsome if satyrish face, on the verge of dissolution. He introduced himself as Harvey Spicer, of Atlantic City, New Jersey, sales representative for Chock-a-Block Toys; and Ian, taken by surprise, characteristically daunted by such aggressive sociability, shook the man's hand, for it could scarcely be avoided, and introduced himself, without thinking, as "Jonathan Hamilton." Spicer was clearly lonely and bored: a fluorescent-pink tropical drink in his hand, his bulk tightly and, it must have been, uncomfortably contained in his swimming trunks, where, like swollen fruit, his genitals bulged. He had a potbelly that looked swollen too, yet rather hard, straining against the elastic waistband of his trunks; and a burly torso, covered in lavish furry hair, most of it gray; and a salesman's smiling, aggressive manner, which filled Ian with despair. For he knew his mood of sun-warmed equanimity was too tenuous to risk in conversation with a stranger.

So he turned back to his book. (*The Political Economy of Bloc Cohesion*, a meticulously documented but not terribly interesting study by a former student, now a professor at Berkeley. He had meant to give a prepublication quote but had failed to read the book in time.)

Yet, feeling his companion's interest in her, Ian could not resist glancing up to watch Bianca in the pool, in her gleaming black rubber cap that looked like a helmet, and her one-piece black bathing suit that gave her smooth rounded flesh a curiously ascetic look, swimming laps, unhurried, methodical, with, at least to the casual eye, an expert's ease and economy—for, among the numerous lessons of her suburban childhood, Bianca had of course been taught to swim, and to swim correctly. Though she had lost weight since her mother's death Bianca was not yet thin, not even slender; she had the full-bodied boneless look of one of Renoir's young women, both childlike and womanly, an opulence rather more of nature than of human artifice. If a Renoir, however, Bianca was one of those with a pearly-pale, not a rosy, rouged-looking skin. Her face, somber in concentration, was strong-boned and, to her father's eye, handsome; the eyes sunk deeper in their sockets than he would have liked, and the jaws clenched in what seemed to him a melancholy stoicism.

How he loved her, and how little he could do for her! Staying out of prison might be the least he could offer, and the most.

Except for an older couple who wallowed and splashed in waist-deep water, and, at the shallow end of the pool, a mother with two small children, Bianca had the pool to herself: was the only swimmer, making her imperturbable way from one end to the other, her strong arms flashing like blades and her feet kicking bubbles beneath the water, in a counterrhythm, or so it seemed, to the piped-in Muzak, bright shadowless tinkly music that spoke of the happiness of surfaces, the bliss of the present tense. Strands of wet hair showed at her forehead and the nape of her neck; a ring on one of her fingers gleamed. Ian wondered what she was thinking and was grateful not to know. He had the idea that the satiny black bathing suit with its low back and crossed straps was one of Glynnis's, years ago relegated to the bottom of a drawer, but this too he did not want to know. Bianca had taken upon herself the task of going through Glynnis's things in an effort to divide them into what would be kept and what would be given away to the Salvation Army, but it was a task she began, and stopped, and began again, and stopped, with no spirit for completing. Maybe it would be best for them to put most of the things in storage, Ian suggested, until they knew what to do, by which he meant, and perhaps Bianca understood, until they knew the outcome of the trial and whether Ian would have to sell the house. Bianca said, simply, No. I want to do it myself.

The man who had introduced himself as Harvey Spicer continued to watch Bianca with obvious interest even as, idly, to Ian's annoyance, he picked at the toenails of his left foot with the plastic swizzle stick from his drink. If Bianca was aware of being so closely observed, she had too much composure to give any sign; back and forth she swam, propelling herself forward in fast hard faultless strokes, while beneath her her equally graceful shadow skimmed the pool's pale bottom like a twin swimmer, of whom she took no notice. Ian wondered what Glynnis would think of Bianca now. In her shiny black bathing cap and black bathing suit, for mourning.

When, at the end of her swim, Bianca climbed up out of the pool, breathing hard, her columnar legs streaming water, and pulled off her cap and shook her long gleaming hair free, Ian heard the man beside him suck in his breath noisily and murmur, no doubt for Ian's sake, "*Jeezus*. Look at that."

"Excuse me," Ian said, annoyed, "that young woman is my daughter."

Spicer squinted at Ian with a pretense of surprise, smiled his broad damp smile, seemed about to wink. Or did he wink? He readjusted his buttocks in the canvas chair, tugging at his trunks to loosen the crotch, and said, in an undertone, one man to another, "Well. Too bad, buddy."

MOTIONS

1.

If the law is a game, or a set of many games uncertainly interlocked, does it follow, Ian wondered, that those trapped in such games are players? That their experience, for all its anguish and its greater tedium, is a kind of play? He thought such thoughts with no bitterness, for he discovered in himself, now he'd crossed to the other side, surprisingly little bitterness. He had come to this place by his own effort, after all.

Each time the trial was set—for September 8, for November 30, for January 11—Nick Ottinger succeeded in getting it postponed. That the man was brilliant, and brilliantly obfuscating, Ian did not doubt. It was for that he was being paid.

At the time of the first postponement, in August, Ian protested. "I want to get this thing over with. If I could begin it tomorrow morning, I would."

Ottinger said, reprovingly, "Fortunately it has nothing to do with you. Every postponement is to your advantage."

"But I want to get it *over* with and move on with my life."

Ottinger regarded him speculatively, as if Ian were mildly, one might almost say amusingly, mad. And said, finally, with a smile that struck Ian as both pitying and smug, "Oh no you don't, my friend. Oh no you don't."

ONE OF THE motions Ottinger was filing was for dismissal, pure and simple. The prosecution had no case: no witnesses, no evidence, no motive. No crime.

Another motion, following upon the failure of the first, was for change of venue: the "lurid and ludicrous" publicity surrounding the McCullough tragedy had made it impossible for his client to get a fair trial in or near Cattaraugus County.

Another motion, for postponement, involved the absence of a probable defense witness, Miss Sigrid Hunt, who was in fact being sought by both the prosecution and the defense, thus far without success.

And another motion . . .

Ian listened, or tried to listen. The band around his chest was so tight he could scarcely breathe; his thoughts jammed in sheer misery.

This is hell, nor am I out of it.

Following the indictment and, indeed, the "lurid and ludicrous" publicity, had come a nightmare barrage of interruptions and intrusions: reporters, media people, uninvited visitors to both 338 Pearce and the Institute; anonymous letters, telegrams, packages; handwritten prayers and threats; sporadic acts of vandalism against the McCulloughs' property, primarily their mailbox. (The damned thing was toppled from its post so many times, presumably by neighborhood teenagers, Ian finally gave up on it and rented a post office box in town.) His home telephone number had long been unlisted, but unwanted calls came for him each day at the Institute, where the staff—increasingly weary of such calls, and of him—had been instructed to say that Dr. McCullough was on "extended leave" and could not be reached. The calls were from strangers with advice to give Ian McCullough or advice to ask; from people who claimed to know Sigrid Hunt's "whereabouts"; from people, deranged or otherwise, who seemed simply to want to talk. There were invitations from radio and television interview shows suggesting that Dr. McCullough might want to "tell his side of the controversial story" before the trial began.

Ian threw most of the mail away, would not have had the time to open it had he had the inclination. He had quickly learned to recognize crank mail, so-called, by the very look of the envelope: the block lettering, often in pencil; a certain crumpled, even soiled quality of the paper itself. *You are an evil man, I hope you die in the electic chair and rot in hell.* Or, *Doctor McCullough I will pray for you. Its not too late for you to save your soul through Our Lord Jesus Christ our Shephard in all things.* Or, *The Governor of this state acting in principal with the F.B.I. has wiretapped private households in order to trap innocent citizens into jail. I beg of you Dr. McCullough to use your influence to put an end to such Nazi methods and misuse of taxpayers money.* Some of the envelopes were so light as to appear empty; they contained clippings from various newspapers, as far-flung as the *Boise Citizen-Ledger,* the *San Antonio Gazette,* the *Toronto Star,* the *Nome Evening News.* An early story, the one headlined HAZELTON-ON-HUDSON SCHOLAR INDICTED IN WIFE'S DEATH, had been sent out by way of the UP news service, everywhere in North America it seemed. My fame flies before me, Ian thought, reading the clippings in fascination, then tearing them into shreds, dropping them into his wastebasket. Sometimes he sat at his desk for long catatonic moments staring into space; sometimes he sank forward to lie with his head on his arms, face hidden.

Though Ottinger had warned him against becoming obsessed

with his case, it was difficult for him to block certain thoughts. Repetitive and fruitless they were, and exhausting in their very futility, but irresistible. Where had Sigrid gone, for instance, and why, and was she living or dead? If living, she had cynically abandoned him, for she must know by now of his arrest and indictment; why did she not come forward to exonerate him? If dead . . . but he could not bear to think of her dead. (And who but her Fermi would have killed her?) Ottinger had allowed Ian to read part of the sworn testimony Fermi Sabri had given to the grand jury (under the New York State statute the prosecution was obliged to provide the defense with lists of witnesses they intended to introduce at the trial, and copies of their statements) in which Sigrid Hunt's exfiancé, whether out of malice, derangement, or simple confusion, spoke of Ian McCullough as Sigrid's "married lover." His testimony was rambling, repetitive, and frequently incoherent, but the gist of it was clear enough: Ian McCullough had come between Sigrid Hunt and himself and was responsible for the breakup of his engagement. (Sabri spoke of the wedding date as having been set, for April, in Cairo. Which was the first Ian had heard of it.) Asked if he knew where Sigrid Hunt was, Fermi Sabri denied knowing anything about her since her disappearance in May; raved at length about Ian McCullough, who had seduced his fiancée with money and promises of marriage and turned her against him; and accused McCullough alternately of having "enticed her away from me to stay in hiding from me" or of having murdered her "out of jealousy over me." Ian, reading the transcript, shuddered to think of the jurors listening in silence to Fermi Sabri's mad testimony, without any idea that it was sheer fabrication. Sheer fantasy! No wonder they had voted to uphold the prosecutor's case. And how could he defend himself against such reckless accusations?

Ottinger, seeing Ian's face, said quickly that the witness would very likely not speak so emotionally in a court of law; and that in any case he would be rigorously cross-examined and broken down. "If he's the lunatic you say he is, and he certainly sounds that way, he'll expose himself," Ottinger said. Recalling the single time he'd seen Sabri, in, so very ironically, his own house—why had Glynnis opened their door to such monsters?—he believed that the man would make a strong impression on the jurors. He was educated, attractive, had a high-paying job, dressed well, carried himself with a certain style. No doubt it would be revealed that his Egyptian background was upper-class, if not aristocratic. Ian could imagine it! He could imagine it! A sordid love triangle, two men and a woman, a "flame-haired dancer and model." And poor Glynnis the casualty of their passion.

"It's a simple thing, the bastard wants my heart," Ian told Ottinger.

There were other rude surprises for Ian. The prosecution had subpoenaed his bank account, so the $1,000 check payable to Sigrid Hunt was a matter of public record; the prosecution had subpoenaed his account with New York Bell, as Ottinger had anticipated, so the numerous toll calls he'd made to Sigrid Hunt's Poughkeepsie and Manhattan numbers were matters of public record; the results of the ignominious Breathalyser test—"a blood alcohol level of .14, when anything above a .10 reading is considered legally intoxicated"—were a matter of public record; as were medical reports from the Hazelton Clinic, Ian's and Glynnis's both. (Ian's injuries were minor, mere lacerations to the face and hands, but there was a notation that the cuts on his right hand seemed to have been caused by a knife blade. Glynnis's injuries were manifold, so bluntly stated, in clinical terminology, that Ian could barely force himself to read it. The crucial notation was that the skull fractures were on the back of the head, thus "the victim would appear to have been pushed forcibly backward.")

There were police witnesses: the patrolmen who had been called to 338 Pearce to investigate what neighbors called "the sound of a violent quarrel"; the detectives Wentz and Holleran, who had interviewed McCullough in his own home. There was the lengthy, repetitive transcript of Ian's own testimony at police headquarters, on May 29. (How many times had Ian said, *I don't know,* and *I'm afraid I don't remember.*) There was a garbled account by a Mr. Horace K. Vick, identified as caretaker for the residence at 119 Tice Street, Poughkeepsie, where Sigrid Hunt rented an apartment, to the effect that Ian McCullough—or a man who strongly resembled him—had visited Miss Hunt there several times over the winter; might or might not have "stayed the night, sometime around Christmas"; and, when Miss Hunt was not home, sometime in the spring, insisted upon being let into the apartment to see if something might have happened to her. (Vick said, in what must have been a pious tone, "This McCullough party, he offered me money to unlock the girl's door, but I said no thanks, mister. Told him it was a private residence and I didn't want to get mixed up in no kind of murder case if that's what it turned out to be.") Ah, Ian could imagine it! He had entirely forgotten Vick until this moment.

More upsetting, and far more shameful to read, were the testimonies of several friends. Ian had known they were being subpoenaed, or had half known, but had suppressed the knowledge; it would have pained him too deeply to imagine these people answering questions about him in so hostile an atmosphere. But now, in stark computer print, was the testimony of Roberta Grinnell, who had said that on the afternoon of April 23 she'd had a telephone conversation with Glynnis McCullough, during the course of which Mrs. McCullough had spoken to her of her husband's "alleged love affair" with a young woman named Sigrid Hunt. Mrs. McCullough was "extremely upset, as upset as I've ever known her," and "broke off our conversation rather suddenly." So far as she knew, Roberta stated, there was no substance to the accusation that Ian McCullough was having a love affair or did not love Glynnis, et cetera. Next, to Ian's considerable shock, was Elizabeth Kuhn, whom Glynnis had telephoned around noon of April 23, to ask for advice regarding her husband's "alleged infidelity" and other marital problems. Elizabeth too reported Glynnis's "distraught state of mind" and stated that, to her knowledge, Ian McCullough had never been unfaithful to his wife; indeed, the two had always been "an ideal, happy young couple, with a lovely daughter and a lovely house." Denis Grinnell made a brief, laconic statement, to the effect that he was "morally certain" that Ian McCullough was *not* having an affair with any woman; that the McCulloughs were *not* going through any kind of marital crisis; that they were *not* in the habit of drinking heavily, or quarreling, still less given to physical violence. Amos Kuhn, Malcolm Oliver, June Oliver, Vaughn Cassity, Meika Cassity, Leonard Oppenheim, Paul Owen, Dr. Max, Dr. Max's wife, Frieda, colleagues at the Institute, a dozen others gave statements, all of them brief, of the nature of Denis Grinnell's. Ian read them with a growing sense of hope. So many witnesses on his side! So many voices in support of his innocence! He might almost believe, reading these pages of the transcript, that he *was* innocent.

There was more, but this was enough. Ian handed the document back to Ottinger. He lit a cigarette—he'd recently begun smoking again, having quit fifteen years before—and said, "I understand now why the indictment was handed down. It is an ingenious story the prosecution has invented, sheerly fiction, but plausible. And then, you know, people want to believe. They have a sort of savage instinct for believing in romance."

Ottinger said carefully, "It *is* fiction?"

"Most of it."

" 'Most'—?"

"Most."

"But not all?"

Ian shrugged. "I've told you I don't care to talk about my private life," he said. He added, ironically, "My private sexual life."

"Your sexual life, it seems, has become public."

"It has *not* become public."

"The prosecution argues that you killed your wife, and did so intentionally, because you were in love with another woman and wanted your wife out of the way. And, on the face of it, the canceled check, the telephone calls, this Fermi Sabri's testimony, and the caretaker's—"

"A fabrication. A sequence of small truths that add up to an enormous lie."

"Obviously, you were involved with Sigrid Hunt. Otherwise you would not have given her money or telephoned her. Or visited her in Poughkeepsie. *Did* you visit her?"

"Once, because she called me. It was"—Ian hesitated, filled with rage at Ottinger for asking these questions—"it was a friendly visit, and nothing more. Not even 'friendly' as such because we weren't, the two of us, really friends. We were hardly acquaintances. She had met me, I don't remember where, it might have been at our house, a party of Glynnis's, a large cocktail party of Glynnis's, sixty or seventy people perhaps, and Sigrid Hunt and her fiancé were there, I really don't know why," Ian said, his voice quickening, and his face hot, "and there, suddenly, I turned around, and—they were *there*. And some weeks afterward she telephoned me, to ask help of me, as it turned out to borrow money of me, and I drove to her apartment in Poughkeepsie not knowing why she had called me or why on earth I was going there, like a man who has suspended all volition, simply coasting along as in a dream. And I did not know why, nor do I know why, even today. I only know that I deeply regret having done all that I did, and would give my very life if I could undo it. But the hourglass runs in one direction only. Its sands run in one direction only."

Ottinger regarded him closely. "You visited Hunt only once?"

Ian looked away. "I visited her only once but, yes, there was another time, the time the caretaker spoke of, when I'd been worried about her, not having been able to contact her, and I—yes, I did drive down, simply to see if . . . she was all right. I mean, if she might have been in trouble."

"And you asked the caretaker to let you in her apartment, and he refused?"

"He did not refuse. He let me in. He accepted twenty-five dollars from me. She was not there, of course." Ian picked a fleck of tobacco from his tongue. He wanted very badly to strike Ottinger in the face and wondered if the man sensed it, if that was why Ottinger was staring at him so keenly. "I had worried that she might be dead. That her fiancé might have killed her. She told me he treated her brutally, at times; she told me she was frightened of him. And somehow I was caught up in it. As I said, I don't know why. It must have been because I'd wanted to be."

"So she asked you for money?"

"I don't think she did, I think I offered it to her."

"And she accepted?"

"She accepted."

"And your wife found the canceled check?"

"Yes. Famously. As is known through North America."

"Do you know what the money was for?"

"An abortion."

"And was the father this Fermi Sabri?"

"As far as I know, yes."

"And not you."

Ian cast Ottinger a look of pure hatred. "And not me."

"So you were not having an affair, in the usual sense of the word, with Hunt."

Ian shook his head and did not reply.

"You were not in love with her, and you did not want to get rid of your wife in order to marry her. And Glynnis was mistaken in thinking . . . what it seems to have been she thought."

Again, Ian shook his head.

"But she became very upset, and very angry, and she accused you, and—"

"No. I don't remember."

"Is it possible that Glynnis attacked you, and you fended her off in self-defense, and—"

Ian got to his feet. "I've told you I don't want to talk about it," he said. "I will not talk about it. I will not violate Glynnis's privacy; I will not desecrate her, goddamn you, do you understand?"

He left Ottinger's office, plunged blindly down a flight of stairs, hurried out into the street. He'd wanted so desperately to strike Ottinger with his fists, he had to get away. But *I am not the sort of person who behaves like this*, he thought, in amazement. *Am I?*

OTTINGER CALLED HIM that evening, at home. "I've hired a private investigator to look for Hunt," he said. "We can't sit back and wait for Lederer to find her. He's a fellow I've worked with in the past, with some success." When Ian did not reply he added, "Of course, he doesn't come cheaply."

"Do any of us?" Ian said, and hung up the phone.

2.

At Glynnis's grave. In the early evening: a damp greeny quiet, swarms of gnats in the shadows. And mosquitoes: Ian slapped repeatedly at his bare arms, and at the back of his neck. God*damn*.

Bianca, squatting in her white shorts, white cotton pullover top, was picking away dead blooms and leaves from a geranium plant in a pink foil-wrapped pot. In the warm airless humidity of the August evening her skin glowed whitely, as if damply; her hair had been braided, not very expertly, and fell in a heavy rope between her shoulder blades. It was a habit father and daughter had fallen into, of visiting the cemetery twice a week, often, for expediency's sake, as they were tonight, on their way to somewhere else. (Ian, at least, was going to the Cassitys', to an outdoor barbecue. Bianca had been invited but would probably not come along.) She said, casually, "I was thinking, Daddy, it wouldn't be any trouble for me to take the fall semester off. And stay home—if you wanted me to."

Distracted as he was, invariably, at Glynnis's gravesite, for what after all does one *do*, what does one *say*, in such a place, where even grief seems crude and self-assuaging, Ian nonetheless heard his daughter's voice waver: for she'd meant to say, in a voice of heart-rending kindness, stay home with *you*.

He said quickly, "Of course not, honey, don't even think of such a thing. The trial has been postponed until after Thanksgiving now, and Nick is trying to get it pushed back again." Ian smiled at his daughter, who was looking so earnestly at him. What, he wondered, did she see? Was the man in her vision, as in her imagination, anyone with whom he might reasonably identify? He said, "He is busily filing motions, or writing briefs, whatever it is lawyers do with their days, ostensibly in the service of humanity. He is certain that things will turn out well, and I am certain they will, too. There's no need for you to interrupt your studies; I wish, really, you could put the matter out of your mind. And if . . ."

His words faded. He could not think what he meant to say.

Bianca said, as if enthusiastically, "I could stay home and work here. Reading, I mean. At school, that's mostly what I do, read; it seems so easy to stay away from classes."

Ian said, "I thought you were involved with other things too. Theatrical productions, dance. . . ."

Bianca looked at him oddly. "Dance? I was never involved with dance. And you wind up spending so much time, you need to have so much energy, for performance things. Things that people do together, in a group. So much effort goes into making one another believe, you know, that it's worthwhile; that it's real enough."

"But isn't it fun, too, working with other people? You seem to have enjoyed it, in the past."

Bianca crinkled her nose, as if she were trying to remember. The past? Which past? She said, stubbornly, "It requires a lot of faith to make some things real, that's all."

Ian had developed a fatherly distaste, a nervous tic of a reaction, when Bianca drifted onto her subject—it had become so specifically *hers*—of what is "real" and what is "not real." He said, "I suspect that all things are equally real, and that's the problem—how to choose."

"No," Bianca said, with her maddening serenity, "it isn't a problem for all of us."

Ian smiled and fumbled for his cigarettes, which, it seemed, he had left back in the car, or had not brought along at all, and said, more energetically, "Of course I don't want you to sacrifice another semester for me, Bianca. You've done so wonderfully; in fact I am filled with awe at you, not only your academic performance last spring but—how can I say it—*you*. You have held us both together, somehow. Everyone says—"

He paused, and added, "Not that I think it has been easy for you. My God, no."

Bianca frowned, picking now at another plant, one of those voluptuous flowering plants with the enormous blooms that looked, and perhaps were, dyed: this one was deep blue. Hydrangea? There were a half-dozen potted plants at the head of Glynnis's grave, each quite large and surely expensive; all were overblown, now, and required trimming. You could see, quickly scanning this section of the cemetery, that Glynnis McCullough's was a *popular* grave.

And would that please her? Ian wondered. As, in life, it had meant so strangely much?

Bianca was saying, in her low, murmurous, rather too restrained voice, ". . . as things work themselves through, in another year or so; I'm not impatient and I can wait, but—well, when they do . . . maybe my junior year . . . there's this program in Thailand, for teaching English and just sort of helping out, in, I guess you could call them, rural villages. . . . It's no big deal: nothing like the Peace Corps. What I'd hope for is that I'd learn, you know, from the Thais. Their way of life, you know, and their tradition. I'd learn, I'm sure, a lot more than I'd be teaching *them*. Then I could come back and get my BA, East Asian Studies probably, and I'd have an advantage; I will have learned the language, and learned about the religion, the specific kind or kinds of Buddhism they practice . . . it's all very complex, you know, like a language with any number of dialects. The only way to learn anything genuine is from the inside, Daddy, don't you think?"

"A program in Thailand? Teaching English?"

"Actually it's in Burma, Ceylon, Laos, and Nepal, too. But from what I've read, and people have told me, Thailand seems just right."

"You'd spend a year of your life in Thailand, teaching English in a village?"

"Did I say a year? It might be less than that, or more. The program sets you up, you know, it's all very structured; my adviser at school was saying . . ."

Ian listened to Bianca and did not interrupt. He saw, in her hopeful face, in the glisten of her wide intelligent evasive eyes, that if he loved her he must not interrupt. His daughter was plotting the desperate way she might escape from him, while, beneath her, so very literally and precisely beneath her, the dead woman who had been her mother lay in her ebony coffin, sheerly matter now. Matter disintegrating into its elements. How Bianca might escape him, and how she might escape *that*.

Bianca said, "Mainly I just want to *learn*, I want to be filled with something—well, I don't know how to put it, something that isn't, you know, just *me*." She paused and wiped at her damp upper lip. "Just—*us*."

"Of course, honey. I see."

Still, on the way home, Ian, always the professional, the professional father it might be said, thoughtfully named the friends, acquaintances, colleagues, professional contacts of his who were involved in one way or another with East Asia and who might be of help to her: economists, anthropologists, political scientists, historians; an ex-student of his in population research and demography, at the Center for East Asian Studies in Washington; an old classmate from Harvard who was deputy chief of mission at the embassy in Rangoon. Bianca listened politely and did not interrupt.

3.

It was a season of stasis: each day interminable, unimaginable. Had it not been for his work, the consolation of hours—for there is no end to statistics, nor to the ever more refined programming of variable futures—he doubted he could endure. For one must live after all in the present tense: the next five minutes is the great challenge. Except for accepting an invitation to Cape Cod, to spend a few days with Denis and Roberta, at the cottage they usually rented for the month of August, Ian had made no plans for the summer except to get through it.

Yet he was cheerful enough, with an air of energy, resigned good-will. Smiling when necessary, proffering his hand to be shaken. Hello, how are you! Hello, how are *you!* These many months, he could not once recall being rebuffed. For those colleagues, acquaintances, former friends who wished to shun him were discreet enough to do it without calling attention to themselves. Hazelton-on-Hudson was one of the civilized places of the world.

Of course, social invitations were down. The telephone rarely rang. Glynnis would have been crushed, mystified. What has happened to us, she would have said, what on earth has happened to us, we tried so hard, we tried so very hard, what has happened?

4.

The kind of s.o.b. you'd like to stick a hot iron up his ass, see how he likes it. That was Ian's father's voice: unbidden, unanticipated, asserting itself ever more frequently in Ian's consciousness, in that uncertain state between sleep and waking, when the soul is thin as a wisp of smoke. He had not heard the voice in years, in decades, had not wished to hear it, and had not supposed its recall his prerogative. His father had been a complex man, Ian supposed, in retrospect: clearly intelligent, and yet deliberately stupid; suffused with anger, yet insistently maudlin, if not sentimental; a chronic alcoholic, yet given to frequent campaigns of reform. *Your mother will have to meet me halfway,* Ian's father often said to Ian, and Ian, a small child at the time, had a confused and frightened vision of his mother walking something like a workman's plank stretched between buildings, or a tightrope. *I can't do it alone and the bloody woman well knows it, wants me to fail I wouldn't doubt, but I'm my own man and I do what I want to do, self-righteous bitch like all of them in her family.* The words were incoherent when most impassioned, but his son always understood their meaning.

A small-time merchant with a store, rented, on a block of failing stores, in a "transitional" neighborhood in Bridgeport. A sales representative for a failing company, working out of his car—a Nash? Studebaker?—driving hundreds of miles a week. *Think I'm made out of money* the voice intoned, in the midst of thudding noises, the kitchen chairs knocked about: *Bloodsuckers,* the refrigerator door opened and shut, hard, in a fury of disappointment; *Think I don't know you're listening well I know it and I don't give a good goddamn, hear me? Don't give a shit.* Ian and his mother were hiding in the back bedroom; Ian's mother had dragged a chair against the door, as if a mere chair were adequate to keep that fury at a distance, a mere door adequate to muffle the terrible droning voice.

But there was little physical violence. Ian recalled some slaps, shoves, punches with closed fists, yet, strangely, could not recall if these were directed against his mother, or against him, or against them both. Most nights, the rampages in the kitchen played themselves out; the ravings came to an abrupt end; Ian's father would collapse on the sofa and begin almost at once to snore, or slam melodramatically out of the house and stay away for the night, or for days, or, eventually, for weeks. His presence was reduced to infrequent and unexpected telephone calls that terrified Ian's mother as much as the man himself had done.

So gradually did Michael McCullough disappear from the life of the household, with so much the waning energy of a moribund comet, there was never an hour, still less a profound moment, when his son might have said, *At last we are free,* or, more somberly, *I will never see him again.*

My father did not die, Ian realized. His death had merely been reported.

It was Roberta Grinnell who telephoned Ian, from Cape Cod, to remind him he was expected to visit. To stay for as long as he liked. And why didn't he bring Bianca along? There were plenty of beds.

"Our sons," Roberta said, "are off on their own this summer. Jobs in Maine and Colorado; did Denis tell you?"

"Yes," Ian said, though he wasn't sure Denis had told him. "And Bianca too has a job."

"That YM-YWCA thing she did last summer, at the camp? Swimming lessons?"

"Yes," Ian said. He thought it touching that Roberta should remember what his daughter had done the previous summer. He wasn't certain he would have remembered, himself.

Still Roberta persisted, as if they were really talking of something else, "Why *don't* you bring her along, though? Labor Day weekend. The camp breaks up about then."

When their children were younger, and life had seemed, strangely, for all its surface difficulties, far easier to negotiate, the McCulloughs and the Grinnells had often spent parts of their summers together: at Cape Cod, or in Maine, or near Lake Placid in the Adirondacks, where Glynnis's family owned a camp (the "cottage" slept twelve adults, the property consisted of five hundred acres of pine forest); one memorable time the Grinnells met up with the McCulloughs in Italy, in Bellagio, where Ian was concluding his residency at the Rockefeller Center, and, in a rented van, the families made a tour through Italy, Greece, the south of France, Spain, and Portugal—an adventure of some six extravagant weeks that would one day be reduced, with the anecdotal economy of picture postcards, to a very few vignettes starring one or another of the principals. Do you remember, Denis would say, that night in Milano; do you remember, Glynnis would say, that dreadful hotel in Valencia;

and Roberta would press her hands over her ears, and Ian would laugh and threaten to stalk out of the room: no more tales of tainted seafood in Majorca, Rome in clamorous traffic, the polluted air and maniacal street traffic of Athens, the scavenger birds over Apollo's shrine at Delphi, the melancholy fact, taken from an unusually frank guidebook, that Sophocles' Colonus is now the site of an industrial slum. Ian himself had frequently risen to the occasion, travel-weary, insomniac, dyspeptic, reciting Oedipus' "I have been saved / for something great and terrible, something strange" at his most inspired hour. But he could not remember what followed, or had preceded, that hour. Diarrhea, perhaps.

"We were always so happy together," Ian said.

Roberta said, "What? This line is buzzing."

"Our summers. We were always so happy."

"Yes. Oh, yes, of course. That's why," Roberta said, speaking quickly, "we want you to come stay with us. And bring Bianca too if you can."

Ian said faintly, "Yes, yes, I'll try," and hung up rather abruptly.

He thought, But am I free to leave Hazelton—with the trial set for November 30? He would have to check with Ottinger; he really didn't know.

He thought, Of course I won't take them up on the invitation, they are only being kind.

HE DROVE UP to Cape Cod alone at the very end of August, nervously apprehensive of the visit—for Glynnis's absence would be more potent than any presence, in such close quarters—but innocently content, even at times rather ecstatic, with the drive itself. It was not a long trip, as trips go: not quite three hundred miles. But he was determined to enjoy each mile.

He fantasized Jonathan Hamilton, who had never sinned. Or had yet to sin.

When he arrived at the cottage the Grinnells had visitors, not houseguests but visitors from Provincetown: friendly enough people, they seemed, their names passing too quickly for Ian to catch, their handshakes quick, too, though sincere enough; or so it seemed. It was the sort of situation in which Ian quite naturally depended upon Glynnis to remember names and to attach them to the correct faces; he'd long ago stopped making any attempt at all. Denis shook his hand happily and Roberta embraced him, a bit stiffly, Ian thought, but kissed his cheek, invariably the right cheek, out of years of habit, and welcomed him, seemed quite genuine in welcoming him, remarking upon "how dramatically different" he looked—his hair combed forward in the new way, the green plastic lenses clipped over his glasses. The several bottles of wine Ian had brought were taken from him, with thanks, and if any of them, Ian included, had an impulse to look around for Glynnis, that impulse was discreetly blocked.

Denis, whose breath smelled, not disagreeably, of beer, was wearing swimming trunks and a sweat-stained T-shirt; his mood was aggressively sociable, as Ian rather liked it. He opened a beer to hand to Ian and said, "Where's Bianca? I thought Bianca was coming?" and Ian said, "No, she has a job with the—" as Roberta interrupted.

"I *told* you, Denis, Bianca has a summer job; she couldn't come," Roberta said irritably, looking now at Ian and, beyond him, at the others. "He never listens to me; he nods and agrees but doesn't *listen*," and they all laughed, Ian included, and, after a moment, Denis. One of the women said, as if to ingratiate herself with the company, "Albert is exactly the same way."

Roberta, hair tied back in a scarf, shoulders, arms, legs warmly tanned, slender in a shift of some crinkled Indian-looking fabric, led Ian into the house, into "his" bedroom, with its double bed, its floral-print wallpapered walls, its dramatic view of the beach, sea, sky. Is this a bed in which Glynnis and I have slept? Ian wondered. He supposed it must be. Yes, the nubby white bedspread looked familiar. The floor of dark blue painted planks, the handwoven oval rugs, the filmy white curtains blowing in the breeze. Ian bent to the window and inhaled the salt air, and his eyes filled unexpectedly with tears. "We were always so happy," he said. "We seemed to be living in a sort of golden age that went on and on and—"

"You don't mind sharing the bathroom, do you, Ian? It's out in the hall, through here . . . you probably remember."

"I remember."

Ian let his suitcase fall on the bed. He caught a glimpse of his reflection, blurred in motion, in the bureau mirror: the tinted lenses gave him a sporty look, edged with something sinister; or was it a sinister look, edged with something sporty. He had started a mustache a few weeks ago but shaved it off at Bianca's insistence. ("You look like Richard Widmark in the Late Movie," Bianca said, giving a little scream of laughter, as she so rarely did now. "The psychopathic sympathetic killer.")

Roberta stood in the doorway, arms folded beneath her breasts, telling Ian about their guests for the evening: who was staying for dinner and who was not, the man who did documentary films for Public Television, the botanist from Harvard, the woman violinist with the Boston Symphony. . . . As if, Ian thought, I give a damn for any of them except you.

She was looking very attractive: the ocean air suited her. The dark-gold strand of hair at her temple looked burnished as if with health.

Ian opened his suitcase, quickly, before Roberta could slip away, and turned brandishing an ebony cane, did a Fred Astaire sort of shuffle with it, and, as Roberta stared, unscrewed the cane's grip and let its contents fall onto the bed: a rolled-up backgammon board, chips, and dice. "Remember this crazy thing?" he said, grinning.

Roberta laughed. "What on earth *is* it?"

"The birthday present you and Denis gave me," Ian said. "I mean, one of the presents. A backgammon set. I thought we could play, if . . . if we had time." The joke, if it was a joke, seemed to have misfired; Roberta was staring at him in incomprehension. "Didn't you give it to me? You and Denis? For my birthday?" Ian asked, embarrassed. His face had gone unpleasantly hot.

"No," said Roberta, "it wasn't us." Then, seeing Ian's face, his look of hurt and chagrin, she said, "But maybe Denis did, on his own. I don't exactly remember. It's his sort of humor, isn't it?"

THAT EVENING THEY ate on a picnic table overlooking the beach: Roberta, and Denis, and Ian, and a couple named Hicks, and a couple named Braun, and a middle-aged woman named Molly, a fading beauty in a sunburst sun hat, who fixed her gaze upon Ian McCullough with so singular an intensity, Ian understood she must know who he was; what he'd done. Of course, the Grinnells had thought it necessary to inform their guests, before his arrival. He did not blame them in the slightest.

Denis grilled tuna steaks, and delicious steaks they were. And Roberta served German potato salad, and corn on the cob, and sourdough bread, and chocolate mousse from a charcuterie in Provincetown. They drank beer, and Ian's gift wine, and several other bottles of wine. "Like old times!" Denis said, raising his glass, and everyone said, "Like old times!" without knowing what he meant. They passed around the bowl containing the chocolate mousse until its lovely creamy substance was scraped clean away.

Ian and Albert Hicks fell into a conversation of some seriousness and drifted away from the others, walking, with difficulty, in the sand, Ian barefoot and Hicks in sandals, each smoking a cigarette from Hicks's pack of Luckies. Hicks was the documentary filmmaker, a big man, muscular yet soft-bellied, with kindly crinkled eyes and a pointed, clipped beard, like a nineteenth-century dandy. He knew, he said, who Ian was. He'd read about it in the papers. McCullough was the name, too, of distant relatives, so there was that connection; not, of course, that it *was* any connection . . . just the name. He told Ian a story that was, in his words, a true story; it had happened to him when he was nineteen, a Sigma Chi at Cornell. "This was a long time ago, of course, we're talking about the early 1950s, and we'd had a beer party, the fraternity, and went out sailing; I got a little crew of us to go out sailing, a nasty gusty April day, on Lake Cayuga, and I was blind drunk I mean I was stoned and these fraternity brothers of mine were as bad if not worse and I was supposedly the sailor, the expert, and we got out there in the middle of the lake and the wind was rising and a rain started and next thing we knew the sail was in the water and we were in the water and one of us didn't make it, this boy I'd liked a lot; it turned out he couldn't swim, or couldn't swim well enough to save himself, and being blind drunk like he was he couldn't hang on to the boat, and when we were picked up there were just three of us, and his body was lost; and you know, there isn't a day of my life when I don't think of it, and of him," Hicks said, spreading his fingers and staring at them, "though the lawsuit his family brought against me, for criminal negligence, was settled out of court, and they didn't get all that much. They were nice folks but they hated me; I mean they hated my guts, could have torn me open with their teeth, but *my* folks fought it in court, my father's lawyer, and we came off all right, and it wasn't that bad, I mean in the newspapers, but I transferred to Colgate and deactivated from the fraternity;

it seemed the best thing to do. I feel that I am blameless, yet of course it was my fault, the shithead sailing idea was my fault; in my heart I know I'm responsible but I never talk about it. I never did then, and I never do now. My wife doesn't know. I mean, she doesn't know much. She'd just say, 'Al, you mustn't blame yourself'; she'd say, like they all do, 'Al, you're too hard on yourself, it was just an accident, why don't you forget it?' There is a limit to what you can tell people because there is a limit to what they can hear. Beyond that point you're only talking to yourself. . . . It's a lonely predicament."

Ian agreed, it was a lonely predicament.

IN THE MORNING, Denis said to Ian, quizzically, "What were you and Al Hicks talking about last night? I hope he didn't bore you."

"Not at all," Ian said.

"He's a sweet guy but he can be terribly intense. Does these prize-winning documentaries on AIDS victims, runaway children, battered wives. . . . I hope he didn't bore you or upset you, or whatever."

"Not at all," Ian said, smiling. "He didn't bore me in the slightest."

Denis looked at him as if he wanted to ask something more, but said nothing.

It was a warm windless hazy morning, with a fishy odor, a taste of brine. The surf was subdued, its percussive rhythm muted. Ian said happily, "Last night I slept deeply for the first time in a long time; I don't remember anything, any dreams. I seemed to have been borne along somehow by the water, as if I were in the water, lifted up and let down, lifted up, let down, *in* the water, and no margin of consciousness to interfere." He looked at Denis with wide shining eyes. "I'm so very grateful, you know, to you and Roberta. I told Roberta, over the phone," he said, not remembering if he really had. "In all this misery, you have been so . . . kind."

He had been intending to say "faithful."

Denis smiled guardedly and clapped Ian on the shoulder. "Well," he said. "Now it's morning."

Denis was unshaven; his eyes lightly netted with blood, his face rather puffy. At breakfast he'd complained amusingly of a headache, a hangover headache, those people the night before had stayed so late and what's to be done, you can't ask guests to leave after all. . . . (Roberta had inconspicuously slipped away from the party around midnight; Ian, not long afterward. He had slept in such a bliss of oblivion, exhausted, alcohol- and surf-lulled, he'd had no idea when the party had broken up.) "You *can't* ask guests to leave after all," Denis repeated, with emphasis, and Ian understood that the remark was directed at Roberta, who stood, her back to the men, at the stove, preparing breakfast, removing strips of bacon from a large iron skillet and laying them, as neatly as Glynnis had done, on a paper napkin, to absorb the excess grease. She was barelegged and barefoot; wore a red polka-dot halter top of a kind a teen-aged girl might wear, showing much of her smooth, freckled, golden-tanned back; white linen Bermuda shorts that hid, to a degree, the disproportionate thickness of her legs above the knees. Her hair was again tied back in a scarf, tightly knotted, and her silence, her very posture, possessed a disturbingly renitent quality Ian would not have wished to goad, as Denis clearly did.

But no response was forthcoming, no quarrel provoked. Roberta set the men's breakfast plates down before them and smilingly accepted their thanks, but did not sit with them. She'd already eaten, she said. She had a dozen chores to do this morning . . . the weekend was coming up so quickly. She drifted off, barefoot, coffee mug in hand. Ian looked after her with longing and regret. Was she angry at him? Was she angry at all? Minutes later the telephone rang, and he could hear her voice in another part of the house. He could make out no words, only the sound of her voice: clear, high, uncomplicated, melodic. He felt a sharp pang of envy, thinking, She will never greet me like that again.

Perhaps Denis was thinking the same thought. He hunched over his plate, and grimaced, and said wryly, "Christ. I can guess who *that* is. 'Roberta, we just happen to be in the vicinity . . .' "

That afternoon, driving into Provincetown in Denis's car, Denis said casually that, as Ian had probably noticed, things were "unnaturally tense" between him and Roberta lately.

Ian said, "I hadn't noticed."

Denis shrugged. He said, embarrassed, evasive, "It isn't important, really. I hate to mention it. I just thought you might have noticed and felt uneasy. This is supposed to be a holiday for you, after all."

"It's a marvelous holiday," Ian said quickly, his voice flat and unconvincing in his own ears. "I hadn't noticed any . . . tension."

"We never quarrel. She doesn't have the temperament for it. A few words exchanged, and she's exhausted . . . she claims. But there is a feeling of something cold, hard, indifferent, unjudging. Sometimes I'm frantic with rage; the woman just *stands* there, won't *say* anything, just *looks* at me as if she's looking through me, with that SpiderWoman look of hers, under the eyelids . . . yet at the same time she's the woman you know, the woman we all know, patient, gentle, warm generous hospitable unfailingly good-hearted . . . *good*." Denis pressed down harder on the accelerator, barreling along the crowded highway. His jaws clenched with feeling; his eyes seemed to strain in their sockets. "Sometimes I have the feeling, Ian, that they are all playing a game of some kind, the women we know: our women—with the exception of Glynnis; I don't care to talk about Glynnis at the moment—the women of Hazelton, the wives, playing an elaborate game . . . behind our backs. *We* are the game, but we can't see it. The way they simulate happiness, answering the telephone, opening the door to guests, where, a moment before, there was something very different . . . from happiness."

Ian, not liking the drift of Denis's argument, said, "But we are all like that, aren't we, to a degree? It isn't hypocrisy; it's simply a sense of decorum. Our obligation to one another: to be pleasant, agreeable, *civil*." When Denis said nothing, he added, "There is a lovely observation of George Santayana's I read years ago: 'Masks are arrested expressions and admirable echoes of feelings once faithful, discreet, and superlative. Living things in contact with the air must acquire cuticles, and it should not be urged against cuticles that they are not—"

Suddenly Ian could not remember the rest of it. And Denis did not seem to be listening. He said, bitterly, "She said she'd forgiven me, you know, for that time a few years ago, that affair I'd had, which I think I told you about . . . that mistake I made. But it seems, beneath it all, she has not. Maybe she can't. Maybe, in her place, I would feel the same way: reluctant to forgive. There are certain aboriginal instincts in us; or maybe they are metaphysical, even linguistic. How did you phrase it? 'Things once said can't be unsaid.' One might add, 'Or forgotten.' "

Ian wondered, with a stab of anxiety, if Roberta had told Denis of his behavior toward her: his desperate embrace, his faltering plea. . . . She would not have been so cruel, he decided. Even if she detests me.

"So, it seems, I made two mistakes. The first, becoming involved with another woman; the second, confessing the fact to my wife. Yet Roberta assured me she *had* forgiven me. . . ."

Denis cast Ian a fleeting sidelong glance: a look, Ian thought, of raw appeal; yet there was a defensiveness in his tone, a thick stubborn squareness about his jaws, that spoke of another motive. He was driving both aggressively and absentmindedly, often, to Ian's discomfort, lifting both hands from the steering wheel at the same time. The conversation had become a monologue to which Ian was a privileged witness.

"And then I'm so lonely sometimes. All these parties we go to and give—or used to, before last spring. And in a family, at the very hub of a family, a household . . . it can be so much more intensely worse. Because you know you should not be lonely there. Because you know you have no right to be; it's selfish, self-pitying. And, too, there is a sort of taboo about talking about it. . . ."

Ian, whose loneliness was less theoretical, murmured a vague assent.

"The boys are grown; they have their own lives, a network of friends, plans for the future that exclude us. Of course I understand completely—*I* had my own life at that age and would have suffocated if I had not—but still, when it happens to you, it's something of a shock. That they so clearly prefer not only the company of others but a type, a texture, a *quality* of company so different from our own. . . . And in the center of it, as women are invariably in the 'center,' there stands Roberta, watching me, not even with suspicion now but with a cold unblaming unjudging eye, beyond suspicion." He paused and said, in a burst of sudden feeling, "She doesn't love me any longer—"

Ian said, "Don't be ridiculous. Of course she loves you."

"—but she won't admit it. The words, the actual words, she can't bring herself to say: *I no longer love you.*"

"Obviously she—"

"Since last spring. Sometime last spring. I think it began when Glynnis was first hospitalized and we were all so upset, so disoriented, as if some sort of law of nature had been suspended . . . or violated. Roberta took Glynnis's death very hard, as I did, and of course," Denis said, quietly, "it is still very much with us. It remains a *fact* prominent in our *data.* I needn't tell you that. . . . In any case, it began then, this sort of estrangement, simply not talking to each other as much as we always have, a gradual atrophying of . . . whatever it is that keeps people together. The frustrating thing is, I hear her on the telephone all the time with her women friends, or her sister, someone *not me* to whom she feels she can talk. (And she's quite close to Leonard and Paul, too; *that* kind of man, they can relate to. Glynnis was the same way.) I don't mean that I eavesdrop. I would never eavesdrop." He looked at Ian and smiled bitterly. "But if you do overhear, you know, by accident, they never seem to be talking about anything substantial. Laughing a good deal, and interrupting each other, finishing each other's sentences. Possibly they talk in code. I wonder if anyone has ever attempted a deconstructionist analysis of women's conversation, or something in the style of *The Raw and the Cooked*."

Ian said, "We men talk directly, is that it? In a vocabulary untainted by ambiguity."

But his irony seemed to make no impression on Denis, who was saying, in the same hurt tone, edged now with resentment, "So long as they *love* you they are one sort of being, but when they've decided to stop *loving* you—by which, incidentally, I don't mean *liking, tolerating, enduring* you—they shift into another sort of being altogether, a wholly other consciousness. Even the way they look at you changes: the very pupils of their eyes contract! It's a weird thing, obvious maybe, even banal, maybe, but when it happens to you . . . it's a considerable shock, as if the earth had shifted beneath your feet. You can feel it *spinning*."

Denis had begun to speak rapidly and incoherently. Ian laughed and said, "But we spin with the earth, don't we? It's all a single motion." He laid a tentative hand on Denis's forearm: not to silence him, still less to rebuke him, but to waken him to a sense of where he was (downtown Provincetown) and what he was doing (looking for a parking place). The congestion was dismaying; even the side streets were clogged with traffic; pedestrians, many of them gay men in fashionable resort wear and styled haircuts, arms slung around one another's shoulders, were crossing streets in defiance of, or indifference to, traffic lights, passing dangerously close to Denis's car.

"She accuses me of not hearing her, when I hear her very well. Of not seeing her, when I see her very well. I 'see' her regarding me with a look of utter pitying disdain; as if, knowing that I love her, that my life, for better or worse, is bound up with hers, out of inertia, maybe, if not out of passion—though inertia at our age *is* a passion, and should never be underestimated—she knows she has me trapped. To be separated from Roberta would be death for me, now that"—and here Denis faltered slightly, not looking at Ian—"other things in my life have come undone."

Ian said, pointing, "There's a parking place. If you maneuver quickly—"

But it was too late. Denis blundered on and turned a corner, headed for a parking garage up the street at whose entrance SORRY: FILLED had been posted.

"Shit," he said, braking at the entrance. He backed up, turned another corner, drove on. He said, as if his monologue were uninterrupted, "There is a sense in which Roberta's accusations have some grounding in fact, because lately I have had trouble seeing: I mean quite literally with my vision. It's the left eye that gives me the trouble. Most of the trouble. I went to the optometrist and he seemed baffled: it isn't nearsightedness, or farsightedness; in fact my eyes are rather good, he says, for a man of my age—I don't need reading glasses yet, and there are friends of ours, for instance Vaughn, who have had bifocals for years. And you?—yes?—you have bifocals, don't you? In my case it's something else, as if, now and then, the light and color drained out of things, I keep glancing up at the sky as if the trouble were there, a massive cloud over the sun, or an eclipse. Then there is a glowering hazy light, *this* light in fact, as if a photograph were overexposed. A scrim of bubbles, sparks, emptinesses, like black holes—except they are filled with light, blinding light, and not . . . nothing. I'm on the stairs and suddenly the stairs disappear, and I reach for the railing that both is and is not there; not that I stumble, exactly, because ninety percent of my life is automatic; I'm on automatic pilot like most of us, I suppose; but *I* know, and it's disconcerting. When I read there sometimes seem to be patches of blank on the page, that are filled in, slowly, with words; or, if I manage to read quickly enough, at my usual pace, I can keep ahead of the patches of blank. Even my dreams are affected, sometimes," Denis said, laughing, "fading out, blanking out, dissolving to nothing. Have you ever heard of anything more absurd?"

Ian said, "But didn't the optometrist refer you to a—"

"Oh, yes. Of course. An ophthalmologist. I'll see the bastard after Labor Day. But I doubt he'll be able to help me."

"Why do you say that?"

Denis shrugged loftily. "It's a feeling I have."

He found a parking place at last, brazening out, to Ian's embarrassment, a young woman in a Volkswagen who had gotten there first but had pulled too far forward. And in the grocery store, and in the beer and liquor store, he was all business: brisk and genial and in no mood to linger. "Don't you hate it sometimes, this constant buying, spending, consuming?" he asked Ian, who had to fight lapsing into a mild trance in such places, dazed by an excess of stimuli. "A steady stream of food and drink processed through us as through reeds. Was it Pascal who said, 'Man is a thinking reed' or was it Aristotle?"

"Aristotle said, 'Man is a thinking animal.' "

"Thinking *animal*, thinking *reed*, what the hell. It comes to the same thing in the end."

The cashier, a college boy with long straggly hair gathered into a ponytail, had been listening to their conversation, observing them through his eyelashes. As he rang up Denis's purchases he said with a shy smile, "My favorite philosopher is Lucretius. 'The swerve of the atoms.' He had no instruments, but he knew it all."

"He did," Denis said, enthusiastically. "The son of a bitch, he did. Left nothing for the rest of us but filling in the blanks."

ON THE WAY home Denis drove less compulsively; their talk was of professional matters: news of the Institute, who was coming for fall/winter residencies and to give symposia; who was traveling where and doing what and for what purpose. They drank Anchor Steam, a beer new to Ian, from cans, and Ian quite liked the dreamy hazy air through which Denis's car moved, punctuated by stops and starts and the intrusion of other vehicles as a dream is punctuated by external sounds, yet not interrupted. He liked too the sharp darting pain between his eyes that accompanied his first beer of the day, especially if he drank it down quickly. Was it the beer itself or its metallic iciness? he wondered. She was waiting for them at the beach. Her eyes would lift smiling to his when he appeared.

Denis was talking of being courted—"with a truly flattering aggression"—by the Arhardt Center for Strategic and International Studies in Washington, one of those mysteriously funded foundations that address themselves, usually quite publicly, to such issues as the defense budget, antiterrorism, nuclear stockpiling and World War III, and the like: pimping for the generals, Ian thought it, since it was no secret that the Pentagon funded certain of these foundations or arranged for funds to be channeled into them. Before the ruin of his reputation, Ian McCullough too had been approached, upon occasion, by the Arhardt Center—or the Georgetown Center, or the La Jolla Center, or the McIntyre Center: invited to participate in symposia, to act as a consultant, to accept a full-time position as a "senior fellow" in such seemingly academic divisions as Third World population growth. Of course, like all his liberal-minded colleagues, Ian had politely declined these invitations.

Now Denis complained dryly, "I wish the bastards would leave me alone; I don't quite see myself ending my career as a professional Père Joseph," and Ian said, "I don't quite see that either," though he felt uneasy with the subject and wondered what Denis was getting at. It was no secret that, having been passed over as a candidate for the director-ship at Hazelton, and having been interviewed no less than three times by the prestigious Mellon Foundation for a high-ranking position there, and again been disappointed, Denis was feeling professionally slighted: personally wounded, if not insulted, in one of those career phases in which abrupt, dramatic, but not invariably wise decisions are made to spite those who have valued us less than we imagine we deserve.

"It's your association with me," Ian said.

"My what?"

"Your friendship with . . . Never mind," he said. "I'm thinking of something else."

"You've turned the Arhardt people down once or twice, haven't you?" Denis asked. "What was it, some sort of fellowship? Or was it administrative?"

"I don't remember," Ian said, "I didn't give it much thought." Not meaning to sound so smugly superior he asked, "What do they want with you? A touch of glamour?"

"There's an extravagant new chair of 'political economics' they are establishing, with a six-million-dollar endowment," Denis said. "Of course it's out of the question. It's a think-tank Disneyworld, toadying to the Pentagon, the President . . . if not worse. I've stopped returning their calls; if I set up there I'd have to shave without a mirror, to avoid looking myself in the eye."

Ian said, thoughtfully, "It isn't that difficult, in fact, to shave *with* a mirror and not look yourself in the eye."

"Isn't it!" Denis said, embarrassed. He drained his can of Anchor Steam, and asked Ian if he'd be kind enough to open him another.

After a moment he asked, guardedly, as he invariably did when approaching this subject, "How are things going, Ian?—with Ottinger, I mean. And all that."

Ian said simply that things were going well, as well as might be expected; he liked Ottinger and respected him, though he did not much respect the law—its adversarial structure, its endless proliferation of detail, its mind-numbing tedium. He would have wished, he said, to get the trial out of the way by now; to have his fate decided for him. "Not, of course, that the issue of my guilt or innocence will be irrevocably decided," Ian said in a neutral voice. "If we lose, there is always the appeal."

Denis said, "Don't be ridiculous: you're not going to lose."

They drove for a while in silence. Ian shut his eyes, grateful for the wind against his sunburnt face—he'd swum that morning in the surf, and the Grinnells' suntan lotion had not been strong enough to protect his fair, thin skin—liking the smell of the ocean and the heated sand. Liking too the fact of his friend beside him: not any friend, but Denis, placating him with quick nervous assurances that, however unconvincing, were enormously comforting to hear. *Don't worry,* voices must console us, *you will be all right,* we must be told, *this will only hurt for a fraction of a second: steady!* Loving murmurous voices: *Trust in us.*

Ian opened his eyes and said, "I'd halfway wanted to plead guilty. To get it over, at the arraignment. Had you heard that?"

"I did," Denis said, "and I think you were out of your mind."

"They thought so too. But we could have plea-bargained; you know what plea bargaining is, the salvation of the criminal justice system: a murderer agrees to charges of manslaughter, a manslaughterer to charges of assault, the rapist to charges of sexual misconduct. But Nick Ottinger says I am innocent and will be completely vindicated by the trial; he says there has been no crime, consequently nothing can be proved 'beyond a shadow of a doubt.' So there is that hope. There is always that hope. And, technically speaking," he added, "I *am* innocent."

"Of course you're innocent," Denis said.

" 'Innocent,' under our law, 'until proven guilty.' "

Denis did not reply; Ian's banter grated against his nerves, perhaps; it was not a side of Ian McCullough he wished to encourage. After a pause he asked, "Do you think about it all the time?"

And Ian, without giving the question a moment's thought, said, "Yes. Of course."

"Even when you're thinking of other things, I suppose," Denis said speculatively.

And Ian said, "Yes, even when I am thinking of other things."

"It sounds like hell, frankly," Denis said.

Ian said, thoughtfully, "There is the trial, and there is Glynnis: her death and her burial. And our married life leading up to the night of the accident. My entire life, in fact, leading up to that night. Leading up to this very moment." He laid his hand against the doorframe, where the window was rolled down; the metal burned his fingers. "Other things are real enough, other people," he said, thinking of his daughter, and of Roberta, "but on the other side of a sort of barrier from me: a gigantic pane of glass. This time I don't want to break the glass."

Denis pulled into the sandy rutted lane that linked the cottages along their stretch of beach, and, quickly, secure in the knowledge that they had no more than a few minutes to talk, Ian said, as he'd wanted to say for weeks, that Ottinger had gone through most of the grand jury's minutes with him; that he had seen the list of witnesses and read the witnesses' testimonies; that he'd been deeply moved by the things that Denis had said about him. Denis said, "For Christ's sake, Ian, what did I say about you that isn't absolutely self-evident?"

"Nonetheless," Ian said, "in the context of . . ."

"I don't know about any context," Denis said, staring, "but please don't thank me for saying things that anyone in his right mind would say about you." He spoke loudly, incredulously. "I'm sure that all of us who were subpoenaed by that prick Lederer, and who will testify in your defense at the trial, said the same things I did. For Christ's sake, don't make an issue of it; let's drop it right now. You seem to be forgetting . . ."

"Yes? Forgetting?"

"Who you are."

LATER THAT DAY, when they were having drinks on the beach, the Grinnells, and Ian, and some visitors from Cambridge—among them an attractive couple whom it seemed Ian had once met, though he could not in all conscience recall their meeting: the man a freelance writer of biographies, as he identified himself, the woman, much younger, an artist and photographer, as she identified herself—Ian made the company laugh, made Denis snort with laughter, in fact, by wryly acknowledging his "altered status" in the intellectual community. "The great advantage of my situation," he said, "is that, now, virtually no one asks me for letters of recommendation; my ducklings have all paddled away."

Denis said, "*My* ducklings, bless their hearts, I'll have until *I* paddle away."

So they laughed, as if with relief, that the air (perhaps) had been cleared; except for Roberta, who, smiling, stared into the tall frosted glass in her hand, a plain fizzing drink of some kind, very likely club soda, into which Denis had dropped a neat crescent moon of lime.

"IF YOU'VE BEEN avoiding me, I mean being alone with me," Ian said, "I quite understand. I don't, you know, want to embarrass you. I don't . . ." He paused; could not think what he meant to say, standing in Roberta's kitchen, tall, slope-shouldered, rather too thin, self-conscious as an adolescent boy. He wore khaki shorts and a T-shirt, white, freshly laundered, that fitted his torso loosely; his legs, thin also, bony-kneed, covered in fine fair hairs like down, seemed to him unnaturally pale in this healthy sunny seaside setting. ". . . don't after all want you to *dis*like me."

Roberta laughed nervously and smiled at him, or made the attempt, a blush like an imperfectly realized birthmark rising from her neck to her cheeks. She said, "How could I dislike you? You are our closest friend. You, and Glynnis, and Denis, and me. . . ." And her voice too trailed off; and they stood, smiling, embarrassed, oddly happy, looking at each other as if across a small abyss, while outside, from the beach, came shouts and laughter—an impromptu volleyball game had begun, at Denis's instigation, since there was a volleyball net, slack, rather ripped, yet serviceable, slung between poles, and there were now enough players; as the long Sunday waned, several more friends had turned up. Ian's heart was beating violently. He thought, Why am I doing this, what am I saying? Why am I here?

Ian had followed Roberta into the house, they'd been talking of other things, and now, as gracefully as possible—with, Ian was thinking, the forced ease of an experienced speaker, who, having made a mistake in his speech, simply continues, without breaking his rhythm, as if nothing were wrong—he reverted to one of these subjects: Denis's recent disappointments, his mood of professional dissatisfaction, for which Ian felt some responsibility; he felt that Denis was contaminated, to a degree, by his friendship with him and was at a loss what to do about it.

"Are you serious?" Roberta asked, staring at him. "You can't be serious."

"I most certainly am serious."

"I don't want to talk about it, it's too absurd," Roberta said. "Don't you think Denis has qualities of his own, sufficient qualities of his own, to make even people who admire him not care to hire him for sensitive positions? You know what he's like in close quarters."

"I know that there has been a good deal of adverse publicity, and when the trial begins—"

"Why don't you try not to think about it! Since you're here with us; it's Labor Day weekend; it's"—she made a gesture, as if of appeal, toward the beach, the ocean, the sky—"it's another world, here. Or we are trying to make it one."

"I wish there were something I could do," Ian said. "I've put you all in such an awkward position. And my colleagues at the Institute—"

"Did *he* bring it up?"

"Denis? Of course not."

Roberta looked doubtful, as if not believing him. "He isn't perfect, you know."

Ian laughed, happy again. "I'd thought he was!"

So they talked for a while of other things, like, Ian was thinking, children skidding and swerving down a snowy hill on makeshift sleds, and Roberta asked Ian that discreet codified question, How are things going? and Ian asked Roberta how, with her, things were going; and from outside the shouts, cries, screams of laughter of the volley-ball players came like a raucous music, a counterpoint and a check to solemnity inside. Though Ian's heart was still beating uncomfortably fast, and Roberta seemed unusually breathless, her face heated, her eyes shy, damp, shining, even as, as if unconsciously, she maintained a certain distance between them. Ian, not drunk, but not as fully sober as he might have wished, thought it an odd, ironic, yet appropriate fact that, were he to tell Roberta Grinnell he loved her and would give his life for her and would—ah, how happily, how desperately he would!—marry her if, ever, she were free, his declaration must be made in the kitchen of a rented seaside cottage, amid a clutter of kitchen debris: cooking utensils and things soaking in the sink, things on counters, things in Styrofoam containers, things named and unnamed, the paraphernalia of food and drink and their consumption. There was a lingering smell of grease, from breakfast; a lingering smell of oyster shells, from lunch; a smell—Ian's mouth watered though he wasn't hungry in the slightest—of puff pastries heating in the oven.

Out of nervousness Ian lit a cigarette and saw Roberta tolerate it, the thin curling smoke, until, as if unobtrusively, she waved the smoke away; and Ian quickly stubbed the cigarette out. "I always hated Glynnis smoking," he said. "Of course she hated it, too, and was always trying to stop."

"It's said to be more difficult for women to stop than men," Roberta said. "I have no idea if that's so."

"When Freud was dying of cancer of the mouth . . ."

"Oh I know! Wasn't that—"

"Pathetic."

"*Tragic*."

They had spoken at once, and Roberta went on, as vehemently as if Freud were a friend of theirs, of whom one had a right to expect better things, "That he couldn't give up that wretched pipe of his, even after the operations to his jaw! That the addiction to his pipe was greater than the addiction, if it can be called that, to life. I used to wonder how such things were possible, but now . . ."

Ian laughed helplessly, sadly. "Oh, well. *Now.*"

The volleyball players were hooting someone's comical blunder, and then they were applauding someone's inspired or lucky shot, and Roberta said she didn't really mind if Ian smoked if he really wanted to smoke and Ian said of course not, it was a filthy habit he intended to give up soon; his daughter was disgusted with him, strongly disapproved. So they talked for a while of Bianca, and, for a while, of the Grinnells' sons, and Ian stared at the timer on the oven, clicking away, eight minutes to go, five minutes. . . . Roberta said, "I can't take her place, you know; I'm sure that's what you want," and, when Ian did not reply, as if, however improbably, Ian had not quite heard, she continued, in the same voice, quickly, guiltily, as if this were what they had really been talking about, or what she had meant to say, "Denis says I don't need to explain, but I should explain, I know you've seen the grand jury's minutes by now, I know you've seen the transcript of my testimony, which is what I will have to give at the trial too, if I'm called, and Denis says of course I will be called, that terrible man, that manipulator, won't let anything get by that might help him with his case. You know I was subpoenaed, we were all subpoenaed, we hadn't any choice . . . it seems civil rights are suspended in such instances . . . something I had not known . . . I was forbidden to take the Fifth Amendment since I was not charged with any crime and could not incriminate myself by anything I said. It's tyranny, isn't it; I told them that, that terrible man Lederer and his assistants; I told him it was like Orwell's *1984*, the thought police prying open our skulls."

She paused to draw breath; she looked as if she were about to take hold of Ian, to seize his hands as, he didn't doubt, she would have done, in those more innocent days before he'd embraced her in the courtyard of his house and begged her for whatever it was he'd begged her; he supposed it had been love.

"You know, Ian, don't you, that I had no choice but to tell them about my conversation with Glynnis, that final conversation, and I had no choice but to try to answer their questions as honestly as I could; I couldn't perjure myself even in the interests of friendship, even though I am so . . . even though I love you, Denis and I both love you, as a friend, our oldest closest dearest friend—"

Her voice broke, and Ian said quickly, "Of course I know," smiling hard at her, his hands involuntarily lifted as if in appeal. "Of course. Of course I know."

Roberta spoke of the ordeal of appearing before the grand jury; of the questions put to her, which were insidious, snide, unfair, and unjust; of the fact that, as Ian perhaps knew, she had tried, like all his friends, to represent him as he truly was: Glynnis and him, their marriage, their family life, their significance in the community. She had tried, and she believed she had succeeded, to the degree to which the prosecution had allowed her to speak her heart. Of course, at the trial, she would be cross-examined by his attorney, and it would then become clear to the courtroom, if any ambiguity remained, that she was not a hostile witness but a friendly witness, a "character" witness in fact. She would tell all the world what a good man he was: decent kindly generous gentle *good*.

And Ian listened and nodded, his face very warm and his eyes smarting; yes he knew yes he understood yes of course of course but is there no hope of you loving me apart from your husband's "love" of me? Is there no hope? No hope?

Then the timer on the oven rang, and Ian volunteered to take out the tray of pastries, but, foolishly and so very typically, he nearly forgot to use potholders; and Roberta gave a little scream and stopped him, ending, as Glynnis had so often ended, doing the little task herself.

Ian said, "Those smell delicious," and Roberta said, "There's crabmeat, minced mushroom, sausage, would you like one?—no, wait, they're too hot," taking them from the baking tray and setting them on a platter.

Ian watched and said again, "They do smell delicious; you're a wonderful cook," and Roberta glanced up at him as if he were teasing and said, "Of course I didn't make these myself, I bought them; I'm not a purist like Glynnis was."

Ian waited a bit and said, as he'd said some minutes before, that if Roberta had been avoiding him this weekend he understood; didn't blame her in the slightest; she knew, he thought, he *hoped*, how he felt about her, and—but here she interrupted to say that she seriously doubted that *he* knew: he was under a terrible strain, Glynnis's death and the other, the rest of it; he really didn't know what his feelings were and couldn't be expected to know. He said, smiling, his lips so dry they felt as if they were about to crack, that the high regard he had for her, the love he had for her, was as genuine as any in his life, in his entire life, but he quite understood if being told this simply embarrassed her. "There is nothing worse than being loved when one can't love in return," he said, wondering if this were true, and why *he* was volunteering it, since he'd had so little experience along those lines. Had Glynnis simply told him? Was all he knew of love, to the degree he knew of love, nothing more than what Glynnis had told him?

Roberta said, "I don't think we should talk about this now, Ian; this isn't the ideal time to talk about it."

Ian said, "I only want you to understand that, having said what I've said, I *do* love you, I don't want you to think that I expect any sort of reciprocity, any response on your part at all, even a . . . even a calm and considered refutation." He smiled, and his eyes filled now frankly with tears; and Roberta looked away, as if too deeply, keenly, moved; and he said, hoping she would not interrupt, but hear him out, "I dread your thinking this is some sort of emotional blackmail. Please don't think it! My feeling for you is as disinterested as it can be, though I—I will admit—I will admit I think about you a good deal," he said, beginning now to tremble, and speaking rapidly, daring to take Roberta's hand in his, then both her hands, in his, trapped in his, as if to hold her still; to make her listen. She did not resist, nor did she return the pressure of his fingers. How like ordinary hands our hands are, Ian thought; how ordinary it all is, after all; while somewhere up the beach a dog was barking in a series of high piercing yips, and the volleyball players were throwing themselves about—Ian could see them through the screened window, had been keeping Denis in sight all along—and the rich warm delicious smell of the pastries lifted from the platter.

After a moment Roberta drew her hands out of his but did not step away. She said, "May I ask you something frankly, Ian?"

"Yes? What?"

"About Sigrid Hunt."

Ian hesitated. "If you must."

"Well, no then," Roberta said evenly. "It isn't that I *must*."

She picked up the platter, to take outside to her guests. Would Ian like to sample one of the pastries? she asked, and Ian, his glasses misted over, standing very still, frowning, said politely, "No thank you, I'm not hungry," and Roberta said, "Of course you are, you were swimming this afternoon, weren't you?" and Ian obediently picked up one of the pastries and bit into it, scarcely knowing what he did or what he chewed except, yes, it *was* delicious.

He said, smiling, "You are all too good to us."

SO THE LABOR Day weekend passed. Like sand slipping through his fingers.

He left early the following day, before lunch, though it was a clear cloudless lovely day at last, and the ocean had never looked more beautiful: slate blue waves, white-capped like mountains, and the fishy salty smell edged with an autumnal coolness. Denis urged him to stay another day, and Roberta urged him, with a look almost pleading, to stay at least for lunch, but Ian thanked them for their hospitality, shaking Denis's hand hard and embracing Roberta in their quick polite ceremonial manner: feeling her initial stiffness, then her pliancy, the warmth of her lips brushing his cheek. He drove away, waving out the window of his car. The Grinnells stood waving after him, side by side; then their hands dropped and they continued to look after him, he saw in the rearview mirror, until he had passed out of view, and they were lost to one another.

6.

That fall, Ian began volunteer work at the Short North Rehabilitation Center in Newburgh, a twenty-minute drive from Hazelton. He taught in the adult illiteracy program, Monday and Thursday evenings; his course was advertised as Remedial English for Native-born Americans.

At the Short North, so far as he could make out, no one knew him; his name meant nothing; the color of his skin marked him off not only from his students—three black women, middle-aged, and one youngish black man, on parole from Sing Sing for attempted robbery and felonious assault—but from the majority of his fellow volunteers. People looked at him, sometimes stared thoughtfully at him, but he knew himself invisible.

Had it occurred to anyone to ask what had brought Ian to the program, he intended to tell the truth: he really didn't know. He had happened to read about it on a communal bulletin board in the Hazelton public library; it had sounded like a good, helpful, charitable thing, a way of filling in the hours, biding his time. In prison, he thought, if he went to prison, he would sign up for similar programs, teaching inmates to read, even to write.

No one asked. But he had his answer prepared, in any case.

BY THE END of October the trial had been postponed another time: to January 11.

Ian, who had been marking off the days on his calendar, thought, It will never end. It will never even begin.

There was a rumor too that Sigrid Hunt had returned to the area. She was to be a witness for the prosecution; a witness for the defense. Nicholas Ottinger, who had, in secret, hired a private investigator to find her, told Ian that the rumors were unfounded, unfortunately. "It's quite possible the woman is no longer living," he said carefully, as if the word *dead* might be too strong for Ian's nerves. "But the body probably won't be found either," he added.

Ian winced inwardly but made no reply. Why was Ottinger looking at him so closely? What was he supposed to say? That *he* had not killed Sigrid Hunt and did not know who had?

FOUR

THE TRIAL

1.

So frequently, and with such hallucinatory vividness, had Ian Mc-Cullough anticipated his trial, had in fact dreamt of it for months, that, on the first day, a snow-muffled morning in late February—for Ottinger had cannily succeeded in getting it postponed another time—many of its proceedings had the air, to him, of an imperfectly recalled dream: alternately monotonous and jarring, predictable and disconcerting. He had been prepared for the opening of the prosecution's case, but he had not been prepared for the disjointed nature of the session itself: its several delays and false starts, its many interruptions—most of them, in fact, by his own counsel, for Nicholas Ottinger was quick as a pit bull to the attack, rising to his feet to object, to raise points of law, procedure, and propriety. He had been prepared for a crowded courtroom but he had not been prepared for so much seemingly unco-ordinated activity in the area of the bench, nor for the initially appealing but finally rather disappointing candor and lack of pretension of Justice Benedict Harmon, who seemed intelligent enough for the authority of his position, but only enough. ("Benedict Harmon is the best of second-best," Ottinger had told Ian, "which, in the larger context, is after all quite good.") He had been prepared for the substance of the prosecution's case against him but he had hardly been prepared for Samuel S. Lederer's theatrical, repetitious, and heavily ironic performance: that air, beneath the public servant's zealous vigilance against all things evil, of something mean-spirited and mendacious. Above all he was not prepared for his growing, and numbing, conviction that, though "Ian J. McCullough" was the still point of all procedural motion, and his formally rendered plea of "not guilty" to the charge of murder in the second degree its mainspring, he himself, in the flesh, sitting beside his counsel at the defense table, was irrelevant. I am being tried *in absentia*, he thought.

In the first row, behind him, sat Bianca; beside her, Glynnis's sister, Katherine. (Who had very little to say to Ian McCullough, these days.) Scattered throughout the courtroom were familiar faces: friends, acquaintances, colleagues whom Ian's eye nervously sought even as it recoiled from them in shame. (One of the faces, the mouth very red and the pale skin smooth as porcelain, belonged to Meika Cassity.) Most of the men and women who had crowded into the courtroom on the second floor of this rather churchly courthouse were strangers to Ian McCullough and certainly had not known Glynnis. Who were they, Ian wondered, and why, on this freezing icy morning, had they made the effort to come to this place, to crowd into pews, to observe *him:* to be spectators at *his* trial? What did they, seeing him, *see?*

The setting, and the crowdedness, reminded Ian of Glynnis's funeral service at the First Unitarian Church. Where the casket bearing his wife's body had been, Ian himself was now seated; where that spare yet eloquent ceremony had dealt with death, and with life's accommodation of death, this ceremony, protracted, graceless, subject to constant interruptions and derailments and that air, ingrained in the grime of the hardwood floor and the shiny scrim of dirt on the windowpanes, of the defiantly anachronistic, was to deal with punishment. For justice in its ideality can only be measured in terms of punishment, Ian thought. Without punishment there can be no justice.

The Cattaraugus County courthouse in the county seat of Cattaraugus, New York, an easy half-hour from Hazelton along a scenic country highway, had been built in the heyday of Greek Revival fashion: chunky granite columns, with a flurry at their tops of Corinthian excess; numberless granite steps; a stately portico; and, inside, a stately foyer, opening onto yet more stairs of the same smooth-worn stone, rising to the second floor, curved and splendid as a staircase in a mansion. To enter its poorly lit and poorly ventilated interior was to enter a place of, paradoxically, solemnity and cacophony: for the acoustics were terrible, and voices, even when raised, even when rebounding from wall to wall, were difficult to hear. Decades out of date, badly in need of renovation, if not actual demolition—in the right frame of mind, Ian was inspired to note such grandiloquent architectural monstrosities with an architect's unsentimental eye—the building did exact from those who entered it a measure of frightened awe. And the high-ceilinged and many-windowed courtroom with its marble pillars, its oak pews and wainscoting, the judge's raised bench, the heraldic insignia of American justice and the faded, limp, yet still imperial American flag at its front, did suggest a significance scarcely to be named: though those who entered it were dwarfs, those who inhabited it, at its highest echelons at least, were giants. A self-referential little American world, staffed by females, ordained by males.

Entering the building in the company of his daughter and, of course, Nick Ottinger and one of Ottinger's young assistants, Ian had felt, despite his resolve to feel nothing, a stab of physical pain and apprehension, a despairing sense that, however his fate might be decided in this place, it would not really relate to him: would fail to define, to him, the nature of his crime, his guilt, and even his punishment.

THE NIGHT BEFORE, at the Cassitys', Meika had said, as if impulsively, laying a hand on Ian's arm and squeezing with surprisingly strong fingers, "What we should all do, you know, is reject *them;* reject their damned au*thori*ty; fly away, the three of us, to someplace nice, like Majorca or Rio. Have you ever been to Rio? Yes? It's lovely, isn't it? If you stick to the right quarters."

AFTER NUMEROUS DELAYS, including, for some confused and rancorous minutes, the possibility of the trial's opening being postponed until the afternoon—a document, pertinent to the prosecution's case, having been misplaced, or lost, and demanded by the court—the trial was finally formally convened: the case of the *People of the State of New York v. Ian J. McCullough,* on charges of second-degree murder, announced by the clerk of the court, at 10:35 A.M. of February 26, 1988. The prosecutor stepped forward to identify himself, and the defense attorney stepped forward to identify himself—and to request that the court enter a plea of "not guilty" to the charges pronounced against his client. There was a lengthy discussion, in which Ian had no part, before Judge Harmon's bench: indeed, a surprisingly lengthy discussion. Then the procedure began again, like a faulty engine kicking to life, and, with a certain degree of dramatic flourish the jurors—seven men and five women, all white, most of middle age—were led into the courtroom and took their places in the jury box. They looked at Ian McCullough, and, circumspectly, with a dizzily pounding heart, Ian McCullough looked at them.

Nick Ottinger had seemingly taken countless pains with the selection of this particular jury; had done everything within his power as defense counsel—so he assured Ian, and so Ian believed—to make certain that none of these men and women was so much as "latently" ill-disposed to Ian McCullough.

So it begins, Ian thought.

He saw the members of the press, a veritable platoon of men and women, rather like a second jury, seated at a long table against the farther wall and in the first two rows of benches, until now slack-jawed with boredom, begin to quicken in interest and to take up their pens. He felt suddenly very like the way he felt in his doctor's examining room, when, having reported stoically for his annual checkup—the dreaded one involving an examination for cancer of the lower bowel—he was forced to wait so long that his anxiety became dulled. Where visceral fear had been, an anesthetized resignation had settled in. Almost.

For his appearance in court Ian wore his dark gray pin-striped suit minus the vest, which fitted him rather loosely now, as if it were another man's. Glynnis had selected it, years ago, for an honorific occasion now long forgotten; Bianca had selected it more recently, having conferred with Nick Ottinger, for this occasion. And a white shirt with modest cuff links, and a tie of some somber hue and fabric, and polished shoes. His hair, faded almost entirely to silver and receding from his high forehead—catching sight of himself unexpectedly, in mirrors, Ian was now in the habit of thinking, *Who* is that man?—had been trimmed to the perfect length, neither too short nor too long.

Though, from having seen the grand jury transcript, Ian knew beforehand the substance of the prosecution's case against him and, more or less, what Samuel S. Lederer would say of him in his opening remarks, it was a daunting thing to sit, in so public a place, and hear himself accused of having caused the death of his wife of twenty-six years "with intent"; of having killed her by fracturing her skull in an action "as deliberate, and as cruel" as if he had bludgeoned her to death with a hammer. "This is a simple case," Lederer said. "A case of lust, greed, and barbaric selfishness." He had lowered his voice dramatically; he addressed not only the jurors, who were staring at him with rapt, it seemed very nearly hypnotized attention, but everyone in the court-room. Ian felt a spasm of nausea, a threat of immediate physical distress. He thought, I cannot bear it.

The defendant McCullough, Lederer continued, had a very spe-cific motive for wanting his wife dead and out of the way: he had en-tered into an adulterous liaison with a young woman, "a young woman half his age." Though a highly respected faculty member of the Institute for Independent Research in the Social Sciences and an allegedly well-liked member of his community, McCullough lacked the patience, or the moral integrity, to sever his marital ties in an aboveboard manner, or perhaps he did not want to give up any portion of his estate in a costly divorce settlement. In any case. . . .

Ian stared at Lederer through a mist of pain as the man paced about before the judge's bench, with a veteran's sense of how to use the space and how to use his gesticulating hands to advantage. How confi-dent he was! How unhesitating, in the dreadful things he said! His eyes shone like chips of glass in his broad, ruddy, creased face; his gleaming head, which seemed disproportionately large for his narrow shoulders, had a look of being hard and was fringed with graying red curls. Ottinger had so long spoken disparagingly of Lederer, questioning not only his in-tegrity in bringing charges against Ian but his knowledge of the law and his competence as a prosecutor, that Ian was disconcerted by his perfor-mance; for much of what he said was convincing, however exaggerated for theatrical emphasis. My enemy, Ian thought. Who wants my heart. But the man was of course a fellow professional, going about his job.

As Ottinger had explained to Ian, the prosecutor's task was to construct an agent, a hypothesis, to account for a death that had come under his jurisdiction, a death that might not seem accountable in ordinary—i.e., noncriminal—terms. If he charged murder in the second degree it was probably with the hope of winning with manslaughter; there was no third-degree murder charge under the New York State statute. In the normal course of events—if, for instance, Ian had had prior convictions—he and his attorney might have plea-bargained with Lederer and settled for a lesser charge. It was unlikely that murder could be proven without eyewitnesses, and on circumstantial evidence of the kind the prosecution had assembled; yet in an American law court, given the jury system and the notorious unreliability of witnesses, not to mention the deviousness of certain members of the bench, anything might happen. Anything! Particularly if Ian refused to take the witness stand and defend himself; and this Ian did not want to do. So now, listening to Lederer, to a careful description of witnesses and exhibits to come, Ian could see all too readily the logic of the man's argument: his invention of an agent, and of a motive, to account for the death of Glynnis McCullough. None of it was true but all was logical.

And why not simply kill yourself, he thought, and escape them all; make a noble Roman end of it? *In all that you do or say or think, recollect that at any time the power of withdrawal from life is in your hands . . .* as Marcus Aurelius taught. He'd been with his friends, and they'd been drinking—Ian McCullough too had been drinking a bit more than usual, a bit more than was usually associated with that upright self-conscious citizen "Ian McCullough"—and the subject had come up; or was it an issue, suicide, a moral issue, not entirely serious yet not entirely playful either? and Meika Cassity had said, baring her lovely teeth in a grimace, But why cut your throat? There are so many others ready to do it for you.

Another time, Meika had said, There are better things to do. Besides dying, I mean.

Samuel S. Lederer was concluding his presentation. It had gone on a long time. At the very end he stood in silence, as if exhausted by his effort. His manner had by degrees become heavily ironic; challenged several times by Ottinger, the ever-vigilant, he had acquiesced, with an expression of disdain, before Judge Harmon could rule against him. Indignation oozed like oil from his pores: he wiped his heated face with a handkerchief and still did not move from the spot until Judge Harmon made an impatient gesture and invited him to step down.

"Certainly, Your Honor," he said.

Now Nicholas Ottinger rose to his feet and began his rebuttal. He too would present the case as a simple one: no crime had been committed, and no crime could be proved to have been committed. No crime and no criminal; no proof and no case. The prosecutor, Mr. Lederer, was faced with reelection, and, having no record of distinction with which to run, he was "desperately grasping at political straws," using any means at his disposal to court public favor and to get his picture in the papers. (Here, a mild ripple of laughter ran through the courtroom, at Lederer's expense. Those who had avidly followed his words only minutes ago now smiled at his reddened, surely not very photogenic face in skeptical mirth.) Similarly, the Hazelton township police were engaged in a personal vendetta of sorts against Ian McCullough, as a consequence of Dr. McCullough's involvement in an American Civil Liberties Union case of some years ago. (Of which, more, in time.) There was no adulterous liaison with the young woman named Sigrid Hunt, who had been Mrs. McCullough's friend primarily; there was no marital discord, but, as friends of the McCulloughs would testify, a long, happy, mutually respectful relationship; Glynnis McCullough had died as a result of a tragic accident, an accident *sui generis*—"which is to say, unique of its kind"—for which no one, absolutely no one, could be blamed. As for the accused: Dr. Ian McCullough, for sixteen years a senior fellow on the political science faculty at the Institute for Independent Research in the Social Sciences, Hazelton-on-Hudson, was one of the most admired, respected, and loved men in his community: one of the most brilliant, industrious, and productive men in his field, the comparatively new field of demographics. ("That is," Ottinger carefully emended, yet in such a way as to suggest that no one would be expected to know so exotic a word, "population study.") To imagine that Dr. McCullough, of all men, a devoted husband of twenty-six years, a loving father of a college-age daughter, the most reliable of friends, neighbors, citizens, would so much as wish injury to another human being, let alone commit it, was self-evidently ludicrous; to imagine that he would wish injury to his wife, let alone commit it, verged upon the obscene. The public prosecutor of Cattaraugus County has misused the power of his office in an effort to. . . . The defense will show. . . .

Ian sat very straight and very still, his hands clasped together, hard, on the table before him, his head raised, alertly and respectfully, as if he were listening. Through a tall narrow window beyond the jurors' box there came a dull but harsh winter light, of the color of bone marrow, and Ian willed it to flood his consciousness: to muffle all sound, sight, motion. He understood with a part of his mind that his "counsel" was performing beautifully on his behalf; that the mood of the courtroom had shifted; that it would, again, and yet again, who knew how many times, shift: like sand, like water, like molecules, the flood of atoms swerving through the void. *He had no instruments, but he knew it all.* He would learn to retreat, Ian thought, to a place beyond karmic illusion. He would get there, and he would survive.

2.

Meika slapped Ian, lightly; she wanted him, she said, to be *awake*. For he had to leave soon didn't he and their time together was precious wasn't it she wanted him to be fully *awake*. "Yes and I do too," Ian said, smiling but very sleepy, groping for her hand, her hands, which were so warm, busy, fretful, proprietary.

He squeezed the hands in his, the small light bones, a sparrow's bones, until she winced.

". . . love you."

"Yes and I . . . do too."

"Loved you for such a damned long time. But *you* know."

"Do I . . . ?"

"You know now."

"Yes. I suppose I do."

But he kept falling asleep. Images, bright, blurred, as if seen fleetingly through water, passed through his vision, toppled over, disappeared. Meika leaned over him and kissed him and ran her tongue, and her teeth, over him, laughing quietly, the length of her body warm and insistent against his, as intimate as if they had been lovers, like this, for a very long time. Though of course he did not know the woman. Did he. Meika Cassity who is Vaughn Cassity's wife, old friends of Glynnis's and mine; we are all old friends, belong to the same circle of friends, entertaining in one another's homes for years, a circle of friends, unknown to one another. Meika was stroking his belly, his thighs, his penis, at first lightly, with feathery touches, then more firmly, assuredly; Meika was kissing, tonguing, his nipples, biting his nipples, her breath warm and damp against his chest, her hair with its ashy-dry synthetic smell in his face, strands of it against his mouth. She'd been lazy and yawning and fucked out, she said; now she wanted to fuck again and damn him she wanted him *awake*—laughing in his ear, sticking her tongue in his ear, pummeling him, tickling him hard, and again taking his penis between her fingers, with a rough proprietary air, like milking a cow's teat (she'd said the other night, rather shocking him), and Ian, laughing, struggling to breathe, felt all the blood of his body rush as if panicked to the organ between his legs; limp and boneless it had been, like the man himself, exhausted, emptied out, sucked dry; but now, as if in defiance of his will (for, sleep-dazed as he was he nonetheless knew he *must* get up and get home, *must* get up and get home, there was Bianca, in bed, he hoped in bed but surely not asleep, well aware of her father's inexplicable lateness, her father's really quite mysterious lateness, returning from supper at the Cassitys' and expected back hours ago), gradually hardening, becoming erect, a rod of vengeance, delirium. Oh God I love you I'm crazy about you came the hot urgent breath in his face as she straddled him, grunting with effort, panting, her thin body slippery and snaky and dank with sweat; come inside me I'm *dy*ing for you. But he kept falling asleep.

IS IT MEIKA, is it you and Meika, why now, why her? Bianca so clearly wanted to ask; are you that desperate? that reckless? that *mad?* But of course Bianca had not asked: Bianca was no longer that kind of daughter. And Ian had not explained himself to her.

He tried not to think of Bianca and of Meika in the same dimension at all.

IAN HAD KNOWN, he supposed, that, over the years, Meika Cassity had been . . . interested in him; but it was difficult, given the rhetorical nature of certain of his friends' beliefs, to distinguish what was genuine from what was merely playful, whimsical, or frankly spurious.

If a woman in Hazelton talked of the "politics" or "consciousness" of women's liberation (as, frequently, Glynnis herself had talked of such matters), did it invariably mean that she believed herself liberated, did it mean that she was sexually adventurous, or did it in fact mean nothing at all? Ian had only vaguely concerned himself with such things because, married as he was to Glynnis and deeply immersed in his work, he simply hadn't time; sexual adventures were not his style. Or had not been.

Thus the affair with Meika Cassity, beginning abruptly as it did, and, in time, to end abruptly, had the resonance of a dream: a dream's air of highly charged potency and meaning. The week before Christmas, Ian had driven to the Short North Rehabilitation Center to teach his Thursday evening class, only to discover, to his disappointment and chagrin, that only one student had troubled to show up: Mrs. Myrna Castle, a heavyset black woman with a sweet shy gold-toothed smile, dressed as if for Sunday, the least confident of his students and the one most despairingly hopeful of learning to read. (It was Mrs. Castle's desire to be able to read, before she died, the Holy Bible, and to be able to deal with supermarket ads and coupons.) Ian spent ninety minutes with Mrs. Castle, going through adult primer material unfamiliar to her—in class, Ian always dealt with new material since, otherwise, students would memorize assigned material and appear to be reading when in fact they were not. The lesson went slowly and painstakingly. Mrs. Castle forgot words she knew, sometimes misreading the same word in a single paragraph or seeing "they" for "the," "our" for "are," and while Ian lost himself rather pleasurably in the effort of teaching her, as if immersed in an element challenging, if not alarming, to each, like a patch of quicksand, the mood quickly faded when the lesson ended. It was then that he had to drive back to Hazelton-on-Hudson, in the dark, to resume, with dread, his own life. He did not know if what he did at the

Short North could be considered teaching; someone had spoken rather derisively of it, not long before: Denis, probably—Denis was becoming, of late, less and less tolerant of what he called cheap liberal conscience-placating gestures—and he thought of Mrs. Castle and felt a helpless sort of pity for her, the tinge of conscience (for of course Denis was correct, though cruel in being correct) a white man of his class and status might naturally feel for a black woman of her background, her hard luck, her fate. Ian had assumed that Myrna Castle was older than he, but she was in fact two years younger: a former alcoholic, a serious diabetic, the widow of a man who had died in prison fifteen years before, grandmother of seventeen living children and mother of nine, one of whom, her best-loved boy as she called him, was in the state penitentiary at Dutch Neck. Serving two life sentences, Mrs. Castle told Ian, for a deed he had not committed but a friend in his company that night had committed, the both of them serving the very same sentence: is that justice? Mrs. Castle asked of Ian; and Ian could say only, I'm sorry, I'm so sorry to hear that, Mrs. Castle, but maybe he will be eligible for parole someday, and Mrs. Castle said, looking up at him with bright, angry eyes, Oh no he won't Dr. McCullough, the law has seen to that.

When, that night, Ian returned home, to the empty darkened house, to the house of death, he'd felt so low, so absolutely rotten, it was self-evident that there was nothing to be done with the remainder of the night (it was only eight-thirty) but to drink himself into oblivion, to get shitfaced smashing drunk. And the telephone rang, and it was Meika Cassity, inviting him over for a drink. Some friends have dropped by, Meika said, her voice light and melodic; we were thinking maybe we'd all go out to dinner; there's that new seafood restaurant by the square, have you tried it yet? Or do you have other plans?

Ian laughed. Ian said, "I adore you."

THE CASSITYS' OTHER guests were Leonard Oppenheim and Paul Owen, whom, Ian realized, he had not seen in months. Like a fool he said, unthinking, "I haven't seen you in months . . ." even as he realized, from the men's stiff smiles and expressionless eyes, and their conspicuous failure to get to their feet and shake his hand in greeting, that they were no longer his friends. They think I am a murderer, Ian thought, rocked back on his heels.

Meika must have called him without consulting them; or, bent on mischief, as Meika so frequently was, she had called Ian under the pretense of not knowing how they felt. He was deeply embarrassed, wished he might turn around and walk back out the door.

They were primarily Glynnis's friends, Ian thought resentfully. They were never my friends at all.

Leonard and Paul left the Cassitys' after a polite five minutes, making their excuses, and Meika said, shrugging, after they were gone, "It's just as well. They've become so dour, those two, they've lost all their sparkle and wit, and if gay men display no gaiety what is the point really of it all? I really do think there might be truth to the rumor . . ."

"Meika," Vaughn said reprovingly.

". . . that one of them is, you know, ill. Seriously ill."

"Seriously ill?" Ian asked.

"Seriously ill," said Meika. She regarded him with wide damp oyster-white eyes and a grave downturning of her mouth. "Or, that is, has tested positive for the disease."

"Meika," Vaughn said, more sharply, "we don't really know that that is true."

"You must mean AIDS," Ian said, thunderstruck.

"I think it must be Leonard who has it," Meika said thoughtfully. "He has been looking so sallow lately and seems to have lost weight.

But of course if one of them has it the other has it too. My God, it's so ghastly, isn't it? So sad."

"You really think that Leonard has AIDS?" Ian asked.

"As I said, I think he may have tested—"

"Meika, *please*," Vaughn said, so exasperated he'd begun to laugh, "we don't know that the rumor has any basis in fact. It is only a rumor, and you know what Hazelton rumors are."

"Yes," said Meika, "I know what Hazelton rumors are. They are likely to be true."

"Since neither Leonard nor Paul has told us yet himself, I think we should do them the courtesy of keeping silent. It's the least—"

Meika laid a hand on Ian's arm in mock restraint. "Ian won't tell, will you, Ian?"

"I—I'm very shocked. I hadn't heard. I—"

"You're so innocent, off in your sequestered little world, you probably never hear much of anything anymore," Meika said, slipping her arm through his and leading him to the mirror-backed Japanese cabinet where the liquor was kept. "Even about yourself."

"Meika," Vaughn said again, reprovingly. "You know what you promised."

Meika laughed. She was looking unusually attractive tonight, really quite beautiful: her ash-blond hair curled gamine-style about her narrow face; her almond-shaped eyes, enlarged by mascara and shadowed in silver, warm, alert, and shining; her reddened mouth smiling and animated. Like Glynnis, Meika had always been a superb hostess, if less scrupulous than Glynnis—the elaborate food she served her guests was not inevitably, as she confessed, of her own preparation— she seemed to enjoy herself, at others' parties no less than at her own, as much as Glynnis had. The two women had resembled each other in certain superficial ways but were, Ian thought, profoundly differ-ent. Perhaps it had to do with Meika being childless . . . and Vaughn so much her senior. (Vaughn was approximately fifty-seven, to Meika's probable forty-five, and had been looking, of late, rather older, his skin dry and lacking in tone, with a curious stippled appearance: as if he were precariously convalescent, though Ian had heard of no illness.)

It had always seemed to Ian that the Cassitys were the most mys-terious of their friends, since, in their sociability, there was something both profligate and withheld; in their presentation of themselves—as, in society, we are continually "presenting" ourselves—there was something indiscriminate yet calculating. It was generally known that Vaughn, as a young architect, had met Meika during a visit to Paris in the mid-fifties; that he had fallen in love with, "in adoration of," Meika, at the time a fashion model—"But *very* young, and *very* naïve," as Meika never failed to interject, "with *no future at all* ahead"—and had broken off his engagement with a girl back home, to pursue her, court her, make her his bride. Meika, seventeen at the time, was Parisian but not French: the daughter of an American foreign service officer (himself of Anglo-Irish blood) and a Belgian woman, a translator, who had elected to dissolve the marriage, and to return to Brussels, when Meika was a child of five. In a version of the story Ian recalled from years ago, when he and Glynnis were first introduced to the Cassitys and flattered at being told such presumably confidential matters, Meika's mother had been an exotic beauty involved in some undefined way with French intelligence—that is, a wartime spy—which had to do somehow with her disappearance; for, in Meika's account, the woman had simply dis-appeared: there was no trace of her. In another version of the story it was Meika's father who had been involved in covert intelligence activi-ties: for the CIA during the fifties, however, and not during the war; at the time Vaughn met Meika her father had in effect disappeared as well, though in one way or another he kept in contact with his daughter, who lived with a French bourgeois family, and supported her generously enough, it seemed. "Meika's father set a standard to which other men must only aspire," Vaughn frequently said, with a lover's doting smile, even as Meika waved him into annoyed silence or pressed a cautionary forefinger to her lips.

Vaughn Cassity had an excellent professional reputation without being of the very highest rank of American architects: the consequence, observers said, rather more of a lack of ambition than of talent; though, to be sure, the man was ambitious enough or would not have made the small fortune he had. Glynnis had thought him charming if, at times, rather willful and self-absorbed; he was famous in Hazelton for day-dreaming while conversation swirled about him, and for murmuring mysterious expletives under his breath: "Well—!" and "You *see*—!" and "And *now*—!" with no recourse to others' remarks. There was, or had been, a minor drinking problem; rumors of health problems, never clearly defined. Vaughn had always been kindly, if characteristically vague, in his relations with his friends, and seemingly devoted to Meika. The house he had bought for her, in Hazelton's older historic district, was a beautiful red-brick Georgian of the size of a small mansion, furnished with antiques, to which, at the rear, Vaughn had added rooms of his own design, spacious, glass-walled, and aggressively contemporary, like the one in which Ian now stood.

"What will you have, Ian? Scotch? Martini? Your usual dry white wine?"

Dry white wine had been Glynnis's drink. Ian said, "Martini, please."

So Vaughn made Ian a martini, and Ian accepted it with thanks and slightly trembling fingers, which he hoped no one would notice. Meika was watching him with a singular, flattering intensity: a hungry concentration. The perfume that lifted from her was sweet, heady, with an undercurrent of something astringent; she wore a long-skirted dress of white cashmere, beaded and sequined in gold and black, and high-heeled open-backed sandals, also gold. On both her wrists, which were very thin, she wore numerous gold bracelets; on her left, a jewel-studded watch with so darkly vitreous a face the numerals were invisible. "A Christmas present?" Ian asked, pointing, and Meika laughed happily, showing her perfect white teeth, and said, "You see, Ian *is* observant. Glynnis used to complain he wasn't."

"It's my Christmas present to Meika," Vaughn said, smiling.

"And it's lovely," Meika said, slipping her arms around her husband's neck and kissing him on the cheek. "Absolutely *lovely*. I don't deserve it, but then one never does deserve anything . . . nice."

"Meika is a Calvinist at heart," Vaughn said, chuckling.

They sat on a long, curving, elegant white couch: facing the fireplace, which was made of white marble, and massive; warmed by a splendidly burning fire—a fire of such lovely iridescent colors, Ian supposed it must be made of composition logs, artificial logs, and not the real thing. But it was splendid, nonetheless, and did not overheat the room.

They drank their drinks, and Ian and Meika smoked cigarettes, and Vaughn teasingly brandished, but did not unwrap and light, a Cuban cigar, and the Cassitys' Chinese girl brought out fresh appetizers, liver pâté and French bread, and generous hunks of Brie, and Gloucester, and Stilton cheese ("I love Stilton," Vaughn said, smacking his lips; "it smells of unwashed feet"), and smoked oysters, and Christmas nuts of various kinds, and it was nearly eleven o'clock before Meika remembered dinner, but of course no one wanted dinner by that time, particularly not Ian. He had stuffed himself with Meika's rich delicious food and had had two, or was it three, of Vaughn's massive martinis, and looked happily from Meika's smiling face to Vaughn's, and from Vaughn's to Meika's, thinking, These people are my friends, these people understand. Since Thanksgiving, when he had been invited over for a drink, and not for dinner as he'd hoped he might be, Ian had seen disappointingly little of the Grinnells: he played squash with Denis on an irregular basis but had not spoken with Roberta or so much as seen her in weeks. The Kuhns were traveling in Africa but the Olivers were in town, and though Malcolm had spoken warmly of getting together over the holidays, Ian had heard nothing since. And he thought, with a stab of bitterness, as much for Glynnis as for himself, They had such a good time, all of them, at my birthday party.

As if reading Ian's mind, Meika interrupted a story Vaughn was telling about one of his eccentric millionaire clients and said, "You've heard, Ian, of course, about Denis and Roberta?"

"What about them?" Ian asked.

"Roberta isn't simply out in Seattle visiting her sister," Meika said. "I mean, she *is*, but it's really the start of a trial separation."

"A separation?"

"I thought perhaps you knew."

"A legal separation?"

"You and the Grinnells have always been so close. You, and Glynnis, and the Grinnells."

"I didn't know," Ian said. His heart knocked against his ribs. "No one told me."

Ian thought, I should leave, and go at once to Denis's.

He thought, I can telephone Roberta; I will find out her number from him.

But he did not leave; and the subject of the Grinnells, so abruptly taken up, was abruptly dismissed; for Meika had questions to ask of Ian, how legal matters were proceeding . . . whether Nick Ottinger was the hotshot people claimed . . . whether "that young woman" (Meika fastidiously shrank from pronouncing Sigrid Hunt's name) had yet been contacted, and whether, if she returned for the trial, she would be a witness for the prosecution or for the defense. Ian shrugged and said he didn't know. He did not seriously believe that Sigrid Hunt, were she to return, would testify for the prosecution, except, perhaps, as a hostile witness, but he saw no reason to tell Meika Cassity this.

"Or is she dead, do you think?" Meika asked, looking rather too levelly at Ian. Her eyes, of no distinct color, a mild pewter-gray, sparkled with a febrile sort of innocence in the firelight.

Ian said stiffly, "I don't know."

"Ah, of course! You don't know, how *could* you know!"

Ian said nothing; Vaughn murmured, *"Well!"* as if in vehement agreement; for a moment no one spoke. Meika, who had tossed her cigarette into the fire, reached absentmindedly for Ian's, burning in an onyx ashtray close by, and said, contemplatively, "There was a side to Glynnis very few of us knew, a jealous, fearful, vulnerable side. . . . That Glynnis of all people could feel jealousy, even envy, of others—of other women, I mean—endeared her to me. It made her, you know, so much more human. It made her so much less perfect."

"Perfect?" Ian said. "Glynnis was not perfect."

He laughed, not bitterly, he hoped, and surely not ironically, and reached for his drink. "Hardly more than I am perfect, in fact," he said.

"Ah," said Meika, smiling her sweet-sly smile, narrowing her eyes to slits as if she were suppressing laughter, "but you *are.*"

And she reached out to give his hand a surprisingly hard squeeze, as if to reassure him.

She said, "If you and . . . your young woman friend . . . were close, I mean simply close, as friends . . . I don't blame you for not wanting to talk about her; our private lives must remain private. Some of the factual information printed in the papers, let alone the 'anonymous' opinions, have been grotesquely inaccurate, in a way insulting to us all. And, damn it, there is no recourse; no way for us to collectively sue, for instance, the *New York Post* for criminal libel. Aren't they bastards, though! All of them! Someone was saying, the other evening, Once the trial begins, it will be like a circus around here. . . . All of Hazelton is being scrutinized. And Glynnis was always so *proud.*" She paused, breathing rather hard. "You are our dear friend, Ian, and we love you—I speak for both Vaughn and myself, don't I, Vaughn?—and we loved Glynnis, of course, and it is all so, so . . ."—for a painful moment it seemed to Ian that Meika's composure might break, her carefully made-up face crease like a baby's—"so unanticipated."

Vaughn leaned across Ian and touched Meika lightly on the knee. "Meika? Dear?"

Meika said, ignoring him, "Like that terrible play . . . *Lear,* I think . . . in which some perfectly nice old bawdy man is blinded, his eyes gouged out onstage while you sit staring, unable to believe you are seeing what you *see.* And yet . . . there it is." She had begun to tremble; a light in her eyes flared up, whether in grief or anger Ian could not have said. "I know I've had too much to drink," she went on hurriedly, appealing to Ian, as if Vaughn were not present and regarding her with husbandly concern, "but I identify . . . so helplessly, and so strangely . . . with you, and with Glynnis. At first I must have been as stunned by the—you know—the event, the accident, the death, as everyone else; then, it seems, I entered into a period of . . . suspension, you might call it. But now, lately, I suppose it has to do with the holiday season and all the parties we'd have been going to, and giving, together, and Glynnis would have had one of her dinners I'm sure . . . and probably an open house . . . she had one on Boxing Day, the last three or four years; I'm sure she meant to continue it. And we would have had you here, of

course; I never did reciprocate that lovely birthday party of yours. . . .
We were so happy then, weren't we! Vaughn was saying just the other
night, It doesn't feel like Christmas this year; something is missing."

Ian swallowed hard and said, embarrassed, "I'm grateful for your
sympathy, Meika. I—"

"I think of her more now than I did while she was alive. I mean,
more obsessively. We were never close, I mean not in the way she and
Roberta were close, but, since her death, I mean, since it happened . . .
the accident . . . since then I seem to be thinking of her more often;
and of you."

There was a brief, pained silence. Then Vaughn, his heavy face
rubescent in the firelight, reached out again, to take hold of Meika's thin
hand, and said, "We really should talk of other things, dear. We don't
want to upset Ian, do we?"

"Are you upset, Ian?" Meika asked, nudging him coquettishly
with her shoulder.

Ian said, "I'm fine."

"He says he's fine," Meika said curtly. "Perhaps you should let us
alone, dear."

It was nearly midnight. Ian got to his feet, not very steadily, with
the intention of going home; but both Meika and Vaughn expressed
surprise, and disappointment, and insisted that he join them in a final
drink, a nightcap—"It's the holiday season, after all." So, against his
better judgment, Ian found himself accepting another drink: a liqueur
glass of wickedly powerful Armagnac.

He said, "You are both extraordinarily kind."

Meika said, smiling, "We are both extraordinarily fond of you."

They talked for a brief while of Ian's class at the Short North
Rehabilitation Center, of which neither Meika nor Vaughn had heard,
though they knew from mutual friends that Ian was involved in some

sort of volunteer effort. "Teaching adult illiterates to read?" Meika said, narrowing her eyes in disapproval, "*You?* It's too absurd."

Vaughn said, frowning, "A white man of your sort, with, you know, your particular background, and manner . . . it seems to me a naïve and dangerous enterprise. Some evening when you go to get into your car—"

Ian said, annoyed, "It isn't that bad at all, really. It isn't bad at *all,* really. The parking lot is well lit and perfectly safe."

"What of your students, aren't they mainly black? Drug addicts, and alcoholics, and parolees—"

"They are black," Ian said, less forcefully than he would have wished, "but they are perfectly fine people. Decent, good, serious, reliable."

"Have they made any progress?" Meika asked.

"Progress?"

"In learning to read."

"Yes, of course . . . some progress."

"Ah, well! *Dei gratia!*" Vaughn murmured, with an expulsion of breath: signaling, perhaps, that the subject was to be dropped. He rubbed his hands together briskly and said, "I have an idea. Why don't we go upstairs to my studio for a minute? I can show Ian my secret portfolio; and you too, Meika, since you haven't seen the latest additions. These past few weeks—"

"I'm perfectly content right here," Meika said lazily. "Though I would like another brandy, please. And where are my cigarettes?"

"My dream project, I call it: an experiment of many decades," Vaughn told Ian, with a shy sort of excitement. "I've shown it to very few people . . . mainly Meika. And one of my teachers, a very long time ago. The man has been dead for twenty years."

He poured Meika more brandy and refilled Ian's glass as well and though Ian supposed he should go home he heard himself responding enthusiastically to the invitation. Yes of course he would like to visit Vaughn's studio. He had not been up there, he said, in a number of years.

So they all went upstairs, by way of a spiral staircase, and Vaughn switched on lights, saying, "It's an experiment of a kind, an exploration of the poetics of pure space, done in the interstices, so to speak, of my 'real' work: the heartrending real work that pays the real bills. Unless the dream work is real and the other is false. Who can tell!"

Meika, out of breath from the climb, leaned playfully against Ian as if she were faint, and yawned like a child, and, her mood having shifted, complained of the mess in the studio—like the interior of a madman's skull, she said—and that smell: such stale, stuffy air, with a strong undercurrent of cigar. "There is a draft from the skylight and it's freezing in here," she said irritably, "yet, paradoxically, it *smells*. How is that possible?"

Vaughn, opening a large portfolio, said, hurt, "I never smoke while I work."

"Then the odor is you," Meika said cruelly, nudging Ian as if inviting him to share the joke. "The unmistakable odor of Vaughn Cassity's soul."

Without meaning to do so, Ian laughed; he was light-headed from the spiral climb and, yes, there was a curious smell in the studio, an air of something dry, scurfy, indefinable. He had not remembered that Vaughn's studio was quite so large, or so cluttered. Against one wall there was an enormous filing cabinet, most of whose drawers were, to varying degrees, pulled out; there were several worktables and two desks; several full-scale drawing boards, each with work on it, projects *in medias res;* hundreds, perhaps thousands of sketches, drawings, blueprints, designs, photographs; dozens of small models of buildings, residential and commercial. . . . Vaughn was turning pages with care, tall stiff sheets of parchmentlike paper, murmuring excitedly under his breath. "Here, Ian, this will give you an idea of the project; step over here," he said. Half-moon reading glasses, low on his nose, gave him an owlish elderly look. "Meika?"

In the fluorescent light, chill, lunar, Meika looked like a mannequin: unnervingly pale and without expression, her eyes bracketed by shadow. She draped her arms across her husband's and Ian's shoulders as Vaughn led them through his "poetics of space," a magnum opus of some thousand pages, still in progress, of course, a work entirely visual in concept yet, here and there, amplified by words; but the words, at least to Ian's confused eye, were of no language he knew: rather like hieroglyphics.   Buildings . . . landscapes . . . cities . . . "temporal dimensions" . . . "spatial hypotheses": the drawings were architectural in execution yet fantastical in conception, elaborate—indeed, dizzyingly elaborate—composed of numberless fine filose lines, like a spider's web. Ian tried to concentrate, tried very hard, thinking, as Vaughn led them through this altogether mad yet beautiful and surely original curiosity, that *this* was the man's soul: and must be honored.

As if not quite knowing what she did, Meika was leaning heavily on Ian's shoulder, breathing warmly against his ear. She began to stroke, knead, caress, his upper arm; drew the tips of her fingers lightly across the nape of his neck; even as, so very happily, Vaughn explained his project's gestation thirty-nine years before—"More of a visitation, really"— and his sense of what it portended, what its significance might one day be in terms of architectural theory and in the history of architecture itself. He did not know, he said, whether he should begin publishing it piecemeal or wait until it was completed. The problem of course was that he did not know *when* it would be completed, or *if.* "A posthumous celebrity would be a melancholy thing," he said slowly, in so neutral a tone that Ian thought he must be joking, and laughed; as Meika did, fairly dissolving in a spasm of giggles. She pinched her husband's ruddy cheek and said, "A posthumous celebrity is better than no celebrity, isn't it? Just as *nouveau riche*, like us, is a fucking lot better than no *riche*. Isn't it!"

Ian, disturbed by Meika's provocative behavior, which he did not quite know how to decode, eased away from her, his breath short and his senses flooded, the very hairs at the nape of his neck stirring as, unmistakably now, with a playful boldness, she caressed him on the neck and ran her hand slowly down his back, to the small of his back and his buttocks, then drew it, yet more slowly and caressingly, up to his neck again, and to his head: all the while looking, with a schoolgirl's mock attentiveness, at the extraordinary drawings Vaughn was showing them.

Vaughn said, as if talking to himself yet with apparent reference to Ian, "More and more, this past year—since last spring, I mean—I seem to be concentrating on the Poetics. My imagination seems naturally to swerve in this direction. Almost, though I shouldn't say so, I wish the San Diego commission would go to someone else. Those massive public structures are so . . . external. They seem to weigh so much, pull so heavily on the soul. Ah, here: can you see, Ian? This is a subterranean city, a sort of metropolis not of the future but of the past, the classical past—Athens, note; and a bit of Pompeii; and—"

Ian was by this time so enormously excited, so sexually, it very nearly seemed angrily, aroused, he could not attend to Vaughn's words at all but stepped frankly away from Meika and looked at her as if to say, Stop. And so, as if chastised, Meika did stop: her mouth blood-swollen and pouty, her eyes sleepily narrowed. She said, in a voice that startled, it was so calm, so measured, so presumably sober, "Vaughn, I'm going to bed; you and Ian can continue but I'm going to bed; please don't keep Ian too long; you know how you are, when professional men get talking together," turning to leave, waving a hostess's warm kiss in Ian's direction, mouthing "Good night" and "Love you!" and disappearing down the spiral staircase. Ian stared after her for a full minute or more, sick and giddy with desire, his brain so besieged he could not think at all.

Moving a thick forefinger along one of his labyrinthine designs, this one conical, with a series of machicolated projections not unlike that of a terraced garden superimposed upon, say, the interior of a television set, Vaughn said, in a voice both reverent and critical, "This is the means by which one moves from one plane to another." He glanced toward Ian and emended, wryly, "If, of course, one *can* move from one plane to another."

AND SHORTLY AFTERWARD, within twenty-four hours in fact, Ian McCullough and Meika Cassity were lovers.

And for the space of such time as they were together, or times— for adultery, in so public a place as Hazelton-on-Hudson, makes of us, by necessity, as unsentimental as coroners in the art of dissection: "time" becomes an hour this afternoon, two hours on Thursday morning, a miraculous stretch of three, late Saturday afternoons—Ian forgot the tragedy of his life: or nearly.

He told her, How beautiful you are, how beautiful: warmed by her body as a convalescent is warmed by the sun. And she told him, seemed at times to be vowing to him, that she loved him, adored him, had adored him in fact for years. (Meika reminisced about their first meeting, many years ago, which Ian, unhappily, could not remember. No matter, Meika said curtly, kissing him in forgiveness; I remember.) She worshiped his body, she said, embracing him fervently, standing on tiptoes to kiss him and, when they were unclothed and lying in her bed, hugging him passionately about the hips . . . kissing the tip of his penis . . . taking his penis in her mouth . . . as Glynnis had never wished to do. She looked up at him in triumph, a greenish fire flaring in her eyes, and eased her slender snaky so very thin yet strong little body over his, to guide him into her, to draw him inside her, yes, like this, ah exactly like this, I adore you damn you fuck you you ignored me and I did, I always *did*, adore you . . . just like this.

3.

There came, on the first day of testimony, such surprising good news Ian could scarcely, at first, grasp its significance: Fermi Sabri had returned suddenly to Cairo, without having informed Lederer, and would not be testifying for the prosecution.

Thus the man's malicious account of Ian McCullough's "affair" with Sigrid Hunt would not be admitted as evidence; under the statute, no testimony from any witness not physically present at a trial was valid.

Ian asked why this was. "For the obvious reason that the defense doesn't have the opportunity to cross-examine," Ottinger explained. "This witness was lying, and I would have exposed him to the court."

"But why do you think he ran off? Do you think—"

"I don't 'think' at all about him; now that he's out of the picture he doesn't exist for me."

"But he might know about Sigrid; he might in fact have killed her, and hidden away her body, and—"

Ottinger waved him into silence. In a gesture resembling eerily a characteristic gesture of Meika's, he pressed a forefinger to his lips. Ian stared at him and could not guess what this meant. That Sigrid was not dead; that Ottinger knew of her; or, that, being out of the picture, nothing Fermi Sabri had done was of immediate, pragmatic interest?

Ian did not pursue that subject but asked Ottinger, "If a witness gives valuable testimony to a grand jury and subsequently dies or disappears or is in fact erased by the defendant himself, is his testimony nonetheless invalid in terms of the trial?"

"Certainly," said Ottinger. "It happens all the time. When you are dealing with professional criminals, I mean. With organized crime."

THE PROSECUTION WAS to require four weeks, with numerous interruptions, delays, and adjournments, to present its case, the main argument being of course that the death of Glynnis McCullough was not, as the defense claimed, an accident, but had been committed both "in the heat of the moment" and "with intent": and for a self-evident motive, to be proved by the testimony of witnesses and evidence.

There came, one by one, like a procession in an old morality play, Mr. Lederer's witnesses: known to the defense beforehand and repeating, with some deviations and embellishments, their grand jury testimonies, but subject now, in court, to rigorous cross-examination by Mr. Ottinger. (The "cross," as Ottinger referred to it, quite intrigued Ian, who had never before attended a trial. How like a game the process truly was, a game of squash, say, in which the ball, slammed back and forth between the players, was the witness.) Each stepped to the witness stand, and each, with varying degrees of confidence, swore to tell the truth, the whole truth, nothing but the truth so help me God. Ian wondered how one could tell the truth if one could not know the truth.

But the "truth" was presented, at least initially, as a sequence of objectively verifiable events. The prosecution's first witnesses took the stand to give factual testimony: one of the paramedics who had been summoned to the McCullough residence on the night of April 23, 1988, by an emergency telephone call of Ian McCullough's, put to the Hazelton Medical Center . . . one of the young police officers who had been summoned by neighbors "to investigate a disturbance" at the McCullough residence . . . the chief physician in the emergency room at the Medical Center, to which both Mrs. McCullough and Dr. McCullough were brought, the one unconscious and requiring immediate neurological testing, the other "inebriated but lucid," with minor lacerations of the face, arms, and hands . . . even Jackson Dewald, who avoided Ian's eye but would not be led by questioning into claiming that the disturbance at his neighbors' house was "part of a pattern" of similar disturbances.

Each witness in turn was required to formally identify Ian McCullough. "Is the defendant present in this court?" he was asked. "Would you point him out, please?" And Ian, pointed out, duly rose from his seat at the defense table: Yes, I am he. It was a curious ceremony but one, he supposed, he could understand. For what if the wrong Ian McCullough had been apprehended?

And there came, one morning, Dr. Morris Flax, who also avoided Ian's eye and remained resolutely neutral in his testimony, willing to be led by neither Mr. Lederer nor Mr. Ottinger. "The trauma to Mrs. McCullough's head might have been an accident," Flax said, "though of course it might also have been something else."

During the neurologist's lengthy, technical testimony, which involved a display of magnified X rays, measuring about two feet by three, for the jury's inspection, Ian began to tremble and worried that he might break down, this episode to be duly reported and headlined in the next day's papers. How quiet the courtroom was, and how reverently everyone, not excluding Judge Harmon, listened to Flax's clipped, cautious voice, the voice of the professional dealer in tragedy, as he described the numerous injuries to Glynnis McCullough's skull; showed, with a pointer, the shadowy brain areas, the fractures in the bone, the blood clot that was removed by emergency surgery from the upper left side of the cerebral cortex. Suppose the patient had lived, Lederer asked, in a dramatically lowered voice, would she have had a full recovery, or would there have been permanent brain damage?

Dr. Flax hesitated for the first time and for the first time allowed a flicker of an expression to pass over his face, a look of regret, annoyance, disdain. "I really cannot say. But I would guess, if forced to do so, that the patient might have sustained some brain damage, and a partial paralysis."

Ian shut his eyes quickly. He had not known this, had he? Had Flax told him?

He began to cry; yet so quietly, with such gentlemanly constraint, sitting as always straight and tall, his head high, he did not think anyone noticed. For the jurors, even with their unimpeded view of his face, were staring at Dr. Flax, fully absorbed in the X rays and his terrible teacherly pointer.

There came then, more aggressively, a Dr. Albert Frazier of the State Department of Health, a forensics expert, a Special Command liaison officer between police and district prosecutors in the state, who testified, and would scarcely be budged by cross-examination, that in his opinion the trauma to the skull and to the brain of the victim—for "victim" was Dr. Frazier's conspicuous term, and not "patient"—could not have been an accident. Again the X rays were exhibited, and again the pointer brought into play. Again the fractures in the bone, the injuries to the brain, the hemorrhaging, the blood clot, the subsequent hemorrhaging, the death. Bruises on Mrs. McCullough's shoulders suggested, Dr. Frazier said, that she had been seized and pushed backward with a good deal of force; had she merely stumbled backward and fallen against the window, her own weight would probably not have been sufficient to account for the trauma. And when Ottinger challenged him he simply repeated what he had said: in his judgment the trauma could not have been caused by an accident.

"Yet you say that the weight of Mrs. McCullough's body would 'probably' not have been sufficient to account for the trauma," Ottinger said. "Which leaves the matter ambiguous, doesn't it?"

"Probability *is* ambiguous," Frazier said. "It is 'possible' that the ceiling of this courtroom will collapse on us in the next few minutes, but it is not 'probable.' "

"It is then 'possible' that the weight of Mrs. McCullough's body would not have been sufficient to account for the trauma, but is it 'probable'?"

Frazier said meanly, "It is both."

Ottinger asked, "But you say categorically that the trauma could not have been caused by an accident. Is this a scientific judgment or just your opinion?"

"Since I am a scientist, it follows that my opinion is scientific."

In a tone of mild incredulity Ottinger asked, "Can you be absolutely certain, Dr. Frazier? Beyond a shadow of a doubt?"

For the first time the witness hesitated, shifted his shoulders inside his coat, conceded, slowly, "One is never absolutely certain of anything one has not seen with his own eyes, of course. And even then . . ."—he paused so long it seemed he had stopped speaking; then added, as if the words held a mysterious meaning for him—"and, of course, beyond the 'shadow' of a doubt. . . ."

Ottinger thanked him and stepped away. Ian was beginning to see that in the courtroom, as virtually everywhere, the trick is to behave as if you have won a point; in which case, perhaps, you have.

BUT THE NEXT item of business was a highly visual and highly dramatic demonstration, staged by the prosecution, to bear out the charge that Glynnis McCullough must have been pushed, and had not simply fallen, into the plate-glass window: the testing of the strength of a sheet of plate glass, identical in size and thickness to the window that had shattered. Much was made by Lederer of the fact that this sheet of glass had been manufactured by the same company that had manufactured the sheet of glass in the McCullough's dining room; it had even been purchased from the same store. A canvas sheet was laid on the courtroom floor and a makeshift shelter set up, to prevent glass from flying out into the courtroom; a faceless mannequin of the approximate size and weight of the deceased was pushed, shoved, thrown against the window, with increasing violence and frustration, until finally the glass cracked: but did not shatter. Ian watched in horror and lifted his hands to shield his eyes. How terrible, how terrible, he thought. He saw again Glynnis's contorted face, the blur of motion that was her body and his, saw again the window careening toward them, and remembered it breaking so easily: as if it had already been broken, in readiness.

Like the magnified X rays, the "window demonstration," as it would be called in the press, made a powerful impression upon the courtroom; but Ottinger calmly and, it seemed, logically dismantled its underlying argument. He objected that no one in the courtroom, except possibly his client, could speak to the condition of the window that had broken: whether it had been previously cracked, for instance; whether it had been fitted in its frame to the degree to which the glass in the demonstration had been fitted in its frame; and so on and so forth. And it was surely erroneous, and a violation of common sense, to claim that a sheet of glass purchased in March 1988 was identical to a sheet of glass purchased as long ago as 1965, when the McCullough house had been built. . . .

So Nick Ottinger rose to the occasion and, for all Ian knew, might have salvaged it. But the image of the mannequin thrown against the glass, and picked up, and thrown, and again picked up, and again thrown, with increasing force, and the simulation of rage, stayed with him. How terrible. How clearly I too deserve to die.

THERE CAME, IN their turn, Police Detectives Wentz and Holleran, Ian's old companions, who answered Lederer's questions unhesitatingly and succinctly: there seemed to be no doubt in their minds that a crime had been committed; thus a criminal had committed it, though they did not quite say so in those words. To Ian's embarrassment the lengthy, rambling, inconclusive interview of May 29, taped at Hazelton police headquarters, was played to the court: and seemed, like so much else that both did yet did not represent him, to make a significant impression upon the jurors.

The voices of the several police detectives were distinct but the voice of Ian McCullough was indistinct: indeed, vague, evasive, and toneless. *I don't know.* And: *I don't remember.* As a consequence of Ottinger's presence, Ian had at least managed to say nothing to incriminate himself: that, he knew; yet he squirmed in misery, hearing his voice so lacking in resonance and spirit, a dead man's voice, the voice of a clearly guilty man. How unfair it was! How unjust! A voice on a tape, of necessity bodiless, lacking all the qualifications of the physical self's condition, at that time and in that place: that morning, Ian recalled, of grief, exhaustion, despair.

The tape ran, in its entirety, for over three hours; it was repetitive, circumlocutious, and spaced out by long silences yet exerted a curious spell, even a kind of slowly accumulating tension. For one waited—Ian found himself waiting!—for a break in the accused's demeanor: a sudden admission of guilt, or a declaration of innocence.

AFTERWARD IAN ASKED Ottinger why the prosecution had not edited or summarized this interminable tape, and Ottinger said, "To punish us, I suppose"; then, more seriously, "I wouldn't have wanted it summarized, in any case."

"Why on earth not?" Ian asked.

"Because it's your voice on the tape, for one thing, which the court won't otherwise hear," Ottinger said. "Unless you change your mind, as I hope you will, and testify." When Ian said nothing Ottinger added, "My instinct is, your existence must be established. It should seem after all more substantial than that of . . . the person whom you have been accused of killing."

Ian was struck by this remark, which he could not quite comprehend. "My existence? Has it been in doubt?"

Ottinger smiled his ambiguous smile, in which, depending upon one's mood, one could read sympathy or contempt. "Hasn't it?"

AND THEN CAME what Ian had long dreaded, the prosecution's dogged pursuit and amplification of the "motive" for the crime: the matter of Sigrid Hunt, missing since the approximate date of the defendant's arrest, on May 30, 1987.

This aspect of the case was taken up with gusto by Lederer, who called Mrs. Elizabeth Kuhn to the witness stand, and Mrs. Roberta Grinnell, "intimate friends of the deceased"; and Mr. Horace K. Vick, caretaker for the rental property at 119 Tice Street, Poughkeepsie, where Sigrid Hunt had lived, at least intermittently, from September 1984 to May 1987. Elizabeth, whom Ian realized, with a sinking sensation, he had not seen in a very long time, gave almost verbatim the testimony she had given to the grand jury: handsome, white-haired, rather regal in responding to Lederer's questions, and resisting when he tried to lead her where she would not be led—into acknowledging that there might be grounds for believing that Mrs. McCullough was correct in her assumption that Mr. McCullough was involved with another woman. Yet she made Ian uneasy by the sharpness with which she replied to Ottinger's questions, as if she cared to make no distinction between him and Mr. Lederer. The carefully worded, very nice things she said about Ian McCullough—"One of our dearest most beloved most loyal friends"—sounded, to Ian's ear, rather forced, as if rehearsed; and the smile Elizabeth directed toward him, as she stepped down, seemed to him forced as well. How she had aged, since Ian had seen her last. . . . Someone has broken her heart, Ian thought.

And then came Roberta Grinnell, looking rather drawn and resistant, regarding Lederer with an expression of frank dislike, hands nervous in her lap, voice nearly inaudible, the streak of gold in her hair strangely dulled, as if by the opacity of the white winter sky beyond the window. (But why did she refuse to look at him? Had someone told her about Meika?) Her testimony was terse and ungiving; several times, Harmon instructed her to speak louder. It seemed clear that she was a hostile witness, which fact did not endear her, Ian suspected, to the court.

He had not spoken with her in weeks. He had intended to telephone her . . . but somehow he had not.

Roberta was recounting her grand jury testimony, point by point: the telephone call to Glynnis McCullough; the startling conversation that followed; Glynnis's distress, incoherence, anger; Glynnis's conviction, which Roberta knew to be unfounded, that her husband was having an affair with another woman.

"Did Mrs. McCullough tell you about a check she had found in her husband's desk made out to 'Sigrid Hunt,' a mutual friend, for the sum of one thousand dollars?" Lederer asked.

"Yes, she did," Roberta said.

"But still you thought her suspicions unfounded?" Lederer asked.

"Yes I did," Roberta said.

"But why, given the apparent evidence?" Lederer asked.

"It didn't seem to me . . . that it was evidence," Roberta said.

"Mrs. McCullough was one of your closest friends, wasn't she?" Lederer asked. "Yet you chose not to believe her."

"I didn't 'choose' not to believe her," Roberta said nervously, "it just seemed to me that she was exaggerating the situation, overreacting, as people sometimes do when they think they have been hurt."

"Was Mrs. McCullough in the habit of exaggerating?" Lederer asked.

"She was an intelligent woman but she could be emotional; she had a temper; you could say she had a dramatic personality," Roberta said.

"And Mr. McCullough—"

"Much quieter, much more in control."

" 'In control'? Of himself, or of others?"

"Of himself. Ian was not in the habit of controlling, or trying to control, others."

"You knew them both well, you and your husband?"

"I think I could say that, yes."

"And you found it absolutely impossible to believe that Mr. McCullough might have been involved with another woman?"

"I found it unlikely."

"Because—?"

"Because I knew him, and I knew Glynnis," Roberta said, her voice rising. "Ian wasn't the type."

"And of this you were absolutely certain?"

"What can I say, except to repeat what I've already said?"

"It is such an extraordinary thing, in your circle of acquaintances, that a husband might occasionally be unfaithful to his wife, or a wife to her husband, it simply cannot be believed?"

"Of course not, you're distorting my words."

"But in the McCulloughs' case, it could not be believed? At least by you?"

"In their case . . . yes."

"And you base this on your intimate acquaintance with them, and with their marriage?"

"I base it on common sense."

"There were no marital difficulties that you knew of?"

"There were no marital difficulties that I knew of."

"Had there been, do you think you would have known?"

"Glynnis, or Ian, would have told us, I'm sure . . . would have told Denis or me. I'm sure. Or we would have known, the way friends know what is happening with one another."

"You would have known, you think, if there had been marital difficulties?"

"Yes."

"You would have been told?"

"Yes, I think so."

"Yet on the day, when Mrs. McCullough called you—"

"I called her."

"When you called her, and she tried to tell you about a crisis in her marriage, you didn't believe her."

"You distort everything!" Roberta said sharply. "My primary motive that day was to calm Glynnis, to reason with her, not to make things worse. I knew she was probably exaggerating something very minor that Ian could explain, and I tried to tell her that. I tried to tell her that several times. And she got angry with me, and wouldn't listen, and hung up on me; and that was that."

Later, when Ottinger questioned her, Roberta spoke more readily, even passionately, insisting that Ian and Glynnis had been a "perfectly happy couple," "a perfectly matched couple"; that the McCullough family was "an ideal Hazelton family." Watching her, Ian felt only a dim stirring of emotion, and that, mainly of regret, as if they were separated by a medium that was not quite transparent: badly scarified glass, for instance. Meika had interceded; Meika had made her claim; it was too late.

The Grinnells were formally separated now: Denis had moved out of the house; Roberta had moved back in, but only temporarily, for the house was to be sold. Denis had explained the breakup as the consequence of "irreconcilable differences." But what on earth does that mean? Ian asked, and Denis merely shrugged, saying, When a woman stops loving you that's that; it's like touching dead meat. And Ian had recoiled from his friend, who had never in their long acquaintance spoken so vulgarly, or in such despair.

AT LAST, WITH a dramatic flourish, as if these items constituted absolute proof of the defendant's guilt, Lederer introduced as evidence a facsimile of the check for $1,000, made out by Ian McCullough to Sigrid Hunt and dated February 20, 1987; and a record of the toll calls, eight in number, made from the McCullough's telephone to Hunt's Poughkeepsie number in the spring of that year. "Mr. McCullough has never explained the check to Hunt or the telephone calls," Lederer said, with an air of pique, as if Ian had personally offended him. "When asked, he has refused to answer. The matter is a 'private' one, he says: 'no one's business but his own.' " Lederer regarded the court, in particular the jurors, with an expression of mild disbelief. How was it possible that any man, charged with murder, should be so arrogant? so defiant? so self-destructive?

Ian squirmed in embarrassment and willed himself to retreat, to withdraw, to disappear into that space, whether in his soul or in his brain, where such indignities could not follow. For it seemed now publicly clear that Ian McCullough was not only a liar but that his longtime friends Mrs. Kuhn and Mrs. Grinnell were actively involved in lying on his behalf, or had been duped by him.

But there came, next, as if for comic relief of a kind, Mr. Horace K. Vick, caretaker of the rental once occupied by Miss Sigrid Hunt: the very man Ian had inveigled into unlocking the apartment; though, on the witness stand, having sworn to tell the truth so help him God, he lied with extraordinary ease and an air of self-righteousness, claiming that he had resisted Dr. McCullough's offer of a bribe. He wasn't that type, he said. To snoop on tenants. Vick was wearing a shiny black suit, with a white shirt and a bowtie; his hair had been brutally trimmed for the occasion; his wizened, malicious face fairly lit up with pleasure as Lederer led him, with ever more insinuating questions, through his testimony. He pointed at Ian with an accusing forefinger, to identify him as the man he'd seen visit Sigrid Hunt several times, oh, three or four times it must have been, over the winter; maybe stayed the night, around Christmas; and, in the spring sometime, asked to be let into the apartment. 'Cause he was worried she'd been hurt or something, maybe killed. 'Cause she had other boyfriends too.

Despite Lederer's effort to rein him in, Vick began to embellish his story, adding extraneous details, smiling and grimacing, as if, with the attention of the court upon him, he were demonically inspired. He spoke of Dr. McCullough's "fancy red sports car, some kind of Eyetalian make," and Dr. McCullough's fancy fur coat, "or maybe it was a coat with a fur collar—either way, you don't see many men that's normal men, I mean that go for women, with an outfit like that." He spoke excitedly of wild parties in Sigrid Hunt's apartment, and people from the college where she used to teach—"the college that used to be all women, you know, what's it, Vassar"—cars parked in the driveway and music and noise and "some coloreds" on the scene too, though this was before McCullough showed up. Or somebody who looked like him.

"Then there was this poor s.o.b., another one of them old enough to be her father, that turned up one night, knocking on my door and asking for her . . . says he's her brother. So I says to him, I says, 'Yeh and I'm her brother too, there's a whole long line of 'em that's her brother.' And I says—"

"Please, Mr. Vick. Stay with the line of questioning."

"You *asked* me, I'm *tell*ing you," Vick said, flaring up in anger. "You want to know, or what?"

So the witness discredited himself and drew a rebuke from Judge Harmon, and Lederer tried, with little success, to salvage what he could; but the damage had already been done. Under Ottinger's skillful questioning—What sort of car did Dr. McCullough drive? What sort of coat did Dr. McCullough wear? How many times had Dr. McCullough visited Sigrid Hunt? And when had he visited? And when was the party? And who were the other guests?—Vick was made out to be not only a wholly unreliable witness but a malicious one. And when he stepped down, having been several times rebuked by Harmon and threatened with contempt of court, he could not resist making an ambiguous gesture in the direction of the judge's bench, which of course prompted an immediate, and very angry, response and some minutes of courtroom flurry and suppressed merriment, when it looked as if Horace Vick might be carried out bodily by police and put into a detention cell.

Ian smiled, with the others; it may have been his first smile in this terrible place. He could not, for the life of him, comprehend why Vick disliked him so; why, in all his rambling about Sigrid Hunt and her men, he had never once mentioned Fermi Sabri; why he had focused his venom upon Ian McCullough. Had $25 been too small a sum and, in retrospect, injurious to Vick's pride? Or had he forgotten he'd been given any money at all?

Asked, afterward, about Vick's probable motive, Ottinger had said indifferently, "Who gives a damn? The witness is gone, dead, *finito*."

IN THE REAR of Ottinger's elegantly cushioned car, returning to Hazelton and to home, Ian lay back and shut his eyes, made an effort not to sleep, for sleep was out of the question, but simply to clear his mind of that day's accumulation of griefs. The others, including Bianca, were talking about the trial; of course they were talking about the trial; there was nothing else to talk about but the trial; there would never be anything else to talk about, in Ian McCullough's life, but the trial. The prosecution would be closing its case in another day or so, and then the defense would present its case. And then, and then. The summations, the judge's instructions to the jury, the jury's deliberations, the verdict. And then.

Ian thought of that day, that day of such extravagant innocence and recklessness, in Bridgeport: the wood-frame duplex in which they'd lived, painted its bright inappropriate blues; the old neighborhood streets; the elementary school and the junior high school; the melancholy little park. He had felt a yearning so palpable as to be almost physical, like sexual desire. And for what? And why? It had brought him to this, a stranger's Mercedes-Benz speeding along a country highway, in the dark of an interminable winter, toward the house he could think of in no other terms than home.

He thought . . . not of Glynnis, who was after all dead and could not help him . . . but of Meika Cassity: approaching the defense table, not altogether prudently, at the end of that afternoon's session; rising pertly on her toes to kiss his cheek, and squeeze, with a schoolgirl's passion, his hand; whispering in his ear (which burned and must have turned bright red), her splendid dark-burnished sable coat slung over her shoulder and her jeweled earrings flashing. Meika's skin was pale but heated; her eyes were unnaturally bright. Seizing Ottinger's hand in hers she congratulated him on the afternoon's performance: "You are going to save Ian, aren't you? Prove his absolute innocence to all the world, aren't you?"

He adored her. He was terrified of her.

4.

By ignoring it, they said, when asked how they dealt with the publicity.

Of the trial coverage in the daily newspapers, in one of the two major news magazines, even, to their chagrin, in the Sunday supplement of the *Newburgh Times*, Ian and Bianca took no account: Ian on principle (for in fact he'd never wasted his time reading such things in the old days of his anonymity, thus why now?), Bianca because her capacity for outrage, indignity, and hurt was finally exhausted. A glossy New York magazine, part fashion and part scandal, approached her with an offer of $50,000 to write "your father's story from *your* point of view." When she declined they returned with an offer of $75,000.

Bianca was preparing material for publication, however: Glynnis's *American Appetites.* She had taken the spring semester off from Wesleyan to be with Ian during the trial; the rest of the time she worked on the manuscript, sitting at Glynnis's place at the kitchen table, industriously typing up notes, collating recipes, talking on the telephone with friends of Glynnis's who had shared her interest in cooking and with Glynnis's editor in New York City. It was now March: the publisher hoped for a more or less complete manuscript by the first of June. "I had never realized there was so much to cooking, to food," Bianca told Ian, and others, in his hearing. "If you want to do things correctly, it's a lot of *work*." And: "I really enjoy doing this, I would never have thought I *would*." And, over the phone, to an unidentified friend: "I really feel close to Mother, for the first time I guess since I was a small child." The air of happy conviction in his daughter's voice struck Ian as insincere, though he hoped of course that it was not.

The actual cooking, begun tentatively, took up more and more of Bianca's time. Glynnis had left variants of certain recipes, as many as six for a single dish, for instance, and Bianca could not decide which was the preferred one. A lentil soup from Pennsylvania Dutch country, with cumin, garlic, ham hocks, and fresh spinach. A heavy stew, pozole, from the Southwest, made with chilies, pork loin, chicken, and hominy. Texas hash, with Tabasco sauce; classic American meat loaf, with chopped olives, mushrooms, thyme, toasted wheat germ; Maryland fried chicken; Charleston chicken hash; New England Indian pudding, with cornmeal, dark molasses, and cinnamon. In the semihysterical aftermath of a trial day Bianca even attempted sauce *velouté*, fillets of sole *en papillotes*, paella *à la Valenciana*. The more ambitious meals were likely to be served as late as eleven o'clock, at which time Bianca would seek out her father (who might have fallen asleep, fully clothed, on top of his bed, having meant "just to rest my eyes"), excited, nervous, apologetic beforehand: "I don't think this has turned out absolutely perfectly, Daddy, and I'm terribly sorry to have taken so long, but—" Ian, sleep-dazed, mildly hung over from the several quick drinks he'd very likely have had earlier that evening, smiled and took his place at the dining room table, where candles were burning, their delicate flames trembling with his approach.

Though Bianca fussed over her mother's recipes and spent hours in the kitchen, she had very little appetite for the meals she prepared; oddly, Ian thought, and worrisomely. Nothing seemed to please her, for, as she said, watching Ian eat (these evenings, he ate slowly, seemed to lose concentration even as he chewed and swallowed), Glynnis would certainly have made it better: *had* made it better. Bianca messed her food about her plate, trying a few mouthfuls, frequently murmuring, disappointed, "Not quite, not this time," and making a face, which rather exasperated Ian, who recalled (for, dear God, how could he not recall) those many hours at the dinner table when, balky and pouting, Bianca found her mother's superbly prepared food not to her taste. Those meals had begun in hope and ended in strain, wounded feelings, intemperate words. Now it was her own food Bianca was refusing.

And she was losing weight steadily, Ian saw. Even in the midst of his own self-absorption, he saw. Her clothes swung loose, her cheeks were becoming hollow. A grim sad satisfied look to her face in repose.

So he said, with a father's chiding smile, a father's smiling frown, Why don't *you* eat, and Bianca said quickly, Oh, I *am*, believe me I *am*, but sometimes I can't keep it down.

5.

He spoke with Meika at least once a day, whether in person or on the telephone, but dared not see her in private, to make love with her, more than once a week in the evenings. Depending upon Vaughn's schedule— whether he was in Hazelton, in New York City, or elsewhere—they met, or tried to meet, on the weekends. On both Saturday and Sunday. For as many hours as they dared.

Did Vaughn know? Ian wondered. And, knowing, did he care?

That strange, sad, mysterious man. My friend of so many years, whom I don't know.

MEIKA SAID, LAZILY, "Vaughn and Glynnis—you know they had something going, once, don't you?—so this is tit for tat."

Ian said, "Vaughn and Glynnis? Are you serious?"

"*They* were serious. But nothing came of it."

"What on earth are you talking about?"

"Your wife, my husband. Didn't you know?"

"When was this?"

"Don't get so excited, Ian," Meika said, smiling her sweet sly slanted smile. "As I said, nothing came of it."

Ian started at her. She was lying with her arms behind her head, the hollows of her underarms exposed shaved and powdered, so intimate a sight, for all their present intimacy, Ian felt it wrong of him to look: as if he were taking advantage of a child. He said, more calmly, "Are you serious, really, or are you teasing? When did this all take place?"

"I don't think we should talk about it," Meika said. "Since it seems to upset you so."

"Of course it upsets me," Ian said, laughing angrily. "To be told so casually that my wife—"

"Oh, 'my wife'—that sort of thing is anachronistic too," Meika said, sitting up abruptly and reaching for her cigarettes on the bedside table. " 'My wife,' 'my property'—the very usage is outmoded." Moving, as she did, her small yet rather flaccid breasts swung: as if the delicate, slightly puckered envelope of skin contained jelly, or water, and might be easily punctured. The first time they had made love, on the eve of Christmas Eve, some weeks before, Meika had drawn Ian's fingers across a thin sickle scar on the outside of her right breast, where a cyst had been removed—"Don't worry: benign"—a few years ago.

Though Ian was Meika's lover, and, in an outmoded style of speech, Meika Ian's mistress, he had yet to become accustomed to her ease in her flesh: or her indifference. He thought her body dazzlingly lovely, though so thin, rather epicene: the narrow boyish hips and long legs charmingly knobby at the knees; the flat smooth stomach and belly (for Meika had never, of course, been pregnant); the small breasts; the collarbone and ribs upon which her skin seemed so tightly, even nervously, stretched. Away from this body he was apt to dream of it, even, fiercely, to will his thoughts upon it: that he might be shielded from thinking of other things. And when, as now, he was with Meika, her presence so flooded his senses, the curious authority of her soul so crowded his own, Ian found it difficult to think at all. Repeatedly he told her, "You are so beautiful, Meika. So beautiful," in a voice of wonder, and Meika seemed to accept such homage as her due; yet teased. "If I'm so beautiful now, why not until now? Why did you never see me before? I loved you, you know, for years," she would say, accusingly, dreamily, "and you never knew; never cared to know; looked through me; cruelly snubbed me," kissing him and caressing him as she spoke, and, as she spoke, as they began to make love, Ian had the uneasy sense that Meika was improvising, inventing, creating for the two of them, now they were lovers, and given an imprimatur of a kind by the physical act of loving, a fictitious but univocal past by which the present, so vertiginous in its forward movement, might be explained.

Most of the time, most of their times, were spent in Meika's bedroom—that is, Meika and Vaughn's bedroom—a spacious, airy, beautifully furnished room with a skylight of glazed, or milky, rather than transparent glass. Though this room was in the older part of the house Vaughn had redesigned it considerably: there was a small dressing room, mirrored, for Meika, and a wall-length closet for the Cassitys' many clothes; a shelf of books, most of them oversized art books and photography books; an enclosed sun deck, opening from a louvered door at the rear, roofed with a specially tinted glass that withheld the sun's more corrosive rays. In this room, with its potted and hanging plants and cushioned white wicker furniture, Meika frequently, on sunny winter days—as Meika had, earlier this morning, demonstrated for Ian—lay nude on a lounge chair, covered by a thin muslin cloth, in order to both absorb the sun's rays and to be protected from them. Her skin, she said, was too fair and thin to tolerate much sun: like, she guessed, Ian's own.

"I realize that Vaughn and Glynnis liked each other a good deal," Ian said, reasonably. "I know Glynnis admired Vaughn, as an architect, and spoke of having him build a house for us some day—"

Meika interrupted. "No, it was to be an addition to the house you have."

"But, still, I find it difficult to believe that—"

"Glynnis loved that house, as you must know. She wanted never to leave it."

"—difficult to believe that it was anything more serious."

"Perhaps then it wasn't," Meika conceded, smoke streaming thinly, yet luxuriantly, from her nostrils. "It becomes increasingly difficult, with time, to know what 'serious' means."

Meika asked if Ian would like another glass of wine, more of the freshly opened Bordeaux she'd brought upstairs with them, and Ian shook his head no, but may have meant yes; so Meika poured him another glass, which Ian drank down, distractedly, as if it were water. She asked would he care for another of the cocktail sandwiches—smoked salmon with dill on crustless white bread, *pâté de la campagne* thickly smeared on pumpernickel—she'd brought up on a platter, delicious though slightly stale; they were leftovers from a party of the previous evening. (Ian had come to the Cassitys', as he'd rather falteringly told Bianca, for Sunday brunch: so very coincidentally, since he'd come there for Saturday brunch only the day before.)

Meika had changed the subject and was talking, complaining

rather, of the trial: its many interruptions and delays; the interminable slowness and opacity, not to say obfuscation, of certain of its procedures; the collective disappointment felt by onlookers when, so seemingly willfully, Judge Harmon stopped proceedings and adjourned with counsel to his chambers. She seemed to think that the trial, Ian McCullough's trial, was an entertainment: or intended to be so. And while she admired Nick Ottinger immensely, she did not like Lederer: did not like him at all. "Isn't it a sobering thing, to realize the power a public prosecutor has, under our system," she said. "To haul perfectly innocent people into court. To make them prove their innocence. And to say such things about them: the *fucker.*"

She looked at Ian, who had not quite been following her line of thought. "He's ruining all our lives," she said. "And yet, he has made them all so . . . significant. Did you read that thing in the *Times?* That sort of personal-interest feature, I guess you would call it, really quite well written, and in its way insightful, the townspeople's vision of the Institute, and of us—'American elite' we are called—the whole thing linked up, I think totally unfairly, in fact outrageously unfairly, with 'white collar' and 'corporate' crime. The rise in statistics or some such thing. But you don't read the newspapers, do you?—I just remembered." She made a sympathetic gesture, pursing her lips in a kiss, of the kind one might offer a person who has suffered a very minor, if not comical, hurt. "You're much better off, not."

Ian felt a sharp pain between his eyes. He said, setting down his wineglass, "I think I had better go home."

Meika said irritably, "You are *always* saying that."

"Not always, surely. But it's nearly three o'clock. Nick Ottinger is dropping by today, to go over some sort of argument, or motion, or brief on my behalf he wants to present to—"

"I think, you know," Meika said, sliding back into bed, her wineglass balanced precariously as she kicked at the covers, "that men like you are terrified of intimacy, of any sort of public acknowledgment of intimacy. Basically you are terrified of something happening to *you* outside of the properly defined contexts of your lives."

"Meika, don't be cruel," Ian said jokingly, as if Meika's very real capacity for cruelty were only play. "It isn't at all flattering to hear an expression like 'men like you.' It suggests—"

"Having a heart attack, for instance, in someone else's bed. Another man's bed. His *property*: like his wife. And, dear God, how proprietary he is, about *his* wife! As if butter wouldn't have melted in Glynnis's—"

"Meika," Ian said, flinching. "Please don't."

"—vagina, then. To maintain our elite vocabulary."

Ian stared at her, really quite baffled. It was not the first time in recent weeks that Meika had become so suddenly, and, it seemed, so inexplicably, furious with him. And there was a nerved-up glow, even a sort of glare, to her skin, and to her pewter-colored eyes, that suggested her extreme pleasure in such fury.

"One of the Rockefellers died that way," Meika said, resting her head back on the pillow and half closing her eyes, as if dreamy with memory's effort, "I forget which. Not Nelson. (Or *was* it Nelson?) And I knew a woman, an old pal," she went on, regarding Ian with amusement, "—having a love affair with a man not unlike you, a straitlaced professional man, very distinguished in his field, very properly married—'happily' as the saying invariably goes—and she adored him, and he claimed to adore her, and this went on for years, a sort of stalemate on both sides, both of them (did I say this?) married, of course. And one day, in a Manhattan hotel—I think it was the Plaza actually; the two of them took it all quite seriously and romantically, though, as I said, it had been dragging on for years—one day, the poor man had a heart attack . . . a coronary thrombosis . . . and *died*, actually *died*, right there in the hotel room, in the hotel bed, in the very act, I suppose, of making love. Jesus! Can you imagine! My friend panicked, she said; had a kind of blackout, or delirium; threw her clothes on and left the hotel and took the train back to Greenwich, where she and her husband lived, and their children, *she* was happily married too; and her lover was left behind—his body, I mean. And when she got home she telephoned the Plaza and said, 'Something has happened to a man in room'—whatever. And she hung up the phone. And that was the end of *that* love affair."

Ian, dressing, rather clumsily, a salmon sandwich stuffed in his mouth, laughed; and, thinking how intensely he hated this woman, said, "Meika, darling, you are impossible." It seemed to him precisely what a lover of Meika Cassity's, dressing clumsily, a salmon sandwich stuffed in his mouth, under her bemused and critical scrutiny, would naturally say.

"Yes," Meika said, "but you don't love me, do you."

"Of course I love you. It's just that I must leave; I really must. Nick is—"

"Oh, the hell with Nick. And Bianca. And Vaughn. And—the rest. The fact is, you hate me."

"Don't be ridiculous."

"You hate us all."

"Meika, for God's sake, please. This has been such a lovely day for me, such a—"

"Tell me: did you hate Glynnis when . . . when it happened?"

"When what happened?"

"The accident. That night. Did you hate her, then?"

Ian felt the pain, sharper now, between his eyes. He said, "I'm going. I'll call you tonight."

"But *did* you? I can keep a secret; really I can."

"I never hated Glynnis; please don't say such things," Ian said, "and I don't hate you."

"Oh, yes you do."

Ian stooped to kiss her goodbye, as if nothing were wrong, for, for all he knew, his senses in such a tumult, his heart beating so alarmingly fast, nothing at all was wrong. Perhaps this was all play: love play of a kind to which he, in his straitlaced long-married propriety, was not accustomed.

Meika slipped her arms around his neck and said, her mouth swollen as if with hurt or desire, "Yet you want, don't you"—her eyes opened wide, yet dreamy and occluded—"so badly to hurt me. Right now. Don't you. Tell the *truth.*"

COMING UPON IAN that night, sitting at his desk with his head cradled in his arms and his glasses beside him, upside down as if removed in haste, Bianca said softly, "Daddy?" and Ian stirred guiltily, hearing her voice: so familiar a voice, yet not one he seemed, in this strange new mood that had come upon him, to have expected. "Are you all right, Daddy? Are you"—and Bianca paused, unable to bring herself to lay a hand on his shoulder, as if in fear of overstepping the amorphous but seemingly irrefragable border between them—"all *right?*"

Ian looked up and groped for his glasses, saying, "Yes, yes of course," smiling at her. "Of course. I was just resting my eyes."

Bianca apologized for the fact that dinner was so delayed. She'd begun, she said, at seven o'clock, and it seemed, now, to be nearly ten. "You must be starving," she said.

"Oh, yes," Ian said, still smiling at her. "Yes, certainly."

HE HAD MADE up his mind that he would not, simply could not, see the woman again, let alone touch her, make love with her: grovel in her. For all that she'd said that day, or had taunted him with, was true; even as it was, of course, not true at all; in fact obscenely contrary to the truth.

So he telephoned her and said, "Meika? I don't think we should see each other again for a while."

Meika said, "I was thinking the same thing, actually."

There was an awkward pause. Ian could hear music in the background, a harsh calypso beat; could hear voices.

Meika said, as if apologetically, "Ian, dear, the problem is that you are so easily *hurt;* I suppose I'm not accustomed to a man quite like you. It's as if the outermost layer of your skin has been peeled off. Have you always been like this, or has it . . . does it have something to do, you know, with . . . the things that have happened to you?"

Ian said flatly that he didn't know. And that he had to hang up.

Next morning, in court, he did not see Meika and was able, for the duration of that day—a day that passed in a haze of pain, involving, as it did, Samuel S. Lederer's summary of his case against Ian McCullough—to forget about her; or, at any rate, not to think about her. But that night Meika called, merely, as she said, to say hello and to ask how the day had gone, and Ian broke down, and began to weep, and said, pleading, "Meika, I didn't mean it, I hope you know I didn't mean it, I love you, I want to see you again soon, tonight if I can, if we could"—while Meika, in a pretense of surprise, made comforting sounds over the telephone—"I'm not ready yet, I need you, I want to marry you, I love you, I love you more than *he* loves you; do you think, Meika, don't answer me now—not yet—we might be married? Someday, when all this is settled, when . . . when we are both free, when—"

When Ian's extraordinary outburst had run its course, Meika said gently, it may have been pityingly, "Why of course, Ian, I love you too, and I'm not ready yet either; of course I want to see you again. But not tonight, darling: I'm afraid Vaughn is back from San Diego."

6.

Ian thought, It is as if I am attached to a great machine, Death. A robot with no will, no volition, no intelligence of my own.

He was trying to urinate but could not. His muscles clenched in alarm . . . the muscles of his belly and groin. He was standing before a urinal in some place not known to him, of a clinical tiled white; but, badly as he wanted to urinate, his bladder bloated to the point of pain, nothing happened. And then—

He woke, in his bed, on the verge of having urinated in his sleep. But woke in time. I am becoming an infant, he thought. They are killing me.

THE TRIAL WAS entering its fifth week.

After the prosecution completed its case, the defense duly filed a motion that the charge against Ian McCullough be dismissed and the trial itself ended. Ottinger's argument was that the prosecution had failed to prove that any crime had been committed, de facto; the death of Mrs. McCullough had followed from an accident for which no one could be held accountable. He argued too that the prosecution had presented insufficient and merely circumstantial evidence; that there were no eye-witnesses to the "crime"; that there had been no motive established. And that the "vendetta" against his client was politically motivated.

This, Judge Harmon seemed to seriously consider but in the end denied. So the trial continued, and, on the morning of March 24,

Ottinger began his case, rising to remind the court (how diplomatic, Ian thought: "remind") of the famous admonition of the fourteenth-century English philosopher William of Occam (i.e., Occam's Razor): we are warned "never to multiply entities beyond simplicity."

For it was Ottinger's central argument that no crime had been committed; though he and his client knew why a crime had been hypothetized and publicized. "The prosecution has said that this is a simple case, motivated by lust, greed, and barbaric selfishness," Ottinger said. "And so, in a way, it is. But the 'lust, greed, and barbaric selfishness' are not attributes of my client; they are attributes of the authorities who have brought the outrageous charge of second-degree murder. . . ." And so it went.

The argument offered by the defense, or, as Ian thought it, the narrative, was, of course, the very obverse of the prosecution's. Where, previously, Dr. Ian McCullough had been a man of "deceptive civility," a "passive-aggressive personality" of a kind prone to "repressed" violence, and susceptible, by way of alcohol or drugs, to an "explosive liberation" of said violence, Dr. Ian McCullough was now a man of "unfailing courtesy," "kindness," "generosity": a model husband and father, a model citizen, a model of professional "brilliance" and "reliability"; admired by his colleagues, loved by his friends; "even-tempered," "rational," "reasonable"; even, in the passionate words of an Institute colleague (Denis Grinnell), "the most civilized man of my acquaintance." Where, in previous weeks, he had been a "devious and systematic" adulterer, a "faithless" husband, sufficiently "coldhearted" not only to betray his wife but to lie to her and, as the evidence would seem to have shown, to commit an act of grievous physical harm against her, he was now an "unfailingly faithful and devoted" husband to his wife of twenty-six years, a man who "has always divided his time equally between his family and his profession," with a reputation for . . . and so on and so forth. Ian recalled that the gods of antiquity observed a rule: none must cross the path of another's humor.

Yet he felt, with the passage of days, as the procession of defense witnesses came forward to take the stand in Ian McCullough's behalf, to swear to tell the truth the whole truth and nothing but the truth so help me God, a yet more profound sense of shame. For now others, these so innocent and well-intentioned others, were publicly involved in his fate.

FROM THE START, Nicholas Ottinger had made an excellent impression on the court. He was articulate, yet not too articulate; forthright, yet not overbearing; inclined at times to irony, but never, like his older adversary, to sarcasm. He seemed to possess a photographic memory and knew many things Ian was astonished to discover he knew (the make and date of Ian's car, for instance), since Ian could not recall having told him. An attractive, well-dressed man of youthful middle age, with his dark tight-rippled hair and look of combative vigor; a sudden startling white smile; springy on his feet, yet dignified; and clearly very intelligent: a man, Ian thought, one would not wish for an enemy.

His strategy, he told Ian, was to establish Ian's "real" character in the jurors' minds. This being done, he then shifted to the circumstances of the accident, drawing testimony from, among others, a Manhattan forensic specialist who claimed that the fractures to Glynnis's skull "might easily have been caused by a fall." (Again the X rays were evoked; the pointer brought into play. Again the jurors, so sedulously courted, looked on rapt with attention.) He re-called to the witness stand the chief paramedic; one of the young police officers who had entered the McCullough's house on the night of the accident; the admitting physician at Hazelton Medical Center; even Dr. Flax, who repeated much of his testimony verbatim but became, under Ottinger's persistent questioning of his medical career (i.e., the malpractice suits brought against Flax in 1983 and 1987, each settled out of court for an "undisclosed" sum), suddenly rather defensive. There was an entertaining sequence, taking up, in all, three full trial days, involving witnesses who had known Sigrid Hunt during the two-year tenure of her dance instructorship at Vassar and during the period of her engagement to Mr. Fermi Sabri: six young women and three young men, each of whom denied any knowledge of a "relationship" or, even, a "friendship" with Ian McCullough. ("I never heard of him, frankly." "The name is unknown to me, except, y'know, from reading about the two of them in the papers.")

The most articulate of these witnesses was a young woman friend of Sigrid Hunt's who had attended dance classes with her in Manhattan, years ago, and was now, like Hunt, an ex-dancer "on the fringes of the dance world": living in SoHo and working as a waitress in a Seventh Avenue jazz club. Her name was Ichor Matthews—"Yes, sir, Ichor is my baptismal name"—and she had prematurely white hair, a high pale brow, a rapid, brittle, yet rather seductive voice. She wore a black jumpsuit with conspicuous silver buckles and zippers and high-heeled black boots.

Ottinger asked, "To your knowledge, Miss Matthews, did Sigrid Hunt ever speak of 'Dr. Ian McCullough'?"

Ichor Matthews said, "Sigrid knew all sorts of people, she might have mentioned his name, or a name like that, but I truthfully don't remember. People go in and out of all of our lives. . . ."

"You don't remember the name 'Ian McCullough'?"

"No, sir, I do not."

"Did she mention other men's names, which you do remember?"

"Oh, yes, certainly. We had friends in common. And there was this man, this Egyptian engineer, from a millionaire family in Cairo I think; she'd talk about him all the time because she was afraid of him, I think. But she was in love with him too; they were supposed to get married."

"Was it a formal engagement?"

" 'Engaged' is the word Sigrid used, yes."

"And what was Miss Hunt's fiancé's name?"

"Fermi Sabri. But I think his real name was Sharif or something; I wasn't ever clear about it."

"And how would you describe your friend's relationship with Mr. Sabri?"

"Dramatic."

"Meaning—?"

"Dramatic is an understatement, actually. I happen to know that Sabri bullied her, threatened her, even beat her sometimes, though she never reported him. She might have been afraid he would have killed her, or she might have wanted to protect him because she loved him."

"Did you ever witness his 'bullying' of her?"

"Oh, no. Nothing like that. I'd see her sometimes bruised around the face and neck, maybe the wrists; once there was a large ugly purplish-yellow bruise above her knee . . . but she said she had done it to herself. And I didn't want to argue; I didn't want to get into that. Because women like that, who let themselves be hurt by men, are almost always lying to protect them; and it makes me sick. Frankly."

"Did Miss Hunt appeal to anyone for help, to your knowledge?"

"No. Not to my knowledge."

"How long were Miss Hunt and Mr. Sabri engaged?"

"About eighteen months. Until she had an abortion, which he didn't want her to have—which, in fact, he forbade her to have—and that was that."

"You say that Miss Hunt had an abortion? And was Fermi Sabri the father?"

"Oh, definitely. Nobody else."

"When did the abortion take place?"

"Maybe a year ago, about this time."

"And where?"

"Sigrid was so worried about it, so frightened, I set it up for her myself, at a clinic called WomanSpace in Chelsea . . . staffed by women doctors, nurses. A wonderful place, and very safe. No men allowed anywhere on the premises. Sigrid didn't want Fermi to know what she was doing; this was one of the times she was hiding out from him, staying with me or other friends."

"Did she ever, to your knowledge, stay with anyone in Hazelton?"

"In Hazelton? Not to my knowledge."

"And you say she never, so far as you can remember, spoke of Ian McCullough?"

"Sigrid did know people up in Hazelton, connected with the Institute, I think, older people, middle-aged people; I got the impression they were intellectuals, writers and such, and fairly well-to-do. She had this side to her, an utterly conventional side, admiring, even envying, people like that, a sort of bourgeois romantic streak. There was a woman in particular she admired, a food expert I think, but I don't remember any names, and maybe she didn't mention any names. Sigrid was the kind of girl, you might think you knew her, but it would turn out eventually that you didn't; she would have another life somewhere else, an entirely different life . . . like the other side of the moon."

"In any case, Miss Matthews, Sigrid Hunt's emotional life, during the time of which we're speaking, was focused upon her fiancé primarily, and not upon another man?"

"Oh, yes, certainly, I'd say that. No doubt about that."

"And what was Mr. Sabri like?"

"I never actually met him, that's the strange thing. I saw him a few times, the two of them in his car. . . ."

"And what kind of car did Mr. Sabri drive?"

"A Ferrari sports car, I don't remember the name. Bright red. Blood red."

"A distinctive car?"

"A distinctive car. He'd bring her places, or pick her up, but he wouldn't get out; evidently didn't want to be introduced to her American friends. He was jealous, possessive . . . that type."

"Was he jealous even of Miss Hunt's women friends?"

"I think he had the idea we were all lesbians or something. Because we looked after one another. He was crazy to take her back to Cairo with him . . . he just wanted her for himself."

"And where is Mr. Sabri now, do you know?"

"Supposedly, he went back to Egypt. Afraid of being involved in this trial. Or for being blamed for Sigrid's disappearing . . . whatever happened to her."

"What did happen to her, do you know?"

"I have absolutely no idea, sir. I have answered that question quite a few times now."

"Put to you by whom?"

"By the police."

"Had Sigrid Hunt ever disappeared in the past, to your knowledge?"

"Yes she did, maybe not disappeared exactly, because someone always knew where she was, but she's the kind to slip away, go into hiding, if things get unpleasant. Like I said, she's the type to have another life, or lives, the way a dancer or an actor has roles, other modes of being. Not that Sigrid was consciously devious or anything, though I suppose, conventionally judged, she was, or is; it's really just her character, the way she was born. She had been a quite promising dancer for a while, before the life began to wear her down like it does most of us, and finally she injured her foot, and that was that. Too much pain. And she was getting old. Like me."

"How old are you, Miss Matthews?"

"Oh, Jesus! And I'm under oath! I'm twenty-seven. Going on twenty-eight."

AND THEN, ON another day, came Malcolm Oliver, to tell the court, at Ottinger's invitation, about the Thiel-Edwards episode, as it had come to be called: the case of police brutality in which Ian McCullough and other Hazelton area members of the American Civil Liberties Union became involved in early 1986.

It seemed that, at approximately 2:00 A.M. of December 26, 1985, Henry Thiel, a thirty-one-year-old high school teacher from Mount Kisco, New York, was driving a friend, Darryl Edwards, twenty-eight, a Ph.D. candidate in economics at Columbia University, home from a party in Hazelton-on-Hudson, when, on Charter Street (a narrow one-way street one block from and parallel to Hazelton's main street), a vehicle that turned out to be an unmarked police car approached them head on, headlights blinding, and forced them to a sudden stop. At the same time, another unmarked car pulled up short behind them, its brakes squealing. Thinking they were going to be robbed and assaulted, if not murdered, Thiel and Edwards ducked down in their seats. Within seconds they heard three shots, and the windshield of Thiel's car was shattered. With no warning, or no warning that either Thiel or Edwards heard, a police officer in the car in front of them had fired his pistol. At once, a second officer joined him, firing three or four times. There followed then, as witnesses (residents of a nearby apartment building) described it, a "barrage" of bullets, as police officers from both cars opened fire, shooting out most of the windows of Thiel's car. Several people called police, and more units arrived at the scene. By this time Thiel and Edwards had been dragged out of their car, overpowered, beaten, kicked, and handcuffed, and forced into one of the squad cars. They were to be accused afterward of "resisting arrest" and "forcibly resisting arresting officers," though no evidence would be offered to corroborate these charges.

Both Thiel and Edwards, after being booked at Hazelton police headquarters, were taken to the Hazelton Medical Center, Thiel with a broken nose, severe facial lacerations, and several broken ribs; Edwards with similar facial injuries, broken ribs and fingers, and a fractured skull from having been, in his words, "struck repeatedly" with a billy club. (Why was Edwards beaten more severely than Thiel? Malcolm interjected, putting his question to the court. Because Edwards is black.)

It would turn out that the Thiel-Edwards arrest was a case of mistaken identity. The plainclothes police were looking for two suspected robbers, a white man and a black man (though in fact the "black" man had been described to police as a light-skinned Hispanic, with a mustache: Edwards was clean-shaven), who had held up a liquor store on Route 9. The thieves were reported having driven away in a late-model dark sedan; Thiel's car was a 1986 metallic-blue Honda Civic. The five police officers involved in the episode insisted that there had been no brutality, nothing in excess of "necessary force." Under oath, they testified to a grand jury that Thiel had allegedly driven his car into a police barricade and was himself responsible for his and Edwards's injuries and for the damage to his car; more minor injuries were caused by scuffling, pushing and shoving, and "resisting arresting officers." Though the case received a good deal of publicity locally and in *The New York Times,* and was taken up immediately by the state branch of the ACLU, no public explanation or apology was ever made by the Hazelton police; nor were the officers involved disciplined, other than to be reassigned to different units. Eventually, after months of stalling, a public hearing was held, sponsored by the ACLU, and the county prosecutor, Samuel S. Lederer, was finally prodded into action. A grand jury was convened, and the officers brought before it but the hearing was undercut by Edwards's refusal to testify and Thiel's obvious reluctance to provide jurors with information. Thiel told ACLU officers afterward (among them, Malcolm Oliver) that he had been "frightened and intimidated" by telephone threats from anonymous callers. Like his friend, he intended "never to set foot in Hazelton-on-Hudson again."

More than one hundred Hazelton residents, the majority of them active members of the ACLU, took part, for approximately an eighteen-month period beginning in April 1986, in a series of protests following the grand jury's refusal to hand down indictments against the police officers. A petition was drawn up and signed; letters and telegrams of complaint were sent to relevant agencies, including the office of the Governor of New York and the district attorney general; a number of meetings were held in private homes, including the home of Ian and Glynnis McCullough. (Ian McCullough had been a dues-paying member of the ACLU since 1963.) Though police denied the association and, again, were to advance an excuse of "mistaken identity," three state police officers went to the McCullough home in the early morning of September 21, 1986, where, under the pretext of looking for neighborhood vandals and without identifying themselves, they pounded on the front door of the house, waking the McCulloughs and upsetting them considerably. Though the officers shone flashlights into the house, they did not shine them on their own uniforms or badges, according to the McCulloughs. Afterward, they were to claim that they had only rung the doorbell and had gone away almost at once, without any further disturbance.

Though Dr. and Mrs. McCullough were outraged by this act of harassment, and Dr. McCullough made a number of formal protests, by telephone, by letter, and in person—he insisted upon seeing, among others, the State Commissioner of Police—there was never any explanation for the officers' behavior, other than their claim of having been looking for neighborhood vandals (teenagers had set off firecrackers in some mailboxes in the neighborhood earlier that night), nor was there any apology.

Ottinger duly asked, "And do you think, Mr. Oliver, based upon your experience as an ACLU officer and your acquaintance with Dr. and Mrs. McCullough, that the Hazelton police were deliberately harassing the McCulloughs on the night of September 21, 1986?" and Malcolm said, "Yes, I certainly do," and began to elaborate, speaking rapidly and angrily; for this was a subject about which Malcolm had long had passionate feelings, whether altogether justified or not. Ian, blinking and squinting through a headachy malaise, like a tortoise peeping out of its shell, took pride in his friend's testimony; felt a thrill of nervous elation in sensing the mood of the court and seeing, it seemed so plainly on their faces, the mood of the jurors. For everyone, or nearly everyone, was swept up in Malcolm Oliver's dramatic recital of injustice and inveigled into, as if by the back door, a tacit sympathy for Ian McCullough. Why, the man was a martyr!—a local hero!

Ian thought, But I did so little. Thiel and Edwards would not even know my name.

There followed then Samuel Lederer's crudely aggressive cross-examination—for the man was very angry—which allowed Malcolm Oliver to demonstrate his own lawyerly talents. One-on-one combat, here as on the squash court, excited him and enlivened him; he got the better (or so Ian sensed from the amused response on all sides) of the public prosecutor at every turn. "Do you have any proof that the Hazelton police, collectively or as individuals, were involved in a 'vendetta' against Ian McCullough?"

"I am basing my judgment on my experience of nearly thirty years involvement with the—"

"Mr. Oliver, do you have any proof, I am asking do you have any proof?"

"—with the law-enforcement agencies of the state and with the alleged upholders of the law like yourself."

"Mr. Oliver, I am asking you, what proof do you have?"

" 'Proof' could only be supplied by police testimony, and, as all the world knows, no officer will inform on his fellow officers, under pain of—"

"Mr. Oliver, for the last time, I am asking you, what proof can you—"

"—censure, harassment, maybe even brutality, who knows?" Malcolm said sharply, before Judge Harmon could cut him off. "Only *they* know, and *they* won't tell."

THAT EVENING, SHORTLY after Ottinger dropped Ian and Bianca at their house, the telephone rang; and it was Vaughn Cassity. With whom Ian had not spoken in weeks.

He had heard, Vaughn said, in a hearty, belligerent voice, that Nick Ottinger had had a brilliant first week, that things were looking very well for Ian at last. Why didn't they, then, all go out to celebrate tomorrow night? "You and your daughter, of course, and Nick, and Meika and me. What d'you say?"

"Celebrate?" Ian said. "Surely it's a bit premature to celebrate."

"My party. I insist. That new seafood restaurant in the village. What d'you say?"

"I really don't think . . ."

"I've been so busy, I haven't had time to get up to the courthouse, but Meika tells me your defense counsel is winning every round now, or nearly. Meika tells me it looks very, very good. Don't read the damned papers, says Meika, they give you the wrong impression!" When Ian made no reply Vaughn went on, still belligerently, "And I'm lonely, these days. D'you know what it is, Ian, to be lonely? Married and lonely?" He mumbled to himself; perhaps he was laughing. It sounded as if the telephone receiver had been dropped. "Though I guess you wouldn't know, would you. Since you're not married now. You're of widower status. And you're not lonely."

Ian stood mute, accused. He felt a quick stab of pain between the eyes. He had the strange, unsettling idea that Meika was standing close by Vaughn, or was even, slyly, on another extension, listening in on her husband's call.

Vaughn said, "Hello? You there? Ian? Still there?"

Ian said, "Yes."

"Hell, Ian, I know you're going through . . . hell. Whatever happened with you and poor Glynnis, it was just something that happened. It wouldn't happen again. Right? I've had a little too much to drink but I think I can make myself clear. Right?" He paused; Ian could hear him breathing. "Meika, are *you* on the line?" he asked suddenly.

There was no reply.

Vaughn said, "Meika, *are* you?" He waited, and again there was only silence. "Bad puss, if you are."

Ian said, embarrassed, "Vaughn? I don't think I can make it tomorrow night. But thank you."

"Another time, then? When the trial is over? When you're acquitted? Free and clear? We can all go out, then, right, and celebrate? Not like it would be hubris then, or anything. Challenging the gods. Once you *are* acquitted."

"Yes, fine," Ian said, desperate to get away.

"You're my friend too, you know."

"Yes," said Ian.

"We're all friends. We don't judge. Fundamental principle of civilization."

"Yes."

"When you die, you die alone. But when you live, you can't live alone. Can't bear to live alone." He paused again; again there was a sound of mumbling, or laughter. Perhaps it was sobbing. "I've been exploring some of these problems—I call them 'problems'; to an artist all substance not yet given a structure represents a 'problem' to be solved—in my Poetics, of course. You saw my Poetics, didn't you? Back around Christmastime."

"I'm afraid I can't talk now, Vaughn. Bianca and I have only just arrived home—"

"Let's make it another time, then. You and your daughter, and Nick Ottinger, and Meika and me, shall we? Celebration dinner. Vaughn's treat. Right? Shall we?"

"Yes," Ian said quickly. "Yes, good. Good night."

"Good *night*."

7.

On the night of March 29, near midnight, Nick Ottinger telephoned Ian McCullough and said, in a voice that fairly trembled with excitement, "Ian, I have a surprise for you, can you guess?" and Ian, who had been sitting in the darkened kitchen of his house, drinking Scotch and thinking of his wife's snow-covered grave, which he had not visited in weeks, and of Sigrid Hunt whose face was now a dim dreamy blur in his memory, said at once, "Sigrid Hunt. You've found her."

And so it was.

SINCE THE START of Ian McCullough's trial there had been rumors, some of them very public indeed, that Sigrid Hunt—"the Missing Woman," "the Mystery Woman," "the 'Other' Woman"—would appear: initially, to testify for the prosecution; then for the defense. Concurrent with these rumors, though antithetical to them, were rumors that Sigrid Hunt was dead, had (in fact) been murdered. (And if Hunt had been murdered, who was the "likely" murderer?)

So, on the morning of April 4, when Sigrid Hunt did at last appear in court, taking the witness stand beside the judge's high bench as naturally—which is to say as hesitantly and as self-consciously—as any other witness, there was a truly palpable air of excitement and anticipation in the courtroom: crude, melodramatic, yet contagious; an assumption too, particularly among the press, however erroneous and however frequently denied, that the defense had timed its coup deliberately. (But this was not the case. Sigrid Hunt had only just been contacted, by a private investigator in the hire of Nick Ottinger, the week before, in a coastal village west of Guadalajara, Mexico; Ottinger had then been required to spend a total of four hours talking with her on the telephone, to convince her that she was in no way under arrest or in violation of any state statute, before she agreed, and then with reluctance, to fly back for the trial.)

An extra row of benches had been reserved for the press, and television camera crews and photographers crowded about on the sidewalk outside the courthouse, waiting, with a determination and a sort of defiant communal cheeriness Ian rather admired, for those confused, fleeting moments when the "principals" appeared. The heightened interest today was of course focused upon Sigrid Hunt and not on Ian McCullough; or, if on McCullough, it was minimal and cursory; for the man's tall spare rangy "professorial" frame was familiar to the regulars by now, and his face, and now silvered hair, yet more familiar and unyielding of dramatic surprise. Over the long months, Ian had grown not only accustomed to but philosophically accepting of the childlike appetite of the press for material, substance, essence, *life;* its elaborate formal structure existed, in contradistinction to Vaughn Cassity's Poetics, *a priori,* and must be filled. Glynnis had told him, following one of her television interview shows (it had consisted of an eight-minute sequence requiring approximately six thousand miles of air travel) that the thing most dreaded on network television was silence. Not the collapse of a performer, or even his death, for that could be accommodated by the media, if not energetically exploited; but, simply, silence. So with the newspapers' blank pulp pages, which must be filled.

He had spoken himself only briefly with Sigrid Hunt, and that over the telephone; he had not much wanted to see her and had not been much moved by Ottinger's relaying of messages from her, to him, to the effect that she was sorry for her behavior and asked to be forgiven. ("Why didn't she ever write to me, in all these months, then," Ian said indifferently. "She says she did write, but couldn't mail the letters," Ottinger said. "She says she has saved them all." Ian allowed himself the indulgence of an expletive for which there is no genteel equivalent: "Shit.")

But they spoke, finally, on the telephone, and the conversation was not very satisfactory. Hearing her voice, which was so thinly nervous and agitated he would not have recognized it, Ian felt little excitement and even less resentment; rather a dull flat vague clinical curiosity about what the young woman would find to say to him, after so long. And of course she'd said she was sorry, so very sorry; simply could not express in words how sorry, et cetera; then asking, "Oh, Ian, is it terrible, those people, all those crowds of people, those strangers, that you can't control, staring at you, and thinking about you, and judging you?" and he'd realized she was asking not of Ian McCullough's ordeal but of her own, the ordeal shortly to be hers. He said, "Yes. It is terrible."

"AND WERE YOU 'involved' with Dr. McCullough during this period of time?"

"If you mean romantically involved—"

"Romantically, sexually—"

"I was not."

"You were not?"

"I was not his lover. I was not his friend, really. Though I would like to have been. I would like to have been a friend to them both . . . I admired them both so very much."

Sigrid Hunt gave her testimony in a voice that occasionally wavered but was, for the most part, steady, calm, and audible, fixing her attention for nearly two hours on Nick Ottinger, as if oblivious of others in the courtroom, except, from time to time (such times as she faltered in her speech), glancing at Ian McCullough, seated only a few yards away . . . a look of appeal, of, oddly, hurt: for he had been very chill in his greeting and had stared at her, and stared at her now, as if she were a stranger to him.

Yet he thought, She has come back from the grave to save me.

Or was it rather—and he did not understand this either—she has come to save me in my grave.

Sigrid Hunt was still, though perceptibly changed, a young

woman of unusual beauty, with her dead-white skin, her quaintly asymmetrical features, the way in which, not at all stiffly but with a pose of utter naturalness, she held her head, her shoulders, her arms. Oversized plastic-framed glasses, with tinted lenses, made her features appear the more finely cut, as if in miniature: the elegant nose, mouth; the wide-spaced eyes; the rather high narrow forehead; the tips of the exposed ears. She had brushed her long glossy red-gold hair back severely from her face, and parted it in the middle of her head, and coiled it up, at the nape of her neck, in a chignon; she wore a black costume—for Sigrid Hunt was the sort of woman upon whom clothing is not mere clothes but costume—of some soft wool fabric, an overblouse and a skirt that fell to mid-calf; no earrings, no necklaces, no bracelets, no rings. How tall she was, and how odd, teasing, fascinating, the asymmetry of her features, which had the look of being willed and not accidental, like nature. Ian thought of Modigliani and of Parmigianino; he stared and scarcely heard what she was saying, though all that she said was about him and for him.

Whether by way of the defense counsel's skillful questioning or by way of the repentant young woman herself, there now unfolded a narrative in which Ian McCullough emerged in yet another mode of being, rather more victim than agent: a person of enormous sympathy and generosity, though perhaps something of a fool. For Sigrid Hunt confessed both to "admiring" and being "very attracted to" Ian McCullough even as she confessed to "hoping to manipulate him" for her own purposes.

"I was desperate then. I was rather crazy. I'm not at all proud of that time in my life, and I look back upon it with loathing. I had been involved with a man, in love with a man, who wanted to marry me and wanted me, as he said, to have his son, though at the same time he often spoke of killing me and of killing himself. 'We can't be any more miserable than we are now,' he'd say, 'if we were dead.' And though I knew this was madness I saw the logic of it, so to speak. I saw the logic of it quite clearly. At the time. But I was desperate, also, to get free of it . . . of him. There has never been a time in my life when I have not felt a profound sense of shame for what I seem to be doing, a sort of role I seem to be performing, that isn't me, truly isn't me, but a sort of mask I am wearing, yet of course it *is* me since it can be no one else after all. And this was one of the most shameful times. . . .

"I should also say that, at the time I became involved in this love affair, I was feeling ill-used and embittered about losing my job at Vassar. I had been hired to teach dance; I was what's called an adjunct instructor, which means expendable; and so I was. But that doesn't have any bearing on this situation; it certainly has nothing to do with Dr. McCullough or his wife, whom I met around this time, through artist friends in Hazelton: Glynnis McCullough, who was so lovely to me . . . for a while. I liked her very much; there are some women, not many, whom I like immediately and enormously, as if they are larger than life, sort of . . . Amazonian; but it's usually just in my imagination.

"Mrs. McCullough was one of these women, and she seemed to take to me too for a while, as I said, introduced me to friends of hers, some very nice women friends, all of them her age, older than me, of course; and I liked them, too, and felt some sort of . . . envy, I suppose . . . jealousy . . . that their lives were what they were, and mine was what mine was: so shabby, by contrast, and so stupidly desperate. I felt—oh, I've always felt, so often!—I felt I deserved more. I envied them their marriages, and their families, and their expensive houses, which they took for granted, or so it seemed.

"Glynnis had everything, I thought, and when I met her husband, at a party at her house, the single time I was invited to her house, I looked at this man and thought, 'That's the one,' though I knew it was all absurd, simply childish and absurd, and, as I said, I was really in love with this other man; I was caught up in this love affair which seemed to be sucking all the life from me. It was just a state I had drifted into . . . a pathological state of the soul. I looked at these people, so comfortably middle class, I should say upper middle class, with their glass-walled houses, and shelves of books, and the expensive food and drinks they served, and their careers—most of the men were attached to the Institute, and the Institute is so famous, even the grounds are so beautiful—and some of the women I met had done things too, had their own careers, like Glynnis McCullough.

"And there was Ian McCullough, of whom, frankly, I had never heard, though I quickly found out his position at the Institute, and his reputation, the things people said about him. And I envied too the friendships the Hazelton people seemed to have, which seemed to me very different from the friendships my parents had, very different from the friendships I've usually had; which fascinated me but primarily made me angry and resentful, because I couldn't understand it. Like, you know, there's a riddle put to you, like the one the sphinx put to Oedipus, and it's something so close to you you can't see; the answer is obvious as something written on your forehead, or it's the nature of the mask you're wearing, but, because you're wearing it, you can't see. So I fell in love with Glynnis McCullough's husband . . . and that same night forgot about him.

"Then we met again, by accident. Though I'd gone to Hazelton hoping I might meet him, or someone like him. That something might turn up. Along with being unlucky I've always had intermittent bits of luck. . . . And I met Dr. McCullough that day, wholly by accident, this was in November, a year ago last November, and we talked for a while, and he seemed quite friendly, and I thought afterward there was the possibility he might call me and want to see me; but he never did.

"Glynnis had not called me in some time so I understood that she'd dropped me; I don't mean that she had deliberately dropped me, just that, busy as she was, with the social life she managed and her family and all, and her writing, she hadn't time for me; I slipped through the cracks of her life, the way I'd slipped through the cracks of other people's lives in the past. And while I understood the situation, and felt I'd behave the same way in her place, I also felt angry with her, as if I'd been cheated; as if some sort of friendship that was meant to be, or destiny, had been broken off, and it was her fault. And that was another thing I envied in these people, and resented, that they were so damned smug and secure in their lives, in their circle, in their precious homes, and they'd take you up or let you down at will. And in fact there was one man who did call me . . . a Hazelton husband . . . but I wasn't able to see him when he wanted to see me . . . and . . . it sort of trailed off into nothing. But that man wasn't Ian McCullough; if Dr. McCullough had called me, I would have seen him.

"But he never called, and I got pregnant, and more and more desperate, taking drugs sometimes, I don't mean seriously, or that I was a junkie or anything because I never was, but there were times when I wouldn't have cared if I'd OD'd. And one of these really bad sort of crazy times, when I hadn't slept for two or three days and had had a bad fight with my fiancé and was afraid of him, I telephoned Dr. McCullough at the Institute, and I don't even know what I said to him, just asked for help, more or less, begging for help, for someone to talk to, though at the back of my mind there were two things: that I'd ask him for money and get an abortion, and that I'd make him fall in love with me. He came to see me in Poughkeepsie and saved my life, I do mean that literally, and I must have asked him for money because he lent me a thousand dollars, just wrote out a check for me, trusted me; I told him I would repay him and he believed me, or seemed to . . . he was that kind of man. I don't remember the details of that visit because I was so spaced out, but I remember that he stayed an hour or so, and talked with me, and reasoned with me, and I think he might have found some pills I had been taking, some tranquilizers, and flushed them down the toilet. And I think he wanted to call a doctor or an ambulance but I said no, I was terrified of being committed to a psychiatric ward. . . .

"That was the only time we were alone together in my apartment, I think, or anywhere. After that I called Dr. McCullough a few times, and he was kind enough to call me, to see how I was; and that was the extent of it, really. Of course I never repaid the thousand dollars; I'd never intended to. I might have gotten it from my boyfriend or from some other man, to repay it, but I never did. I was attracted to Dr. McCullough, as I've said, but I had a grudge against him too: because he didn't seem to like me quite as much as I wanted him to, and because he was who he was. He was just too *sweet.* He was too damned *nice.* I thought, There must be more to him than that, another side to him, as there mostly is to most men, but it never came out. So I thought, That thousand is mine. (The abortion only cost about four fifty.) I've earned it.

"Then, later, when I read in the newspapers about Glynnis's death, and Dr. McCullough arrested for it, and began to see my name linked up with his, I couldn't deal with it. So I ran away. I can't even say that I panicked, because it was reasoned out enough, but I ran away and figured things would work out by themselves. I did this shameful cowardly childish thing, this absolutely selfish thing, for which I knew beforehand I'd be ashamed: I simply ran away; I got some money from a friend and flew to Mexico.

"I suppose I should say, since I'm under oath, that I got money from a number of men, the kind of men you go out with exclusively to get money (not that I was a hooker or anything, though I am not on principle opposed to making money by turning tricks)—and I flew to Mexico, where I knew some people, not friends but friends of friends, but I used another name with them, called myself Coco Stephens, and no one knew me there as Sigrid Hunt or would ever have made the connection if they knew about Sigrid Hunt, which they didn't. I told them I had a teaching diploma but couldn't get a job in the States, and that seemed reasonable; nobody much cared, nobody asked many questions of me or of anyone else. I felt guilty about running away, but it wasn't the first time I had run away as a solution to my problems. I thought I should telephone Dr. McCullough, or write him a letter, and I did write letters but didn't mail them; I was afraid of the mail being traced.

"Then I got sick, and recovered, and traveled around, and got sick again, and went to Panama and Costa Rica, and spent some time in Mexico City with a person who was nice to me, more or less, but never knew who I was, or much of anything about me. A sort of amnesia came over me. I liked it that way. I was comfortable that way. People in my former life were on the other side of a kind of barrier, a one-way mirror, through which I could see them but they couldn't see me. I don't know how long I could have lived that way—until I got sick again, or my luck seriously ran out—but . . . it came to an end."

And Ian sat, staring, in a transport of wonder. And thought, for the first time since Glynnis's death, I want to live.

8.

That she loved him or might love him, that his life had not after all ended, that he was not condemned to a posthumous existence after all . . . but a life like the old life, even more wonderful than the old, for its impurities had been blasted away: this seemed to him the miraculous, the unspeakably miraculous thing. And it was within his grasp, was it not? So close, so tantalizingly close, was it not?

So he told his attorney that he would testify after all. In his own behalf, after all. And at the trial's next session he took the witness stand and told the court the truth the whole truth and nothing but the truth so help me God, to the extent to which he could remember it. And this in a fairly clear and coherent and reasonable voice, for he was, after all, the most civilized of men.

He did not believe, he said, that he was guilty of having murdered his wife. But he did believe he was guilty of having killed her: of having killed her by accident, reacting blindly, in an animal panic, and pushing her away from him, without knowing what he did or what the consequences would be. "She had been drinking, and she was furious. I tried to reason with her but failed. I could have prevented the accident if I had walked away, simply walked away, but I didn't walk away, and I have never understood why. I had been drinking too, I was drunk, but even drunk I should have known the wisest thing to do, the only thing to do, was to walk away. But I didn't. I seemed drawn to her, to the quarrel, eventually to the fight, the physical scuffling, as she was drawn to it, helplessly, and I have never understood that. It was as if everything, the very fabric of our lives, had been turned inside out . . . exposed in reverse, like a photograph negative.

"She had found the canceled check for one thousand dollars. And she was hurt, and angry, and we began to quarrel . . . quite violently . . . as we had never before quarreled in our lives. The quarrel became a struggle, an actual physical struggle; and Glynnis slapped me, and I pushed at her; and she took up a knife, a knife she'd brought to the table with her, a knife with a long sharp blade, swiping at me with it, as if she wanted to stab me; and I thought, Of course she doesn't mean it, Glynnis would never hurt me; but she was so angry. . . . And I seem to have rather stupidly closed my fingers around the blade and cut them badly. And the knife may have fallen. And Glynnis was screaming at me.

And I reacted instinctively; I must have taken her by the shoulders and shoved her from me, in a sort of animal fright, because of the knife. . . . She struck the window and fell through. And that was how it happened. That quickly, and that irrevocably.

"I did not mean to kill my wife. I did not mean even to hurt her. I wanted only to protect myself from her, I suppose, at that moment, when things were so . . . confused. So unlike anything in our previous lives, anything we could recall. It had seemed to me that the furious woman who attacked me was not my wife but a stranger, and my response to her was a stranger's response; and I loathed both people. The man, the woman . . . the strange and terrible connection between them. A sort of madness coursed through us both. It was like the shock of love, of profound love, erotic, sexual, a violence of which one can't speak, to which one can't give a name. I was utterly helpless; I seemed to have lost all volition. One moment I had been thinking fairly reasonably that I would walk away and leave the house and in the morning things could be cleared up . . . probably . . . and the next moment I seemed incapable of thinking at all. And my wife whom I loved, and who I knew loved me, nonetheless seemed to want to hurt me, had picked up a knife as of course she'd never done before in her life, would never have conceived of doing, yet she was striking at me with it . . . and I shoved her away from me . . . and killed her.

"And I didn't want to tell anyone what had happened between us. Because it was a violation of my wife's honor, and a violation of our marriage. I didn't want to seem to have made her into an adversary when in a very real way she had not been, had never been. It was only this madness that came upon us . . . this sudden terrible fury that has ruined our lives.

"So I refused to explain. I refused to defend myself if it necessitated, as it seemed to do, making my wife into my enemy. I thought, If I am found guilty, then I'm guilty. I will let others decide.

"I thought, I won't lift a finger in my defense.

"I thought, What does it matter if I live or die?—my life is over."

HE WAS SUBSEQUENTLY cross-examined at length, and rather brutally, by Lederer but held his ground, or seemed to, though speaking in an increasingly hoarse voice, with frequent long pauses and spasms of stammering. Lederer demanded of him why, having told police repeatedly that he could not remember what had happened between him and Mrs. McCullough, he now seemed able to remember, and in such persuasive detail. And Ian said, "I want to be cleared of the charges. I want the trial to end; I want to set things straight; I want to resume my life."

"But why now, Mr. McCullough?" Lederer asked, his face mottled with emotion, his voice heavy with sarcasm; "why, so suddenly, now, in the sixth week of the trial?" And Ian drew breath to speak and could not. The courtroom shifted in and out of focus like an ill-conceived dream. He seemed to see himself from a distance, as if through the wrong end of a telescope. Was he dead? Already dead? When he had wanted so desperately to live?

He said, "I have told you. I want to resume my life."

AFTERWARD, THEY TOLD him that he had made a "profound impression" on the jurors and Judge Harmon; and he himself sensed, despite his fatigue, that he had succeeded in moving the hearts of his listeners. I have told only the truth, he thought, as if in protest.

But where was Sigrid Hunt? And where was Bianca?

Ah, there: Bianca. Standing alone a few yards away, staring at him, her coat slung over her arm, one of her gloves fallen unnoticed at her feet. He made his way to her, eager to speak with her, but she edged away and shot him a look of hatred. Her face was clenched like a muscle, her eyes bright with tears. "Murderer," she whispered. And that was all.

She pushed her way into the aisle, and Ian stood, struck dumb, staring after her. What had she said? Had he heard correctly?

But I have told only the truth. I have saved myself, but I have told only the truth.

Epilogue

THE VERDICT

L ate August in Maine, and an eye-piercing day, very blue, a bit windy, tinged with autumn, but they served lunch outside for their guests, on the terrace, at the glass-topped iron table above the crashing surf, and if conversation wavered, or waned—which was in fact not often the case, not with these guests—there was always the ocean, and the sky, and the rocky beach with its sculpted, rebarbative shapes; there was always, as Sigrid said, all that's *there.*

They were self-conscious, to a degree: in truth, mildly embarrassed, like newlyweds entertaining their first guests.

(For of course they were, though not yet married, newlyweds. And Denis Grinnell and Malcolm Oliver were their first guests: their first guests, one might say, from the "old" life. We really can't count having people over for drinks, Sigrid said, just our neighbors here, and the real estate people; they don't exactly count.)

Their guests arrived shortly after noon, in a rented Audi: Denis, who was visiting his brother and his brother's family in Bar Harbor, twenty twisting miles to the south, and Malcolm, who, quite by coincidence, was in Bangor for a week, preparing an article for *The New York Times Magazine*. "How good to see you again," Ian said to them, shaking their hands as hard as he dared; and, "How good to see *you* again," they said, shaking his hand hard, in turn, and looking frankly into his face, which was handsomely tanned, though a bit weathered about the eyes, and the eyes themselves—well, the eyes were hidden, or stylishly obscured, by the dark-green-tinted prescription sunglasses Ian was wearing. "It's been a long time," they said to one another, marveling; "it's been, *how* long?" staring grinning and incredulous at one another, in the way we have when, suddenly confronted with the fact of our friends' existences, apart from our own, we are confronted too with a realization of their, and our, mortality; "three months at least," in the happy nerved-up moments before Sigrid appeared on the deck of the house, in her white summer shift, and waved to them.

Denis said quickly in his ear, "You're looking good, Ian," and Malcolm, giving his upper arm a pointed little punch, said, "You *are* looking good," and Ian laughed and said, "And so are you, so are you both," and led them up to the house. He wore pale blue seersucker trousers, a white cotton-knit sports shirt, and sandals; his hair blew, rather lavishly it seemed, in the wind. His friends knew Sigrid, of course; had spent some evenings with her and Ian, in Hazelton, in the spring. Still, there were some awkward moments.

Sigrid had prepared a superb cold scallop salad, had in fact spent much of the morning on it—for the recipe insisted upon *fresh* squeezed lime juice and *fresh* chopped basil—and Denis and Malcolm had brought two bottles of excellent white Rhone wine, and there would be a kiwi cream pie for dessert, so the luncheon itself, the crucial matter of the food and drink, could not fail; this Ian understood, for food and drink rarely fail us. He hoped in her nervousness Sigrid would let things take their natural pace.

He himself had so anticipated this visit from his friends, he was in a strange exhilarated mood: his concentration fierce, as if he were edging along a high parapet, yet susceptible to sudden breaks or fractures, so that, in the very midst of an animated exchange of his own initiation, his thoughts drifted off; and though he saw his friends, and Sigrid, talking, smiling, laughing, he could not, for the merest hair's-breadth of a second, grasp their words.

Before they sat down to lunch the men climbed out onto the rocks above the beach, where, eddied by the rocks and in some way reflected by them—though the stone itself was a harsh ungiving lightless dark-earthen brown—the sunlight was stronger, shining down directly on their heads. Denis said, "I should have worn my sailor's cap; now my hair is so damned thin my very scalp gets sunburned"; and Malcolm said, "It's certainly beautiful here," shading his eyes, staring at the glittering pocked waves; "how did you manage it?" And though, surely, Malcolm knew how Ian had come to rent this exquisite little white clapboard house on the ocean, at Prospect Harbor, since arrangements had been made through a mutual Hazelton friend, Ian helpfully recounted the brief tale, which had to do with another's misfortune (the orthodontist who had intended to spend August here had died suddenly of a heart attack, and naturally his family had canceled out); and both men listened as if hearing it for the first time, as we so frequently listen, in such circumstances, to tales whose outcomes we already know, or have already been told us by our friends.

Denis said grimly, "I know him, I think. I mean, I knew him. Not that I could remember his face. . . . Bar Harbor, incidentally, is becoming impossible. As crowded as the Cape. And my brother has a half dozen in-laws staying with him."

Ian asked, after a moment's hesitation, "How is Roberta?"

Denis shrugged and said, "We keep in contact, and I know what she's doing, more or less, but I don't know, I must confess, how she is. I can tell you *what,* but not *how.*"

Ian persisted. "Then what is she doing?"

Denis squinted at him in that way he had, a grimace of a kind Ian associated with the squash court, smiling and frowning at the same time, both amused and annoyed. "Don't you keep in touch, the two of you? Has she crossed you off her list too?"

"Oh, I think so, yes," Ian said, laughing. "A long time ago."

"No, you're wrong. Roberta was tremendously relieved about the verdict. She wept, she was so relieved. She and Bianca in each other's arms. . . . I wasn't an eyewitness, but I was told."

"Yes," said Ian. "I suppose that's true."

"She was much more worried about it, the trial, even at the end, than most of us. But I assume you know that."

"Well," said Ian, wondering what they were, so suddenly and aggressively, talking about, "yes."

As if Denis were being purposefully slow to answer Ian's question, Malcolm leaned in and said, "Roberta is doing something really rather wonderful: she's working in a public health program at Goldwater Hospital—you know, the one on Roosevelt Island—giving psychiatric counseling to AIDS victims."

Ian marveled at the news, though in fact he had heard it already, or a version of it: not Goldwater Hospital, surely, but New York Hospital. He said, "It *is* wonderful. It's—"

"It's noble!" Denis said wryly. "Heart-wrenching!"

"—it's the sort of thing one might expect of her, though I can't imagine how long she can bear it," Ian said. He wondered how Leonard Oppenheim was but did not, at the moment, want to ask.

Denis said, "My former wife didn't think, evidently, that I was sick enough, or moribund enough, quite yet, to warrant her ministrations." And the men laughed and clambered back down to the terrace, where Sigrid had set the table with stainless steel cutlery out of the house's kitchen, and inexpensive china, and cloth napkins—for mere cheap crinkly paper napkins would have blown away. The centerpiece was a bottle-green vase in which branches of pale pink multifoliate wild roses had been placed, hanging down like ivy. "Beautiful," the men said, staring.

TEN YEARS AGO, Sigrid was telling them, she had danced in an adaptation of Euripides' *Medea* by a contemporary American composer; not the lead, of course—"I was never to dance any lead, at any time, in my short-lived career"—but a quite good role, brief but spectacular: that of the doomed Princess Creon, Medea's rival for Jason's love.

"The dance was choreographed to give the Princess more space than Euripides gives her," Sigrid said, "so that, while Medea was certainly the central figure, Princess Creon did take the stage as a kind of rival: very young, very innocent, very self-absorbed. I wore my hair long," Sigrid said, fanning her lovely golden-red hair with her hands, so that it rippled and shone in the sun and the men were, for a moment, quite lost in it, "and of course I was young, scarcely seventeen, while the woman who played Medea—our teacher, in fact, a brilliant dancer whose career seemed never to have flourished—was in her early thirties.

"As you know, Medea is bitterly jealous of Princess Creon and kills her by sending her poisoned gifts, a golden diadem for her head and beautiful robes, and the Princess is so innocently vain, or"—and here Sigrid laughed lightly, shutting her eyes for a moment and shaking her head as if she were shivering, in a characteristic gesture Ian had yet to decode—"vainly innocent, she accepts the gifts immediately, and puts them on, and preens in front of a mirror, and dies an agonizing death. 'The flesh melted from her bones,' Euripides says, 'like resin from a pine tree.' She can't remove the diadem from her head, and she can't throw off the robes, they stick to her, and when Creon, her father, rushes in and tries to help her, he is stuck to her, too, and dies the same death.

"First I danced in joy, then in dawning recognition, then in terror and agony, simulating the throes of death: a sort of orgasm, prolonged and hideous, of death, which offended some members of the audience (though no one seems to have walked out of any of the performances) but quite moved most of the others. My father came one night, alone, but thought my performance so 'sickening,' so 'obscene,' he refused to talk about it afterward. In fact he scarcely talked to me at all, afterward. 'How can you do such things in front of other people, in front of strangers?' he said. 'How can you expose yourself so?' He seemed in awe of me at the same time he was repelled." Sigrid paused again, and again shook her head, as if rebuking herself. "Mainly he was repelled."

She stopped abruptly. Her dazzling white cotton shift, with its long sleeves and mock-lace bosom, through which they could see the pale tops of her breasts, made her look, for a moment, like a tall somber child in a nightgown.

Ian said, "You've told me so little about your father." He had spoken as if thinking aloud; their guests were slightly embarrassed.

"Still, it was my triumphant hour, that dance," Sigrid said. "Knowing, really feeling, how the audience was with me, how captivated, horrified . . . how in a sense they couldn't keep any distance between us. It was the music, it was the story, it was," she said, with a shy little flair of bravado, *"me."*

Denis said, "I'm sorry I will never see you dance, Sigrid." He poured wine into all their glasses. "I assume it's never?"

"Never," Sigrid said. She brushed her hair out of her eyes, where the wind was blowing it, in silky glossy tendrils, and smiled, as if with satisfaction, and said, "Look: will you have more? We drove all the way to Bangor to get the olive oil I used in this salad, the recipe called for Italian and all I had was something from the A & P . . . not of course that that's all we got, in Bangor. But, still." She remained seated but started the casserole dish around, to Denis, to Malcolm, to Ian, each of whom took another serving, bay scallops with fusilli, black Kalamata olives, roasted red peppers, lime juice, and basil, and the rich fruity oil. And Sigrid herself spooned a small portion onto her plate.

Denis said, regarding her with frank interest, "It must be a strange sort of art, dancing. So mute, but so revealing. As your father said."

"Oh, everything is 'revealing' enough, isn't it, in its way," Sigrid said elusively.

Ian uncorked another bottle of wine and wondered that his hands were not trembling. Or were they? Invisibly? He had not had a cigarette since noon of the previous day.

THEY TALKED, AND Ian allowed his thoughts to scatter and to drift: less anxious now, now that they'd eaten, and he'd had a glass or two of wine, and he saw that, yes, of course, of course Denis and Malcolm and Sigrid were getting along beautifully, for why should they not, why, indeed, should they not? For after all they were adults, and Glynnis had been dead for many months. I will blow my brains out, Ian had said, smiling, to Ottinger, at one point during the jurors' six-hour deliberation, or I will get married again and begin my life over. And Ottinger had clapped him on the shoulder as if they were, which they were not, very close, even intimate, friends, and said, You'll get married again, Ian, all the signs point in that direction. And so they had. It was really quite extraordinary, how they had.

He had, however, lost Bianca. You might say.

Though Sigrid insisted it was probably only temporary.

That kind of hurt, resentment, rebellion: probably only temporary. She'll get over it.

Will she?

I was like that myself.

Yes?

Impulsive.

Yes.

But she's an intelligent girl, clearly a very intelligent girl. And idealistic.

Oh, idealistic. To a fault.

Still, it was a hopeful sign that, at last, Bianca had sent him a postcard from Bangkok, Krung Thep as it was called, a KodaColor photograph of the Gulf of Siam, at sunset. Spectacular flaming light upon the water, the sun like a fireball about to sink into the sea. *I am fine, I am well, I hope you are well, please don't worry about me, in fact I hope you will not direct your thoughts toward me. "In a moment of time perfect enlightenment is obtained." Love, Bianca.*

The trial, which had seemingly lasted forever, had of course come to an end.

But Bianca had not forgiven him. And he quite understood, he quite sympathized.

By the time the defense rested its case, the prosecution's case had been so severely undermined—both the police report and the medical report appeared to corroborate Ian's story about the knife, for instance:

the defense being, now, classically, "self-defense"—the routed Lederer had had to reduce the charge against Ian to a single count of manslaughter, in the desperate hope of getting a conviction. And Ottinger had passionately appealed to Judge Harmon to drop even this charge—that is, to dismiss the entire case, that his client might be spared the further indignity of waiting out a jury's deliberations. But Ian had not, in a way, minded, had not much minded; being judged by a jury of one's peers is an intriguing prospect from a philosophical point of view . . . an experience not many men and women undergo, after all.

Sigrid had said, I will do anything for you.

Rather fiercely and passionately: Anything.

The hours during which the jury was out, deciding Ian McCullough's fate or, in any case, a preliminary stage of his fate (for, as Ottinger reminded him, we can always appeal), were not unpleasant hours but, rather, hours of suspension; as if Ian were again by Glynnis's bedside in the hospital; as if in fact he were in a comatose state himself, neither fully alive nor dead. One's thoughts scatter, and drift . . . diaphanous as the most insubstantial of clouds.

In a state in which one's soul had not yet been judged, Ian thought, in the interstices of our moral lives, one can at least breathe!

And in that state he thought, quite simply: I will blow my brains out, or I will marry.

In the end, of course, the jurors trooped back into the courtroom with their verdict. And though Ian had vowed not to break down, regardless of the judgment rendered, as soon as the foreman said, "Not guilty, Your Honor," he began to weep: hid his face in his hands in a paroxysm of relief and shame. Everyone crowded around him to congratulate him and to congratulate Nick Ottinger, as if the trial had been, all along, truly a game, a game to be won, at the cost of another's loss: *Mors tua, vita mea.*

In time, Ian shook the jurors' hands, one by one, and thanked them, and was allowed to know, or to guess, by way of smiling innuendo rather than explicit words, that several of them seemed to have favored him all along, from the first; had never been impressed with the prosecution's evidence. Is it possible? Ian wondered, aghast at the possibility. All along? From the first? Never . . . ?

He shook Benedict Harmon's hand too, and, with Ottinger and a few others, stood about chatting; for they were all professional men, successful men, husbands and fathers and citizens of Hazelton-on-Hudson; they understood one another. And it was a splendid April day, chilly, very windy, but clear, the kind of day that whets one's appetite for all that life can offer.

Sigrid had hugged him, had wept in his arms, saying, yet again, "How sorry, how sorry I am, Ian; will you ever forgive me, will you ever, ever forgive me?"

And Ian, overcome with happiness, said, "My darling, there is nothing to forgive."

SO LONG, IN theory, had they been adulterous lovers that the actual circumstances of their first lovemaking—on the very night of the verdict of "not guilty"—seemed to them a confirmation of an old love and not the initiation of a new. There was a sense, too, of déjà vu, their eager reverent kisses and caresses, the urgency, the hunger, the wordless melting pleasure of their sexual union, a sense that they had lived this experience before, many times before, and would live it many times again. In a delirium of happiness in Sigrid Hunt's rather strong arms, Ian McCullough thought, I have loved her all along; I have always loved her.

He did not regret, in that instant, that Glynnis was dead. For Sigrid Hunt would not have been possible for him, had Glynnis not died.

IAN SMILED AND uncorked another bottle of wine. Sigrid was cutting wedges of the kiwi cream pie and easing them, with some little difficulty, onto dessert plates. The men watched her long slender fingers as she maneuvered the knife, the pie, the plates, her smoothly filed nails that gleamed as if they were polished, but were colorless. She wore no rings except a band of hammered gold on the third finger of her left hand: an inexpensive ring Ian had bought for her, only a few weeks ago, in a tiny goldsmith's shop in Rockport, Massachusetts, on their drive up to Maine.

They were talking about Maine, and the end of summer, and how abruptly, in this northerly climate, the summer would end: in another few days, in fact. "The seasons careen by more quickly all the time, don't they," Denis said, sighing. "It's exactly as our elders told us: time accelerates near the point of impact. It really does."

"Yet time is theoretically reversible," Ian said. He had been silent for so long, the others looked at him as if he were obliged to say something crucial. "The mechanics of the cosmos, it's said, can run as easily backward as forward, in the universes of both Newton and Einstein; the past and the future are allegedly fixed. But I have never understood this, and though I've had physicists explain it to me, I have never had the impression that they understood it either. Do you?" He looked at his friends and at Sigrid. "Do you understand it?"

Sigrid lifted her stylish chunky glasses from the bridge of her nose and peered at him through the lenses. Her eyes were round and widened, glassy, lovely, shining: like a doll's perfect eyes. She crinkled her forehead and laughed. "Do we understand what?"

"The theory of time's reversibility."

"That time runs backward?"

"That it could run backward. Though I think, in fact, it never does."

Malcolm said, "I think it's a fallacy. I mean, the applicability of the theory in everyday discourse. It has to do only with subatomic particles, not with—well, us." He laid a hand on Denis's forearm and a hand on Ian's shoulder, as if in consolation. "It doesn't apply to *us*."

"But to memory? Our memories?" Ian asked.

"Bullshit, McCullough," Denis said heartily. "Pass the wine."

"There is a letter of Einstein's, a portion of a letter I've seen reprinted, in which Einstein speaks of someone, a friend, who has left 'this strange world just before me.' But it's of no significance, Einstein says. For the convinced physicist the distinction between past, present, and future is an illusion, 'although a persistent one.' " Ian paused and drew a deep breath. They were watching him, and for a vertiginous moment, there on the high parapet, he had no idea what he was saying or what he was doing or why. The splendid summer day was bleached of color, and even the pounding surf was silent. He had a vague glimmery image of Sigrid staring at him as if she had never seen him before.

Then, in the next instant, time resumed, and Ian felt his blood beat again, warm and surging as always. "But, as I say," he said affably, "I don't understand any of it. I've always wanted to, and I know now that I never will. I am fifty-one years old."

"Oh Christ, McCullough," Denis said. "Give us a break."

They talked for some time of Denis's new position at the Arhardt Center in Washington, which he would take up in January: the challenge to him, as he saw it, to live in the midst of his ideological enemies without succumbing to them. "Dr. Max has assured me I can return to Hazelton whenever I want to, if I want to," Denis said carelessly. "But I know I can never come back. And what about you, Ian? Are you really resigning? I think you're a fool, if you do. You *were* acquitted, after all."

Ian said quickly, "It has nothing to do with that."

"It doesn't?"

"Only that Sigrid and I think it would be better for us to leave Hazelton. To live somewhere else, anywhere else. Surely you can't disagree."

"If you could get another position as good—"

"I'm afraid that isn't likely."

"Hasn't Dr. Max tried to talk you out of it?"

"He has; he's been very kind, very considerate, of course, but he's retiring in another week or two. And his successor, as you know, is no friend of mine."

"He's no one you know at all. No one any of us knows."

"That's what I mean."

"One of the 'new breed' of historian," Denis said, in a sneering sort of aside to Sigrid. "Be frank with me, Ian: are they forcing you out?"

Ian shook his head wordlessly.

Denis said, "After all you've done for the Institute!"

Malcolm said, "But, Ian, *are* you resigning? I've heard such different versions of all this. Where will you go? What will you do?"

"He's going to do independent research," Sigrid said defensively. She laid, gently, a proprietary hand on Ian's hand, a gesture that did not escape their friends. Sigrid Hunt's hand, and Ian McCullough's. There on the glass-topped table amid the wine bottles, the glasses, the dirtied steel cutlery. "He has a contract to write a book. About history."

Ian said, frowning, "I simply think it would be better for us all if I sold the house and moved away from Hazelton. My legal fees, for one thing. They're rather more than Nick led me to expect. And Bianca, for instance—"

"Where *is* Bianca?"

"—is in Thailand; and when she comes back to the States she doesn't plan to live with Sigrid and me. There is no need to retain a home in Hazelton any longer."

Denis said heatedly, "You *were* acquitted, for Christ's sake!"

"That has nothing to do with it."

"It has a good deal to do with it!"

"But Glynnis is dead."

Denis stared at Ian as if he had said something obscene.

Sigrid said quickly, linking her fingers through Ian's and gripping them hard, "Ian has a contract with the Harvard University Press, to write a book. What is the subject, Ian? Nineteenth-century theories of—"

"An overview of historiographical theory," Ian said, embarrassed. He wished that Sigrid had not brought the subject up so casually; it meant too much to him. He said, smiling, quite explicitly changing the subject, "And, as I don't doubt you know, others have approached me about writing books, signing contracts. My 'experience' as a man who has been tried for murder."

"Yes," said Sigrid, "and I've urged him to consider it, seriously. An editor—"

"Sigrid, it's too absurd."

"—with an excellent New York publisher, a high-quality house, wrote him a remarkable letter, a really intelligent and sympathetic letter," Sigrid said, looking at Denis and at Malcolm, as if to enjoin their support, "urging him to write a sort of memoir, a meditation, with facts of course and background information: a journal of his experience and an analysis of its effect upon him, and his family and friends, through the months. The editor said that no one has ever seriously attempted a project of this kind: something in depth, in a European style; it could be a unique and important document that would"—Sigrid paused, sensing Ian's annoyance; he had withdrawn his hand from hers, was slapping at his pockets for cigarettes that weren't there—"tell what it is like, from the inside, to endure a trial. And that the trial would be representative, of course, of the various trials we all endure, and their effect upon people around us." And here, again, breathless and passionate, Sigrid paused: too intelligent a young woman, for all her bravado, not to register the hollowness of her own words and the way in which they struck her listeners.

"So demeaning," Ian said, "even if done in 'a European style.' " But he was smiling, very nearly grinning, and lifting his glass to drink. He said, "Still, I might do it. I've been offered a contract."

Denis said, poking his arm, "With a considerable advance?"

"Do you know about it?"

"Meika was telling us the other evening, actually. Though I think her facts were askew, as usual; she seems to think you have already signed the contract."

"Dear Meika," Ian said, pained. "No. I have not 'already' signed it."

There was a brief silence. Sigrid said, "There's more of this delicious pie; would anyone like another piece? And I should start the coffee—oh, Christ, I forgot. Who would like coffee?" She took their orders but remained seated, her silky hair blowing, as if in tatters, into her face. The wine had visibly heated her skin, had suffused her with a girlish commandeering confidence; she smiled without knowing what she did, as if her perfectly shaped lips lapsed quite naturally, in repose, into a smile. She said, "This is the most beautiful, the most lovely . . . the most special place, to me . . . in all the world."

When she left and the men were alone, Ian immediately asked, "And how is Meika? And Nick?"

Denis laughed in delighted scorn and said, "Christ, that is *the* subject in Hazelton, isn't it, Mal? You can't go into the lavatory, or wait in line at the post office, without somebody coming up and asking. The last I've heard, Meika and Nick are subletting an apartment—"

"Vaughn says they are jointly buying a condominium, actually," Malcolm said.

"Really? *Buy*ing? Is this the place on Fifty-third Street, up the block from the museum?"

"He said, I think, some new place, a glass tower he called it, on Fifth Avenue. Within walking distance of the Metropolitan. Maybe that's what you're thinking of."

"I'm sure I heard Fifty-third Street," Denis said, frowning. "But, hell, what's the difference, now that Nick has this virtual new career, this 'esteem of his colleagues'—was that the wording in the paper? Some high-sounding garblegese like that—now that he's been taken up by the trade as a brilliant criminal lawyer, you can bet he'll be able to af-ford anything he wants. He snubbed me, actually, the other day, at the club. Coming off the squash court—"

"He didn't snub you, Denis," Malcolm said. "He didn't see you."

"He *saw* me, he looked right *through* me. Don't tell *me*."

So they talked for some animated minutes of Nick Ottinger and Meika Cassity, and of poor Vaughn Cassity, crushed with hurt and shame, unable to comprehend how, after all these years of devoted husbandhood, of indulging his wife, with the tacit understanding—"I assume," Denis said, "it *was* tacit"—that she would never publicly be-tray him: and, of course, never leave him; he loved her so much. And Ian listened, finding himself, to his surprise, rather keenly interested: as one might dip one's finger in a sweet syrupy batter, and lick it, and want more. At the same time he was thinking, Who are these people? Why am I connected with them? He had long since given up his search, if it could ever have been called a search, for Glynnis's phantom lover. It might have been Denis; it might have been Malcolm; it might have been . . . but did it matter? No man would confess to having been a dead woman's lover, for, after all, the dead are no longer loved.

Ian said, laughing and stretching his arms in the warm sunshine, "Meika was so sweet to me, actually, you can't imagine."

"Oh yes I can," Denis said.

"And so can I," said Malcolm.

SIGRID BROUGHT THE men coffee, borne on a red plastic tray that shone blinding with reflected sunlight. It was getting time, Denis said, glancing at his watch, for them to start back; though *he* assuredly did not want to return to his brother and sister-in-law's, in Bar Harbor, where he was obliged to stay the night. Nor did Malcolm, who seemed to be enjoying himself thoroughly, much want to leave. He was in Bangor to interview a prominent politician for a piece on yet another environmental outrage, and this was, he assured them, the *ne plus ultra* of outrages, involving a half-dozen states along the Atlantic seaboard, and *The New York Times Magazine* was sitting on a scoop, perhaps even Pulitzer Prize–quality material; but, dear Christ, how tired he was of raking others' muck. He said, in a tone of jocular envy, "You were certainly fortunate, Ian, to find this, this place," gesturing, Ian thought quite tactfully, away from land, out to sea. Out to the very horizon.

"It's quite foggy in the mornings, most mornings," Ian said, by instinct urged to qualify another's admiration or to disparage his own position—out of a muddled sense, Glynnis had once told him, of humility and charity—"and then of course there are days when it rains all day, and we just stay inside." He stopped; his face heated; he felt absurd and exposed, very like a newlywed husband. He said, "I'm still editing the *Journal*, of course. Martha sends me stacks of mail at least once a week."

So they were deflected onto the familiar subject of the *Journal*, about which Ian and Denis could talk for hours, now recounting, for Sigrid and Malcolm's benefit, a small delicious scandal of the previous winter, when a senior political scientist at the Center in Palo Alto reacted rather unprofessionally to a rejection letter from one of the associate editors and fired off two telegrams—one to Ian McCullough and one to Max Kreizer—and followed these up with a lengthy letter to Denis, whose friend he'd believed he was. "And naturally I was drawn into the fray, good-hearted Grinnell, trying to explain to this 'distinguished' academic that the rejection was nothing personal; but nothing professional either—in terms of the high quality of his work, I mean—but that, due to the vagaries of publishing a journal and the timeliness of certain subjects, the editors are forced, now and then, 'and I do mean *forced*,' to reject first-rate material. But now—"

"Now he is feuding with Denis," Ian said, laughing, his cheeks flushed. "Now he goes about saying—"

"—the most libelous, ridiculous things about me," Denis said. "Impugning, even, the integrity of my scholarship. As if he knows anything about my scholarship!"

So Denis and Ian told the story, almost, at times, in concert; and Sigrid laughed, seeming genuinely amused, charmed, Ian supposed, by Denis, who was at his best, his funniest, this afternoon; and Malcolm, though he'd doubtless heard the story before, laughed as well. "We are all so extraordinarily vain," Malcolm said, with a wide white grin. "I suppose it's all we have, you know, to keep going."

"Oh, surely not 'all,' " Ian said. For some reason his heart swelled with gratitude; he loved his friends and would have liked to seize their hands, perhaps would have done so, had Sigrid not been present. He thought, Denis and I will never tell that story again. I will never see Denis again.

And how do you know?

I just know.

Yes, but how?

I will blow my brains out when the season turns.

They talked about Hazelton acquaintances, colleagues at the

Institute, one of the research assistants who had just had a baby—"Great-looking baby," Denis said, "and it looks nothing like me"—and again Ian thought of Leonard Oppenheim and wondered how he and Paul were managing, but, irresolute about the correct pronunciation of Leonard's illness—Kaposi's sarcoma?—did not want to ask. Denis was saying what an extraordinary coincidence it was that both the McCullough and the Grinnell houses would be on the market at the same time, and competing. "Who could have predicted it, a few years ago!"

Malcolm said, "Christ. We were all so happy." He paused, and added, as if it might, for Sigrid Hunt's benefit, be required, "In those houses."

Ian began to say, "In all our houses," but Denis was speaking and cut him off. "Roberta says she will oversee the packing, the moving, all that. She knows my nerves can't bear it."

Malcolm said, "Roberta is a saint."

"But she doesn't ask after my health. She so very conspicuously doesn't ask after my health," Denis said.

"How *is* your health?" Ian asked. "That trouble with your eyes—"

Denis made an impatient gesture. "My phantom brain tumor? It's gone away, I think. I try not to notice." He laughed and looked at Sigrid, warmly, frankly, as if, being a woman, merely, and not a woman of some physical distinction, she might naturally be sympathetic with his plight. "I have other troubles now, in other regions of the body, but they come and go. I try not to notice."

Malcolm asked Ian, "And what about Bianca? How long will she be in Thailand? June seems to think that Glynnis's book, the cookbook she was working on—"

"*American Appetites,*" Denis said. "I love the title."

"—is going to be published after all. She said that Bianca was finishing it—"

"Don't you love the title?" Denis said, nudging Sigrid's arm. The wine had made him both aggressive and somnolent; at such times his eyelids drooped as if with secret wisdom. "I love the title. She was such a—an imaginative woman, you can't imagine. Such a lovely woman."

"I know," Sigrid said quietly. "I knew her."

Denis frowned in surprise. "Oh. Of course. That's right. I'd forgotten you had."

Stubbornly, even primly, Sigrid persisted. "She was my friend too. Glynnis."

The statement seemed to hover in the air as if unheard.

Ian said, "But it *is* going to be published. Bianca finished it the week she left. Glynnis's publisher, the same publisher, is bringing it out, next January in fact, they're going to rush it to get books in the stores before Christmas—prepublication copies I mean. For the Christmas trade. Glynnis always did so well, you know," he said, "around Christmas, in paperback . . . in paperback especially." They were looking at him, he thought, uneasily. But surely they could not know how suffocatingly hard his heart was beating in his chest. He said, as if to round the subject off and retreat from it, "Bianca did a marvelous job. Typing on the word processor, hours at a time, determined to get it done before she left. And she did."

"How long does she plan to be gone?" Malcolm asked. "You know, Thailand is a beautiful country."

"It is," Denis said, nodding vehemently. "And so is Vietnam."

"I know, I've been there," Ian said. "I've been to both countries. Yes," he said, trying to keep his concentration, though there was a sharp pain between his eyes, and his voice sounded suddenly distant and tinny, "Thailand is beautiful. Beautiful."

"And the people—"

"Beautiful."

Ian could not remember what he was saying, what the question he'd been asked was, and did not want to inquire. He recalled, with pain, how, in those final months at home—though no one had known at the time, of course, that they were Mr. McCullough's final months at home—his father had frequently repeated himself, asking questions he'd asked an hour before, angered when answers weren't immediately forthcoming. His brain had been muddled by alcohol and, Ian now saw, so very simply, despair.

The party had fallen silent. Sigrid drew breath to speak, yet seemed not to know what to say. For Sigrid Hunt had her story too, did she not, her surely fascinating life's story, up to and beyond the point at which it intersected with the McCulloughs' tragedy? And it baffled her that none of the men at the table seemed to want to hear—at this juncture in time, at least—no matter how their eyes lingered on her, or trailed after her, or lost themselves in her silky windblown hair.

But she did not take offense. She was not that sort of girl. She was quick, shrewd, inspired, leaning forward, smiling, scarcely minding that her long loose floppy white sleeves trailed across a stained plate or two, and saying, "This kiwi pie, there's nearly half of it left; who wants more? Won't you all have just a little more?"